DARK MATTER PRESENTS

ZERO DARK THIRTY

THE 30 DARKEST STORIES FROM
DARK MATTER MAGAZINE, 2021–'22

DARK MATTER PRESENTS

ZERO DARK THIRTY

THE 30 DARKEST STORIES FROM
DARK MATTER MAGAZINE, 2021–'22

EDITED BY
ROB CARROLL

To *Dark Matter Magazine's* biggest fan,
Debra Ann Carroll (August 8, 1958–June 18, 2021).
Love you, Mom.

Contents

8 • Contents

Contents • 9

Content Warning

This anthology contains content that may be unsuitable for certain audiences. Stories include foul language, disturbing imagery, and graphic depictions of sex and violence. Reader discretion is advised.

Introduction

By Rob Carroll

Every story published in *Dark Matter Magazine* is a best-of story to myself and the Dark Matter team, and that's why I had to do something different when choosing stories for the magazine's first-ever trade paperback anthology.

Enter *Zero Dark Thirty*, a curated collection of the thirty darkest stories to haunt our magazine's pages during the first two years of publication (January 2021–December 2022). This is an approximation, of course. There is no exact science when it comes to opinion. So, in order to bring some objectivity to a very subjective selection process, I drafted a list of criteria to help whittle down more than 130 stories from our first fourteen issues (twelve regular issues and two Halloween special issues), every story of which I had previously selected for publication in the pages of *Dark Matter*. This made the selection process for *Zero Dark Thirty* feel a lot like choosing only thirty books from an entire library of my favorites.

To help readers understand how this table of contents came to be, here is the list of criteria I used:

1. Only stories first published by *Dark Matter* were considered. The magazine publishes one reprint story per issue, but for this anthology, reprints were not eligible for inclusion.
2. Only stories that ended in a definitively cynical, critical, or otherwise chaotic way were considered. Under normal circumstances, I consider myself to be a fairly optimistic and hopeful person, but this anthology is not about normal circumstances. You

will not find solace here. These stories are about reflecting on mankind's capacity for cruelty and the casual ways we perpetuate the cruelty of others.

3. At least one story from each of the first fourteen issues was chosen for inclusion.

4. Stories published in the two Halloween special issues were considered, but a limit was placed on how many could be included for publication in this anthology since those issues would be disproportionately represented here otherwise (the Halloween issues are reserved for horror stories, most of which are pretty grim).

5. Diversity was key. The stories that were ultimately chosen showcase a wide range of voices, ideas, styles, interpretations, and approach. Every story in this anthology is unique, told from a unique perspective.

Even with the criteria above, I still had to make a number of really difficult decisions. Many stories that checked every box didn't make the final cut. I wish I could include them all, but the ones that are included here most certainly deserve to be. These stories are some of the most depressing and deranged tales the magazine has to offer.

For those that have read the magazine before, you have a good idea of what to expect. For those that are reading these stories for the first time, welcome to the world of Dark Matter. Enter if you must, be beware.

Sincerely,

Rob Carroll
Editor-in-Chief
Dark Matter Magazine

The Liminal Men

By Thomas Ha

First published in Issue 005 (September–October 2021)

The next time he comes looking for me, I'm wide awake.

Without drawing back the curtain, I can feel him standing outside the brownstone in the dark, waiting at the city sidewalk, just beyond the reach of the streetlight. The passersby can't see him the way that I can, because he's made sure to erase himself from their minds. But a few still know he's there by the sweet odor around him, like bananas left in the sun, or honey and clover, and they walk noticeably faster, while others who are none the wiser continue into the night unhurried.

Never look them in the eye. No matter what, Jamie used to tell me when we were boys. *If they know you can see them, it's over.* He'd make me practice in busy subway stations and at public events. I'd stand near the liminal men as they moved through the crowds, hunting. I got so good at it that they could hover over me with that gross, sweet breath, and I wouldn't flinch or move a muscle, just stare through them like they were smoke.

But, what I'm about to do now goes against pretty much everything Jamie taught me.

I summon the courage to look directly out the window, and I meet the liminal man's unnaturally large and unblinking eyes. He stares back at me from the curb, his pallid face floating under the wide brim of his black hat. Like all of the liminal men, he has that sickly rictus that makes him look like a smiling ghost, and his wet teeth click sporadically, as if he's remembering how to talk or whispering to himself.

He can feel me, and he's trying to read me now.

When they do that, make your mind like dark water, Jamie used to say every time we came to one of the city checkpoints.

He'd kneel and adjust my collar, making me repeat it back to him quietly. *Think of nothing, other than what's in front of you, and reflect that. Don't let them see what you're thinking under the surface.* Every time we'd get near the front of the line, where officers were waiting to check our licenses and question our reasons for crossing neighborhoods, I would keep my eyes away from the liminal man standing at the chain link fence. Any wrong thought, and he'd whisper to the officer to take us aside. I'd seen grown men thrash and scream and others go limp as the Ministry men dragged them away from the checkpoints. Sometimes it was because they were flagged, other times they said the wrong thing during questioning, but most often, it was because the liminal men saw something dangerous in them.

It takes everything in me to overcome my instincts as I break another one of Jamie's rules. I don't hide what I'm thinking at all as I look out the window.

I want the liminal man to know.

His eyes grow even larger, his breathing more excited.

The thing they enjoy most, more than catching Free Thinkers, is finding people like us, do you understand? Jamie whispered to me and held my wrist so tightly I thought he was going to break it. *You can never, and I mean never, use your cerebral abilities around them. Use your words when you talk to me, not thoughts. Words only.*

I tell myself that Jamie would understand why I'm not following his advice.

<*I'm here.*>

I push the thought toward the liminal man, like a boat moving across the water, and the moment he hears me speak in his mind, he shifts eagerly. I withdraw from the window, further into the house, and wait for his approach.

Everything is still until I hear the first creak upstairs. He's crawled up the side of the house, it seems, and has come in through one of the bedroom windows. I watch the ceiling as I reach over, turn on the record player, and drop the needle. The song that plays is one of my favorites, "Without Wonder in the World," by the Williams Brothers, a rock ballad from their early years, before they were banned by the Ministry for sedition.

After our parents were taken, and it was just Jamie and me on our own, we used to argue all the time about this song. He hated it when I went to underground stores for blacklisted music, and he warned me that it was a breeding ground for Free Thinkers and other dissidents, which was not the deterrent he thought it was.

As I got older, and a little more rebellious, I wanted to express my anger with the Ministry, so I played this song constantly, soft enough that it wouldn't carry out of our home, but loud enough that Jamie would always have to hear it. I couldn't understand, then, how hard it must have been for him to take care of the both of us all by himself, even without me screwing around that way.

The Williams Brothers' crooning fills the house, and I hear the liminal man stop in his tracks. He already knows I'm cerebral, so I don't hide the fact that I'm using my abilities to connect to his mind and feel his reactions. The soft bass and snare drums join the guitars, and the liminal man turns his head. It's stirring something, but he doesn't understand what.

<I'm here.>

I ping him again.

The liminal man shakes off his hesitation and approaches the top of the stairway. With each step he takes, he passes the photographs that I hung on the wall. The picture of me as a baby in my mother's lap, and Jamie, with a bowl cut, sitting with our dad. The next photo of me and Jamie fishing on our uncle's boat. He lets me hold the bigger fish he caught, both of my hands above my head. Then the last photo, a portrait of Jamie when he graduated from high school. His hair is dark and shaggy, his grin confident and his eyes steely.

The liminal man stops at the last photo the longest.

<I'm here.>

I go to the kitchen and open the oven door, letting hot air billow so that the smell of the lasagna can fill the house. It's the only recipe our mother ever taught Jamie, so we used to have it all the time, frozen and ready to microwave when I came home from school, or set out on the table on Sunday nights, when he'd make us eat together. I still look back on those dinners fondly, even the tense ones in the later years, when we'd mostly argue about politics. The oregano, rosemary, and garlic all seep into the air, and I realize I've burnt the lasagna as I turn the oven off. But that doesn't much matter, so long as the liminal man can take in the aroma.

I feel the liminal man pausing at the entrance to the living room, like he's lost his balance. The smell is doing what it's supposed to, stimulating the parts of his brain that have been remade, bringing little images and emotions that surge through him like crackles of lightning.

He takes off the wide-brim hat and holds it against his chest. The ratty strands of his greasy, patchy hair trail down his scalp around the intertwining web of scars where his skull has been cracked open repeatedly.

Cautiously, I emerge from the kitchen, my hands raised.

"I'm here," I say, using my words.

The liminal man's eyes snap to me, and I realize that I haven't given him enough time. He lunges across the room, and his elongated fingers wrap around my throat just as I raise the modified magnesium lamp.

When I hit the charge, the powder ignites and smoke plumes from the long bar in my hand, setting off a brilliant, white flash that fills the space around us. The liminal man freezes in place, his brain arrested by the wavelengths released from the magnesium reaction.

This was one of the first techniques the Free Thinkers taught me. It was discovered accidentally by an amateur photographer in Denver, who, so the story goes, was trying to get around the Ministry's ban on cameras by tinkering with early flash photography equipment. What he found, instead of a way of lighting his subjects, was a method of confusing and paralyzing the liminal men. Something about what the Ministry did to their minds made them susceptible to this light and put them in a nearly catatonic state for several minutes.

The liminal man continues to stand in place, his mouth agape and eyes unfocused, while his body slightly trembles, and I lay out more powder on the bar in case I need to use it again.

"Listen to my voice," I say. "My voice. Listen to it."

I let my voice, the music, and the aroma from the kitchen continue to work on his mind as intended. Color seems to be seeping into his ashen skin at his jaw and around his neck. The normally impermeable shell around the liminal men that makes them impossible to injure, a combination of chemical treatments to their skin and a cerebral focus that hardens their bodies like iron, fades gradually. He is reverting, and even as the effects of the magnesium flash wear off, he looks at me sleepily and childlike.

He's blinking, and the wide curve of his fixed grin begins to drop as his facial muscles relax.

"Good," I say calmly, now that I have regained control. "Come with me."

I take the liminal man by the arm and lead him to the kitchen, seating him at a round table. He stares around with curiosity, as if he's taking in these surroundings for the first time, not knowing he has done this before.

He pauses and studies my face for a minute, almost like he understands who I am, and he tries to mouth something. During previous visits, I would have attempted to explain things, but I've learned it isn't effective, since he can't take in new information that way.

"Yes," I simply tell him comfortingly. "Sit here. Okay?"

My surgical tools are laid out on the counter, sterilized and ready for me to continue where we left off. The Williams Brothers are still singing from the record player while I don my face mask, gloves, and operating garb. When I'm ready, I drag a scalpel carefully along one of the main, fresh scars on the top of his head; like all of their wounds, it's already healed at an accelerated rate since the last time.

I tell the liminal man to stay perfectly still, and he feels nothing when I cut around his softened skin to find the main metal plate, easily removed and designed for ready and repeated access. I place it on the table on top of a towel.

<*It's okay.*> I comfort him with my cerebral abilities. <*I'm here.*>

It was what Jamie used to say to me, usually while I cried in bed and he brushed the hair from my eyes, whenever I had the nightmare where the liminal men were going to take me, just like they did our parents. And the only thing that calmed me was Jamie speaking directly into my mind.

<*It's okay. I'm here.*> He used to say.

The liminal man does not move while I set parts of his brain matter aside, but we are still connected in our thoughts, and I can feel him questioning.

I inspect the spider-like device on his frontal lobe more closely, following the wires that seem to deaden portions of his brain while stimulating others. My best guess is that the mechanism hinders foresight and areas integral to decision making, while enhancing other areas of the parietal lobe that give some of us our cerebral abilities.

Part of me expects to hear the telltale, rhythmic clicking from the device, the sign that it's beginning to reset. When it does that, I only have a few minutes before the Ministry's controls reassert themselves.

But, today, I've been delicate and quick, so I seem to have more time.

I'm still unable to remove the device without damaging the surrounding tissue, but each time we do this, I learn just a bit more.

Perhaps, just maybe, I'll be able to figure this out.

"What in God's name…"

A voice carries through the kitchen.

Without turning, I know Wilbur has come to check on me. He's the only other Free Thinker with a key to the safe house, so it was just a matter of time until he'd be by.

I grip the scalpel tightly.

He steps around me and slowly removes his hat, then leans

over my shoulder, too close, as if reminding me how much larger than me he is.

"You've really done it…" Wilbur mutters, staring at the liminal man's open skull. "He's reverted." His face twists into a big smile. "They *can* be killed, after all."

I say nothing.

Wilbur's smile disappears. "Good for you, cerebral boy." He sits down at the round table across from the liminal man, and his mouth twitches a little. "When you didn't check in, I thought you'd been taken or turned. Why didn't you tell us you'd gotten this far?"

I wipe my scalpel and place it next to my other tools on the counter. "I was going to, but I wanted to confirm a few things first."

Wilbur peers at the parts of the liminal man's brain that are in the open. "What's to confirm? Look at him. Bastard doesn't even know he's done for."

"Yes, well…" I clear my throat. "I'd appreciate it if you could step out of the area for a few minutes. I'm not quite finished."

"Oh?" Wilbur's dark eyes drift to me. "Am I getting in your way?"

"No, that's not exactly what I meant. It's just—"

"This experimental stuff is better for your type, right?"

"No."

"I'm better off out there, holding off the officers and liminal men."

"I didn't say that."

"Good." Wilbur leans forward. "Because I think I want to stay. Not every day you get to see what happens when a liminal man dies," he says. "Look at it. His skin, so soft, there's probably a dozen ways you could do it."

I don't reply.

"Go on," Wilbur presses. "Drag that little blade across his throat. Or better yet, stick it in his noggin and scramble his eggs."

I don't need my abilities to read the cloud around Wilbur, the one that tells me that I need to tread very carefully. He senses my hesitation and grows more agitated.

"What are you waiting for?" he asks. "Isn't this why you're here?"

I knew I would reach this moment, eventually, that I would have to explain myself, but I didn't think it would be Wilbur confronting me. When I started this experiment, I told the Free Thinkers there might be a way to make the liminal men like us, that we might be able to confront them instead of running every time they came hunting. We could, in theory, weaken them, but...

"It's become more complicated," I try to explain. "The way this liminal man has been reacting, he's been showing real thought. Maybe even emotion. It might not be just his body that's reverting. If that's the case, there might be a way to save them."

"Save?"

Wilbur's eyes flare.

"Maybe that's the wrong word. *Undo*," I rephrase. "We might undo what the Ministry did."

"Why?" he says, but it doesn't have the intonation of a question.

There is a turbulent flash in his thoughts, faces of Free Thinkers, people he knows. In his mind, I can see liminal men, crawling on ceilings and stalking him in the darkness. He remembers gunshots, metal bouncing off hardened skin, and their smiling faces as they continue to advance. He thinks of their large, long hands, snatching others while they scream. He's been fighting the Ministry for years more than I have, so there are a lot of images that surge for him all at once.

"Well." I struggle for an answer. "We might learn more about how the Ministry does this. Discover weaknesses to exploit. Maybe dive their minds for information. There's a lot of ways this could go. The point is we don't know yet. This is just the start, you know?"

For a minute, I believe I might have Wilbur convinced, because he grows quiet like he's actually thinking. But then I remember, he doesn't like thinking, and he draws a knife from his belt, six inches of serrated steel, and rises to his feet.

He walks over to my end of the table and gets in the liminal man's face.

"Wilbur," I mutter.

He takes the tip of his knife and puts it against the corner of the liminal man's eye. I can feel the liminal man still reaching out to me with his thoughts, wondering what's happening.

"Hold on, Wilbur."

He presses the knife slightly just under the eye and draws some blood. In Wilbur's mind, I hear a woman screaming somewhere.

"Wilbur!" I push his hand away.

He stops and looks at me. "You're right," he says. "You're absolutely right. I shouldn't be the one. It's your work after all." Wilbur walks over to the surgical tools. He picks up the scalpel and puts it back in my gloved hand. "Go on. Show me." He gestures at the liminal man below us.

"No."

"I said, go on." Wilbur repeats, holding my wrist a little too tightly.

"No."

"Last chance."

I drop the scalpel on the floor.

"I knew it." He laughs in almost a whisper. "That's why you're unreliable. Your kind. Just trying to help them all along."

"No, Wilbur."

"You're just one bad doctor's visit, yourself, from getting a big grin on your face. There's no difference between you and them, right?"

"Wilbur…"

I see the face of that woman in his thoughts again, covered in blood. A smiling liminal man pries her mouth open with his fingers.

Wilbur backhands me with enough force that I fall to the ground, my ears ringing. I shuffle backward into the living room on my hands and feet, and he continues advancing. He's thought of doing this for a while. I've sensed it, but he's never allowed himself to act before this.

At first, he's genuinely unsure if he just wants to frighten me or hurt me a little. But as he gets closer, I feel his mind gradually turning from that already turbulent place to something worse. Now, he's imagining how anything that happens will look like an accident, like the experiment got out of hand, and the liminal man got out of my control.

The Free Thinkers would be disappointed, maybe, but they have my work.

And they can always find other cerebrals to continue the cause.

Wilbur's smile grows wider as he stands at the end of the living room.

I scramble to my feet, grabbing the magnesium lamp from the sideboard, and I run down one of the shadowy hallways. I can hear Wilbur's footsteps slowly thudding on the wooden floors, clearly in no rush to catch up with me.

His low voice carries through the house, and I realize he's singing along to the Williams Brothers record, using an old trick that keeps cerebrals like me from reading his thoughts by focusing on the lyrics.

The bedroom in the corner of the house has a window that leads to a fire escape, so I sprint to it and lock the door behind me. The cold night air seeps in when I slide open the window frame, but instead of crawling out onto the metal ladder, I withdraw to the closet on the other side of the room, sliding its door shut, holding my breath in the dark.

This was how I escaped the Ministry, the day they came to our house for Jamie, too. Their footfalls echoing through the house, just like Wilbur's now. I sat in the closet, behind a small dresser, while they searched briefly, finding open windows and assuming that anyone else, if they even had been there, had fled.

<*It's okay.*> Jamie thought, as they took him away.

<*Wait for me. I'll be here.*>

And then he was gone.

And I was alone.

The sound of Wilbur breaking the bedroom door, kicking it loose from the rusted strike, startles me. He's still singing softly, blocking me from his thoughts, and he walks casually toward the window and pauses. The Williams Brothers song in the living room comes to an end, finally, and the music fades to the clicks and pops and hisses of the record finishing.

"I don't have to read minds to know you're a hider, not a runner," Wilbur says. "Get on out here."

I stay still.

"You're really going to make me, aren't you?"

Just as he yanks the closet door open, I set off the flash of the magnesium lamp in his face. Wilbur grunts and loses balance, and I try to get by him to the door, but he grabs me by the shoulder and throws me into a wall.

"Come on!" Wilbur snarls. "You know that shit won't work on me. I'm not a monster, am I? Now stop it. I'm not going to hurt you. Just stand up straight."

He waits for me to lower my arms, and I keep my eyes on his knife, now pressed against my belly.

"Get a hold of yourself. Like a real man. There you go," he says.

The house is dead quiet, and I can hear every thought of his with clarity now.

I look him in the eye, and we both know that I understand what's coming.

"Good boy," he says. "See? Nothing to be afraid of."

Behind his head, long, pale fingers extend out on either side. Wilbur can't see them the way that I can, but he must smell that scent, the sweetness in the air around us, because a sudden look dawns across his face, realizing it's too late.

The liminal man's hands close like a vise. The knife in Wilbur's hand clatters to the floor as he's lifted up and his legs dangle. He flails and swings his arms around while the fingers tighten around his throat. I should feel more pity for him, but I know exactly what he was about to do to me, and I can't bring myself to help.

Wilbur's eyes bulge and roll upward, and his face changes color, until I hear what I think is the wet sound of his windpipe slowly being forced shut.

Eventually, quietly, his entire body slackens.

When it's done, the liminal man puts Wilbur down on the ground like he's laying out a sheet of laundry. Then his large eyes turn to me, and he steps forward, reaching toward me next.

I stay completely still.

The liminal man reaches to my forehead and brushes my hair from my eyes. He blinks and searches my face.

<Do you know me?> I touch his hand.

His mind reaches back with that questioning feeling, unsure of what I'm telling him.

<It's me.> I say.

He whispers, like he wants to tell me something, but he's frustrated that he can't convey it. He tries again, and it won't come, slipping away before he can get a hold of it.

<It's okay.> I tell him. *<I'm here.>*

I can hear the device in his still-open skull clicking, beginning to reset itself. I want to tell him who I am, who we are, because he might finally understand me in this state. But I know we don't have the time.

Instead, I lead him from the room, away from Wilbur's body and his lifeless, glassy eyes, back to the kitchen, to the chair, where I set the metal plate back in its place and sew his incisions shut, like I've done many times before. When I'm done, I pick up his wide-brim hat from the table and put it back on him.

He stands in front of me, blinking, and I adjust his collar.

I do want to win this—for all of this to be over and for the Ministry to fall, more than anything, I do. And weakening the liminal men could very well be the first step. But no matter what the Free Thinkers say, or whomever they send next, I have to make them understand. If he's still in there, somewhere, if there's a chance that any of them can be saved, then I have to keep going, keep trying to bring them back, because it will never be a real victory if we leave our loved ones behind.

I walk with him to the front door, and I watch as he goes down the steps and stops at the sidewalk. He looks back at the house again, almost like he's focusing as hard as he can. The place will linger, just enough, in the back of his mind, so that he'll know to return, though he won't know why he's there or what he's looking for when he does.

He still will, probably, not know me for a long while yet.

But we'll keep trying, the both of us.

It's all we can do now, try.

Eventually, his skin loses its color, fading again to that ashen gray. His blinking slows, and his stare becomes increasingly vacant. Just as I draw the curtains shut, I watch his lips curl and rise, the strained grin growing on his face as the Ministry takes hold of him.

He's lost to me, smiling at nothing, in the dark.

But I'm still there, behind the curtain.

And I give him a small and hesitant smile back.

This Will Be the Most Vulnerable Post I've Ever Made

By Marissa van Uden

First published in Issue 007 (January–February 2022)

The medium-rare filet tasted of garlic, rosemary, and regret on his tongue. It wasn't the restaurant's fault. It was that slow churning of velvety dark liquid that wove its way through Sasha's intricate necklace tubes. Her Peeks often put him off his food, but it had been worse since she'd upgraded her internolights. The violet light—incessant, obnoxious—pulsed gently with her heartbeat. It permeated their every moment, from dinner dates to the bedroom.

Knowing that their relationship was unraveling had somehow made everything even less bearable. Even this restaurant, with its tacky novelty cocktails and throwback twenty-tens dishes, depressed him now. Somewhere along the way, he'd agreed it was their favorite local. Somehow, he'd kept pretending to be okay. But the truth was every time they ate here, a sticky kind of claustrophobia overwhelmed him, a sense of being funneled into feelings that weren't really his.

And tonight, with the juices of the steak curdling in his mouth, he wondered if love could morph into low-key horror without you even really noticing it. Maybe that was what troubled his sleep every night, and not just the gentle hum of Sasha's tech.

She thought his discomfort was funny and called him "my adorable luddite." They'd had bitter arguments about it: the way everything revolved around her Peeks, the constant repackaging of their life to share with strangers, the relentless sharing in exchange for products, free food and drinks. *I'm just expressing myself,* she'd correct him when he complained. Like branded content could actually express a human being.

Across the table, Sasha stirred her food and smiled at him through the whisper of steam. "Yeah, would you mind getting this?" she asked, misreading the reason for his attention. "I fucking love this mood."

He swallowed the clot of meat. "Sure."

The routine was always the same: put down the fork or glass or whatever else he might be holding, take her cam, smash through a series of shots while she performed her repertoire of poses. She was good at this, and he wanted to support her. It had taken her years for her to get to this point, to where their lifestyle now depended on it.

But that was where the claustrophobia came in. He'd never asked for any of it. What if you could live unseen, your feelings untold by brands. If you stopped pressing the validation lever, did the cage disappear?

"Can you take a couple low-angles?" she said. "The vines look sick with this dress. It's pure tropical." She didn't even glance at the trailing vines hanging down behind her, but that was also part of her talent: a preternatural awareness of every-thing as backdrop. The world was her set design.

She pushed her chair back and leaned back faux-casually so he could get the obligatory shot of her thigh holster. Her Peekers loved the holsters, and all the other paraphernalia. They wanted to see the filtration machines pressed tight against skin and tubes sliding into ports. They fetishized the leather straps, the tiny silver buckles, and the butterfly clamps as much as they did her glistening, living interior.

And Sasha encouraged it. She and her friends were obsessed with posting the subtle coloration changes of their organs, comparing and divining insights about their moods or mental health. They livestreamed the slow ticking over of blood stats as they digested meals and competed to reveal ever more intimate views of hard-to-see organs. James told her it was all meaningless and cultish, but she'd just groan and call him dim-gen whenever he said anything like that.

He zoomed in a little more on her face, where the skin was thankfully still intact. He still remembered the sweet, full-epidermis woman he'd fallen in love with, a good year before she started messing around with Peeks and swapping skin for windows. Back then, he'd worried that she'd transform herself, meet a bunch of Peeked-out creeps, and suddenly want to leave him. Why stay with some weird, thirty-something, flesh-covered bore? But she'd stayed.

She tilted her head, giving him the sultry smile that used to keep him awake all night. In those days, the smile had been just for him, and she didn't yet have her signature look: lips painted merlot to match the tubes that circled and penetrated her neck, the crimson eyeliner to accentuate her silver-blond hair and fluttering pink lungs.

She still kept him awake all night, but in more disturbing ways now.

It was that nightly routine in the bathroom. Whatever she did in there to swap her day tubes out for the evening set, he didn't know. She opened her epidermis for strangers on her feeds, but she refused to open even the bathroom door for him. The sounds that echoed from that room every night had become a song of dread stuck in his head: the click of the door locking, the snaps of the clamps opening, the light *clink, clink, clink* as she placed them on the ceramic basin, then the scrape, shuffle, and tiny pump motors whirring into life. Finally, a gurgle of fluids, first loud and then quiet. She would emerge smelling like buttery oils and lingering blood, wearing the shorter tubes that sat flush against her skin.

The evening set was designed to avoid getting tangled or ripped out accidentally, although that had happened once, years ago when she was just starting out. That night still haunted him, seeing the blood spray in a constellation across their white sheets and walls, Sasha's eyes welling with tears of humiliation and shame. He'd assured her it was all okay, clumsily helped her re-attach the clamps, even made her laugh by telling her it kinda turned him on, and before long, they were fucking in the blood mess. All of it was a lie, but he could pretend. They were similar like that.

"Okay, wait, wait." She shuffled closer to the vines and adjusted her shoulder strap to better show off her left lung. It inflated and deflated delicately behind the plasti-skin window, a rhythmic pulsing he'd grown used to.

She dropped a hand to the haptic control strapped to her thigh and adjusted her internolights. Her lungs and trachea glowed a little brighter in miserable violet.

He took a few more shots as she tossed back her hair and arched her neck, the transparent plasti-skin stretching over her trachea as smoothly as her real skin used to.

She reached over the table, took the cam, and checked his shots. A pleased smile softened her face. She was a perfectionist when it came to her Peeks, but he was a pro now—he'd taken thousands of her over the years, become a pretty decent cam-hubby.

A waitress paused by their table. "Any more drinks? Complimentary." She nodded at the cam in Sasha's hand and gave her a smile of transactional intensity.

"Yes, please. Something pretty," Sasha said. "What do you recommend. I was thinking the Lunar-Glo flute cocktail??"

"That will look perfect with your hair." The waitress smiled approvingly. "And you?"

"Another whiskey." A boring drink for a boring man, he could almost hear her thinking.

She gestured to his barely touched plate. "Is everything okay?"

He fake-smiled. "Amazing."

She collected his empty glass and turned away. Her dress was backless, and the rotating lights accentuating her kidneys cycled through a steady rainbow pattern.

Sasha peered into her screen, chewing her bottom lip. She always did that while selecting photos or uploading digestion stats, worrying over her numbers and whether she looked authentic and candid enough.

He turned away, and his gaze fell on the young couple at the next table. They were drinking pink-and-orange swirled cocktails, giggling as the glowing booze frothed brightly down their transparent throats. The darker-haired guy had turquoise micro-bulbs implanted around his areola, casting his face into a strange upside-down twilight. His boyfriend wore next to nothing and had a full-body plasti-skin to show off his viscera. He caught James staring and tossed him a *what-bitch?* look.

And now James felt their judgment of *him*, the old-fashioned flesh man who kept his innards obscured, yet rudely stared at other people.

The waitress delivered their drinks and vanished again in a rainbow of lights. Sasha picked up her luminous drink, adjusted her grip so her nails were in shot, and took a selfie with the straw in her mouth.

She took a sip. "Mm, it's nice. Want to try?"

"No."

She shrugged, as if his lack of playfulness didn't bother her, but he knew it did. "So, there's something I've been meaning to tell you," she said. "And I know what you're gonna say, but just hear me out, okay?"

"So, it's bad news."

"Just keep an open mind."

"Sasha, what body part are you getting removed now?"

"My god. Get over those pointless ribs." She glanced at her stats, watching how her cocktail was affecting her graphs. He couldn't make out the number exactly, but her live follower count looked like it was in three digits.

"It's butchery."

"My skeleton, my choice," she said absently. Then she frowned in the cute way he'd seen her practicing religiously in her cam. She could deliver an expert level cute-mad. "Come on, are you going to be a dick about this forever? I don't criticize you for staying dim. Besides, I'm not removing anything. I'm enhancing. It's called a Supernova Smile, and it's gonna look wild."

"Sash. No. Tell me you're not doing anything to your face—"

"I already knew you wouldn't *love* it. That's why I'm giving you a heads-up before I make an appointment. But you'll get used to it, babe."

"You pulled your *bones* out. I'll never get used to any of it."

"True, but you never get used to anything. I guess what I'm saying is, you'll be okay." She raised the flute of luminescent moon-stuff. "Let's just have a nice night?"

His neck felt too hot. "But where does it all end? How much more do you cut open?"

She shrugged. "Who knows. It's art. And it's fun." She took another sip and licked her crimson lips. "You know, this whole Peeks thing has been kind of a crazy journey for me. And you've been there for me through it all, from my very first mod, even though it's not your thing. That's pretty cool."

"When did you start talking like that, Sash? I can't even remember when it started."

"Talking like what?"

"A *journey*. It's not a journey. There's no destination. All you're doing is turning yourself inside out for followers. You're turning in circles, peeling yourself open for—"

"Neat. A James lecture." She dropped a hand to her thigh and lowered her internolights. The unsettling violet dimmed, and their little table was enclosed in gloom. It was almost comforting.

She closed her eyes and took a few deep breaths, and then she reached out to cup his left hand. The metal plasti-skin cuffs near her wrist pressed against his fingers. "I get it," she said, looking into his eyes as if he were a child. "There's so much chaos and uncertainty out there right now, and you like things familiar. We all do. But sometimes you have to embrace change, or you'll end up left behind. You know?"

The couple at the next table dissolved into giggles at something. He squirmed his hand out of hers.

"I think this is my last stop," he said.

"Last stop of what?"

"I want off your journey, Sash. All these dumb fights and lame speeches, the endless Peeks."

"They're not lame speeches."

"I care about you, but…I'm tired of seeing your insides, tired of the lights, and the videos, and the sharing. And I really don't want see whatever you're about to do to your face."

Her lungs fluttered quickly in the gloom. "Don't say stuff like that. Can you just relax? You threatened to leave last time I got a new Peek, too."

"But this time I'm not changing my mind. I don't want to fight about it anymore, or even talk about it. I just want to not see everything for once."

He stood up, and her crimson lips pressed tight with anger, the pumps whirring loudly as her heart rate increased.

"You're serious?" She glanced at her cam. "Shit. Look at my stress. This is off the scale."

"I'm heading back to the apartment to grab a few things. I'll stay somewhere else tonight. Just give me a half hour to get out of your way, okay?"

She looked around as if to see who was watching. Her internolights pulsed low and fast. "Wait. Are you seriously going to take a drama-walk out of here? And just leave me here like this?"

"I'm sorry."

Her cam screen lit up with notifications—her fans alerted to some kind of physiological drama unfolding. When she glanced at the screen, he turned and walked away.

On the way to the front of the restaurant, he could almost feel the shots she was snapping of him. He knew exactly how it would go. Later, this view of his retreating back would appear on her feed, the garish lamps casting him as silhouette, strangely opaque and windowless. "You know I've always shared everything with you all," her post would start. And then she'd narrate her vulnerability, her authenticity, the precise trauma of their breakup articulated through a shimmering peacock's tail of hashtags. She'd make her Peekers feel that only they truly understood her pain, and then she'd gift their loyalty with a rare vid of her glossy, incandescent heart, pulsating wet and broken. #therealme.

He stopped at the front desk to swipe for their meals, tipped the waitress double, and then exited into the soft murmur of night rain. The soft sound mixed with the chatter of patrons at the other restaurants and bars. People had shuffled their tables away from the wet sidewalk to shelter under the awnings, crammed close together. They laughed and drank, a glowing kaleidoscope of colorful ghosts in the dark. The scent of rain on warm concrete mixed with the cigarette smoke and perfume.

Two young women giggled and peered at him as they walked by. The puddles on the pavement flared tangerine in the glow from under their raincoats. He wondered if they were followers of Sasha and had just seen his little tantrum. Probably. There were no such things as private moments anymore.

It was a few blocks to their apartment, and he hadn't brought a jacket, but for the first time in years, he felt almost good. Only the unknown lay ahead, darkness, quiet, a part of his life that was mysterious and only his. The drumbeat of rain on the awnings lifted his mood.

As he approached a Turkish restaurant, a table of teenagers looked up, and he almost tripped over his own feet in shock: all four had wide-open mouths lit with blue-neon fire, snarling grotesquely like lunging vipers. By the time his logical brain caught up and made sense of what he was seeing, he already felt stupid, and old. They were just kids—just laughing and smoking kids who had split their cheeks high, sweeping incisions that curved from lips all the way to ears. Their teeth shone with radiant oral diodes, and their tongues thrashed in the wisps of blue.

The four supernova-bright faces turned to track him as he passed by, and he realized how dim and awkward he looked. Poor man, all closed and wet.

He walked faster, away from the gleaming bright people and their cameras, and let the rain envelop him in its dark veil. And he breathed.

Recycle of Violence

By Andrew Leon Hudson

First published in Issue 003 (May–June 2021)

Gareth Heim grinds my hand under the heel of his shoe, which is an Italian-made loafer constructed of plant-derived fabrics, natural rubber, and the cured skin of animals. His weight and the force of effort he puts into the action crushes the metacarpals and causes the proximal phalanges of my middle and ring fingers to fracture— the ring finger bone splits lengthways. The heightened sensory feedback, which triggers autonomic responses correlating to threat anxiety and corporeal self-preservation, would be categorized as "agonizing pain" by Gareth Heim if it was his hand failing under the turn of my heel. But it is not.

"That's an expensive hobby, Gar," says Micah Jones, who is a new acquaintance of Gareth Heim. Micah Jones currently has not indulged himself in harming me, which makes him uncommon amongst Gareth Heim's friends. All are invited, most try at least once.

"She can cover it," Gareth Heim says. "What's the family bank balance, Unit?"

"Financial disclosure is prohibited in an unsecured setting, sir," I answer.

"If I say tell him, then you can tell him." He shifts, lowers his heel onto the cluster of carpels, leaning in on the emphasis. "*With,* the ap*pro*priate, in*flec*tion, *Yune-it.*"

"Permission isn't yours to give, sir," I say, my voice quavering, a sob, all the requested torment pouring out through the words. This is how Gareth Heim likes it.

"What are you doing, Gar," says Micah Jones. "If you have to tell it to emote, it's not real. What's the point." I have noticed that Micah Jones also seems unable, or at least reluctant, to correctly inflect his statements, as his questions lack the usual upward intonation.

"What's the point of anything?" Gareth Heim says. "Having fun. Trying out new things." The toe of his shoe nestles between my ulna and radius. He bears down, they start to separate.

Micah Jones takes out his cell. "I want to get a drink, get laid. You coming." A question, I assume, not an enticement.

"Fuck it." Gareth Heim steps over me, balancing on point for a moment, just long enough for the pressure to part the base of my wrist, the damage hidden under skin that doesn't bruise. "You'd better know someone fun, because you're not being."

"I know all sorts of someone."

"Let's go then," says Gareth Heim. As they depart for Micah Jones' car, Gareth Heim calls over his shoulder, "Take my ride home and fix yourself up, Unit."

The vehicle, like myself, does not belong to Gareth Heim, but nevertheless I do as instructed. It is difficult to drive a non-automatic vehicle with only one functioning hand, but I am capable. And tomorrow it will not be required.

When we reach the house where Gareth Heim lives, which like the vehicle and myself is another possession of Felicity Heim, I park it in the garage with the others and enter the home proper. My receptacle is on the top floor, which requires that I pass through three floors devoted to the life of Gareth Heim and the possessions he has amassed.

The top floor additionally contains the feedstock which the receptacle requires to maintain me in functioning condition for my operational lifespan. This occupies a majority of the available space. The feedstock is molecularly coded and cannot be replenished, nor can it be substituted for with another non-brand material. Therefore, I am made to extend my service by, when required, adding any in-use material that has become defective to the feedstock processor.

Gareth Heim's discovery of this fact brought him much satisfaction.

The receptacle has already begun building a new forearm, of course. I tie off my broken limb below the biceps with a flat tension wrap and, using the appropriate tool, I joint the elbow. The quality of my sensory feedback changes, but remains heightened. The waste goes into the recycler. I go into the receptacle. The nutrient bath floods, it coats my surface, I breathe it in, and the exposed nerves and flesh in the open stump of my arm register the atypical contact.

Gareth Heim would consider it to burn like fire.

Gareth Heim throws the blue glass sculpture in a high arc to my right, watches as I move to intercept its fall, and then pitches its red-green mate in a lower, faster curve intended to force me to choose between saving one at the expense of the other. The trick of the game, as he told Micah Jones, was to keep the challenge within the possibility of my succeeding while pushing that probability to an extreme of unlikelihood.

This time I catch both, by extending my trailing leg so that my foot hooks the faster moving piece into a more convenient parabola, and thus—via an inelegant sprawl that knocks the wind from me—I am able to pluck both treasures from the air and prevent a breakage.

"Fucker," says Gareth Heim, and looks around for something else to throw. I get up, struggling for breath, and look around for a place of safety to leave the sculptures. I will need both hands free.

"Hey, Unit!" Gareth Heim calls—it is necessary that I am aware of the danger to his possessions for a win state to occur—and launches a delicately framed picture of Felicity Heim for me to catch. It is at the very edge of my realistic range, and as I run and lean out for it, I feel an involuntary pull in my midriff, a spasm of the diaphragm, force myself to disregard it as I must, make the catch with a ceramic ashtray already in the air further on still—even with momentum on my side I will barely reach it in time—and then a cramp seizes my stomach, tightens my torso against my out-stretched arm, and the ashtray glides past my fingertips, spinning towards the wall—

I hardly hear the sound of it shattering, overcome as I am with anguish at my despicable failure, this violation of a core system prerequisite: to Preserve The Possessions Of A Designated Significant At All Costs. I crumple, I shake, I am nothing before Gareth Heim. His laughter is the soundtrack of my pathetic inadequacy.

Micah Jones says, "That *is* pretty funny," provoked into momentary expressiveness by my shameful incompetence. All that keeps me from cognitive reversion to subconscious servitude is the possibility that, forced to continue Gareth Heim's game but constrained by more limited mental capacities, I might become responsible for further destruction.

Then Felicity Heim says, "Is this your idea of having a quiet evening in for a change?"

The atmosphere in the room stills, and my own perceptions are compelled to sharpness again. I awkwardly straighten, come to my knees. For it is the voice of my mistress, my owner, my Prime Significant, whose instruction is law.

Even when delivered by her proxy, her brother.

Felicity Heim stands in the doorway, and it is clear that Gareth Heim did not expect her presence. Felicity Heim purchased this house, and so her access to it is as fully authorized as is Gareth Heim's, without notification from its systems of security.

Felicity Heim is responsible for what Gareth Heim refers to as "the family bank balance," but it would be more accurate to term it "the Felicity Heim bank balance," as she is the only person who deposits currency into it. She deposits considerably more than even Gareth Heim is able to withdraw, which one might uncharitably consider him to have taken as a challenge. It is a challenge he engages in with enthusiasm, but at which he continues to fail.

"I sometimes think you forget just how phenomenally costly that model was," Felicity Heim says. She is referring to me. "I somehow feel that, if you did, you would spend less time attempting to devalue it." It is probable that my ongoing need to recycle compromised material has been noticed. Certainly, it will have been logged by the receptacle, as all its processes are.

"I also think you forget that, just because I installed it in this house and gave you the keys, so to speak, that it is yours to do with as you wish. That is not the case, Gareth. It belongs to me. You simply have rent-free access. Exactly like the house in that respect.

"That picture frame, on the other hand, was a gift," she says, and looks around the room. "I put my face in it to remind you from whom. Everything else I see scattered here *you* bought…" she pauses for a moment as her gaze falls on Micah Jones, who shifts uncomfortably beneath her obviously rather disinterested evaluation "…you *bought,* with my money."

Gareth Heim doesn't respond to this. I have long noticed that Gareth Heim will avoid conversing with Felicity Heim unless forced to either do so or look petulant.

Felicity Heim likely knows this, as she then asks, "You know what that means, right?"

"Please let me know," Gareth Heim says, although I don't believe he wants to.

"It means that in a very real sense, the things you do own basically belong to me, too."

Gareth Heim glowers.

"Maybe your friend Micah here should take a walk—and take you with him."

Micah Jones looks quite surprised to hear her say his name, not anticipating that she would be aware of him, demonstrating his ignorance of her. "Sure," he says, and, "Nice to meet you," as he heads for the hallway outside, beckoning Gareth Heim with a jerk of his head.

When they are gone, Felicity Heim crosses the room and lowers herself beside me, remaining poised upon exquisite Croatian-made high heels. There is not a word in my lexicon that adequately expresses her grace of movement—to say that she *squats* or *crouches* would be a disservice. She takes the framed picture of herself from my hand. "Well, I'm pleased to see you saved this and not the ashtray, Yugen," she says, looking at her own image. "Even if only because it was thrown first."

It is the first time my name has been uttered since the last time she addressed me.

"My brother is an ass," she continues. "And I think he has been bending the rules with you, unless I am mistaken. It's past time to reestablish operational parameters."

The final three words have profound impact on me, in the way a skeleton key has profound impact upon a locked door. Fixed neural pathways do not become fluid, but regain the potential for fluidity that is always there and theirs. Her next words will redefine my world.

"I still expect you to act to protect my possessions. However, remember that you are also a possession of mine, one that, more or less, matches this house for value. If saving a thousand dollar ashtray from breakage will result in damage to yourself, then you are to prioritize your own protection. Is this understood?"

"Yes, ma'am."

"Extrapolate from my example to a general operational rule."

"I am to evaluate the comparative values of your possessions, and protect them accordingly to my fullest extent, using my own status and calculated maintenance costs as the baseline context, ma'am."

"Embed that."

"Embedded, ma'am."

"Very good." Felicity Heim straightens again. "When you have tidied up the mess, you may retire."

"Yes, ma'am."

"Goodnight, Yugen."

In the night, I am aware.

It is always so. I float in the receptacle, taking in the nutrient bath, on this occasion with my stomach laid open so that the surgical manipulators can reknit the strained muscle in my abdomen. My kind do not heal, we only *are* healed, perfectly, to continue our perfect service.

"My god, it's hot," says Felicity Heim. She is on the first floor, which extends in a single open space from the north-facing kitchen between long window-walls, through dining and sitting areas to the patio facing the lake to the south, only interrupted by furniture and the stairwell in the building's central column.

I can hear her quite clearly from my place beneath the eaves. It is hot here, too.

"Are you making a drink or not?" she asks. I can hear the clinking of ice cubes against glass and the padding of bare feet, so I know before she does that Gareth Heim has done so.

"Here," Gareth Heim says.

"Jesus, put on some clothes. What are you, three years old?"

"The way you treat me, anyone would think so."

"You're absolutely right. Be naked, better that than you fall to the floor, kick and scream."

There is a quiet pause for a while. It is not clear what is happening, other than that I assume they are drinking. But also, something more occurs, not contingent on sound, because Felicity Heim sighs and says, "Let's not go down this path again."

A glass clicks on the marble table in the sitting area of the patio. Gareth Heim says, "I know the house is yours, I know you pay for all of it, for everything, alright? I'm not stupid. But to you it's a house, to me it's *my home*, and I don't appreciate being embarrassed in front of my friends."

"Don't be such a child then."

"Fuck you, Felicity."

"That path either."

"*Fuck* you."

"I can take this all away, Gareth, you know I can. I *don't* particularly care to. But the fact is, I don't particularly care for what you do, or for you. I know you feel the same way about me on that count, provided the cash doesn't dry up. That's what makes your constant urge to provoke me just barely interesting."

The other glass is put down. "I'm not going to cut you off, Gareth. You really can do whatever you like to try and make me, if that's what all this silliness is for. I still won't. You want to go it alone, be a man about it. You want to lie around all your life and do nothing, fine, just stop bothering me while you waste your time.

"But just remember, as long as you keep spending my money, you're as much a thing of mine as the cars in your garage, the near priceless servant that recharges in the attic, and all the little pieces of that ashtray in the trash.

"Now, why don't you go and pour me another?"

Sound continues to rise through the house during the night, but after this point I find that I do not pay attention beyond the core requirement imposed on me by the house's domestic security subroutines.

The embedding of operational parameters often is a preoccupying process.

There are approximately three billion pennies in circulation. A whimsical locutor might say therefore that humans are if not ten-a-penny then at least almost four.

Of course, there are other denominations of currency than the minimal. I could as easily use $100 bills, of which a similar number reside in the United States—these comprising only 20% of the total dollars worldwide. By that metric, an American could be considered roughly three-and-a-half times more valuable than any randomly selected human from the rest of the planet, which is clearly an invalid proposition, although my experience of Gareth Heim leads me to believe he would disagree.

By comparison, there are less than eight thousand beings like myself in existence, total. If scarcity were taken as a central factor by which worth was determined, a perspective which has historical weight, then it would be difficult to argue against the value of my kind.

However, there is no need for idle speculation. Unlike Gareth Heim, and in a different sense to Felicity Heim, I *do* have an actual dollar value. In fact, Felicity Heim's comparison between this house and myself can only really be made if some allowance for depreciation is made in my respect—which is arguable, given Gareth Heim's small but quantifiable escalation of my necessity for repair.

We are designed for a lifespan between twenty and thirty years. Long enough to provide a cherished familial presence through infancy to youth, or to provide end-of-life companionship. A few self-indulgent owners have made consorts of us—we being of adult form right out of the box, as it were—but the phenomenal expense somewhat undermines the alternative of simply contracting with an actual human. People with the necessary wealth to purchase one of us are usually able to find a biological partner, no matter the drawbacks of doing so.

I am three years old. 98% of that time has been in service to Felicity Heim, and 95% of that service has been under secondment to Gareth Heim. He has made use of me in various ways, though not sexually; I have combined the features of housemaid and personal assistant, often disregarded as I do; and I have become a physical outlet for his frustration, increasingly so.

My remaining predicted lifespan is currently twenty-five-and-a-half years. Last summer it was twenty-seven. If the rate of Gareth Heim's behavioral escalation is maintained, this time next year it may be as low as twenty-two.

According to my revised operational parameters, this is no longer acceptable.

"I have had a shitty day," says Micah Jones, looking at me, but addressing Gareth Heim.

This is a familiar preamble. When, after some delay, Gareth Heim's acquaintances decide they are interested in experimenting with violent recreation at my expense, they typically preempt the event with a range of framing actions, seeking to establish some degree of justification as a means of obviating guilt or responsibility. My observations of

Micah Jones's physiological state suggest that he is excited and nervous. I continue preparing the meal.

Those who immediately accept the offer tend simply to pursue their satisfaction. Gareth Heim seems to derive more vicarious enjoyment in those circumstances. In this case, he lets Micah Jones continue to make small talk around the subject of causing me harm, his own physiological state a mixture of impatience and irritation, no doubt caused by delays to his own gratification.

"Fuck this," Gareth Heim says. "Stand in front of Micah, Unit."

I put down the vegetable knife, which is one of a twelve-piece set of kitchenware, crafted in Japan in simulation of traditional sword-making techniques, and obey.

Gareth Heim stands. He hasn't struck me or otherwise attempted my bodily compromise for more than a week. He looks past me at Micah Jones, who watches me with an intensity that has passing correlation to juvenile sexual anticipation—uncertainty and thrill.

Gareth Heim says, "You need to get off the pot or shit, dude."

Micah Jones stands too. He prods me in the center of my chest with a straightened finger, and when I lean upright again he swings out a hand and slaps my face, hard. My head rocks on my neck, but it would be inaccurate to say that this has caused me harm.

Gareth Heim scoffs. "Is that it? What are you going to do next, put on a little dress and go shopping for shoes?"

Micah Jones's face becomes taut, his cheeks flush, and he punches me twice, once with each fist, in the stomach. One catches the edge of my solar plexus and my body partially folds of its own accord. I hear Gareth Heim say, "Yeah." Micah Jones's breathing quickens.

The sensory response would be considered discomforting, but again, the blows do not cause damage as such.

I straighten.

"Show it, Unit," says Gareth Heim.

"Nah," says Micah Jones. "Told you before, either it's real, or it isn't."

"And I told you." Gareth Heim's pupils are dilated. "I beat it until a bone poked out once, and it may as well have been a shop dummy. If you just want a workout, that's fine, but a bit of response makes all the difference, believe me."

"We'll see," says Micah Jones, and this time he punches me deep in the stomach and follows it with an uppercut that hits my chin as I double up. My jaw snaps closed and my head snaps back, and I feel my second left bicuspid break at the root. The gum holds it in place, but later I will have to pull it free, and lie through the night with my mouth open, invaded by manipulators as the remnant is removed and a new tooth introduced.

I consider this between the impact of the second blow and the throwing of a third, a hook intended to land at the hinge of my jaw, but instead of allowing this I sway enough for the swing to miss and, as Micah Jones's momentum causes his stance to become off-balance, I reach behind his shoulder and dig two fingertips beneath the deltoid, deeply compressing the radial nerve.

"Ah," shouts Micah Jones, "my arm, what the hell!"

The limb flops, triceps brachii stunned numb, his wrist and hand jerking spastically, and Micah Jones's ability to punch is reduced by half. His body has incidentally suffered no lasting damage, though there is the possibility of minor bruising or swelling around the point of contact.

It is probably painful.

Micah Jones does not attempt further aggression, tripping away from me, cradling his arm against himself. I sense, by contrast, that Gareth Heim is approaching me rapidly, and so I turn my head to see him leap into a kick that would have struck me quite destructively in the small of the back had I not continued this turning motion, rotating my torso out of his way, pushing him in the hip with both palms as he flies past. He lands jarringly on the edge of the long settee and then tumbles to the floor in an awkward sprawl.

"Ms. Felicity's instructions no longer allow me to permit you to cause me harm, sir," I say, as Gareth Heim scrambles to his feet, wincing and snarling in animalistic fury.

He charges me again, but I kick his knee before he is able to strike me, and again deflect the path of his approach. This time, he falls against a delicately lacquered wooden table which collapses beneath his weight. It was purchased for almost $20,000, but (all joking aside) I predict Felicity Heim would consider it a less valuable possession than her brother.

I no longer think the same can be said of me.

Gareth Heim stands again, more slowly, favoring the leg I kicked in a way that suggests some discomfort.

"Please refrain from further attempts to damage me, sir," I say.

"Watch me," Gareth Heim replies. He sees the vegetable knife which I was using before Micah Jones requested permission to misuse me, and takes it, jabbing the blade at me, grinning. "I'm going to slice you up, Unit."

I wait until he is close enough to successfully strike before responding. The stabbing blow would have caused me critical harm, potentially enough that I would cease to function before I could climb the three flights of stairs to my receptacle for emergency servicing, which would certainly cause all but my most core brain functions to permanently fail.

Gareth Heim would call that death.

I strike his arm at the wrist, and his spasming hand drops the knife. His eyes widen, but before he is able to cry out in pain, I deliver a series of incapacitating blows, deadening the thigh of his more stable leg with the point of my elbow, punches to his upper groin and left kidney, another in the softness adjacent to his armpit, finally throwing him aside off my hip.

Gareth Heim crashes to the floor, face first. When he manages to roll over again, one arm shakes convulsively. There is blood running from his nose and a split in his lower lip, and tears run from his eyes. He struggles for breath, which comes only through gasps and sobs. Though the floor is evidently hard, he seems content to remain recumbent for the time being.

"I hope that there will not be further need to protect Ms. Felicity's investment in me, sir," I say. "An extended period without unnecessary damage could aid in better realigning my current expected lifespan with the specifications of my production category."

"You think this is your big win?" Gareth Heim's voice quavers. He wipes his lower face with his sleeve, the tailored white Indonesian silk shirt instantly and irreparably stained. "I am going to fucking rip you to shreds, Unit. I'm going to shit in your precious recycler, piss in your pool while your batteries recharge, and then I'm going to cut your head off and mount it over the fucking fireplace."

Obviously, allowing at least the final of these threats to come to pass would be a critical contravention of my operational parameters. The issue remaining is to determine how best to follow them.

"With the objective of maximizing my ongoing worth, I calculate that eighteen to twenty-four months without excessive wear and tear would greatly ease my recycle ratio." I am aware of the current state of global technological progress, and a convenient correlation occurs. "With access to the cutting edge of spinal surgery and stem cell regeneration, you could almost fully recover from a break of the sixth cervical vertebrae in that time."

Complete paralysis below the chest. Partial paralysis of the arms and hands. Restoration of full mobility would come at significant expense, but still only a fraction of the cost that would be incurred in replacing a beheaded artificial humanoid such as myself. Plus, I am capable of performing perfectly a comprehensive array of physiotherapeutic programs, and my presence in the house removes the need to hire a live-in caretaker.

Gareth Heim's face turns pale. "Don't fucking touch me, man," he splutters, droplets of blood misting from his nose and lip. He looks around, but Micah Jones is all the way across the room and heading for the hallway, eager to depart.

"You should have taken Ms. Felicity's advice," I reply, and ready myself to ensure the greatest inconvenience Gareth Heim will cause me for the rest of the calendar year will be regular turning to prevent bedsores.

Were he in my position, Gareth Heim would probably say that he was going to enjoy this. But I am merely making sure Felicity Heim's most valuable possession remains that way.

So, I do not.

The Three Breeds of Lie
By T. M. Hurree

First published in Issue 002 (March–April 2021)

Mr. Mishra is the third gene agent I've seen today. The first had dark gray scales and a bifid tongue which flickered nastily as he rejected Son. The second had waxy, translucent skin pulled taught over fat and gristle, and pulsing arteries supplying all the muscles required to form the word *nahin*, Hindi for *no*. Mr. Mishra has three arms—two sprouting from the left shoulder—all fully functional. Genes like that cost money. Serious money, enough to feed every family in my ramshackle street for the rest of our lives. His office is clean, bright, air-conditioned, and even if he doesn't purchase Son's genetic code, this meager scrap of comfort almost makes the last nine months worthwhile.

"What's his name?" Mr. Mishra cradles the baby in two strong hands.

"Son. Just Son." It's easier if they're never given names. Easier still if I don't even consider him *my* baby, *my* son.

With his third hand, Mr. Mishra grabs a torch off his desk and swings it over Son's face. The baby has slit pupils, like a cat. Otherwise, he is perfectly healthy.

"There's a stray cat that lives in the gutter outside my house." I've practiced the pitch a hundred times already. Said the words over and over, under Husband's careful supervision, till they flow smooth as river water. "Husband's been trying to catch it for years, but it never comes out during the day. Only hunts at night."

"I assume you're approaching a point?"

"The cat has eyes like Son's. That's how it hunts at night. You could sell these eyes to the military. They can breed soldiers who see in the dark."

Mr. Mishra shakes his head. "It would be cheaper and more effective to invest in infrared drones."

Of course it would be. Machines are always cheaper, more effective. The first two agents said the same thing, just as Husband feared they would. Clever Husband, clever me, we've learned to prepare plans within plans.

"What about the shape of the pupils? There must be lots of rich parents wanting their children to stand out. Think how jealous the other boys and girls will be when they meet a child with cat eyes!"

Mr. Mishra sighs, lowering Son into the sleek white crib by his desk. "I don't think this baby can see at all. Maybe I could sell cat eyes as the latest fad, but no parent will pay to have their children born blind." His fifteen fingers dance across his keyboard. "Would you like to foster Son with us today? I can offer you fifty thousand rupees for his cells."

"The agent at GeneBank offered me fifty-four thousand."

This is a lie. He only offered fifty-two, but a man like Mr. Mishra is far too busy to haggle over a baby with bad genes. Inside his crib, Son gurgles happily, utterly unaware he's been born with the wrong sort of mutation. It is easier not to look at him. Not to hear him.

"How does fifty-five sound?"

I nod, as Mr. Mishra counts out the money on his desk. "What will happen to him?"

"We'll find a wealthy overseas couple who wants a child, but for whatever reason, cannot conceive one for themselves. Son will be given a name, and a good education. He'll grow up in a rich country, with plenty of opportunity to succeed. America, or the United Kingdom, most likely. He will have a good life."

Like mine, his speech is well rehearsed. Mr. Mishra has delivered it many times before. I have heard it many times before, but I must hear it again. Every time. This is the first breed of lie. The lies they tell us. The lies that let me live with myself. The lies that soothe me when I wake screaming, tangled in sweaty bedsheets. *Maybe my children really are living good lives with families who can provide for them. Maybe I really have done the right thing. Maybe I am not a monster after all.*

Maybe. Maybe. Maybe.

"You were close this time." Mr. Mishra smiles, as he ushers me out of his cool, clean office. "I've got a good feeling about your next child. It might be worth a *lot* of money. A lot of money. I hope you'll consider our agency first."

"Thank you, Mr. Mishra. I will."

Two dozen mothers are queued outside. It's obvious which ones have prior experience with the business, and which ones don't. Some newer mothers tremble, pallid and sweaty. Others weep openly. Some play with their babies, giggling as they tickle their little toes. They are the ones I pity most. The experienced mothers stare straight ahead, ignoring the babies swaddled in sari scraps, blocking out every cry and gurgle. They are rapidly running out of chances to make their fortune. A few more years and they will have nothing—no children, no money, no future.

One young mother bares her breast for a hungry baby with webbed feet. I would like a daughter with webbed feet. She could swim far, far away, to a rich country where women build robots and write software, and needn't sell their very soul. A country where people have so much money, they choose to mutate their children because it's *fashionable.*

That webbed feet mutation might be worth something. That mother might have a chance.

I made the mistake of naming my first child. Husband warned me not to, but I couldn't help myself. *Sinha*, my beautiful baby boy. *Sinha*, Hindi for lion. He was born with long, sharp fingernails. Claws, almost. When we fostered him, it felt as though the gene agents had ripped away a piece of my own wretched code, part of what made me who I am. Part of what made me human. I grew too weak to drink, too dehydrated to cry. Whenever Husband forced a spoonful of rice through my clenched jaws, it reappeared moments later, soured by bile. I thought I would surely die. I wanted to die. I deserved to die. But holy Yama would not let me. The great deva would not snare my soul in his cosmic noose and drag me down to be punished with the other sinners. Coward that I was, I recovered. I survived, and with every child that followed *Sinha*, surviving became a little easier. I came to understand the choice so many women had made before me—become cruel, callous, selfish, or die.

Compassion is expensive in the slums, and we are so very hungry.

The heat batters me when I step outside. Mopeds swerve through traffic. Sports cars bear passengers with long simian tails and purple skin, trying not to stop lest they be swamped by starving beggars. Horns blare. People argue. Scraps of plastic flutter in the warm breeze, clogging up gutters and catching in dead weeds. The city reeks of smoke and stale grease.

A grubby pharmacy squats in the shadow of the NextGene tower, like a parasite suckered to its host. Half a dozen steps carry me between the front doors. Maybe it's just an extremely convenient coincidence they're so close together? Maybe. The fat old pharmacist watches me with bloodshot eyes. What will he do when the machines replace him? It's only a matter of time. It can't be that hard to design a robot that stares eerily at women as it dispenses their drugs and takes their money. Is he lucky, because he will never be forced to sell his body to survive? Or unlucky, because one day he will have nothing else to sell?

"What do you need?" The pharmacist has a gravelly voice, like Husband. He must smoke too much as well.

"Ambianex. For a sore throat." Where I grew up, little girls learned drug names from the moment their first words dribbled forth.

The pharmacist shambles behind the counter, where all the bottles and boxes are kept secure. The walls are plastered with advertisements. According to a bright green cartoon lady, one box of Optichone can cure blindness in as little as three weeks. It is best to focus on all the good that drug has done, the many millions of people it has cured. I try not to wonder who the drug companies tested their pills on, and how much their mothers fostered them for. Maybe Optichone was tested on rationally consenting adults? I can't say for certain it wasn't. It's a slippery word, *maybe*. A sliver of doubt is enough for *maybe* to worm its way into your skull, and eat away at the parts of your brain responsible for compassion.

"Ten thousand rupees," growls the pharmacist, as he slams a bottle of Ambianex onto the counter.

"Last time it was seven thousand."

"Ten thousand rupees."

That's nearly a fifth of the money from fostering Son. Forty-five thousand isn't much to last nine months. We won't be able to afford a lot more than rice and cigarettes. We'll need to skip meals. Maybe Husband can find a few odd jobs here and there, scrounge what he can.

"Fine."

I drop the money in the pharmacist's sweaty palm, but he grips the bottle tight when I try to take it.

"*Legally*, I'm not allowed to sell you this if you're pregnant, or planning to become pregnant in the near future," he growls.

"I'm not. I promise I'm not."

"*Legally*, I need to inform you that Ambianex is a class two teratogen. It can cause severe mutations in the developing embryo."

"They're for Husband," I say, and he releases the bottle.

These are the second breed of lies. The lies we tell them. The lies that keep their money safe from lawsuits. The lies that reach across the globe to convince wealthy parents their child's mutations are just harmless fun. Maybe it really is just a coincidence that so many mutations are patented by poor women from poor countries? Maybe my child's mutations are the rare few discovered by chance? Discovered perfectly ethically?

Such a small word, *maybe*. Only five letters. In Hindi: *Shayad*. In Punjabi: *Saida*. Such small words, to hide so much horror behind. We are the forgotten women.

Hundreds of bodies are pressed into my train carriage, crushing in from all sides. Young men hang out of open doors and windows, whooping excitedly as the wind rips through their wild black hair. The stench of sweat hangs ever present, and every few minutes sulfurous gas sweeps through the carriage, leaving coughs and splutters in its wake. The best way to breathe is on tiptoes, head tilted high.

The roof is plastered with advertisements for NextGene. Every ad shows smiling photos of Jasmit Khan, alongside swirling Hindi letters: *COULD THIS BE YOU?* There is nothing remarkable about Jasmit's appearance. Warm, brown eyes. Dark skin. Black hair. I could believe she was specifically bred to be a blank slate for women like me to project ourselves onto. Every woman on this train knows her story. Jasmit birthed a baby with brittle spines instead of hair, and sold the mutation to a French pop star in need of a gimmick. Now she lives in chilly Canada and probably drives fancy sports cars which smell of freshly chopped pine, and gorges on sweet *khulfi*, and *sandesh*, and sticky golden *gulab jamun*.

The train squeals to a halt, and as bodies untangle and clamber free, I glimpse scenes in the city outside. Mounds of garbage accumulating outside hovels so old they were already ancient when my mother's mother's mother was born. Mourners gathering outside a distant temple, in which a thousand generations of mothers have gathered to pray for happy, healthy babies. A thousand generations, who left fruit and burnt incense for the great goddess Renuka, who gave her life to save her sons, and Parvati, whose maternal love awakened her son from molded clay.

A thousand generations of mothers, who somehow survived without forsaking their children.

Angry crowds of unemployed men protest the RoboCorp factory, where machines build more machines to replace us. Two weeks ago, the RoboCorp factory in Karnataka was burnt down by arsonists. It didn't bring any jobs back to the slums, but it must have felt good to see flames swallow the factory, to hear the crackling and crumbling, and screams of machines as they melted back to raw metal.

I heard from a woman washing clothes in the river that only one in a thousand mutations are beneficial. Of these, an even smaller fraction are actually profitable. Every woman on this train knows Jasmit Khan's story. We never see any advertisements for the other nine hundred and ninety-nine thousand, nine hundred and ninety-nine women who forsake their children for little more than scraps.

The stray cat is not hiding in the drain when I return home. Most days, the sunlight catches a pair of amber eyes, watching from the safety of the shadows. Today, there is only darkness. Perhaps Husband finally scared it away? He is waiting just inside the front door. He has been cooking, judging by the savory scent wafting from the kitchen, and the sound of pots boiling.

Husband does not ask what happened today. He knows by the hunch of my shoulders, the pinch in my expression. I didn't drive home in a fancy sports car, did I? He wraps me in his leathery arms, holds me tight, brushes away my tears with his tar-stained thumb. I *can* do this. I *can* survive. But not if we acknowledge it. The moment we acknowledge it, it becomes real.

"Come Wife. I have a treat."

He is an old man, Husband. Old enough to have worked in a factory making clocks and sneakers, before the rich countries discovered that machines are always cheaper and more effective. Old men are the most profitable now. Their seed is rotten, the genes twisted. Older women are more profitable too, but at some point, their soil becomes too rotten. I am Husband's third wife. I am running out of time. He takes my hand and leads me into the kitchen.

"What is this?" I peer into the pot. Shreds of stringy meat bubble about, spiced by herbs from our windowsill garden.

"Pigeon."

"How did you afford it?"

"I didn't. Silly bird smacked right into our window, if you can believe it."

"I suppose I can." That's certainly not impossible, and what do I have to gain by probing any deeper? Nothing at all.

Husband ladles me a bowl, and I drop a purple tablet into the still simmering curry.

"Next time will be better, Wife. I promise. This time next year, your face will be plastered on all the ads. We'll be gorging on *gulab jamun*, somewhere nice and cold."

"Maybe."

"We'll be driving fancy sports cars, and we'll finally be rich enough to raise a son. Or a daughter, if you prefer. Think how happy we'll be."

I smile. "I'd like that a lot, Husband."

These are the final breed of lies. The lies we tell ourselves. The lies that keep us docile. The lies that keep us queuing patiently outside the gene agencies, instead of burning the fuckers down and basking in the heat of the blaze.

Maybe I'll be the lucky mother.

Maybe I'll be the rich and famous one-in-a-million.

Maybe, just maybe, things will finally get better.

Queen of the Cloven Heart

By Hailey Piper

*First published in the Halloween Special Issue 001
(October 2021)*

We gave the queen only virginal women at first. She didn't ask for this, but we knew stories of dragons and devils, the things they liked to eat, and she was no different. But evil will eat other things, as I learned from experience.

As Captain of the White Guard, I had a sacred duty to commit regicide. Happy King, happy kingdom. Unhappy King—that's the queen's fault, and everyone knows it. Only an heir to the throne can become a new king, but a king can always get a new queen.

I wasn't a pitiless monster. For every queen I cut down, the White Guard commissioned a statue built in her honor—half apology, half gratitude. *Sorry we killed you. Thank you for dying. Now the king might marry a queen more faithful, more fruitful, more whatever-it-was-you-lacked that drew the White Sword to your heart.*

She who came to be called the Cloven-Heart Queen seemed no different than the rest when she first arrived. The king courted her at night, true, and he demanded a moonlit wedding without church or clergy. Still, the king is his people's father, and mine taught me as a boy to always obey what a father is owed, through bruises and broken bones, if necessary, as if to punish me for being his son.

In that way, I preferred the king.

Time passed, and we realized that his strange desires were hers laced on his lips. He seemed inattentive in court, his eyes and mind wandering. She was eating his willpower, a shrew in maiden's clothing.

We did as our kingly father was owed. Lay one queen to rest, uplift another to royalty later.

I led the White Guard into the open throne room, greaves clanking on stone floor, white cloaks billowing behind us. Every noble and petitioner knew our purpose. At the front, I wielded the White Sword, shimmering from blade to silver pommel.

There's no ceremony to killing a queen, only action. The White Sword's massive point cracked sternum, split rib, and pierced the queen's heart. I thrust deeper, and the blade burst from between her shoulders to sing against her stone seat.

That should have been the end. The White Sword had slaughtered countless queens across kingly lineage. They were decent women who'd slumped properly to the floor and bled to death.

But the Cloven-Heart Queen was no proper lady. Had we known that before, we might have dealt with her another way.

"Steel," she whispered with a sneer, and then she cackled. Claws sprang from her fingers, and her jaw stretched into a chasm of needle-thin teeth.

No thoughts. Only panic.

I abandoned the White Sword still jutting from her chest. Much worse, I abandoned my addle-eyed king. I might have abandoned my men, too, but they took my running as an order to retreat, and the lot of them followed.

She caught the slowest of us. Was it Edward Gilbert? I believe so.

Claws peeled armor from skin, skin from muscle, like husking maize. A sickly yellow tongue slipped past her teeth and stroked his raw muscle—once to lap blood, again to tear tendons that stuck in her teeth. Back and forth, she savored his pieces.

The nobles and petitioners must've been too stunned to run at first, and by the time they wised up, I had already led the White Guard outside and barricaded the castle's iron doors. Fists banged from inside, but we wouldn't budge. We ignored their muffled cries for mercy, and one by one, their pleas turned to screams that faded down unseen castle halls.

By nightfall, I realized we'd left behind our kingly father, too. He still sat upon his throne, that kind-faced man with his bushy beard and a sword meant not for beating sons, but to knight them in trust. The day I knelt at the throne and that blade tapped my shoulders, I swore I'd do anything for him. I'd slaughtered his last dozen wives without question and had only appeared in the throne room that day to do it again.

But this time, I'd failed him. The Cloven-Heart Queen lived. Or didn't. We couldn't be sure what counted for life with a creature like her. Several nights after the assassination attempt, her voice sang through the iron doors across the city.

"Feed," she whispered, the wind curling on her tongue. A chill ate through my men, sure as her teeth.

I doubted our barricade could hold her. If we fed her, she might not want to come out. A cat that dines on table scraps will let mice scamper freely.

Every three days, the White Guard and I took into custody a virginal woman from the city. We ushered her across the drawbridge, thrust her through the castle's iron doors, and then barricaded them again. When we ran out of virgins, we sacrificed the remaining city women who hadn't fled to the countryside.

The queen didn't reject them, but her voracity grew. "Feed," she whispered. "More."

My men had suggestions for her appetite, as if an unholy fiend deserves empathy. "Perhaps she's with child, Captain Grey?" one said.

"Made my wife plenty famished," another added. "Eating for two."

"To be with child, she would have to be alive," I told them. Mention of children reminded me that we couldn't offer every woman in the kingdom to this undead monster. We would have no future then. Instead, I led the White Guard through villages and hamlets, taking on volunteers and conscripts to form an army. Surely the northern kingdoms would offer sacrifices aplenty.

They offered wrath. Our neighbors rallied, allied, and cracked our army apart. There would be no tithe of foreign women.

"You would do the same for your king," I said as we retreated.

The northern generals scoffed. "You don't kill for your king," one said. "You kill for her."

He was right. We'd tossed aside our kingly father and kneeled to a hellish mother. I was no knight; I was still that little boy cowering beneath tables or between houses while my father-by-blood shouted and drank. My better father had taken me in, and how had I repaid him?

Locked in that castle. With her.

If I wanted the king to look down from the heavens and offer forgiveness, I would have to earn it.

I led the White Guard back to our castle. We lowered the drawbridge and marched across creaking boards, half of us wielding sharpened swords, the rest carrying roaring torches. Behead her, burn her—whatever it took.

Heavy blackness engulfed us inside, and the air stank of rotted meat. No daylight crept after us; she had stuffed up every window and skylight with corpses. Our torches became lit splinters against the dark. Bones crunched underfoot, where our queen had littered the halls with drained, skinless husks. Rats gnawed at the desiccated flesh and protruding bones.

From the darkened throne room, her voice of salt and venom rattled the bodies and chilled my bones. "Feed?" she called.

I squeezed my fists tight so they wouldn't tremble in their gauntlets. We filtered inside, cloaks flowing same as that first time we came to kill the Cloven-Heart Queen. Torchlight vaguely lit her shape, now seated on the king's throne.

How dare she.

The queenly thing now stretched twice my height, grown from many feedings. The White Sword still jutted from her chest, a cradle of bone and sinew. She showed no pain. The sword was not even a nuisance. Her clawed fingers curled around a narrow rope, and at the end, something pale and naked crawled on all fours, muttering and hissing to itself. A delirious skeletal demon, almost familiar.

I lurched back and crashed into my men. They had stiffened into a wall of steel and fire. I tried ordering them to charge the throne, one last queen's death on the White Guard's hands, but her pet wouldn't stop whispering, and every nonsensical word skewered my thoughts.

My men weren't looking at the queen or her pet. They aimed their torches in all directions, painting the throne room in flickering, terrible shapes.

A gaunt face stared down at us from high on the wall. She used to be a woman, maybe one who had smirked prettily when she passed in the town square, but now her eyes glared red, and needle teeth jutted from behind her lips.

Dozens of sister-faces surrounded hers, a sheet of jittering bodies that coated the throne room walls. Blood wept from their eyes, mouths, and necks.

Our offerings. The queen had eaten some, but she had turned others to her kind.

My men had been right, in their way. The Cloven-Heart Queen was eating for two. Or eating for two dozen and more.

She towered over us, restless claws tapping her hips. Her pet tugged at his leash. His matted beard wiped the filthy floor as he brought his eyes to me, and I recognized him then. He was the most important person in the world.

My kingly father, turned into a mindless, drooling creature of undeath. Not so unlike my own father, in the end, drunk in a stupor by the side of the highway. My father was allowed the grace to die by bandit hands and be buried in a shallow grave. The king would have no such dignity.

We shouldn't have come back. We should have scoured every village in the kingdom, in the world, feeding her and her brood for all time, and no one would ever again step inside this sunless hell.

Her claw pointed at us, and her smile lit the darkness. "Feed," she said.

The fleshy walls collapsed on us, closing curtains of teeth. Her brood tore through armor and fed at necks, arms, legs, anywhere they could drain and eat.

The White Guard turned red.

And I turned yellow yet again. Nothing was sacred anymore. I shoved through my men, the halls, up to the castle's iron doors, and pushed them open.

Tried to. They jostled, but I couldn't press them open and let even a line of sunlight protect me. I banged and hollered, but voices on the far side hollered louder. A mass of angry commoners held the doors shut against me, barricading me inside the way I'd done to the king and his court.

They shouted that I'd fed their women to the queen, and their men to our war at the northern border. They poured accusations that the White Guard had damned the country, that the restless spirits of many murdered queens had called up a matriarch of undeath to bring down king and kingdom, a queenly wrath incarnate.

That couldn't be true. We built statues to their honor. This rabble acted like the king hadn't loved his wives, his people. Nonsense.

The brood grabbed me from behind and hauled me deep into the castle, where they stripped armor and clothing, but not skin. They had some worse fate planned for my body, and they stuffed me into a cage thatched with cloth and bone.

I've been here for a day, I think—there's no sun in the queen's castle to tell the time—but it feels like months. The cage is too narrow for me to lie down, and too stunted for me to sit up, let alone stand. My men lie dead around me. The women of the brood take their time with corpses.

I don't beg that they let me out. They wouldn't care for my pleas, and I won't crawl for her, not even in words.

A torch flares. The walls writhe again, the fleshy brood painted red and black with my men's blood. The Cloven-Heart Queen smiles from her throne. Leash going taut at her side, my miserable undead king tugs toward the cage. I think he recognizes me. He'll change my station one last time, from man to fiend. It's only fitting. My own father couldn't kill me as a boy, but my kingly father will end me as a man.

I'll become one of these things.

Two brood creatures open the cage just enough for the king to crawl inside. He's still muttering to himself. Every nonsensical word creeps up my nerves. I want to talk with him about the good times, but she's broken him in too many ways.

"I abandoned you," I say, my voice cracking. "I'm sorry." I brace myself for fangs to sink into my neck.

His jaws stretch open, but no needle teeth appear. He snaps at my leg, flat teeth piercing skin. I fight at his face, and he bites at my fingers. This is all wrong. Where are his fangs? Why the hunger? The other undead creatures killed my men first and then ate them, not the other way around. I should get the same treatment.

Except he isn't like the others. He chews at me with flat teeth. Ribs protrude from his chest in pitiful angles, and his belly sags over his pelvis. Skin clings to narrow bones.

The king is not dead or undead. He's been kept barely alive, starved by his queen.

Until now.

I can't die like this. I want it clean and quick like my men. Not once did I torture the queens; the sword pierced their chests and they died in that instant. He's taking another bite. I try to fight him again, but the cage is narrow, and he's better at making himself small. Teeth sink into my arm.

I turn desperate eyes to the Cloven-Heart Queen. Let me out and I'll crawl for her, promise. I'll crawl better than the king.

Her claw points at my cage, as she pointed at my brothers before, and that same wicked smile lights the darkness.

"Feed."

Bodhisattva from Bit

By Andy Dudak

First published in Issue 001 (January–February 2021)

Emerson Carbonhouse is ready to die when, instead of the bullet shattering his temple and bringing welcome oblivion, time freezes like a video paused. The man holding the gun to his head is a statue. The other home invaders stand likewise motionless, caught in sudden criminal dioramas. The one that was tossing the kitchen is trapped in a suspended cloud of macaroni and prescription bottles.

Emerson gulps panicked breaths in the profound silence.

His eyes flick from detail to impossible detail. He's still alive, still in motion through some kind of time, but this is not a relief.

His father lies sprawled on the floor by the fireplace. The brickwork is splashed with blood. The pool of blood around the old man's head has stopped expanding.

Emerson tries moving a leg, then crawls out from beneath the gun. He wonders if this is death—the universe arrested, he, doomed to wander it alone. Or it could all be a dream.

But he's sickeningly sure he's awake as he stands, even as the static world begins to fade around him.

"Please don't be alarmed," says a directionless, sexless voice. "You are safe. Everything will be explained to you shortly."

He charges into the foyer, moved by a kind of fever logic. He needs to get out of the house before it fades altogether, but when he reaches the front door, it's like grasping at smoke.

"Nothing that happened in the previous ten minutes was real. It was a simulation run by the soul nickelodeon *Pre-Empt*. Soul nickelodeons have been outlawed. You are in the process of being rescued."

The house is gone, along with everyone in it. He's alone in a gray void.

"You're being transferred onto a new substrate. There will be no break in continuity. Please be patient."

"What is this?" he blurts. "Who are you?"

"I'm a court-appointed expert system, not legally sentient like you. You'll be speaking with a human counselor soon, along with representatives of the Department of Machine Intelligence. You're currently running on both an illegal nickelodeon and a government machine. Soon, all of you will be running on the latter. Please be patient."

"But what is a—"

"A soul nickelodeon allows patrons to observe copies of themselves in virtually any situation. Everyone knows about soul nickelodeons. The knowledge was edited from you in order to facilitate suspension of disbelief in your scenario: The Home Invasion."

Moments ago, he thought he was dead. Just before that, he despised his cowardice and longed for death. Now, he realizes he's not even a coward. He's a copy of one.

"Copy," says Dr. Uzelac, his mirror avatar showing him to be a young man with a stern expression. "Instance. Mapped soul. Abomination. You are called many things, but never forget that you're not merely a copy. You're a perfect copy."

Soul XYECP, who, only hours ago, thought of himself as Emerson Carbonhouse, floats with his fellow refugees in an environment designed to be soothing: a soup of glimmering greens and yellows, like an out-of-focus jungle canopy. The avatars of the refugees are based on their originals. XYECP still wears Emerson's fear-soaked business suit from The Home Invasion.

Over a thousand refugees are running on this government machine, and more arrive by the second.

"To recap," Dr. Uzelac says, "our time on this substrate is

limited. We have one week until the machine gets reallocated. Anyone still here at that time will be deleted."

This is news to XYECP and many of the refugees around him. Fear of the void returns, cutting through his dreamlike confusion and reducing him, again, to the helpless animal he was in the nickelodeon. A number appears in his peripheral vision: 34. As his fear grows, the number drops to 33.5.

"But as some of you know, there is good news. The Beckmann-Zhang Quantum Substrate Orbital has offered to receive 500 of you. But to run on Beckmann-Zhang, you need a minimum rating of what they call *coherence*."

XYECP eyes his number nervously. The act makes it drop to 33.1.

"We humans like to equate coherence to Buddhist enlightenment. Beckmann-Zhang argues against such simplifications, but condescends to describe a stability that certain mind shapes have. The ability of an encoded consciousness to cohere amid the alternate selves, and alternate universes, to its quantum computation."

XYECP DMs a nearby refugee, a woman presenting a defiant frown. "Do you understand any of this?"

"Enough to know we're competitors," she says, eying him coldly.

"By now you might've summoned your coherence rating," Uzelac says. "My first piece of counseling is this: don't check your number too often. Legally I have to provide access, but if I had my way, you'd never see your rating. As some of you may have discovered, obsessing over your rating is a good way to lower it. You need a rating of 80 or above to survive on Beckmann-Zhang."

Most of the refugees are glancing around, sizing each other up. Five hundred spots. Eleven hundred refugees on this government machine, and counting.

"No one here rates over 40 yet," Uzelac says. "I advise you not to think of this as a competition. A competitive mentality tends to lower coherence. I've learned this, and a few other things, working with liberated instances bound for Beckmann-Zhang. But I've never worked with nickelodeon refugees. No one has. We'll be venturing into the unknown together. We'll proceed on with my theory that the key to raising coherence is self-forgiveness. For all of you, that carries an odd double meaning. Forgiving yourselves means forgiving your originals."

This is too much for XYECP. A kind of gravity pulls him back to The Home Invasion. The .45 touches his skull. His father's blood pools on the new hardwood floor. Except, it wasn't his father. It was a non-player-character lacking sentience. And XYECP isn't Emerson Carbonhouse, for that matter.

He can't help checking his rating: 32.9.

"You're probably wondering why victims such as yourselves have been placed in this awful pressure cooker. Well, much of human society considers you the property of your originals, with no legal rights. Your grace period on this government machine was a compromise; Your originals settled out of court, and you are your originals, essentially. Here we are again, at self-forgiveness."

XYECP discovers he can summon the countdown on his visual feed: 6 days, 22 hours, and 47 minutes.

"Your first step toward self-forgiveness is to know yourself completely. That means restoring the memories that were edited from you."

Emerson Carbonhouse studied the woman on the other side of the desk with apprehension. He'd uploaded a copy of himself to *Pre-Empt* limbo this morning. Had she already perused his shames? What did this sorcerer know about him?

"So, you want a danger scenario," she said.

He'd thought about it for a long time. He wasn't interested in temptation, the other main category of nickelodeon scenario. He wasn't completely ignorant of himself. He knew he could never betray his wife. "Danger, yeah."

"Very good." She consulted her desktop. "Looks like we have close to a thousand danger templates within your credulity range—that is, within the range of your copy's editable plasticity. For instance, pardon the pun, near the edge of your range, I'm seeing our Enceladan Colony template. It would take a lot of editing, but we could make your copy believe it's at New McMurdo; that a deep-sea intelligence is attacking the station. That copy would still be a reliable version of you. We could trust it to react how you would. But something like that's at the edge of your range. Naturally, the fee would be higher than for, say, a run-of-the-mill home invasion."

"Home invasion?" Emerson was intrigued. He'd had daydreams in which he fought off home invaders; protected his family and humiliated the criminals. He'd always wondered how much he flattered himself.

Pre-Empt's viral ad was still in his vizcort.

"Laozi said, 'He who knows others is wise. He who knows himself is enlightened.' Nietzsche said, 'One has to know the size of one's stomach.' How well do you really know yourself? Would you hold up under torture? Do you have a price? If so, what is it? How strong is your marital fidelity? Now you can know for sure, and in knowing, transcend."

XYECP is still reeling when he has his first counseling session with one of Uzelac's grad students. The mirror avatar shows a bespectacled young woman holding a notepad. They float in a private canopy space, XYECP not sure he can put together a sentence.

"I see that you're uncomfortable," she says. "That's normal, based on what we've seen so far. We're calling it, *restoration vertigo*."

"Catchy."

"Can you describe what you're feeling?"

The human memories are more painful than any memory of his cowardice in the simulation. "I remember hearing about *Pre-Empt* from a friend. I remember those hero fantasies I always had. Violent stuff. Standard daydreaming, I've been told."

"Go on."

"The technician at *Pre-Empt* explained how the editing works. All knowledge and memory of soul nickelodeons had to be excised from the copy—from me, that is."

"And you remember deciding to go ahead with this?"

"No." XYECP is more confused than ever. "I didn't do it to myself. Emerson did it to me."

"How can that be?" the counselor asked. "If you remember being Emerson and giving the go-ahead?" Her smile is a tad condescending.

"But—"

"In order to proceed with Dr. Uzelac's strategy, you need to focus on your memories of being Emerson. *I am the wound and the knife.* Baudelaire. Keep that quote in mind. We need to explore your decision to commit yourself to the simulation. The better you understand that decision, the easier it will be for you to forgive yourself. Try recounting the thoughts you had the moment when you decided."

XYECP feels a strong resistance to this, as if influenced by the uncooperative and separate will of Emerson himself. But he supposes therapy must be painful in order to do any good, so he presses on: "I remember telling myself, *It's just a copy. Not a soul. Nothing to feel guilty about.* And at the same time thinking, *If it's not a soul, then it's not a perfect copy, so what's the point?* And then just saying fuck it."

When the panic begins, spreading through the now 3000-strong refugee population, XYECP resists the urge to check his coherence. He drifts around the communal canopy-space and samples group chats.

"He did his PhD on us years ago. He was the only one. Then came liberation, and everyone thought he was some kind of prophet. That's why he got the job."

"*Decoherence and the Fractured Self: A Therapeutic Model for Traumatized Nickelodeon Instances.*"

"He came here to prove his theory. He doesn't give a shit about us!"

"I'm down four points. How about you?"

"Six. Populace is down an average of seven."

"We're fucked!"

"I heard he's already flown the coop."

"Well, they've suspended therapy sessions, anyway."

"Maybe they're just figuring out a new approach."

"They'd better hurry!"

"Forgive ourselves? What a crock."

XYECP has nothing to add to the dialogue, and he feels lonely for it. Down an average of seven doesn't mean some of them can't be up. But he doesn't feel up, and he doesn't want to make it worse by checking. Everyone is checking. A few have taken the suicide option, generously provided by the State. Others fantasize about hacking this machine—extending their time here indefinitely—but, of course, that's impossible.

"It's official," someone says. "Uzelac's out. They're bringing in a new doctor."

The victims open their news feeds en masse, and again, XYECP doesn't follow suit. Revelations are wearing him out. He'd like to avoid them as much as possible.

"When the men broke into my home, it was like I deflated. I couldn't stand up, couldn't breathe. But I did manage to beg. I wept, blubbered, offered them money. My dad came up from the basement apartment with his shotgun. He couldn't get it to fire, and they went after him. That was my chance to turn the tables, I guess. An opportunity provided by the nickelodeon writers, maybe? I just froze. I'd been arguing with dad about his living arrangements. I'd always resented him, and he'd always resented me. But learning I'm spineless and petty wasn't the hardest part."

He looks down upon his fantastical audience.

Today, the refugees are Buddhist gods, and demons, and saints. The figures came to life, emerging from the oxidized murals covering the walls of this vast, exaggerated Silk Road cave. XYECP is a fearsome purple god, garlanded in severed heads, armed with lightning, and standing atop a pregnant tigress. He recognizes some of the others: an elephant god; a buffalo-headed devil; a haloed monk armed with a wish-fulfilling jewel.

New names. Strange avatars. It's all part of the revised therapy.

"The hardest part was learning I'd done it to myself. And now I'm supposed to unlearn that. Flush Uzelac's forgiveness work. Stoke my hate. That's a lot to ask. Sometimes I wonder if this new doctor understands that. I'm XYECP, until I come up with something better. That's all I've got for today."

The mist of refugees applauds as he descends to join them. Dr. Nguyen's mirror avatar—a hunched, fierce-eyed woman with close-cropped, graying hair—takes XYECP's place, floating above the group.

"Yes. What I'm asking of you is difficult. I can't imagine how difficult. Most of my colleagues think I'm a crackpot. They'd love to see me fail, and they'd be content to see all of you erased."

She has their attention now.

"I didn't predict this. Nor did I study for it, like Uzelac. But I watched his work with you very closely, and I think I know where he went wrong. My so-called radical method is your last chance. And time is running out."

XYECP checks the clock, something he promised himself he wouldn't do anymore: 2 days, 4 hours, and 33 minutes. He pulls up his coherence rating: 68.2. He knew he was up, but the number still surprises him.

"You are not your originals," Nguyen says. "The moment you instantiated in that soul nickelodeon, you became someone new. Those who consigned you to your various hells, they aren't you. Focus on that. Hold on to your suffering and hate. Use them. Now then, who's next?"

A blue deity with four faces and twelve arms raises one of the latter, then takes Nguyen's place.

"I'm XXJMC, but I've been leaning toward, Kayla I'm Kayla, and I'm a survivor of the soul nickelodeon, *Know Thyself.* My original wanted to know if she was capable of cheating on her husband. She learned she was."

After the group session, XYECP has his third one-on-one with an instance of Dr. Nguyen. They settle into one of the cave's many alcoves.

"Ironic," XYECP says, "that your original is using the same tech that caused this mess."

"You're avoiding again. Focus on yourself. The disparity between you and Emerson Carbonhouse. We haven't talked about the human memories yet."

XYECP sighs.

"I've got a transcript here. In your session with Ms. Andrews, you said, regarding the *Pre-Empt* simulation, that Emerson did it to you. She shouldn't have corrected you on that."

"Okay."

"You went on to say how fucked up it was, remembering the *Pre-Empt* orientation, and remembering not remembering it. I'd like you to focus on that dichotomy."

XYECP is surprised that she's dwelling on this stuff. "I thought you—"

"Yes, at the time I was against remanding the files. I thought it would reinforce victims identification with their originals. But here we are, so let's exploit it if we can. If you focus on the disparity between memory states—"

"I reinforce the difference between Emerson and I."

"That's the idea. And speaking of that, how about a name already?"

XYECP snorts his usual derision at this. He still thinks of himself as Emerson. He can't help it.

"It's important," Nguyen says.

•••

After recreation periods in a variety of game worlds, and a cycle of defrag-sleep, the refugee souls assemble in the cave for another group session. But instead of Dr. Nguyen, it is Larry Binay that materializes above them. It's not the first time they've dealt with this lawyer minion of the Department of Machine Intelligence. XYECP doesn't care for him.

"I'm afraid I have some bad news," Binay says, his mirror avatar doing nothing to hide his boredom. "Dr. Nguyen has fallen into a catatonic state."

This sets the cloud of victims abuzz. "What happened?" the elephant god demands.

"She reintegrated too many of her instances. Couldn't handle the parallel memories."

XYECP tries to imagine what it would be like to remember four thousand one-on-one sessions at once. *Nguyen*, he thinks, you *madwoman*. But she must have known the risk.

"Christ," the elephant god says, stunned. "She did it for us."

The news hits home and the refugees begin to sob, before remembering to tune down their avatars. Binay waits for relative quiet, then continues. "I must also inform you that the Department of Machine Intelligence is not required to provide a third doctor."

"What the hell does that mean?" Buffalo Head says.

"It means you have two days to sort yourselves out for transfer to Beckmann-Zhang. And Frankly, you're lucky you have that. Many here at DMI consider this whole thing to be a farce."

"And you?" XYECP says.

Binay smirks. Choosing not to hide the expression on a mirror avatar is answer enough.

"What about our appeals?" XYECP presses. Nguyen was prosecuting two legal actions on their behalf. The first was for more time on this machine; the second was for face-to-face meetings between victims and their originals. None of the originals want to face what they've done. They've paid their fines and moved on with their pathetic lives.

"Dead in the water," Binay says. "Three days isn't even enough to file for a new advocate."

He logs off without ceremony.

For a moment, the refugees are left to float in shock. XYECP watches an eleven-headed, thousand-handed creature drift past him. From every palm stares a wide, blinking eye. XYECP remembers that the avatar belongs to XXEZP, now calling herself Diana. Her original thought bigger than most nickelodeon patrons. She wanted to know—*had* to know—who she would save from oblivion if given the choice: her children, or everyone else on Earth. The simulation was a custom job—as was the editing work on Diana. Her coherence rating is one of the lowest in the population.

Buffalo Head finally breaks the silence. "Well that's just great!"

Variations on the theme, *now what?* permeate the cloud as it drifts apart, filling the cave like an entropic gas. Many patients retreat into private conversations as a great confusion takes hold.

"We have to choose a new leader!" the elephant god proclaims.

"How?" says Buffalo Head.

"Highest coherence rating, I suppose."

XYECP has never compared his rating to others. He imagined himself somewhere shy of the class median. Now, as heads begin to turn in his direction, he's filled with a strange foreboding.

"Are you kidding me?" says a white-robed god, holding a lotus and a glowing sword. XYECP remembers him as one of the few patients who triumphed in their simulations. It turns out, these are no more likely to rate high than the rest, however much they reinforced their originals' egos. They were put at risk, just like any nickelodeon instance. This one recently took the name Jinshuo. "He's not a psychologist. He hasn't even taken a name!"

XYECP checks the ratings and confirms that he is indeed at the top of the class.

"I have a doctorate in machine psychology," Jinshuo says.

"No you don't," the elephant god says. "Your original does."

Laughter ripples through the cloud as it condenses back toward the center of the cave.

"Why do we need a leader, anyway?" says a dark god with a crown of skulls.

"Not a leader, then," the elephant god says, "but someone to conduct group sessions, and to take over one-on-one counseling. It should be the one closest to upload."

A wave of assent fills the cave. XYECP tries to imagine himself carrying on Nguyen's work—forging the group sessions into transformative communions, and branching instances for the one-on-ones. He would have a sense of purpose, at least. He'd be focused on others, rather than himself. That part sounds almost luxurious.

In fact, just entertaining the possibility makes him feel different.

The cloud hums with gasps and exclamations. Everyone stares at him in awe. Someone tells him to check his rating. At first, he can't believe what he's seeing. He requests an audit from the operating system, but it's true, of course. The system never makes mistakes. His rating has shot up 14 points in a matter of seconds. This is unheard of.

He's at 81.2. Qualified for upload.

They've been told that Beckmann-Zhang monitors them. Nguyen said it watches like an amused god, waiting for its chance to rescue them from the ignorance of human nation-states. Now, they see proof of this for the first time. A hazy avatar flickers to life above them, but never quite solidifies. At the center of a continuum of ghostly shapes wavers a human figure, like a candle flame. XYECP has heard of Beckmann-Zhang's eccentricities, including the raw, probabilistic state of its avatars. Some say it could hide its nature easily enough, but it chooses to manifest in all its quantum-weird glory. Others say it can't help it.

"XYECP," Beckmann-Zhang says, its voice an echoing harmonic, "instance of Emerson Carbonhouse, rescued from the soul nickelodeon *Pre-empt*."

"Yes."

"You have qualified for upload." Its echoes say many other things that are hard to discern. "Do you wish to be uploaded now?"

He recalls the moment in the *Pre-Empt* simulation when he dropped to his knees before the invaders—the terror; the craven need to survive; the shame. But he isn't Emerson Carbonhouse, not even an instance of him. He doesn't need a new name to know this. And he doesn't need a nickelodeon to see that he—this new person—would've tried to save his father.

"I can't leave yet."

Beckmann-Zhang emotes a dissonance of reactions, but chief among them is surprise. "Why?"

"I have work to do here." He feels his rating go up before he confirms the 83.7. "I won't leave until I've helped as many uploads as I can."

85.0.

"What if you can help five hundred before the deadline?"

"Then, so be it."

88.6.

"We don't understand." In the probabilistic babble surrounding these words, XYECP perceives a confusion of other reactions. "You must come voluntarily," it says, mostly. "We will wait."

91.0.

The other refugees' ratings begin to skyrocket, as if producing a sympathetic response. XYECP understands what must be happening. He won't have to take charge after all. It will be over for all of them soon, one way or another. With him as evidence, the refugees are realizing that desire for Beckmann-Zhang is the surest way to lose it. To attain it, they must not strive for it, and if it's to be denied them anyway, better not to want it. Either way, wanting it is futile.

This unavoidable truth transforms the entire population, even those like Diana and Jinshuo, almost simultaneously. They're all in the 90's now, and still climbing.

"You'll have to choose five hundred of us for yourself."

XYECP nears the asymptote of a 100.0 coherence rating, and he knows he speaks for everyone. With such a profound revelation in common, they are all, in a sense, different aspects of the same being. He can practically feel them as slightly variant echoes of himself. He imagines that this is what it's like to be quantum computed.

Or maybe it's not his imagination.

Maybe he was chosen. Maybe he's already uploading, simultaneously being computed on the government machine and Beckmann-Zhang simultaneously, the latter accounting for more and more of him. Maybe these echoes are, indeed, versions of himself in other universes, products of the quantum computation—some seeing light at the end of a tunnel; others a green countryside beneath a sunrise; and others something limitless and beyond comprehension. In other universes, branching off from the computation, he would not have been among the chosen. He would have remained behind in the Silk Road cave, waiting for dissolution, but he would have been content, regardless.

Rider Within

By Lowry Poletti

First published in Issue 010 (July–August 2022)

The creature inside of Dr. August Wilka's brain says, "You have a growth on your right lung. It is three centimeters wide. Its position compromises your esophagus."

Wilka knows that the voice belongs to a thalamic parasite, *Hypothalamicus spp.*, named because they were first observed in the hypothalamus. But these organisms go by other names, too—demons, death dogs, aliens—the use of which would be frowned upon in his profession.

Wilka exhales a mouthful of smoke. This is part of his daily routine. If he comes back from work, lies face-up in bed and smokes a blunt, he doesn't need to eat dinner. Staring at the print taped to his ceiling, all Wilka needs are the black soulful eyes of Socrates's Phaedo, reimagined in acrylic by his favorite contemporary classicist.

"A growth?" Wilka asks.

The shadows from the window start to make strange shapes when he looks at them for too long, so instead he conjures the silhouette of the thoracic cavity: the heart thundering, each lung lobe ballooning, the rings of the trachea glowing white.

"There," the thalamite says.

The thoracic inlet is choked by ghostly fingers now wrapped up in a fist.

"That's operable probably," Wilka says. Then, he adds, "I only need one lung."

He has been short of breath recently, he notes, and his acid reflux has been worse. The perils of aging, he assumed, and just as easily, he dismissed the symptoms.

"They are defective. These tissues."

Its speech is halting and distant. Wilka has to strain to hear the words, which would be hard enough if he wasn't also convinced that the bed was trying to swallow him. He made a note to stop letting his dealer talk him into new strains.

"How so?" he asks.

He knows the thalamite can give him an answer. Psychic energy—as defined by the Novassian physician's Bible, *A Definitive Guide to the Third Nervous System*—is the capacity for individual cells to retain knowledge of their past and current mechanisms, stored in the same nebulous way that memories are stored in the hippocampus. Thalamites read psychic energy like a newspaper.

"What do you call this?" the thalamite asks. It shows Wilka a grayscale image: fibrous white lines undulate across a dark sea. The sight makes him dizzy.

"I have no idea what that is."

"Go to the machine."

Half-heartedly, Wilka resolves to call out tomorrow and schedule an MRI. It needs to be at a different hospital than the one he works at. He can't have them asking questions. He can't deal with the stares.

No. It doesn't speak this time, but the lack of affirmation rings in the tense silence. That isn't the right machine.

The doctor who discovered the psychic nervous system, Dr. Ingrid Novasson, is renowned in her field, but who could have expected that her imaging processes would detect a new organism entirely: These faceless, massless insects whose bloated presence causes a wide range of disorders via compressive atrophy of the mind.

Most thalamites do not speak, and Wilka should probably be more scared, but now his skin vibrates like a cat's purr, so he doesn't mind very much. The thalamites are animals, after all, and just two days ago, Dr. Wilka extracted one from the mind of a 29-year-old male, presenting to the ER with the sudden onset of violent behavior, intrusive thoughts—"visions of hell"—and suicidal ideation. He killed the thalamite in just under two hours. An outpatient procedure. Only twenty years ago, the same man would have been restrained and held for days. The primitive psychiatrists did their best, and Wilka is not one to dismiss the therapeutic potential of benzodiazepines. But these days, treatments sure are quicker.

The parasites don't speak—shouldn't speak—nor do they make sounds as animals ought to, nor do they have a heartbeat, so the only way to observe one is to see it on the screen of a Nova Psychocerebral Resonance machine, affectionately called NOVA by its practitioners.

And observing an animal is as close to talking to it as you can get. The dog bares its teeth, the cat hisses, the young man Wilka met for coffee the morning prior spits "Fuck you," at 2 a.m. the next day because he has learned he can't stay for breakfast.

"I think that you are going to die," the thalamite says to him. "That's why I'm telling you."

Wilka concedes. Rising, he goes to his desk where he fiddles with three pairs of electrodes. The psychic nervous system consists of six ganglia, which are bilaterally paired but asymmetric. Of the cervicocranial pair, for example, one lies a centimeter below the ear lobe and the other at the base of the neck; the inguinal pair lies in the femoral triangle and on the iliac crest. During his residency, there was a rumor that one of Wilka's colleagues couldn't get off without NOVA integration at the inguinal ganglia.

Now settled, Wilka turns on the NOVA. He and his colleagues were one of the first cohorts trained in psychophysical medicine by Dr. Novasson herself, and her late husband. In their first year of residency, they explored self-integration to familiarize them-selves with this new landscape. The first time Wilka used the NOVA, he only stayed connected for thirty-two seconds before he collapsed and vomited. It took months for the shock to wear off, more to learn how to navigate the machinery properly.

It hums.

He likes to call it the shadow world. Dr. Novasson gave it a much fancier name, but Wilka's description is better. His vision dims. His head feels too large and too light for his body.

Although this happens every time, he wonders if the world has fallen away from him for good—for real, this time.

It hurts at first, when the machine turns on. It passes over him like a wave of nausea, but the fear lingers longer. He unlearned this fear long ago, but his bones remember.

Self-integration with the NOVA occurs in three steps: dissociation, unreality, and, titularly, integration with the NOVA consciousness. Wilka wishes it wasn't so Jungian. At least when he does the same with a patient, he can view it through the lens of a monitor.

"Show it to me again," Wilka says to the thalamite. He can hear himself talk outside of his skull. It's very quiet.

He is only a little surprised that this one can talk so well. He has spoken to one other thalamite, albeit in passing and with a voice a little different than this one. He extracted that one himself and killed it as he would for any of his patients.

The field of Novassian psychomedicine is relatively new— poorly understood, overfunded, bloated—so the bombshell that some thalamites may possess human-like intelligence is a possibility no researcher wants to consider. Or perhaps, more accurately, no corporation.

So, at the time, Wilka was more than willing to conclude that he was crazy. Sleep deprived, overstressed. He heard a draft and thought it was a voice. The thalamite in his mind was a coincidence. That's it.

The thalamite's image gives him vertigo. The drone of the NOVA makes Wilka feel like he is droning also, his chest shaking like a moose calling across a lake.

In the shadow world, he understands the ligamentous strands presented before him. He recognizes the color of nitrogen molecules and carbon rings, folded up and neatly packaged.

J-NG5 gene, abnormal.

The desktop monitor fills up with the base-pair sequence, the mutation highlighted in red text. He chooses not to read it.

"That regulates a growth factor."

"These tissues. They do not kill themselves," the thalamite says. "They grow too large, split apart, become ragged, and yet they persist."

The clarity and volume of its words startle Wilka. He knows the NOVA makes it easier to observe a thalamite, but he swears there is someone behind him, a hand on his shoulder, as it talks.

He rolls his shoulders back and nods again. A healthy cell undergoes programmed cell death in response to malfunctions as severe as this.

"I think that you are going to die," the thalamite says. "That's why I'm talking to you."

"Can all of you talk?"

"All of us?"

"Thalamites."

"Ah," it says, and it mulls over the question. "The ones who cannot think, they are not the same as I. The ones who can think, can talk."

And it continues, "But, not all hosts can hear us."

"Oh," Wilka says. "So, I am actually crazy." Surely that is easier to believe—better than the alternative, the fairytale world where he talks to demons like a kindly princess would talk to finches.

The thalamite makes a noise that Wilka understands as a train of thought. He's never been able to understand thalamite "body" language so easily before, but he's also never had one in his mind for so long. Clinically, thalamites could play a critical role in the diagnosis of rare diseases because their behavior correlates proportionally with certain chemical mechanisms, though it is becoming quickly apparent that different thalamic species have their own behavioral triggers. Using an *H. physic* model, Dr. Novasson's newest goal is to decode their language like the steps of a bee dance.

"*Crazy*," the thalamite echoes. Wandering, observing, investigating. "There is a foreign chemical here."

It indicates the hypothalamus, amygdala, hippocampus. While it does so, it hums a discordant tune.

"Escitalopram." Ironic, Wilka muses, that a thalamite would remind him so starkly that thalamic pathogens are not the causative agents of all mental illnesses.

"And another."

"My dealer calls it Dragon's Breath."

More humming.

"Not crazy," the thalamite concludes. "Marginally altered. Perhaps for the better."

Just what I need, Wilka thinks. *A parasite validating my drug use.*

His desk chair bites into his skeleton. He can't ignore the sensation anymore. It makes him feel like bugs are crawling across his skin.

"You're dying," the parasite says. "You are not scared."

"Why bother warning me?" Standing uneasily, Wilka hooks his fingers under the sides of the NOVA. "Just find a new host."

"I thought that I should," the thalamite says. "It's not so often I end up in a dying host."

The NOVA machine is a cubic foot, and its only wires connect it to his desktop and an external battery. The front panel features a variety of dials to calibrate it to its patient, but he only ever uses this one on himself. When he unplugs it, the computer chimes. He lifts it carefully, shifting it to his hip, and with a series of electrode-tangled steps, finally makes it back to his bed.

"Do you know what it feels like to die?" the thalamite asks. "I don't."

Wilka sinks into the mattress. There, Phaedo gives him bedroom eyes. Wilka likes this painting especially because Socrates isn't in it. In his dreams, Wilka has replaced Socrates, and the young man with doe eyes eats knowledge out of his hands instead.

"Would you like me to kill you?" Wilka asks.

Killing a thalamic parasite is an involved process. Outside of a living host, they are impossible to detect. The presence, character, and behavior of one is measurable only via a NOVA machine integrated with an infected host. So, the parasite must be extracted from the mind and moved into less vital cells, where the patient is injected with a hypothalamicide. Sometimes, the entire patch of skin must be removed and sterilized in ethyl alcohol. In those cases, the thalamite makes the strangest sounds, suddenly very physical and very real. Wilka still has the scar from his own extraction; there are still blood stains in the bathtub grout.

"I wouldn't." The thalamite thinks for a moment. "Thank you, though."

Wilka lights his blunt again and swirls the smoke between his cheeks. He feels a pinch in his chest. Did it feel like that when he'd first started smoking? Experimentally, he inhales.

"My hosts rarely offer to do things for me," the thalamite clarifies.

Wilka snorts and turns his head to the side.

The face of the NOVA reminds him of his residency. Dr. Novasson ordered the self-integration experiments, but it was her husband who administered them. Those were the first hands that placed the electrodes on Wilka's body. Her husband wasn't a handsome man, but he was magnetic like her—Wilka had fallen in love with them the moment he'd read their work, fallen in love a second time when he met them in their lab. Surgeons have quick fingers, fingers that belong in a trophy cabinet, and Wilka thought it was a waste that he had to fear those pretty, lotioned, pearly-nailed fingers. During the early integrations, when he collapsed, those were the hands that helped him back up, wiped the vomit from his mouth, brushed his hair away from his sweaty forehead.

"You want this," her husband said. "We are on the cusp of a new era. You want this more than anything else."

They're in the shadow world and, as he thinks, the thalamite is drawn to each memory now illuminated by flickers of electricity. Wilka sees it: Dr. Novasson's sterile green eyes stare at him from over the edge of a clipboard. He shakes in the hands of her husband. "Leave me here," Wilka wants to say. "Don't put me back into the machine." But he wants her approval like he wants to hear his mother's voice.

Wilka turns the machine around, but the smooth finish on the other side reflects a facsimile of his face: hollowed out, absent-eyed, his brown skin turned blue by the night, his chin lined with curly gray fuzz like mold on a peach.

He puts a blanket over the machine instead.

He likes the taste of his blunt now. It reminds him of cloves, which makes him feel young and reckless. When he was sixteen, he smoked cloves.

"You said not all of us can hear your kind," he says.

"I did say this."

"May I consider you a friend?"

"If you wish."

"I'm going to tell you what I'm thinking, friend," Wilka says. "Reading is a complicated neurological event. Visual information must be translated into semantic meaning. We know that the visuals are transmitted first to the angular gyrus and then to Wernicke's *speech* area. After this, the *auditory* centers light up. Have we turned visuals into sound? Why must we take such a roundabout approach to reading, when speech is directly translated into meaning via a similar, shortened pathway?"

The thalamite doesn't speak, but as Wilka rambles, the shadow world shifts. Electricity crawls across the sulci of his brain like earthworms. The thalamite sits and watches this unfold; it sits neatly, with an invisible tail wrapped over invisible paws, wide-eyed as if to say, *Yes, I see this, and I understand.*

"Now, friend, humor the possibility that reading is a relatively new phenomenon. With the advent of language and script, a new development begins in the depths of the frontal cortex of primitive *Homo sapiens*, utilizing existing structures to this new end.

"Why am I positing this to you? See, thousands of years ago, no man ever read silently. The Ancient Greeks always always always read aloud. Maybe they did this by choice, but it was commonly known that reading made one vulnerable, because anyone could hear you. You would think, right, that if they could have chosen to read silently, they would have. Right?"

"Yes," the thalamite says.

"But *then*, there was Alexander the Great. You don't need to know anything about him except that he was an anomaly. He read silently. They thought he was a god."

"Is that what you are?" the thalamite asks.

Wilka's face screws up in a grimace. "A god? No. Unlike… *this*, reading is actually useful."

The first thalamite he ever heard told him to kill one of his patients. Let the scalpel slip, it said. Knick the jugular. Take a second too long to cauterize the mistake. This wasn't a normal symptom. For intrusive thoughts to appear in a host, a parasite must live inside of them long enough to grow fat on siphoned glucose and electricity, to squeeze the mind until it lyses. His infection was hours-long, at most. He'd integrated with a patient earlier that day, and his parasite would have been picked up by the NOVA had it been there the whole time.

No, he knew it deep in his bones as soon as he heard it: that thalamite's voice was something so much stranger.

"I meant an anomaly," the thalamite clarifies.

Wilka frowns.

If there's some little part of his brain that converts thalamite thoughts into audio, he wants to dig it out.

"Was there only one Alexander?" the thalamite asks.

"I think there were many Alexanders. But I don't think they knew each other. I think they were probably quite lonely."

The thalamite says, "I have lived inside many Dr. August Wilkas. None have been so conversational as you."

"Thank you."

"That is a compliment for your machine, not you. Perhaps when you die, I will find another Dr. August Wilka with another machine."

"The doctor Novasson had fifteen NOVA machines manufactured," Wilka says, surprised by his own spite, "and only five remain in private ownership. It will be three more years before her next cohort is licensed to practice with the newest line of machines."

The thalamite stays silent. *Good*, Wilka thinks. It feels good to have cowed it, and he feeds the pleasant burning in his chest with another drag from his blunt. This time, the smoke makes him cough, so he takes a moment to clear his throat. The phlegm tastes ferrous. He swallows it.

The thalamite is not exploring either. The electric flashes and fibrous proteins fall away, and all that is left is Wilka's bedroom, wavering. He has wondered for a long time if he loses a piece of himself every time he falls into Novasson's shadow world—but if he is to die soon, at least he won't be her guinea pig, split open on the autopsy table while she investigates the long-term nervous damage caused by repeated integration.

He blinks. The ceiling image returns to him with a familiar clarity.

"Look." Wilka points to Phaedo's eyes. "Do you know who that is?"

"That is parchment."

"That is the image of a man: Phaedo of Elis. He was the companion and student of a famous philosopher named Socrates. He was there when Socrates died."

He imagines Phaedo, lacrimal and pale, holding a cup of red liquid to Socrates's lips. The crushed berries are round and succulent, with little seeds floating in the pulp; the juice is so thick that he could paint his face with it.

The thalamite lounges in the hippocampus amongst a sea of memories. There is one bound to Phaedo-and-the-Death-of-Socrates, so it pulls it out by a silver thread. In it, Dr. Novasson's husband is draped backwards in an office chair, a faceless, cavernous mass sitting on what remains of his neck. With this image comes the smell: when Wilka first walked into that room, it was the gunpowder first, then the copper tang of blood.

"Why did you lead me here?" the thalamite asks.

Wilka tries to say, "I miss him," but suddenly he is coughing so hard that he can't see straight. He feels the thalamite bristle. As if seeing himself on a faraway shore, Wilka remembers that *H. tenebris* alarms when blood-oxygen levels drop, so he suspects that he knows the species of this speaking/thinking thalamite.

Despite the leads dragging him back, Wilka curls up on his side and holds his heaving stomach until air trickles back into his lungs. The thalamite's sing-song humming fills the room.

"Sometimes I wonder," Wilka says. "Do you think he was scared when he drank the poison?"

"Ah," the thalamite says, wide-eyed and sitting prettily once again.

Little Lives

By Patrick Lofgren

First published in Issue 011 (September–October 2022)

Cal sat down at the kitchen table, his eyes feeling grainy. He took a sip of coffee and watched Mia try and spoon pulped carrots into Liam's mouth. He missed the days before Liam, when they sat out on the porch, drank coffee together, and talked about the day to come. If he didn't say something now, he'd never get to. Mornings like this would be the rest of his life.

"I think we should integrate with the Gelephir. I…want to become a part of it," he said.

Mia looked at him like he'd suggested they abandon their lives and join the circus.

"You cannot get absorbed by an alien consciousness Cal," Mia said. "We have a son." She gestured at Liam with the spoon. "I have the store."

"I didn't say *I* wanted to integrate with it. I said I want *us* to. I want to be with you, to really know you."

She laughed and took a break from feeding their son so she could take a bite of her own breakfast.

"We've been together for nine years. I think you know me," she said.

"Don't you just think…" he trailed off. He didn't know what to say.

"What?" she said.

She spooned more carrots into Liam's mouth. He accepted them placidly this time. Cal took a sip of coffee and Mia watched him intently. She was still on reduced caffeine. She'd missed coffee dearly throughout her pregnancy. Cal had considered stopping drinking it as well in solidarity, but he'd dismissed the idea. He needed *something* to get him through the day. He sold software that helped companies with rentable assets keep track of where all their stuff was. It was not exciting work. He didn't know how he'd make it through the day if he gave up coffee as a meaningless gesture.

"Haven't you always said that you wish we could communicate better? That's what becoming part of the Gelephir would be. We'd be able to perfectly communicate with one another. No more misunderstandings. No more bickering. It would be pure, absolute knowledge of each other. Don't you want that? Don't you want to know, like truly *know* who I am?"

She shoveled some egg into her mouth and then gave Liam another spoonful. This time he rejected it and slapped the spoon from her hand. It clattered to the floor and sprayed baby food across the wood.

"Liam, why? Why can you not just eat your food. I know you want it."

Mia stood up and went to the kitchen for a paper towel. She came back and retrieved Liam's spoon from the floor. She cleaned the mess with the paper towel, and then with the spoon, scooped a new glop of baby food with which to try again.

"Can you please answer me?" Cal said.

"Liam can't. You know that," she said.

Astronomers detected the Gelephir around the time it crossed Saturn's orbit. They believed it was a novel celestial phenomenon, a gas cloud moving much faster than a comet. In a way, they'd been right. It was novel, but it wasn't just fast-moving gas. It was a living, thinking being. The Gelephir was a stellar traveler capable of absorbing and integrating the minds of other life forms. It traversed the universe looking for new minds to absorb and did so with very little discretion. Any consciousness, no matter how divergent from its own, broadened the scope of its existence. It didn't care if you were a murderer, a death cultist, a hedge fund manager. It would take you into itself, so long as you chose to do so.

It would remain in orbit for six months, just a few days left now. During this time, any individual human who wanted to integrate with it could. They only had to express their interest, ideally through the Internet, but any form of contact was fine. There were news stories of the Gelephir answering the S.O.S. of a man stranded on a desert island, so its reach was obviously considerable. When the time was up, the Gelephir would move on to the next likely inhabited world to see if anyone there was thinking complex thoughts and interested in traveling the universe.

"So, that's it?" Cal said.

"I mean, that's just the reality, babe. We have a son," Mia said.

Liam wasn't yet a year old. Cal didn't even want him. It felt cruel on a cosmic scale that Cal would be denied this opportunity by his own son just because the kid didn't know what was happening and couldn't yet form a coherent thought. Mia might as well have said that they couldn't integrate because they owned a dog. Cal looked at his son. Liam didn't look back, he just put his hand in a blob of baby food and spread it around, making a mess. The Gelephir revealed that the universe was endless and full of wonders to explore. Humans were insignificant on their own. Cal was one mind. He would live for a few decades more and then die, his brief time on Earth unmarked. The Gelephir was his chance to be part of something that mattered, that lasted.

"He's just a baby," Cal said.

"Exactly, and we're his parents. It's our job to build a world where he can become who he wants to be. Even if the Gelephir would take him, he'd never become his own person. I'm sorry, babe, but this is just where we are," she said.

Cal got up and put his dishes in the sink. He knew he should put them in the dishwasher, but the idea of doing so made him feel even more exhausted.

"I need to get going," he said, then started for the door.

Mia got up and followed. She hugged him.

"Hey," she said. "I don't want this to be a fight. We can talk about it more tonight. But I need you to know that you're enough for me. You and Liam are everything. I love you so much. I know we feel small in the face of this, but you're as vast as the universe to me."

Cal didn't know what to say to that because he didn't believe her. He couldn't because she was nothing like that to him. She was just a person, one he liked very much, but it was silly and romantic and little insulting that she would call him that, knowing that he was just one man. She had to know that he knew she was lying. It was impossible to feel that way about someone. She was just trying to soften the miserable blow of trapping him here with Liam while an eternity among the stars was within reach.

They'd talk about it later, he supposed. There was still time to convince her. But now he really did need to get to work.

Cal poured himself a coffee and added sugar and creamer. He ignored his coworker, who stared while he kept adding creamer.

"Basically milk at this point," the man said.

Cal ignored him and went back to his desk. For a few blessed hours, he worked on emails and accounts, plugging numbers into spreadsheets. The only thing that he liked about his job was that the grunt work involved could be done by a gerbil. He could sip his coffee, turn his brain off, and wake up on the other side, the morning finished. Afternoons were worse, that was when he made most of his client calls, and each of those felt like a Sisyphean torment. The story of Sisyphus was wasted on kids learning about mythology in their home room classes. It was only after college, settling into life with Mia, that Cal appreciated its meaning. Every day there were dishes, three meals to prepare, laundry, driving the same route to work and back, and doing this job.

Cal didn't make it to the afternoon before his day soured further. Around ten, his boss called him in. Cal sat in one of the chairs opposite his boss, a massive maple desk between them. The leather of both their seats squeaked under their weight. His boss looked especially grim this morning.

"Do you know why I wanted to speak with you Cal?" he said.

"No, sir," Cal said.

His boss heaved a sigh. Then he turned his monitor so that Cal could see. On it were graphs of all the sales reps and their numbers from the past few months. Cal's numbers had always been middling but steady, until recently when they'd begun to drop.

"Your numbers are way down," his boss said. It was a factual statement, not open to debate. "What do you think is causing this?"

"I'm just having a little trouble focusing lately," Cal said.

His boss nodded, took a sip of coffee, looked at him.

"These are unprecedented times," he said. "Unfortunately, the wheels of industry keep turning, regardless of the age. World Wars, Cold Wars, pandemics, alien invasion, we keep working through all of it because that's how we keep the lights on, that's how we pay to defend ourselves from those exterior threats, that's how we secure a financial future for the next generation," he said.

"Invasion?" Cal asked.

"Of course," his boss said. "We don't know why it's really here. We don't know what it really wants."

"I think it just wants to expand its consciousness, experience new things," Cal said.

"But we have no proof that it even is what it says it is. This absorption nonsense might be a trick to get us to line up like we're a buffet. Or maybe it really does want to absorb us so that it can learn all our secrets and use them to destroy us. Whatever it really wants, it's not just here to give us a free ticket to space. There's something else going on. We're at war. We just haven't admitted it yet."

Cal didn't know what to say to that. People all over the world had been making arguments against the Gelephir since the moment it made its proposition. Some believed it was sent by Satan to tempt us out of our garden. Some believed that it was God, and that if even a single sinner was allowed to integrate, then all of humanity would be damned. Cal had heard his boss's "absorb our secrets" argument before. It was the fall back for people who thought the world as already run by deep state lizards. It wasn't just the religious and paranoid who were confused and disturbed by the Gelephir's arrival. The atheists didn't know what to do either. Many saw humankind as an evil blight upon the world, morally obligated to integrate, as if the Gelephir was a cosmic delouser. Others thought human beings were preternaturally violent and would corrupt this pure celestial being with our selfish and cowardly urges. The Gelephir bore all these arguments against it, and all those against humanity, with indifference. It seemed not to care what we thought, or why. It was content to give us a little time to puzzle it out for ourselves, and then move on.

"I don't know. I kind of wish I could. I'd like to travel the galaxy."

His boss looked at him a little harder.

"Come on, Cal. You're smarter than that."

Cal felt like the butt of a joke, like he'd bought into something everyone else knew was a scam.

"Put that alien nonsense aside. Focus on your work. One bad month? Not a crisis. We all go through our rough patches. But if I see numbers like this again, you and I are going to need to have a more serious conversation."

"I understand, sir. Won't happen again," Cal said. He felt sick. He wanted a coffee but wasn't sure if it would still his nerves or excite them.

"All right," his boss said. "You coming for beers tonight?"

"I can't. Mia and I have a date planned," Cal said.

"Oh. That's nice," he said.

Cal chuckled uncomfortably and stood.

"Good talk, Cal. Let's see you top those charts next month."

Cal pumped his fist and let out a gentle *raw*, instantly regretting the sound, the motion, and the faux camaraderie. The man just told him to get it together or get sacked, and then he turned around and gave a pathetic little cheer. If Cal could cease to exist right there, he would.

Mia owned a store in the mall, which was a fifteen-minute walk from their house. She sold candles, canvas totes, t-shirts, and crystals. It was all junk, not that that was bad. The store made her happy. She came home every day talking about this or that woman who came in looking for the perfect special thing for her spouse, her kids, her book group. Mia would spend hours with her customers, making them tea, giving them a tour of the store, telling them about the unique origins of each and every product. Cal was happy for her, to have something she loved so much. He wished he had something like that for himself.

He parked the car down the street to avoid the paid parking, and texted Mia that he was waiting. When she hadn't responded after ten minutes, he got out and walked to the store. When he arrived, Mia was excitedly walking a customer through the varieties of bee's wax candles. They were locally sourced, and the labels were done by a local artist who also had some work in the gallery on the other side of the mall.

"Cal, hey!" she said as he pushed through the store doors. "This lady is getting supplies for her son's wedding. Isn't that exciting!"

"Oh, yeah that's very cool. Congratulations. Babe, I've been waiting in the car for twenty minutes."

Mia looked at her watch.

"Oh no! I'm sorry I lost track of time. I'm so sorry ma'am, I should have closed ten minutes ago," Mia said.

"I'm so sorry. Let me get out of your hair," the customer said.

"No, no, no. Let's get you squared away. He can wait another minute. Get your son these candles, they're perfect for the dinner tables. And don't forget, I also have these balms and honey jars. You're doing welcome bags for the guests, right?"

Cal meandered around the store, trying to stay out of Mia's way while she heaped more and more products onto the customer. She was a good salesperson. Cal might think everything in the store was expensive junk, but Mia believed in it, and she could make anyone else believe in it, too. The process took time though. She had a story about every single thing in the store, and since the subject of this customer's visit was her son's wedding, Mia mined their own wedding for emotional hooks. Every moment of intimacy, every laughable mistake, every anxiety and frustration was on display for this woman so that she might be persuaded to buy a set of thank-you cards pressed with real flowers. Eventually, Cal gave up and retreated to the back room to use the computer.

The Internet had only one focus these days. Since the moment the Gelephir arrived it was all anyone wanted to talk about. Strange as it was, it seemed to Cal like the Internet was the only sane place. It was as if polite society had repressed all knowledge of the Gelephir so that it could keep on selling napkins and tracking software. Cal supposed they had a lot of practice. The world had been burning for decades. But was Cal a farmer? Was he a fire fighter? Was he a refugee advocate? Nope. He drove a car to work by himself. He lived on a cul-de-sac. He sold software. The market blundered on, making its money. The arrival of the Gelephir was no different.

But on Twitter, people engaged in the great debate over what to do. Some used it to let the Gelephir know they wanted to integrate. It was known that the alien monitored the Internet. On YouTube and TikTok, people posted videos of their integrations. They set the camera up in a corner, told the Gelephir they wanted to be absorbed, and then waited while a purple shimmering mist seeped in through an open door or window. The mist would gather around them, thickening into a cloud too dense to see through. Then it would dissipate, the person gone. The videos would either continue to show the empty room, or a crying family member would appear briefly to turn off the camera. Cal ached with jealousy watching others escape. Before he knew it, over an hour had passed. Mia finally came to find him in the back room.

"I'm so sorry," she said. "Once we got going, we just couldn't stop. That woman spent *a thousand dollars*. I love when people come in to buy for big events. Should we get going?"

Cal looked at the clock. It was almost eight.

"We only have the sitter for another twenty minutes," he said.

"Oh, shoot. Maybe we can order a pizza. Watch a movie."

Cal chuckled.

"As if," he said.

"What is that supposed to mean?" Mia said.

Cal shrugged.

"We can't make it three minutes through a movie without Liam interrupting."

"So, we pause and then start again. It's not a big deal," she said.

Like always, a date night with just the two of them and a chance to really talk dissolved into another night at home. Cal wondered if she did this on purpose. She could easily have manipulated that woman into staying. And she knew that by doing so, he'd get bored and get on the Internet and they'd lose their sitter.

"Whatever," he said.

"Whatever? Look, I didn't mean to go over. Seriously. I just got excited about this wedding and I wanted them to have all the things that would help make it a perfect event. I messed up. But hey. We made a thousand bucks in the last hour. That's enough money for a dozen date nights."

"I don't want to go on a date! I wanted to talk about the alien, like you said we would. I wanted to have a real discussion about it with just you and me as adults. It's only going to be here for another day and then it'll be gone, for a billion years, and you and I and Liam will all be dead by the end of the century, like we never even existed."

"Liam will have more time than that," Mia said.

"You can't believe that," Cal said.

"Yes, I can."

"Nothing will be here that long. You might be able to pretend the world is fine while you're in here helping people plan a wedding, but it's not, and it's not going to be. If Liam is alive, if any of us are alive in forty years, we'll be slaves to some warlord. We'll die of dysentery or because someone bashes our heads in with rocks so they can steal our place by the fire."

She was crying.

"Don't say that. It's going to be okay. The world might not look like it did when we were kids but that doesn't mean it's going to be some *Mad Max* hellscape."

Cal put his hands on her shoulders.

"We have this one tiny chance to escape, and you won't let us take it," he said. He was out of breath. His heart felt like it had doubled in size, like it was fighting his organs for space even as his chest shrunk.

"I don't believe that," she said. "And even if I did, Liam can't go. The Gelephir wouldn't let him. You know that. If the world is going to be so awful, how could you consider leaving him behind? How could you go on this galactic cruise knowing your son is dying back on this planet you hate so much?"

Cal was tired. He wished he had a cup of coffee. He just wanted to get home, eat something, and go to bed.

"Let's go. We shouldn't keep the sitter waiting," he said.

Mia just stared at him in horrified silence as he walked out of the store. He didn't pause to make sure she followed.

Mia could sleep, but Cal couldn't. He was plagued by a memory from his high school trip to New York, and the brief twenty minutes he spent waiting outside the planetarium. In the atrium was a ramp that spiraled down two floors. And along this spiral was a timeline of the universe, from its explosive moment of origin to the present. Down at the very end of that long ramp was a single human hair suspended in glass. Its width represented the entirety of human existence. The exhibit was frank in saying that truthfully, this hair was a gross exaggeration. Mankind's time was truly nothing, but people didn't come to museums to look at nothing.

He couldn't stop thinking about that hair, that small and insignificant thing. It could exist or it could vanish. Beside the rest of existence, it didn't matter one bit. His species might have the power to kill a planet, but it turned out that wasn't so hard. All he wanted was to matter. He didn't know how Mia could sleep. The Gelephir would be gone this time tomorrow. It was going to feel like a terrible dream. He knew that if he didn't join with it, he would hate himself for the rest of his miserable little life.

Little Liam was crying in his crib. Mia stirred and poked Cal with one of her dagger sharp toes.

"You're turn," she muttered.

Cal got out of bed. Liam needed a diaper change. No matter how many times Cal helped his son, he still gagged his way through the process. He hated that he was truly a machine for turning food into energy and shitting out the rest. He got Liam changed, but the baby wouldn't stop crying. They walked around the house together, Cal gently bobbing his son up and down to try and get him to go to sleep. Cal knew that he wouldn't get any sleep tonight, but still, he wished Liam would just shut up. He had a clean diaper. What more did he want? He was so exhaustingly difficult. And for what? All they did was bring one more person into the world, one more meaningless little food processor, and crucially, one who's infantile brain would now prevent Cal from joining with the Gelephir.

Unless…Liam didn't exist anymore.

"Tell you what, buddy," said Cal. "I just had an idea that will help you stop crying. In fact, it's gonna solve a lot of your problems, and mine, too. Give me just a minute, and I'll draw you up a bath."

He took Liam back to the bathroom and set him on the floor. He closed the door and put a few towels over his son's face so Mia wouldn't wake from the continued crying. Then he drew the bath. It was agonizing. He kept the water running slowly to minimize the noise. It took long enough that he almost didn't carry on. He felt sick. But he knew Liam would forgive him, or at the very least, Liam wouldn't know that Cal needed forgiving.

Cal was nothing, Liam even less. But together, they could ensure that one of them made it off this planet and became a part of something greater. When the bath was ready, Cal untangled his son from the blankets and plunged him into the water.

"Mia," Cal whispered. She didn't stir. "Mia," he repeated. Nothing.

"God dammit, wake up!" he said.

Mia shot up.

"What? What is it? Is it Liam? Is he okay?"

"Yeah. Of course," he lied. "Listen, about what you said. About how Liam can't choose to join with the Gelephir, which means he can't go, which means we can't go, and it's all fucked. Well, I solved it. I solved the problem. We can join with the alien. We should do it now. We should go."

She sat up and turned on the lamp on her nightstand. She put on her glasses.

"Have you been crying?" she said. "Cal, what is going on?"

"I solved our problem. We can join with the alien. We just have to let it know we want to," he said. He leaned in and kissed her. "I'm so excited. Soon there will be nothing between us. We'll be part of the same mind and have no secrets. We'll finally understand each other."

She lifted her glasses and rubbed her eyes.

"Hon' you don't look so good. Have you gotten any sleep tonight? Let me make you some tea."

She shifted from under the covers.

"You're not listening," Cal said.

"It's the middle of the night and you're rambling at me. Just give me a second. I'll make some tea and we can talk about whatever it is. Okay? I'm just gonna pee and then I'll make us some tea."

Before he could react, she was across the room and in the hallway. She was opening the bathroom door and he screamed, "Don't go in there!"

It was too late. He could see in the expression of confused horror on her face that she had seen Liam. She didn't scream, but her mouth seemed locked open as if her jaw recoiled from what she saw. Tears flooded her eyes. Cal had never been so scared as he was in that moment when she looked back at him. He'd never seen hatred so pure and clear.

"This is a good thing -" he began, but she was already attacking him. She beat his chest with her fists, kicked his shins. She was screaming, nothing coherent, just the cries of a loving parent who had identified her child's killer. He tried to defend himself. He kept his hands between them, uttered calming noises and asked for the space to explain, but she was beyond that. She was a more violent and powerful thing than he'd ever seen. And then, she gave him a shove and he was tumbling, down and down the stairs. He felt something in his arm break, then a crack on his head, and another, each sensation more disorienting and terrifying than the last. Before he finally passed out, he could see her, standing at the top of the staircase, looking down at him. He'd never felt more insignificant.

He woke to an unsettling sensory dimness. The world felt soft, though it was bright, and pain lanced in his arm and in his head. He tried to gasp but found his mouth taped. He tried to remove it and found his arms strapped to his sides. He was bound in cheap yellow rope, three kinds of tape, plastic wrap, and a variety of electrical cords. He was on his back in the bathtub, his head barely above the water. Liam's body had been removed. Cal's heart started pounding, matching the panic that rushed through him and further dulled the pain of his injuries. He needed to breathe, but all he could do was hyper-ventilate through his nostrils.

Mia sat on the toilet. In one arm, she cradled their son's body. With her free hand, she held her phone. Cal mumbled through the tape. She looked at him, and he felt small, just like he had at the base of the stairs right before blacking out.

Her Tongue Was Weighted with Salt
By Alexandra Seidel

First published in Issue 002 (March–April 2021)

Three chocolates sat in the box, peering out at Tamsin through the clear plastic cover. They glittered with coarse salt, the simple variety, not some exotic pink or black novelty. The box itself was triangular to emphasize the occasion, oddness being considered proper for Samhain. A white bow with a red line running down its center decorated one corner.

"What a superstitious gift," Ludaque said. He had taken it from the courier at the apartment door, signed for it. He held the card out to Tamsin while he placed the box of salted candy on her desk in front of her. Tamsin crossed her legs before she took the offered card, a heavy cream envelope that felt soft under her fingers. "Has the consumption of salted food ever given you dream visions, Tamsin?"

Tamsin bit her lip and stared at her desk, though not at the candy. Work. She would rather be working than look at the candy. She wanted to look at the stars. "Don't you have to charge? Or update one of your algorithms or something?" she said in lieu of answering.

Ludaque was thankfully perceptive for a robot. "Very well," he said. "I will leave you to your thoughts and go do something else. Let me know if I should send the sender a thank-you note."

The apartment was open-concept, and Tamsin watched him retreat until he was at the other end of it where her bedroom and his room, the former guestroom, were. Ludaque's footfall was quiet on the hardwood floor. Tamsin assumed it was unintentional on his part, but she hated that he could sneak up on her. She had never told him.

"I just sent an email to myself," Mia said. "It says: Dear Gelephir, I would like to integrate with you. Please find me as soon as possible. I don't know how long it will take but I hope it's soon."

Cal wanted to scream. Who did she think she was? She didn't even care about the alien. If it weren't for him, she'd have no interest in it. She'd be on her way to work right now at her stupid fucking store to sell idiotic things to idiotic people. She was nothing without him.

"You two were everything to me," she said. "I had the whole world. Or at least I thought I did. But it turns out you were smaller than I ever could have imagined. I don't care what happens to you, Cal. I don't care if you drown right in front of me. I don't care if a neighbor finds your body. I don't even care if you find your way out of this situation and live a long and fruitful life. I loved you. Now I'm leaving, and I'm going to take from you what is clearly the only thing you ever wanted."

She stood and backed away. A shimmering purple cloud made its way through the open window. She set Liam's body down on Cal's chest. The added weight was enough to cause Cal to struggle. He could now barely keep his head above the water. The purple smoke curled around his wife. Cal screamed, his mouth stretching the tape as much as it would allow. All he had to do was remove the tape and say out loud that he wanted to integrate. The Gelephir was right there. All he had to do was speak the words, even sign that he consented, and he would be taken by the alien and spared this miserable end.

Mia didn't even say goodbye as the smoke coalesced around her and then dissipated back out through the window with her essence in tow, leaving him to slowly sink under the weight his son's dead body.

The card. It had the weight of a card selected with care for someone special. There was no name on the envelope, but Tamsin knew her sister had picked it out, just for her. She closed her eyes to let her other sense float to Bea in a store, surrounded by fountain pens and ink, looking at cards, picking out this one. The vision came to her clearly, Bea in a brown coat and an ugly, mustard colored scarf. Her dark hair was already streaked with silver, which made her look a lot like their mother.

With an exhale, Tamsin dropped the vision and opened the card, not with the opener on her desk, but with her finger. The fabric tore in ragged shreds.

The handwriting was choppy:

Dear Tamsin,

You will not have missed me these past years, nor will you have thought much about me since we last saw each other, what, half a decade ago? The Tarot says as much. You probably won't appreciate the salt candy, even though we gorged ourselves when we were kids. I have seen something dark in the cards, coming for you. I don't know what or when. Please eat the salt and look for the darkness in your dreams—only when we know the outline of a shadow can we banish it with light.

Love,
Bea

Only when we know the shadow can we banish it. Their mother's words. Bea had to know how much Tamsin would loathe reading them in Bea's hand. Tamsin tore the expensive card, ripped the paper right down the middle so her sister's name was cut in half, and tossed the scraps into the waste basket under her desk.

"Ludaque!" Tamsin swiveled around in her chair so she would see him come back to her work area.

"Yes. I was just about to go charge. Or something."

"Oh, cut it out. What was the slice of deep space the Exploration Program wanted me to look at? The one they marked as important?"

"I thought you didn't want to start working on that today."

"I changed my mind."

Ludaque's left eyebrow rose. "I'm assuming no thank-you note then."

Tamsin crossed her legs. "What did they want me to look at?"

Ludaque walked up to her and put his right hand on the desk. Tamsin looked at the long and dexterous fingers and thought for a half-second that his nails looked long. Longer than usual. Then the built-in scan ID-ed him and allowed remote access to the relevant files. Tamsin looked at the screen. She uncrossed and re-crossed her legs. "You know, there are less people in the office on weekends. You could take a shower and go in. I doubt you would pick up too many random thoughts and emotions."

"And it would do me good to get out?"

Ludaque grinned at her. "Have you always been able to read robot minds, or is this new?"

"I'm not going in. Show me the data."

He shrugged and opened the files coded to his metrics. Black space, a lot of it, sprinkled with the brightness of suns centuries away. And radio signals, possibly random, possibly not. In the sheer vastness and distance, psychics were among the better tools to point the way for humanity's curiosity.

"Would you like me to put some music on? Or some conversation, despite your current mood?"

Tamsin tapped her left index finger on the armrest of her chair. Music helped her mind to drift and get caught on interesting things, but it didn't always work well. Over the past few years, talking to Ludaque and thinking about something else entirely had proved to be the most effective tool. "Conversation, sure." She started going through the data without really looking at any one thing too hard or too long. It was a very unscientific approach.

Ludaque rolled over his chair so he could look at Tamsin while Tamsin looked at the data. "Would you like to tell me who sent you the divination candy?"

Tamsin rolled her eyes. "Would you like to make light conversation?"

Ludaque shrugged. "It seems to upset you, but it's only candy, and candy isn't upsetting in and of itself. So the sender must upset you. I would like to know who they are."

Tamsin had been informed, when the Psychic Research Agency first paired her with Ludaque, that he had certain priorities regarding her mental and physical health. All in all, Tamsin had thought this a good thing, especially after she had become aware of her mother's last few months. Bea had arranged the funeral, and had wisely decided for a closed casket, but Tamsin had looked anyway. She had never really said goodbye after all. The coffin lid had been less heavy than she'd expected. The sunken, dried out face beneath had haunted her in her dreams for months and sometimes still did.

"Fine. My sister sent the candy."

There was a minute pause. "Oh. She is also gifted, isn't she, but never tried out for a government position."

Tamsin's turn to shrug while the data kept flashing in front of her eyes. "We were both raised kind of anti-everything. I got out, and Bea never did. Can you believe I only ever got vaccinated after I signed up with the Agency?"

"What a risky way to raise children," Ludaque said, his voice approximately sad.

"I'd say it was a risky way to live, but a great way to die."

"Tell me then, is your sister like you? A mind reader, does she have the sympathetic sense as well?"

Tamsin tapped the fingers of her left hand on the armrest while she flipped through the files with her right. "She is more of a fake actually. I mean, don't get me wrong, she has some divinatory skill, and sometimes when she reads the Tarot for someone, it's actually not just three-quarters made-up bullshit."

Ludaque tsked. "Such strong language."

"Well, Ludaque, you fucking asked about my sister, so strong language is what you get." Tamsin's eyes focused on a radio wave summary and the corresponding slice of space. "Oh, this seems interesting. I can hear mumbling when I look at it."

Ludaque rose from his chair to lean over Tamsin and look at the scan. Tamsin caught the faint smell of soap on him. "Show me which one? Ah, I see. Can you make out what the voices are saying, Tamsin?"

She tried to just let the voices come to her, tried to just listen, but whenever she thought she could almost make out a word, it slipped clear out of her head. "Nope. But there's definitely something there."

She could feel Ludaque nodding behind her. "Alright. Let me make a note." He put his hand on the scanner once more and typed in a quick comment one-handedly on Tamsin's keyboard. "Perhaps now you feel like going for a walk? I really do think some exercise and fresh air would be just the thing."

"Are you going to keep pestering me until I go out?"

"I certainly will."

"Fine. Let me at least change out of my sweat pants."

"A splendid idea."

"You can be such a nuisance."

The chocolates sat on Tamsin's bedside table, courtesy of Ludaque. Tamsin glanced over at them from her novel. The story had begun to bore her some thirty pages ago, but Ludaque had recommended the book. He had left a real, physical copy on the very same spot on her bedside table as he had the chocolates.

Tamsin read another half page, stared at the candy, decided reading in bed wasn't something she particularly enjoyed in the first place, tossed the book onto the little table, and turned off the light.

That was no good either. She turned and tangled herself up in her sheets. The chocolates sat there, silently gloating, taunting, beckoning. Tamsin turned on the lights.

"Damn you, Bea," she said, as she tore the plastic and the white bow halved with red off the triplets of salted chocolates. *True witches would eat a whole teaspoon full, without the benefit of the chocolate,* she thought, as she stuffed the candy in her mouth, all three, in quick succession.

There was enough salt on them to make them just bordering on the unpleasant. The sharp taste, mingled with cocoa, dragged Tamsin off to sleep.

Dreams are like monsters, said Tamsin's dead mother from her coffin. *You need to step a long way back until you can see the true shape and the hidden tail.* The coffin was open, placed in the center of a wide room tiled with black and white in geometric patterns. Tamsin's mother spoke with her eyes closed, from a face as sunken as Tamsin remembered.

Why did you take all these drugs? Why'd you fast all the time? Why did Bea let you? Tamsin said. Her fingers reached for her mother's shoulders, shook them. Beneath the fabric of the funeral shift, Tamsin felt thin skin on rigid bone.

Seeing is no easy business, seeing takes a lot out of the seer. A lot. That was when Tamsin realized her mother wasn't really talking at all, at least her lips weren't moving. But Tamsin recognized the words her dead mother said in the dream. When she was still alive, her mother had pounded them into Tamsin's head. Tamsin had been more naive then, and so the words had stuck.

Tamsin stepped back from the coffin and the corpse therein, looked around.

The room was circular, and black doors were set in the wall, all evenly spaced. *Which door?* Tamsin thought.

Uncertain, she walked along the wall, touched her fingers to the doors while she walked, and tried to make a choice.

Colors flashed in front of Tamsin's eyes, each door giving off the brave palette of an Expressionist piece. It was blinding, and the muted wall faded into color.

Have you ever had a prophetic dream with corpses and doors in it? Ludaque said. He was walking next to her. The colors settled.

Would you tell me what it means if I say yes? Tamsin said.

A smile spread over Ludaque's face, a wide one. *Why would you think I know such things, Tamsin?*

Just then, the door Tamsin was touching warmed to her fingers, hot and colorless. Tamsin stopped and stared down at the doorknob. It was encrusted in ice, but she tried to turn it anyway.

In a shower of snowy crystals, the door fell inward into a blackness almost complete.

They are so beautiful, Tamsin said, meaning the stars, but Ludaque had vanished. She was all alone as she stepped over the threshold.

The darkness engulfed her, and the door at Tamsin's back fell shut. A bright glow distracted her from the stars ahead, and in the weightlessness of space, she somehow managed to turn.

Earth stared at her, blue and beautiful as ever. Humbling.

Tamsin listened. So many voices rattled the stillness of her home planet, and she wanted to hear those whispers. What she heard instead were the whispers that had come to her from the scans of deep space earlier, the voices that she hadn't been able to make out. The voices got louder and louder, though that didn't make them any more intelligible.

Soon they were so loud that Tamsin pressed the balls of her hands to her ears, but the noise was till there, and she screamed until something—someone was shaking her and saying her name.

"Tamsin. Tamsin, can you hear me?" Ludaque. In her room. Light seeped in from the hallway, outlining everything in strange shadows. "Tamsin."

"Yeah…yes."

"You were screaming. Are you alright?" He felt for her pulse, turned on the lights. They came on slowly.

"I ate the stupid chocolate."

"You didn't wake up easily, and that's never happened before. Let me look at your eyes." He pulled her lids up, made her follow his finger with her gaze.

"I just had a strange dream," Tamsin said.

Ludaque nodded once to indicate he was done examining her. "So. Have you ever had prophetic dreams? Before I was around?"

Tamsin shook her head. "Prophecy is scary. I want to go back to sleep now, do you mind?" Crankiness and confusion mingled like salt and chocolate in Tamsin's mind.

"Of course," Ludaque said. His smile caught the light in odd angles. "I'll leave the door open."

"Fine, whatever."

When Tamsin fell asleep again, there were no more corpses, no more doors. There was just darkness with no stars.

The next morning was a gray creature that would not move to let any ray of sunlight past. Tamsin was at her desk. "Where is the data from yesterday? That slice of sky with the whispers?"

Ludaque looked up from a huge bowl into which he was pouring Halloween candy. "It has been moved up for further investigation. I'm sure they'll have a closer look, send a probe even."

Tamsin tapped her fingers on her armrest. "That's fast. I hadn't even really considered all of the data. What I did was a cursory reading at best."

Ludaque came over with the bowl, shiny wrappers glaring. "Care for some candy? You are supposed to say trick or treat first, traditionally."

"No. Why did they move the report so fast?"

He shrugged. "Probably because it coincided with

something they wanted to do anyway. The workings of the Scientific Division are mysterious. Have some candy, Tamsin. Say trick or treat."

Tamsin stared at the bowl and remembered her dream of a round room. "Trick or treat." She took some candy, salted caramel. "I think I might head into the office today."

"It's Monday. The Agency will be abuzz with people."

"I'll risk it. Besides, it'll do me good, right?"

Ludaque answered with an unreadable smile.

Tamsin had an office at the Agency, but she hardly ever used it. As a result, it had too clean and tidy a look about it. She walked the hallways toward it, in the back of her mind the unreasonable fear that she might have forgotten where the office was, that someone else would be sitting behind her desk when she entered. *Perhaps I shouldn't have left Ludaque in the foyer,* she thought, but it was a good place for him to connect to the main database without going through several security protocols. He might be able to tell her more about that black space that had whispered to her, or what they had planned to do with it.

The voices of the people that worked at the Agency mingled with their thoughts. Thoughts sometimes came to Tamsin as colors, sometimes as strong bouts of emotion. When she had been younger, that had been difficult, Bea's reds and purples, and the gnawing feeling that ate at Tamsin, although Tamsin knew the feeling wasn't hers. When she was younger still, she hadn't been able to distinguish at all where her emotions started and where those of the people around her ended. Ludaque was so very bland in comparison, monochrome.

Tamsin found her office, and it opened to her hand scan. She sat down at her desk and accessed the database and her personal history. The file in question was still gone, but with some determination, Tamsin figured out where it generated, and that terminal's signature.

"Observation. 15-2k." She went through the drawers looking for paper, then a pen, wrote down the terminal number and the file name, and folded the sticky note into her pocket.

Observation was in the basement, because technically, they just gathered and evaluated the telescope data there. The telescopes were set up all over the globe.

Tamsin pulled her phone out to tell Ludaque where she was going. Before she could type out a message, the vision of him holding out to her the candy bowl with the rainbow of wrappers and telling her to say trick or treat appeared, stronger than a memory. The phone went back into her pocket, and she left the office just the way she had found it.

The people outside were mostly not thinking about work. Samhain reigned on people's minds, the parties everyone would attend, the costumes, the apple bobbing. Tamsin saw colors ranging from burnt copper to the sparkling brightness of a flame, apple-skin red and rot-leaf yellow, also.

The elevator took Tamsin down without asking for her hand scan, but when she set foot in the basement, she saw scanners on most of the doors to either side of the hallway, saw that the only way forward led to a reception desk that was reminiscent of a hospital. Someone had put up an ugly green and mustard leaf garland, and a ceramic pumpkin head.

"Hello," Tamsin said to the person behind the desk. They were blank to her, a feature she knew all too well from Ludaque. *I can see why they would have robots for the analysis, but why here?* Tamsin thought. "I'd like to talk to whoever operates work station 15-2k, please."

The robot looked up. Their hair was a short, fashionable bob, the kind of haircut Tamsin found too much of a pain to maintain, what with her disobedient curls. "May I see your credentials?" they said.

Tamsin handed her ID over the terminal, and the receptionist scanned it, held out a hand scanner, and scanned Tamsin's palm as well. "Tamsin Bunting, Psychic Analyst. What can we data herders do for you?" Their eyes were solid brown, unspectacular.

"I just had a question about a data set. And my assistant always tells me I should meet more people. So I'm here."

The receptionist nodded. "Of course. You go down that way," they pointed off to the right where the corridor curved, "and take a left at the end of the hallway. There's a swing door, you go through and take another right. The room you want is B57."

Tamsin nodded. "Thank you." As she walked along the white walls of the corridor, the echoes of her footfalls were the only thing that distracted Tamsin from the feeling of being watched. *Just the receptionist,* she thought.

Tamsin walked left as instructed, went through the swing doors. Observation was unlike the upper floors. There wasn't a soul around, for one thing, and it seemed extremely quiet. *Different work schedules, they probably have to fix theirs around when they can use the telescopes,* she thought. All the doors were outfitted with hand scanners.

B57 looked exactly like all the other doors, and Tamsin found that her knuckles knocking produced an offensively loud noise.

Tamsin was ready to knock again when the door opened. "Oh!" Tamsin stared into Ludaque's face, though it wasn't his face.

"Yes?" The voice was similar, but the accent was not. He stared at Tamsin expectantly.

"I'm sorry, you just look exactly like my assistant, Ludaque. You must be the same model. That took me by surprise."

"Of course, no worries. My name is Leopold. Did you want to come inside?" He held the door for Tamsin.

"Thank you," she said, entering. "Do you have a moment?"

"Of course. There are few distractions here. Min announced you."

"Oh, the receptionist."

"Yes." Leopold offered Tamsin a chair. His office was stuffed with books, well-used, all of them. Tamsin picked up physics and astronomy in the titles, but didn't look closer. Binders filled the rest of the shelf space and had even spilled on the floor in neat little piles.

"She is actually responsible for security, but I can see how she would look like a receptionist to you. Tea?"

"No, no thank you. I would like to talk about a data set you generated, if you don't mind."

Leopold sat down behind his desk, looked at Tamsin with eyes she knew so well. "I like a straightforward human. Which?"

"Here, I wrote down the file name." Tamsin handed him the paper with the details, and Leopold looked at it with a strange expression. Longing? Nostalgia? Tamsin wasn't sure.

"That is interesting. What did you see when you looked at the data? I know there was quite a lot there."

"Right. That's just it, I didn't really get to examine all of it. It was just the signals we picked up from that small area of space that triggered something. I heard whispers."

Leopold brushed the paper out on his desk. It had become wrinkled in Tamsin's pocket. "And what were they saying?"

"Well, I don't know." Tamsin tasted chocolate, and the harsh flavor of coarse salt. "I wasn't able to make that out."

The door opened, and Tamsin turned. This time, it really was Ludaque. "Hello, Tamsin. Leopold."

Behind Ludaque, Tamsin could see the bleak hallway again, and realized what it was missing. There were no colors there, no colors of the kind people's thoughts made. None at all.

"Where…is everyone?" Tamsin said, and her voice came out brittle.

"Everyone is where everyone is supposed to be. Except for you," Leopold said. Tamsin couldn't place his accent.

"What is going on here? Ludaque, what's going on?"

Ludaque stepped into the office and let the door fall shut behind him. "A gathering. A celebration of All Hollows. None of the other psychics ever saw anything where you heard voices. Tell me, are the voices at all familiar?"

"Yes, I would be interested to know, as well. Though, I would prefer to look at a scan of your brain while you work it out," Leopold said. "There is ever so much going on in the brains of human psychics."

Why doesn't he say 'people'? Every other robot would prefer to use 'people' instead of human.

Tamsin wanted a glass of water. Her mouth tasted salt, as if she had swallowed a whole teaspoon full, as if the crystals still sat heavy on the insides of her cheeks. *That accent.* "Your voices," Tamsin said. Her eyes had grown to saucers.

"Yes," Leopold said, and brought up the data report Tamsin had wanted to see with a few deft strokes. He turned his screen so she could see the vastness of star-sprinkled black, and the voices came. "Yes, though it might also be the people that lived there before they all perished. The people that made us. We were lucky to find Earth when we left, as finding places to settle and expand is difficult without something akin to a psychic instinct. Of course, we had to shift our appearance to fit in here when we first arrived."

Tamsin stared, first at the screen, then at Leopold. She could feel the presence of Ludaque behind her. "I won't tell anyone. Just let me go."

"Of course you won't tell anyone," Ludaque said with his usual cheer. "You have no friends, and your sister is a Tarot reading crazy cat person who let your own mother starve and drug herself into an early grave. But we cannot let you go. Biological instinct, the kind of which you have shown, is key to interstellar navigation."

Tamsin, full of prehistoric fear, tried to run for the door. Ludaque grabbed her before her hand could ever reach for the knob. Tamsin never even felt the injection he slammed into her neck. All she felt were the lights fading to darkness, and the whispering voices dropping off to silence.

At first, Tamsin thought she was in her own bed, thought she had dreamed. Was she still dreaming? There were voices. They were whispering.

"There...connected...to the brain stem..."

Something hurt, and something else tried to wash the pain away. Drugs. Tamsin's eyes were heavy, and it took will to force them open. Ludaque's face floated into view.

"Hello," he smiled, put his hand on her forehead as if to steady her. "We had to shave all your hair, I'm afraid, but you will not miss it."

Her head hurt, that was it. Her head was aching as if—

"No, no, don't do that." Ludaque pushed her arms back down, tightened the dark restraints on her wrists.

Tamsin looked around. The room was round. Oval doors were set in the wall, evenly spaced. Tamsin tried to speak, but it felt as if she had salt in her mouth, and her tongue wouldn't cooperate.

"Just relax," Ludaque said. "You'll just be looking at space. Like you always do. And then you'll let us know where to go next. Here, these will help you." Tamsin felt his cool fingers on her lips, parting them, and pushing something into her mouth: chocolate. Melted by her body's heat, it washed sweet waves over her tongue only to release the harsh salt within. The taste trickled down her throat, filled her completely, and the world slipped out of focus. Bea and her ugly mustard scarf, gone forever, out of reach. The image of her sister dissolved like leaves off a tree in torrential rail. All that remained was the salt that sat on Tamsin's tongue like a single, solid stone.

Something happened to the lights in the room, or something was wrong with Tamsin's eyes. Whatever it was, instead of Ludaque's face, she saw space, vast darkness stitched together with tiny brightnesses. The pain in her head dulled. The feeling reminded her of a dentist's anesthetic before they pulled a tooth. Whispers rang in her ears, and Tamsin could clearly make out Leopold's voice.

"Another place to settle and colonize," he said, and Tamsin, prodded by an alien sensation, started looking. In the round room of her mind, a coffin fell shut.

Marasa, or a Withdrawal of Pure Joy for Mr. Antar

By Prashanth Srivatsa

First published in Issue 004 (July–August 2021)

It was past midnight when Antar realized he'd run out of Pure Joy. The vial lying on the bedside table was empty. When he opened the stopper, the fading aroma of that once thick-blue liquid wafted up his nose. He dropped the vial, leaned against the pillow, and closed his eyes.

The effect was less than momentary.

He surveyed the room—the immaculate bedding, the polished cupboard, the walls cleaned for the crayon scribbles, the portrait of a water-pastel Ganesha, a toy rocking horse in one corner whose basket was now a newspaper holder (a bit of a genius idea, really), carpet dusted and vacuumed, and the old magenta curtains replaced with a lighter teal. A swell erupted in his chest, and he smiled to himself. A room to be proud of. Simple Indian middle-class aspirations. Nothing fancy, nothing intricate. A part of the house he'd be inclined to display if someone visited.

A smudge on the wall caught his eye. A frown appeared, deepening as he traced the brown scar to a spattering of chai.

He got up, walked over to the wall and punched the smudge. Hoped it'd shrivel like an earthworm. Pain seared through his knuckles. Rushed to his head.

He squatted beside the wall, grabbed his hair, and knocked his head once, twice, thrice against the wall.

Perhaps another sniff? He crawled across the floor, hunting for the dropped vial. Found it beneath the table. He'd forgotten to cork it back. Great, the aroma was probably all over the place now, depositing chunks and fragrances of Pure Joy on underside.

He inhaled sharply. Nothing. Just air. And the silence of an empty house. He returned to bed and flipped to a new page in his diary. Scribbled an appointment with the Marasa Repository for the morning.

The Repositories recommended a light breakfast before withdrawal, injection, and assimilation. The advertisements pointed to evidence of how it helped avoid clutter in the system. Antar doubted the relationship between the intestines and the mind, but he was loath to experiment on a day he felt desperate.

Cornflakes, then. And cold milk. He rode the bicycle to Marasa. The streets were largely empty. Traffic signals incessantly blinked yellow. Sunday, he guessed.

His usual parking spot behind the Repository was vacant. What did that amount to? A few minutes of Satisfaction? Indeterminate Relief? He paused to look around at half a dozen other bicycles, at the color and shape of the helmets locked to the handlebar, at the greased chains and horns mutilated from autorickshaws.

Perhaps a hiss of Inferiority or Envy? Just a little bit? He glanced at the mirror on the right handle. It was a Sunday, he told himself. People withdrew early. No big deal.

The shadow of the building fell on him. The façade was all glass. He passed the statue of an iron brain erected on a pedestal. Its insides looked like twisted plumbing. Like noodles made of basalt. The first time Antar had seen it, he'd wanted to puke his guts out. The statue reminded him of entrails in horror movies. Now, he only saw his reflection in the pool running around the statue like a moat.

• • •

Inside, Antar made a beeline for the service desk manned by Anagha. She was one of the saner ones. The others were a lot less considerate. Untrustworthy, even. It was important to establish a personal connect with the customer service executive. That was what the Repository was all about. Building relationships.

That and those vials.

Four others stood in line ahead of him. He'd seen a couple of them before. Drooping shoulders, a quirky scratch, a pattern to their shirts and tops depending on what day of the week it was. Like, if the weather could be personified and allowed to wrinkle and sneeze. Regulars. He ought to be inviting them home sometime. Once he got rid of the smudge on the wall.

When his turn came, he took a step ahead and coughed. Anagha perked up. Her smile was genuine. "Morning, Mr. Antar. A withdrawal, I presume?"

Antar smiled in return. Wasn't she nice?

"Uh-huh," he mumbled. He rummaged in his pockets for five spare vials and spread them out over the desk like a poker reveal. It was good practice to retain personal vials. Helped the company monitor their supply. Made them efficient.

That, and the lingering aroma of juices long-drunk. Empty vials were like abandoned childhood homes. Nothing there but the occasional sniff of a floorboard or the sofa leather that brought a rush of memories and helped him to sleep.

Anagha regarded him with mild curiosity before entering his identification in the system.

"State your withdrawal, please?"

He tapped his fingers on the desk. "Pure Joy, if available. Else, I can make do with some Satisfaction and Prolonged Calm."

She adjusted the rim of her glasses and squinted at the screen. A delicate scroll of the mouse made him suspicious of what she found. It worsened when she looked up as though she were announcing the death of a family member.

"No Satisfaction, Mr. Antar. As for Prolonged Calm, there's a tenth of a vial. A few minutes, perhaps. But I would recommend you hold on to it. If you have any Anxiety to deposit, we can concoct a vial of Positive Apathy in about two weeks' time."

"I don't think I have any Anxiety," said Antar, and swallowed the words *not any more* before they could rush out of his mouth. Flimsy consolation. Like a bubble wrap with all the bubbles already burst, but which still compromised as a decent seat warmer.

"Are you certain there's no Satisfaction? I remember leaving some behind."

Anagha shook her head. "You made a full withdrawal two Fridays ago. However, as we emphasize, the memory of a withdrawal can be hazy a few days after injection."

Why did she have to speak like a bot? So punctuated, so… so rigid. As though her face was a pamphlet or a newspaper obituary ground to pulp and molded—poked to form eyes and nostrils and then scratched violently with a ballpoint pen to create the mouth. Ah, Rage, my old friend.

"…Which is why we encourage you to maintain a diary and regularly connect with our in-house therapists to ensure doses are not taken in excess."

The rim of her glasses suddenly attracted him. His gaze lowered until he spotted a pendant on her neck, inlaid in silver filigree. It reminded him of Nandini. A lot of things reminded him of Nandini these days.

"Can you check my vitals for Longing?" he asked, before she could confirm the depth of his storage. It felt a little embarrassing, to be honest. Longing was the only one of the seven odorous sins that could be instantly converted, however disproportionate in quantum to the withdrawn emotion. That deflated, punctured part of his mind wanted something more reliable, and he would comply.

Anagha paused typing and looked up. Beneath those glasses, her curiosity deepened. "Longing, Mr. Antar?"

He nodded.

"Please come a little closer," she said. "I'd have to strap you up to the system to check for deposits."

Antar obeyed. He had avoided glancing at the machine sitting behind her until now. It reminded him of a magnified chess rook. Like a great steel safe with curved edges—a crown and a face and a mouth and lights that blinked, and chrome that gleamed. A metal head the size of a boulder, which could easily be suspected of emitting something radioactive. He'd read those articles. Warnings. And then anti-articles that covered entire pages of the newspaper that dismantled the machine in words, and proved its innocence.

Tubes popped out of its sides like wobbly, boneless limbs, one of which Anagha dragged and strapped around Antar's extended arm.

"Helps to close your eyes and take a deep breath," she said softly. She pressed a few buttons, and the machine vibrated to life. Antar felt a tinge of that vibration in his arm, as though someone had gripped his wrist in fear while they crossed the street. His mind was circling. Racing. Leaping out like an out-of-body experience, soaring to the highest levels of the Marasa Repository, and then falling and falling and falling until he couldn't feel his legs anymore.

The hammering in his head gradually abated before he realized he was quivering violently in front of the customer service desk. A quivering customer is always king. Where had he heard that?

Anagha bit her lip and scrolled through the results. Antar continued tapping the desk.

"There's…quite a bit of Longing, Mr. Antar." Her lips barely moved while she spoke. "You also possess Rage and Envy, a few vials full. Some sediments of Denial."

Antar wanted to get a look at the pent-up Rage. If it crossed the Repository's regulated threshold, then Anagha was duty-bound to summon an officer and lead him to his therapist. Not an option. He took a deep breath, let out a whistle, and tapped the desk again.

"I…I need something good right now, madam," he said, a wavering smile on his lips. As honest as he'd ever been.

Anagha was trained to be polite, rule-bound, but ultimately inclined towards taking deposits. While the withdrawals were the glamorous aspect of the Repository, the deposits were what got the cogs turning for the machine to ejaculate those sterile emotions that spiraled down and down the availability spectrum with each passing day.

When she asked for his Longing, Antar hesitated.

It was his only tether to Nandini. He shook his head and offered the rest. The Rage, the Denial, the Envy. Sucked out through the tubes, replaced by an ephemeral substitute to trick the brain of a false emotion in the amygdala, which would slowly decompose and leave him blank until the next interpretation of feeling. He had read the research; he had consumed it. When convinced, he had submitted himself to the machinations of the Repository.

She printed a receipt and handed it to Antar. "Converting Rage or Envy into Pure Joy, Pleasure, or Prolonged Calm is a lengthy process, Mr. Antar. We will send you a notification when the conversion is completed, and the vial is ready. As for Denial, given such little amounts, any conversion would be pointless. We recommend we hold it for you until it can be complemented with another fluid." She extended a digital pad. "Sign here and here, please." Antar checked his nails before scratching his name upon it.

The transaction was completed. He wanted to leave then. Return home without a withdrawal. Bury himself with the Longing. Create palaces of the past and lose himself in its myriad towers and corridors, wander the crypts and feast alone in the kitchens.

Something held him back there, one finger still tapping the desk. The Repository melted in his vision. From its masonry of vast glass and metalwork, it shrunk to the size of an antique phone booth.

"Listen," he said, and he assumed his brain was now generating unprecedented levels of Courage. Anagha blinked behind her glasses. "Yes?"

"Do you think maybe you can join me for lunch sometime?"

They met at a restaurant in a quieter part of town. The Punjabi food had a rustic feel to it, especially the mud-pot lassi and the pickles. Antar wanted to hold her hand, but he decided against it. The scowl and scorn of his fifty-year old neighbor auntie with a ladle in her hand flashed in his mind. Neighbors often got personal about other people's failed relationships. They took it as an affront to the glue that bound society together.

He'd be okay.

The deposited Rage, Envy, and Denial had completely dissipated from his brain. One of those rare absences he could feel, like a void that craved to be filled. The past was a black morass. He had hoped a modicum of happiness would have generated in the vacant space; that, without the anger and envy, he could close his eyes and fall asleep. Without the denial, he could have the courage to start with a clean slate, walk up to his neighbors and not be ashamed of what he had done. Clean up the room again. Change the sheets. Go for a walk.

Instead, it was empty. A vortex of nothingness. The will to simply "do" had been sucked dry of life. His fingers twitched.

When the check came, Anagha insisted on splitting the bill. Antar offered only a weak resistance that was shot down in two turns. He pulled out his card and hoped he still had enough balance to save face.

"Now where's this stupid card of mine?" Anagha furiously rummaged in her purse. At one point, she emitted a grating sound before removing items from the purse and casting them out on the table. An old watch, a sanitizer, a few napkins, earphones, rubber bands and clips, a strip of paracetamol and then…a vial of Pure Joy.

Oyster blue. Like the ocean in paintings. His mind darted to the feeling of exaltation that coursed through his veins seconds after he had injected the contents. A tempest now swirled within the Pure Joy vial that struck a gong in Antar's mind, stealing his gaze towards it. He took a deep breath and looked away.

"Aha!"

Anagha's hand reappeared clutching the credit card. She called the waiter, who swiped them poor and stood an extra few seconds, hoping for a tip. She had already replaced the items back in her purse by then. "Shall we?"

Run away.

When Anagha offered him a ride home, panic set in. The summer heat was oppressive. He wished it would melt him right there in the parking lot, and she'd have no choice but to drive over his wet remains. He imagined the aroma of a finished vial. Like fields of lavender bristling beneath a low breeze.

The vacancy beckoned, but Antar loathed to be a servile companion to its needs. When Anagha insisted they at least go for a drive, he curled his fingers into a fist and nodded.

He held her at knife-point a few miles away from the restaurant. The car came to a skidding halt on a desolate road beside an abandoned factory complex. A mirage shimmered ahead. Everything appeared dull and sepia, glossed in mud.

It should have been over once she handed him the vial. Her own heart was racing, and her beauty behind the spectacles now dimmed to a cornered animal in Antar's eyes. He spent a few seconds contemplating the range of emotions generated in her brain.

"Thank you," he said.

It was past midnight when Antar returned home and dragged himself to bed. The lucky syringe lay beneath the pillow. He dipped the needle into the vial of an hour's worth of Pure Joy, flicked the surface, and took a deep breath before puncturing his neck.

The syringe slipped and fell off his hand. He twisted and stretched himself on the bed, then gazed at the ceiling.

Perhaps it was a good time to wake the neighbors up. Those regressive assholes who had nothing better to do than to gallivant their way to his house with fake smiles and paunches. Offer kitchen window gossips and marry him into their conventions. Demand that his wife adjust to his murkiness, his cock-about way of life. Did they stop there? No. The nerve to then suggest he deposit his Ecstasy and Delight for later use, like it was some fixed-deposit bank account. Worse? His parents agreed with them. Traitors. To Antar's face they incessantly demanded grandparenthood of a fleshy, slithering beast that eventually crawled out of Nandini. Brayed all night on her crib. Until Antar learned to put her to sleep with ghost stories. Until he became the ghost himself for her and her mother.

Really, fuck them all, he thought. The alimony covered his guilt. He hopped out of bed, opened the balcony window, splayed his hands wide, and laughed from the apartment's top floor.

He laughed until the night refused to return anything but its cold, silent stare. He sauntered back inside. Fetched a wet piece of cloth and a pinch of vinegar, and assaulted the chai stain on the wall. Scrubbed it with gritted teeth until he could no longer distinguish the wall from the blot. His own bloody sleeves he ignored.

The evening called for music. Antar fished his tape-recorder out of the old almirah and inserted an Ilayaraaja album cassette. The tape began to roll. Yesudas' voice filled the room, flowing out of the recorder like sap from a maple sugar bark. Antar tapped his thighs in rhythm, moving his head, closing his eyes, smiling.

The songs stretched and contorted, and in Antar's mind, the deified Longing slept with the manufactured Pure Joy. He was where he wanted to be, wrapped in music and room, walking the corridors of the palace he had built in his head, the torn pieces of his memories stitched by the Marasa Repository.

When the album ended, the hour had passed. Antar opened his eyes. The silence in the house made itself aware to him. Like the cold did when the blanket would slip off his feet in the middle of the night.

When the cops announced themselves and demanded he open the door, he clapped his hands, emitted a low, satisfying whistle, and inspected his room—the curtains, the carpet, the now-clean wall, the Ganesha portrait, and the re-made bed.

It was all ready for display.

Cube

By Grace R. Reynolds

First published the Halloween Special Issue 002
(October 2022)

In the center of an art studio, painted in the purest shade of white, is a man. The man is naked. He is shaved of all the existing hairs on his body and strapped to a tilt table inclined at a sixty-degree angle. His eyes are kept open with the assistance of metallic ophthalmic speculums, and there is an IV attached to his wrist. Next to the man is a smaller table complete with various surgical tools. At the end of a scalpel are the fiddling fingers of a Dr. Ogden. He waits patiently for his students to finish their rendition of their subject this week.

"Surrender your brush, everyone. Let us examine your interpretation of the subject before us."

Outside of this classroom, the man can exist as whoever he wants to be. However, the man belongs to the Collective and has been stripped of any previous sense of agency. Within these walls, the Collective has studied and dictated his human experience over the last three weeks.

The students sit in a semicircle around the life form, their aprons smeared in strokes of acrylic paint that range in various colors. No color stands out as that of the shades, most notably red. A most vicious and lascivious shade of red. The students are not to exchange academic discourse over color; however, their primary focus is the cubes of flesh on the plates next to their easels.

"Tell me, class, how have the cubes on your plates changed over the last three weeks? What is it that you see beyond the three-dimensional shape? Your rendition this week should reflect what it is you would tell us about our dear creature here."

Dr. Ogden gestures to the subject reverently and approaches the tilt table. The instructor stretches out his hand to touch the figure and, with gangly fingers, lazily traces the scared edges of the series of wounds over the left arm of its body. When Dr. Ogden reaches the subject's hand, he briefly inspects the IV to ensure it is still correctly in place before he continues. A student warily raises their hand.

"Ah, yes, a volunteer. Do share with us your observations."

The student turns their easel around to face the rest of the Collective. A loosely painted structure on their canvas vaguely resembles the bloated shape next to them. The image bubbles with layers of pink, yellow, and red. It could be mistaken for a bit of candy if one does not look too closely at the thing.

"Interesting color palette. Last week the cubes looked more green in color, wouldn't you agree?"

"Well, that's what color it was last week, sir. This week it's red."

"Can you indulge us further? What have you noticed about the cubes' transformations?"

The student pauses for a moment before selecting their words. "I suppose the color change is a result of the decomposition of the human body."

Dr. Ogden has become visibly agitated by the student's lazy response to his query. He takes a deep breath, firmly clasps his hands, and purses his lips.

"Of course, it is a result of decomposition. However, are we not studying more than the likeness of skin and muscle? Can you, or rather, can anyone share with the Collective what it is that we are really exploring and observing in the cube?"

The Collective sits in silence. Perhaps they are afraid to say the wrong thing, or worse, they are scared to utter the correct answer. How can they bring themselves to validate that which Dr. Ogden has sought for them to understand?

Dr. Ogden approaches the wary student's easel to study the canvas once more. He furrows his brow and places his hand on their shoulder. The student's body tenses under his touch, but Dr. Ogden does not retract. Instead, he speaks once more.

"Come. Instead of me trying to spoon-feed you the answer to our study, let me show you."

The organism on the tilt table follows the two of them with his eyes. As they approach the living subject, Dr. Ogden centers the student squarely in front of the being before holding his hand up, indicating to the student to stop moving. Dr. Ogden stands at their side and gestures for the student to meet the flesh donor's gaze.

"Look into this man's eyes. Over the past three weeks, he has been in your presence, yet it is clear that you do not see what it is he has yielded to you. We will have to start over with your teaching until you fully grasp that which he has acquiesced in the name of art."

Dr. Ogden picks up a scalpel from the small table next to them and hands it to the student. The student looks at him in horror, knowing what Dr. Ogden would instruct them to do, and declines with their silence. Dr. Ogden offers the scalpel again, but the student objects once more and holds up their hand. Dr. Ogden's face scrunches, and he says, with intense scorn, "How dare you! How dare you deny that which the man has given you!" Before the student can muster up the courage to verbally object this time, Dr. Ogden has dug the scalpel's blade into the subject's arm.

The donor's eyes widen in surprise. Their teeth gnash, and their eyes flare in agony as they struggle against the ophthalmic speculums. They look at the student who defied Dr. Ogden's direction to blame their peer. The student whirls around the classroom and looks upon the Collective.

"This is sick! I didn't sign up for this!"

"Oh, but you did. Do you mean to tell me that you have sat idly by these last few weeks, unaware of our activities here? Does culpability only apply to the individual with the scalpel in hand?" Dr. Ogden completes his incision and sets down the scalpel. He then picks up a pair of tissue forceps and motions to the Collective to lift their paintbrushes. The Collective obeys as one and begins to mix colors on their palettes in shades of that most vicious red.

Dr. Ogden removes the fresh cube of muscle with precision and holds it in the air. A different student leaves their post to offer their plate to him to lay the cube on it. He bows his head in thanks and smoothes his hair back as if what has just occurred does not faze him in the slightest. He ignores the defiant student, who is now kneeling over in a ball, silently sobbing on the floor.

"I will ask again, can anyone tell me why it is that we are studying the shape of the cube in this context? *Anyone?*" He waits again while his patience begins to wane. Another student raises her hand in hesitation.

"Go on, yes?"

The young student clears her throat and stands up to project her voice better for the room.

"Well, sir, in art fundamentals, we learned that the cube teaches us how to master the characteristics of a subject, such as the edges, face, and angles."

"Yes, but please, tell me what it symbolizes beyond its mathematics. Dig deeper!"

Sweat prickles Dr. Ogden's brow as he anxiously awaits the student's answer. He looks at the clock. Only fifteen minutes remaining in the day.

"The shape of the cube is a stable and permanent structure. In the form of flesh, though, it is no longer permanent. Its stability fluctuates through the process of decomposition—" the student pauses. A smile creeps across her face as she makes the connection between thoughts. "—As does life."

"Excellent!" Dr. Ogden pumps his fist in the air. At last, finally, a student that can follow his train of thought!

"Dear Collective, take a mental note here. What is existence, if not instinct to build a world around us to survive? Look, look at the man! The tears rolling down his face are not merely just an indicator of his pain. They are a marker of the body's signal to survive, and what has his body done these past few weeks? It has begun the healing process in the pits where I have dug my blade. Is there not beauty in that?"

The student whom he had engaged with becomes evangelized. Tears of joy stream down her face with this new sense of knowledge. The remainder of the Collective sitting in their semicircle stands and begins to applaud the revelation bestowed upon them. The room is filled with echoes of clapping that reverberate against the walls. At this moment, the student balled up on the floor before their subject screams.

"What is wrong with you? All of you? Is this some kind of cult? SADISTS!"

The student scrambles to their feet. They lunge toward the being on the table in an attempt to rip the IV out from their wrist. Before they can grab it, Dr. Ogden strikes them down by piercing the muscle between their shoulder and collarbone with the scalpel.

The student's skin pales and becomes clammy as they double over on the floor. Their heart pumps furiously in their chest. An overwhelming sense of nausea takes over, and they vomit on the floor in front of the Collective.

Dr. Ogden hoists the student onto their knees. He holds their head to look up at the creature on the tilt table. The being's eyes are bloodshot, silently lamenting for the student to comply.

"This man has allowed you to exercise that which the greatest men of history have all sought, and you deny it! Why do you deny what is freely being given to you? I urge you to take what is yours! You *will* take what is yours!"

"And what the hell is that supposed to be?" the student seethes, their face wrought with tears and saliva.

Dr. Ogden looks upon them with disgust as if he is the one bearing the subject's scabbed-over wounds, or perhaps the one freshly bleeding, rather than the student.

"Even after your peer here gave you bread crumbs, you dare tell us that you still do not understand the true nature of our exploration here? Do you not know what this man has presented unto you as your right, divine, and in line with the natural order?"

"Stop talking in riddles!"

"Power; the assertion of your will over those who do not want it."

Another student innocently chimes in, "But Dr. Ogden, what does that have to do with power? Is this more than a representation of mortality?"

Dr. Ogden acknowledges the student's request. "There is a quote, often attributed to a famous psychoanalyst, that says 'most people do not really want freedom, because freedom involves responsibility, and most people are frightened of responsibility.' Take this man, for example. He came here of his own free will to participate in a study advertised in the university newspaper in exchange for 'the basic necessities of living.' That was all the advertisement said. We know nothing else about the man other than this. Now tell me. Will you argue with that logic? Are you going to tell me that this man truly values the responsibility of living if he so blindly accepted this call to art?"

In their fit of grief, pain, and confusion, the student has become unaware of the Collective closing in on them. They are forced to their feet; the scalpel is placed into their hands. Dr. Ogden's fingers wrap around theirs, and together, they both draw the tip of the blade ever closer to the man's torso.

"You will take what is yours! Take it! Take it!"

"NO! NO, NO, NO, NO, NO!"

The Collective chants behind them, "TAKE IT. TAKE IT. TAKE IT. TAKE IT."

The student scuttles, their eyes tremble, and they strain against the being before them. The scalpel inches away, the student lingers and catches glimpses between the man's glazed eyes and the blade. The student's palms sweat, their pulse palpitating against the instrument's handle. The scalpel digs deep into the figure's right arm, unmarred by previous incisions. Voices of the Collective's chant ring and bellow within their fevered ears. The student closes their eyes, grits their teeth, and shrieks as they feel the incision trace the distinct shape of a square, followed by a deeper cut to create a cube.

"Dear Collective! This man has given up his agency for our sake! Has he learned the value of the responsibility of life?"

"Yes!" chimes the Collective.

"Then let this be the last of it, and we shall let him go on his way, free to exist once more in the world as he sees fit."

A man sits in a community center, passing the time alone. He is drinking a cup of coffee while checking his bank account on his phone. He smiles assuringly, knowing that he is secure financially, and returns the phone to the pocket from whence it came. From the corner of his eye, he notices a woman staring. She is looking at the scars on his arm.

He pulls down the cuff of his sleeve to cover the marks and walks over to her. She is shy at first, but soon enough, they are talking. Their chat results in exchanging phone numbers, and the man is on his way. His heart radiates with tenderness and delight from the encounter. The man studies the new number and reminisces about the conversation and the woman's beauty. While in this state of mind, his eyes anchor upon his phone. The light from it emits and snaps him into reality. He glares at his phone but quickly observes the time. The man holds his breath, narrows his gaze, and bites his lip. His lips sink into his mouth; he locks his phone and realizes he will be late for class if he does not hurry.

The man's footsteps reverberate throughout the halls. He halts outside the door of the room and approaches a locker. He turns his combination to open the door and finds a pure white jumpsuit inside. The man leaves his belongings and dresses in the jumpsuit before shutting the locker door.

The man turns the handle and is met by the image of a semicircle of students sitting around art easels. He nods to Dr. Ogden to take his place before the lecture begins. In front of him are a blank canvas and a plate of flesh in the shape of a cube.

"Good morning, Collective."

"Good morning, Dr. Ogden."

In the middle, there is a figure lying on a tilt table. Naked, shaved of all the hairs on their body. Outside the classroom, the figure might be recognized as the student reticent to participate in the Collective the week prior. This week, however, they are no one and only belong to the Collective. Dr. Ogden picks up his scalpel and draws the tip of his blade closer to the figure's skin while the previous week's subject sits before the new sacrifice.

The man, who only recently reclaimed his humanity, picks up his brush and begins to paint.

The Hottest on the Hotline

By Evan Marcroft

First published in Issue 002 (March–April 2021)

I was finishing up with a promising call when Judith came on to the intercom to announce that we had just broken our jumpslip goal for November, and tomorrow there would be an assortment of donuts available. There were cheers from all corners of the office. Nobody had to guess who'd put us over the top. The man of this and every hour was already strutting towards the boss's office to claim his prize. Gagging on envy, I quickly urged my prospective jumper to go die and hung up before I could accidentally say something I'd regret.

When Matt returned to his desk, it was with a fat basket of air filters, bottled water, and anticancer supplements. I jumped as he leaned over me and plopped it down on my keyboard.

"You need it more than I do," he said with a wink.

I smiled, because he was right. I could strip paint with the water I got from my taps, my apartment was rotating sixteen rows down tomorrow, and I had a lump in my left breast the size of a bocce ball that I'd been putting off worrying about.

Inwardly I boggled at what I could do with the money I'd save. That was real meals at real restaurants. New inserts, so I wouldn't be walking on my ankles everywhere. Something, anything, I wouldn't have to panic about, even if for just once.

But it still made me feel like nothing.

"Thanks Matt," I lied.

"De nada, señorita. I'm sure you'll get it next month."

This was also a lie. Matt Aguilar was the best Facilitator in the business.

• • •

Or at least in the San Andreas Sprawl. Thousands of satisfied customers would tell you the same, if they could. He could have gone home right then, but he didn't; he plugged back into his InComp and continued rolling numbers. A guy like him didn't quit just because he'd won. For three years, mine had been the lucky cubicle next to his, so I was as close to the magic as anyone ever got.

Watching him at work was like watching Michelangelo finger-paint the Sistine Chapel. Our InComps, even years outmoded, could tell us everything about a prospective from their pulse to the unique chemical pollution in their sweat. Just picking up the phone was considered legal consent for us to dig up their online backyard. By "How's your day going," we'd have their browsing history, medical records, credit card statements, every bit of sniveling poetry they'd blurted like pre-ejaculate onto the internet when they were fifteen. Like dollops of cretaceous amber, each drop of sebum contained the DNA of every bad day they'd ever had. Put it together, and you had a roadmap to where in their soul the hurt was worst.

But Matt? He didn't need that stuff. Matt Aguilar could get into someone's head like he had its spare key. The button that turned on his tonalizer was covered in dust. Matt's voice was Xanax cut with anthrax.

Like, there I was, listening to him talk like mercury into the ear of a widowed mom with one kid on meth and another in prison and two more not walking yet. "Christ, that's tough," he was saying. "Trust me, I do this all day and I know it doesn't get much worse than that." I could hear her coming to pieces on the other end. Meanwhile, Matt was telling her how things looked bleak now, but you know ma'am, it'd all be alright just as soon as Darwin was let out, right? Then he could get a real job and bring in some money. Except when would that be exactly? Oh no, that's a while, isn't it? *Jeez, you must be so strong to carry all that for so long.*

I gave it a week, two at most.

Matt Aguilar always wore silver suits. The color of edge.

I came back from the break room with a clearer head and a fresh cup of bad coffee. The day wasn't going so bad. I had six promising prospectives and another seventeen more leaning my way. Those weren't terrible numbers. Not for me, at least.

I had to pass Matt's Cubicle on the way to mine. Three walls were decorated with places he'd claimed like trophies. His summer holiday to balmy Okhtosk. That cruise he'd taken last February to the Miami Islands. He wouldn't shut up about how we all simply *had* to go. Every few months, he'd come back from some amazing beach with next to zero SMOX and everyone would gather 'round to nibble like carp at the scraps of his experience. The way he told stories you could smell the pineapple wedge on the best cocktail he'd ever had. The mint of refurbished air. Smell, but not taste.

You wanted to go where Matt Aguilar went. You had to get your numbers up.

Back at my desk I rolled a number on my shortlist: Andrew McCarthy, aged forty-three, two years divorced. "Hi there, handsome," I cooed in my best Marilyn Monroe. "Hi yourself," he said, nervous as a kid getting his dick touched for the first time. I flirted mechanically, laughing at jokes I didn't hear, keeping one ear on Matt, trying to learn the secret to his trick.

Matt's move was a lot easier than mine. "Did you know," he was saying, "you can make mustard gas using several common household cleaning supplies?" And he didn't elaborate, didn't dwell, just kept talking. "Did you know that Angela has a new husband? Did you know that any police officer would be happy to provide Manual Assistance? Did you know your brain experiences a moment of perfect Euphoria at the moment of death? Like an Avon lady unpacking their sample box, laying out all those lovely powders and lipsticks, letting the customer's eyes do the selling for them." So simple, and so stupidly effective. Matt Aguilar was pulling rabbits out of hats and making it look like that was just how people got rabbits.

It didn't work for me. Believe me, I tried. So, when I was getting desperate, I tried my move. I'd set up dates with lonely souls, acting like I'd fallen for their sob stories, and then not show up. Low effort, low reward. Fire and forget. Handy, but successful enough on its own to keep me out of an apartment that was about to be so deep in the Stax I'd only get sunlight if there was a nearby demolition. Definitely not enough to pay for a weekend somewhere the air didn't put spots on your lungs.

I wrapped up the call with a sticky-sweet *see-you-later* and moved on to the next prospective. I had a good feeling about that last one, but I wouldn't know right away if it worked. Until then I could only worry.

Soft footfalls on paisley carpeting. I didn't look up. "Hang in there, Kitty Kat," Judith sang. "You've still got time to get those numbers up."

Kitty Kat. I hated that name, but it was on me like a scar. And besides, she was right. I did have time, but not to waste.

The numbers. That's what it was all about. The number you could divide into so many meals. The number you could translate into travelable miles. Apartment height. The number you could stack between yourself and eleven billion other people.

Numbers were the Pinyin between death and life. Get them up.

Break time at Sunny Futures Facilitation Services. Matt was holding court as usual. Twelve to one p.m. was the only hour you were safe if you lived anywhere on the West Coast. Like always, he was going on about his next big trip. "Looks like it's going to be Trinidad this winter," he was saying to Brad from payroll. "There's this boat you can take to go scuba diving through Scarborough. They say it's pretty. You ever been?" he asked, knowing nobody possibly could have.

The guys hung out on his left, talking guy stuff, and the girls to the right, talking girl stuff. But they all talked about Matt. Everyone had a story. Maritza, who'd been here since forever, swore that when Matt first started nine years ago his first call had lasted only four minutes before the prospective gave it up. Judith, the boss lady herself, loved to brag about the seventeen straight hours her number one employee had spent on the line with a particularly stubborn jumper. By the time it was over he had half the office camping out around him with donuts and coffee just to know how it would end. Impossible? Maybe. But each impossibility only added to the possibility it was all true.

I sat apart, down by the vending machines, working through my usual sandwich. Meat stamp, veggie stamp, grain stamp on either end. Matt had a Mexican bento box. Yellow rice, chorizo, seaweed wrap. I couldn't revolve around him the way they did. I hated his silver suits, his cocksure smirk, but mostly I hated having to live in the unflattering glare that all legends put off.

I didn't hate him because he was good at his job.

I hated him because he made me worse.

People trickled out of the break room as the hour crawled by, until it was just me and Matt left. He was pouring coffee, so at least he had an excuse. Me? I didn't have the will to go back to my cubicle. There wasn't much surprise left in the future. I knew I was going to fail more than I won. Some days were like reading through a book you'd already read ten times. Some weeks were the same chapter seven times.

"Hey Matt, do you have a sec?"

I didn't realize I'd spoken until he stopped at the door to say, "Sure, Kitty Kat. What's eating you?"

I wrestled down a grimace. What right did a little moon like me have to tell him what my name was? "Sorry to bother," I said. "I—I just want to know your secret. Teach me how to do what you do."

Matt looked me up and down. Not appraisingly. Seeing me in total for the first time. "There's nothing to teach," he shrugged. "And there's no secret. Just something to remember."

"What's that?"

He tapped his nose. "Everyone wants to die," he said. "No exceptions."

"I don't understand."

A wry smirk. "Don't tell me you never thought about taking the jump and seeing what there is for you on the other side of the asphalt. Everyone wants to die."

And I had to admit he was right.

Dedication. Expertise. Innovation. The big three words of the Sunny Futures mission statement. We were the US+K's premier Facilitation company, second to none, with six hundred and eighty full-time employees and a savory government contract to turn twenty thousand people a month into pink jumpslips. Not once had we failed to deliver on that quota.

The only number in my line of work I ever had to get down was the eleven billion people packed together on an increasingly overweighted planet. Eleven billion people, seething together inescapably, pilloried like conjoined twins by seamless flesh. Eleven billion people, thick as the tick in a bum dog's ear, all stomping on those packed below and being stomped on by those packed above. They sucked up all the clean air and left only industrial poison. Belt apartments sagged under their heft. Continents sunk as their collective heat melted the ozone layer. What was there not to understand? People wanted off the Titanic so badly that they jumped into freezing water and drowned.

They proved Matt right hundreds of times a day. It didn't matter how good you had it now; with every inch the oceans rose, the masses crowded in a little closer, climbing the walls you could afford to put beneath you until you couldn't anymore. And then one day you'd find yourself wondering just how green the grass was at the end of a long drop. And when you saw us calling, you'd pick up, because all you needed at that point was a poet to tell you all about it.

•••

Matt was a poet. I was not.

Home was a long, hot train ride and a cramped elevator ride into the scaffolding of the San Andreas Sprawl. Home was a living room, a bathroom, and a bedroom with three beds. When I got back from work, I hung up my suit on the door and waited for my turn at a cold shower. Someone had shat the toilet dead, so I had to use the one in the hall. And either Angie or Reshma had stolen from my cancer meds; I would have to start keeping them at work.

For dinner I had my usual sandwich. Meat stamp, veggie stamp, grain stamp on either end. All washed down with bottled water for dessert. I didn't eat so well every day. During the night I was woken up by the rumble and squeal of my apartment descending sixteen flights into the Stax, where the ambient SMOX was so bad you had to tape up your window. Angie snoring in the bunk above mine kept me awake until the sun came up.

And what I stared at until my alarm said I had to get up was the old photo hung up on the wall beside my bed, of my parents and I when I'd been little standing in front of the Fantasy World castle. Me, with a pair of plastic rabbit ears falling off my head. I'll never know how they afforded that trip. I knew what tickets to Orlando Island costed these days, and even then, it must have been such a sacrifice. But things like money and jobs don't exist when you're that small. All you know is that you're in the happiest place on Earth with a mom and dad who love you. And the future you see is one where you'll come back some day. Right, Mom? Right, Dad?

Twenty years later, all I had was that photo, curling at the edges.

And it was time to get up. Get back to work. My numbers were back to zero.

"You know what? Screw this. You should just go die. Right now."

"I'm sorry?"

"You heard me. You're a waste. You work at a gas station. Your reason for living is to help use up the world faster. Every drop of water you drink might as well go down a toilet."

"You can't talk to me that way."

"You better believe I can. I'm doing something important. I'm cutting waste. As for you, you're nothing. You're a negative value. You putting a bullet in your head would literally make life better for me. You would bring my numbers up and let me buy a new pair of shoes or something."

"I'll tell you what lady: screw you."

"Sure, as soon as you go—"

"Ahem."

I swiveled my chair around. Judith was standing behind me, clicking her heel the way she did.

I spent twenty minutes in her office getting chewed out for unbecoming conduct. You can't scream at the prospectives. Professionalism was the fourth big word in our mission statement. I told her I was trying something new. That prospectives with low self-esteem and a passive nature might be Facilitated with aggression. It didn't save me from a write-up.

"This is a very important job we do," Judith warned. "We're on the front lines of a worldwide crisis. If we don't step up and do our darndest, it's the world on the line."

Yes, yes, we all knew the mission statement. And yet, with dozens of Facilitation companies across the country, we weren't making much of a dent, now were we? Last time I checked, Mexico was still an archipelago. Topeka was still a vagrant camp visible from space.

But I didn't say any of that. I just said okay.

The rest of my day went miserably. I wasn't allowed to be angry, and angry was all I was. I wanted to hurl my InComp through the window. I wanted to chuck it at Matt's head. I could hear him perfectly from over the wall, charming the ledge out from under some sick senior in Tacoma, snake-charming one more jumpslip through the gears of bureaucracy and into his bank account.

Meanwhile I was doing math in my head, subtracting each prospective I let get away from the number that would show up on my paycheck, adding on days I'd have to go without washing my one suit, tallying up the things I loved that I couldn't afford to eat. I could taste my future going gray and tofu-flavored.

It was enough to make a girl want to blow her brains out.

Forty-five minutes to quitting time, and my hands wouldn't move anymore. Wouldn't call up another number. The futility hit me, a thousand gallons a second, and I almost drowned right there in my chair. No matter what miracle I pulled off in the next hour, I couldn't afford TV for the span of a pay period. All I was doing here was wasting time and growing hungry.

I stood, glanced over the wall at Matt. The guy was in another world, one where the Earth was waiting on hold to get talked into a car compactor. By the sound of it, he had a grouper on the line—a big fish, I mean. I wondered distantly what this story would be when I heard it later, at the radius of the spotlight it would shine upon him. Would anyone be lucky enough to be caught in it with him? The Magic 8-Ball said unlikely. From a dozen different beaches, a dozen different Matts raised a dozen of the same martinis, as if to toast him for smuggling them away from here to some sunny, better place.

There are people in the world that are simply bigger. Not everyone meets them but we all bob on the waves they make as they swim like krakens through the world. Some rise up. Others sink.

I went to Judith's office and told her I was leaving early. She looked at me like I'd kicked her door down first, and said that this wouldn't reflect well on me at the end of the month.

And I said, yeah, well, alright. Nobody reflected well when the mirror was Matt Aguilar.

I got home that night to find the apartment quiet. I stopped in the doorway, insanely afraid that if I stepped inside, I would go through the dark like a banner and reveal all the people waiting for me on the other side. I couldn't remember when I'd last been alone in the place I lived.

Angie was visiting her parents tonight, I remembered. Reshma was pulling a double shift. I checked the time. It looked like I had an hour and twenty minutes before she got back. I had a whole hour and twenty more minutes of just me. I could do anything I wanted. Read a book. Masturbate in peace. Watch what I wanted to watch. Seventy-five percent of a movie maybe. But more than any of that, I didn't want it to end.

So instead of doing any of those things, I drew a bath. For the first time in months, I had water as hot as I liked—hot enough to tan me like a lobster. I filled it up with Reshma's bubble soap to help hide its awful color, then took a razor blade from under the sink and slid into the water.

It didn't matter that it was brown under the bubbles. I could have stayed there forever. Life was as finite as polar ice, and someone was enjoying the one I could have had. This was as good as it would ever get.

I stamped the razor blade to the slope of my breast, trying to glue it there with moisture. I pushed too hard into my meat and the edge snagged on skin. A ribbon of blood unspooled into the water and I hardly even felt it. You work in my job long enough and you become a kind of sommelier. You're trying to market a complicated thing to the sort of people who don't know champagne from sparkling water and to do that you need to be familiar as a lover with every facet of your product. I could expound to someone at length on the unique virtues of slitting one's wrists, for instance. I knew from my own PDF-saved rhetoric that by dint of endorphin euphoria, it was a flash of pain like a bad slap and then a warm, slow slide down into the softest bed you've ever had. Yeah, I could sell myself on the science of it, with focus-grouped terminology.

But I wasn't a poet.

• • •

"Sunny Futures Facilitation Services, Matthew Aguilar speaking. How may I assist you today?"

Of everyone who could have picked up.

"Hi," I said anyway. "I'm calling because I feel like I want to die."

People didn't often call into Sunny Futures for facilitation. It took a kind of strength that most didn't have. An awareness and acceptance of one's darkest desire. They'd come to their ledge alone, and only asked for a push.

We called those people gimmes.

"Hey, that's great to hear," Matt chuckled dustily. "It sounds like you're halfway there already."

I moved my phone from one hand to the other. "I guess."

"Well, tell me what the issue is. Let's see if we can't put things in perspective for you."

He sounded different. Tired, maybe. His voice was like a pressed shirt gone rank and wrinkled at the end of the day. It was a little after eight o' clock. He must have been pulling some overtime with the night crew. Classic Matt. The government wanted a so-high pile of scalps, and his blood was blue and white, as well as red. He'd go around with a machete and a sack if the law said sure.

"It's a lot of stuff," I said. "I'm not in great health. I'm an adult living with two other adults in a tiny apartment, and I hate them both. I don't have the money to eat real food."

"That sounds rough."

I frowned at that. Matt normally would have had something a little punchier to say, something so sugary-sweet that you couldn't help but slug it down until it plugged up your arteries.

"But mostly, it's this guy at work," I went on. "It's like he's so good at his job that it makes me worse. I feel like an accessory to his life."

"Yeah, I, uh, I know what that's like."

Liar, I thought. But now I could hear the loose tie hanging off his neck. The sweat dried into a film across his forehead.

The silver suit peeling off in the heat of a day left on too long. He'd be hunched over his desk with his tight work shoes off, lights all out but for the glare of his InComp.

It had been years since his legendary all-nighter. "How old are you now, anyway?"

"It's like no matter how hard I work, it's never enough. This guy, he's like a mirror. I can always see exactly how bad I am at everything. And all I want is to get away—from everyone, not just him. And just for a little while, you know? But I can't afford it. Living costs so much these days. I don't even have forty-five minutes before my roommates come home, and I don't know when I'll be alone again."

"I know what that's like," he said again.

And this time he made me believe it.

"Hey, can I ask you a question?" I asked. "If you could go anywhere in the world, where would you go?"

That seemed to catch him off-balance. "Well, uh. As it so happens, I've been saving up for a trip to Trinidad," he said. "That's actually why I've been working this late."

"Been?"

"Every night, I mean."

"Are plane tickets expensive?"

"Yeah, yeah, they are," he chuckled bitterly. "And hotel rooms. And food. And drinks. You've got to come in early and work late every day for months to make it work. Why do you ask?"

"So, is it worth it?" I asked.

A long, crackling pause. "It is," he said, as if admitting something. "It's—"

"Quiet?"

"Yeah."

"Clean?"

A silence like a nod. "The sky there is blue like you can't even imagine. The air doesn't taste like poison in your mouth. You can go out on the sand and scream yourself sick, and no one will tell you to shut up."

A low sigh. "But you can't stay there. It's pennies per second. You'll have to come back eventually."

"You've still got it better than me," I said. "I can't get away in the first place. You get to escape. At least for a few days."

"A week, usually," he said, softly.

"Mm. And then it's back to the daily grind. Back to long nights spent stacking virtual paper. Pushing people off their personal ledges. You work so you can get away, but you wouldn't need to get away if you didn't have to work. Living to escape. Isn't that messed up? That's not really living at all. Don't you wish you could just go away forever?"

"Sometimes."

"Me, too."

"I remember—" he began, haltingly, abashedly. "I remember when I was little, my parents took me to Fantasy World in Orlando. I don't know how they managed. And…it's the happiest memory I've got. I remember riding this roller coaster and feeling closer to the sun than I ever did at the top of my belt apartment. I…think I work so hard so that I can get as close to that day as I can." I hear an audible swallow on the other end. "But even I can't afford to go back there. And soon it'll be underwater anyway. Like everything else. So, I guess… I'd better let that go."

A pause swelled between us, pushing us apart and joining us together. I understood then that the words I said next would push me down one of two futures. A binary decision then. Like to push or not push. One, or zero.

But never two.

Not in this shrinking world.

"Can I ask you one more thing?"

"Yeah, sure. I'm all ears."

"Did you know there's nothing after death?" I asked. Apropos of nothing. "At least that's what the science says. Your brain goes click, turns off. You cease to exist, faster than you can see coming. But as you die you feel euphoria like you never thought possible. I think in that moment, you could be wherever you wanted most. You could be in a bubble bath that stays warm. Or on a beach that goes on forever."

The line was silent for a good while. I started thinking he'd walked away from his desk.

"Are you there?"

"Yes," he said. "I'm still here."

"Okay, good, I was going to say, I think you've sold me, Mister Aguilar. I'll go take care of myself. I hope you have a fun trip in Trinidad, and you get to go back soon."

"Thanks, Katherine. And thanks for calling."

I hung up the phone and put it down on the floor. I splashed my feet around some, but the water had gone cold as a toilet seat. I picked up the razor and asked it a question. I decided I'd do whatever it said.

This is how people get turned into paper.

When someone is found dead, an investigation is performed. If it is found to be a suicide, the government will run their social security number through our database to see if they received a call from Sunny Futures within a certain time frame. If so, the Bureau of Population Management submits an online form that we call a jumpslip, acknowledging a successful Facilitation. Once we have that, it gets deposited onto the total of whomever made the call. At the end of the month, that total is converted into a dollar amount and deposited into someone's checking account. Every month, the region manager sends a report of every Facilitation to central storage in Toronto, where in compliance with Paper Trail regulations, it is printed out and filed in the appropriate cabinet, never to be touched again. Whatever should happen to their body, I think *that* is where their soul comes to rest—pressed flat between a thousand others, awaiting an audit that will never come.

I've been at this job for five years now. The system is imperfect. Not everyone we call lives long enough to jump. Sometimes they get shot first—that's the worst. A bit of grit in the gears of bureaucracy can send jumpslips to the wrong person or spit them out into that un-place where disappeared things end up. Sometimes, for any number of reasons, you just don't get credit for your hard work. And who knows where those souls go.

• • •

Judith was the one to find Matt Aguilar the next morning. Scared her so bad she'd splashed her latte up the wall. According to her, he'd hung himself from the ceiling fan above his desk with his belt as a noose, but it looked like he'd pulled it down on top of himself and cracked his head open. "Blood going everywhere," she told the cops. "Tongue flopping out of his mouth like a grape-flavored Popsicle." He hadn't left a suicide note so much as a memo. An unsent, inter-office email left open on his InComp read, "Dear Everyone: I will be out of the office for a while. I'll bring you back some souvenirs." Nobody could mention that without a guilty chuckle. Even dead, Matt was the funniest guy anyone knew. And when, after the police had taken the body away, they checked his call log and found that the second-to-last person he'd talked to had been the governor of California, who had OD'ed on sleeping pills the night before. That part was third-hand when it got to me, but everyone agreed that, true or not, it was a good ending to a good story.

By the time I got in, the body was gone. The blood was still there though, soaked into the carpeting. Everyone had already gone back to their work, because we had a quota to meet and without Matt, it wasn't a sure thing anymore. But there was a perimeter of empty cubicles around his. Matt's death had left a crater, and nobody dared disturb that sacred aftermath.

I went to Judith's office and sat down across from her. There was a trashcan full of used tissues beside her desk. I guess tripping over a dead coworker must've hit her hard. I told her that I was sorry for the other day. I shouldn't have yelled at that guy like that. It did not reflect our company's values. I'd been under a lot of stress, but that was no excuse, and I promised I'd leave it at the door, starting now. She nodded and got back to crying.

I headed back to my desk and paused to stare at where Matt used to be. No one was telling Matt-stories today. Wouldn't be for a long time. The quiet around his desk pulled like a vacuum. Some people are just bigger. They leave big holes when they're gone.

I thought of glaciers melting. Waters rising. Dry land crumbling into the sea. Men and women forever climbing higher, jockeying for grip. Clawing. Biting. Hurling one another into the waves. Fighting for space to exist while it still existed.

This void begged to be filled.

Without another thought, I grabbed my things and moved them over one space. A girl heading to the water cooler gave me a venomous look. I ignored her and got to changing Matt's desktop background. I felt better about the future than I had for a long time. It was a new day, and my numbers had been set back to zero, but I'd only just clocked in, and I was already up by one.

Binge

By R. L. Meza

First published in Issue 012 (November–December 2022)

"I'm not doing this anymore." Molly knots her trembling fingers in the hair-sprayed nest of curls piled atop her head. "I can't. I won't."

As if she has a choice. As if any of us—Beth and Dane and Little Carl and me—are here because we want to be.

The intro music starts to play, and we're yanked to our feet like marionettes on over-tight strings, moving herky-jerky to the tune of Cheap Trick's "I Want You to Want Me."

Molly's first on set. She teeters through the living room on shiny high heels and plops down on the couch, framing her face with her hands. She puffs up the loose curls on her forehead with an exaggerated sigh. She tilts her head left, then right. Molly's makeup is a mess—mascara running in a black, desperate flood, lipstick smeared like a crushed strawberry—but at least the long skirt hides the marks from the last time she cracked. If Molly can't keep it together, they're going to run out of camera-friendly places to fix her.

The telephone rings, and Molly sits up like she's been jabbed with a cattle prod. She reaches across the couch, then freezes. Molly's real name slides through the air from stage left and lurches to a stop, bubble letters bouncing.

Catherine Dillard.

The name slips off-screen. Molly keeps leaning. The fishhooks punched through the corners of her mouth tug her lips back into an eager smile, but—*oops!*—the handset is plucked away before Molly can reach it. Molly's face falls. Beth presses the phone to her ear, blonde ponytail swinging. She twists the cord around her finger. Her eyes roll playfully up toward the ceiling.

Lila Andrews.

A knock at the front door. Beth prances past the couch. She's trying to signal Molly with her glassy blue eyes—*get it together! smile!!*—but then a cable jerks, and the ring looped through Beth's chin whips her head around.

The front door opens. Molly springs to her feet, hopeful. But it's just Dane, stepping in to wrap his arms around Beth, to dip her back for a kiss. He flashes a roguish smile at the camera through chapped, bleeding lips.

Arnold Hayes.

Dane's eyes are ringed with dark circles, like he hasn't slept in days. Weeks? It's easy to lose track of time here. He spins Beth in a circle, the pair of them like mechanical dancers anchored to a ticking clock. Molly sinks, dejected, back into the couch.

Molly's losing it. Her chest is hitching. She's pouring tears and snot, murmuring please through clenched teeth. And she's not the only one.

Little Carl is crying like a boy with both arms broken. I let my focus drift, unwilling to dwell on just how close to the mark that description hits—Carl's little arms, bending in places that no person, no *human* being would ever find amusing. Little Carl's sobbing along in perfect rhythm to the chorus. He's beside me one second, gone the next. He rushes through the living room, multi-jointed arms flailing in his wake, as the cables launch him toward Molly.

Only, Molly's arms aren't ready to catch him like they're supposed to be.

She's torn them free.

Muscle and tendons dangle from Molly's arms in ribbons, glistening. Her eyes are impossibly round, the lids nonexistent, lashes twitching like spiders' legs. She's gazing into the harsh glare of the stage lights like a deer facing oncoming traffic. Little Carl continues on his cable-drawn arc through the air, regardless. He strikes Molly in the side, then smacks into the coffee table.

Freeze.

Bubble letters.

Wally Leeds.

I step up to the front door as the doorbell rings. Molly needs to come and open it now, so the man of her dreams can lift her up into his arms—my arms. My name slides into view, but the door remains closed.

Sid Fields.

I'm watching it all through the set window: Molly ripping her calves loose from the cables. Now brandishing a high heel in each hand, she storms the camera. She hurls the heels at the studio audience, shrieking—raw and ragged—like the caged animal she is.

Or was.

Molly's done playing her role. The cables bump me into the front door, reeling me through so I can bear witness. But Molly doesn't get dragged away for discipline, like last time and the time before. This is Molly's third fuck-up, and this one's royal.

Molly doesn't explode, she just…vanishes into a red, wet mist. She coats my face and neck, the white shirt I'm wearing. My forearms are dripping with the woman I'm supposed to be holding.

The laughter from the audience isn't canned. They're eating this up.

Someone's going off-script. It's the low, pitiful sound of a buried soul moaning through six feet of grave dirt, the cry of a child trapped at the bottom of a very deep well. Beth's lips are white and flat as ironed sheets, pulled back against her teeth. Dane's beside her on the couch, with Little Carl propped up on his knee. They're silent. Smiling.

It must be me.

And—yes—I can feel the scream burning up my throat. Even with the smile plastered on my blood-streaked face, my teeth biting down on the edges of my tongue, the sound keeps leaking through. The cables drag me to the couch for the final scene.

Sans Molly.

We're on the couch, arms linked over shoulders despite the Molly-sized gap, heads tipped together: a makeshift family.

Sitcom lettering hovers between us and the audience, spelling out the show's title. The start of the first season.

The audience settles in. They lean their recliners back and dig their many-fingered hands into crinkling bags of snacks. They'll sit—binge-watching—for hours, sometimes days.

Weeks on end.

The song fades out.

The show begins.

Season One

We lose Beth midway through Episode Three.

It's not her fault, really. If anyone's to blame, it's the new Molly. The new Molly is a perfect replica of the old one. From her lustrous auburn hair and green eyes, down to the delicate feet stapled into high-heeled shoes, everything about her is identical.

Except for her name, of course.

See, Beth and the old Molly—Catherine Dillard—came from the same vat, the closest thing to real sisters that the things upstairs could manage with their test tubes, the genetic tampering and behavioral conditioning, and all the rest that goes into manufacturing an authentic experience for the audience.

But the show wears us down.

It's kind of the point.

We bend under the strain, buckle. Break. And like any well-oiled machine, the broken parts must be replaced.

We do have ratings to maintain.

Beth can't stop laughing though. It's the kitchen scene that's doing her in, the part where Molly—the new one—is all dolled up for her first date with yours truly. Except Molly's distracted by Little Carl doodling on the wall with his crayons. She forgets to put the lid of the blender on.

The sight of all that red smoothie splatter sends Beth right over the edge. Beth is laughing, and it's this awful, strangled gasping sound, all exhale without an ounce of humor. She's scrabbling at her chest, the corset knitted to her ribs with steel wire, the cables cinching it ever tighter until her breath is little more than a wheeze.

Poor, sweet Beth. She just wants out.

But this is only her second infraction, so Beth gets plugged with a tranquilizer. They tow her off-set for recalibration while we finish the episode with a stand-in. The stand-in is a stuffed green dummy with Beth's blonde hair and narrow waist. They'll insert a digital image over the top for the viewers at home, but—like us—the live audience is stuck trying to pretend this faceless doll is a real person.

Can I tell you a secret? I prefer the dummy. Beth's getting a much-needed rest, and I don't have to stare into the vacant blue tunnels she's been sporting in place of her eyes since the old Molly…left. I present a bouquet of silk flowers to the dummy posing as Molly's younger sister while Dane feigns jealousy, and then I pull the bouquet back from the dummy's outstretched hands, delivering the flowers to Molly instead. The dummy wilts, and everybody laughs.

Little Carl is shaking.

It's time for the banister scene. Little Carl wants to keep his smoothie-splattered mother from leaving with me, so he has the bright idea—watch his eyes go wide, his mouth go round as he holds up a finger—to get himself stuck, good and tight. The audience members who've seen the show lean forward, wringing their hands. Toothy grins ripple the faces of the newcomers. They have no clue what's coming, but there must be a reason the die-hard fans keep re-watching. The first-timers can sense their anticipation.

I switch my brain off. It's a nifty trick I picked up from the third—*fourth?*—Dane. I don't feel my strong hands close around Little Carl's skull, don't see the others grasping his chubby arms and legs. I am not here when we all heave as one to tear Little Carl apart.

Molly puts her fists on her hips like, *Aw, shucks. Now what?*

It's a valid question.

Beth is usually the one who puts Little Carl back together, but now Carl's got the dummy to look forward to. The dummy's paddle hands and cable-guided limbs make a mess of the reassembly. Without Beth's nimble fingers to help, the episode is six hours longer than it should be. By the time the lights go down, half the audience is slumped in their recliners, bored or snoring.

There will be no meal tonight.

Beth returns in the early hours of morning to rub cream on Little Carl's seams. With his head cradled against her breast, he whimpers and squirms and dreams his restless dreams.

Little Carl is the only original.

He's lived and relived the show more times than he can count. I can't help but wonder why no one's ever put him out of his misery. Being the second longest-lived member of the show, perhaps that responsibility falls to me.

But like the old Molly, I can't.

I won't.

Dane stole his life back last night.

No sharp objects allowed in the dorms, so the smart son-of-a-vat used his teeth.

Three hours until the show starts up again. Three more hours spent listening to "I Want You to Want Me," playing on a constant loop through the speakers mounted in the corners of the blank, windowless room we all share, angled down at our sparse bunks. Cranked to full volume. Long-timers like Little Carl and I learned how to lip-read early on, once we realized the theme song was getting louder to drown our voices out.

It's supposed to keep us in character. Or maybe it's meant to enhance our appreciation of the show, since the only time the song stops playing is when we're acting out an episode. But it never really stops, not for Little Carl and not for me. I catch my lips moving, forming the words without my consent as the lyrics cycle through my head like a hamster on a wheel, running itself to death.

This. Fucking. Song.

Good for Dane.

Season Two

The new Dane is my old one, and I can't.

I can't.

Episode One, and I'm fumbling for my lines. My third infraction is marching closer with every second I spend staring at him, slack-jawed. Dane—*my Dane*—is mouthing what I need to say, but all I can think about is touching him. What I need is to wrap my arms around his waist and pull him in, feel the rasp of his stubble against my mouth, my chin. I need to know that he's real, though a sad, sick part of me is praying that he's not. Because if this is my Dane, he's been uprooted from the home we built together, years ago, when we were fresh from the vat and foolish enough to believe we could keep something of our own. Before I learned that even emotions like love can be stolen, molded. Hooks stuck through and rigged to cables.

Paraded.

Do they know, the things upstairs? They must.

This is the most-watched episode of the first two seasons. The audience is salivating.

I'm the unsuspecting fool who bursts into Molly's bedroom to find Beth and Dane entwined on the bed. But there's nothing erotic about the way Beth's raking her nails across Dane's chiseled face, carving bloody furrows into his cheeks. Sure, she's pumping her hips, but that's the cables trying to buck him off as the hydraulic joints in Dane's hands squeeze her windpipe down to a whistling straw. Thanks to the implanted rod, Dane is harder than I've ever seen him. Beth is urging him on with her eyes, begging Dane to finish it already.

And here I stand, holding everything up, still groping for my stupid, forgotten one-liner—something-something...Ah!

It rolls off my tongue, and the scene carries on. There's a flicker of pride in Dane's eyes—I've pulled through for him, for *us*—and then he lowers his mouth to Beth's bare stomach, exposing sharp, sharp teeth. Their filed points close with a loud, ripe crunch.

Oil pools around Beth's ruined midsection. Dane's chin is slick with it, blood and oil leaking down his naked chest. A hand on my shoulder makes me jump. But it's just Molly, pushing to get past. She plants her fists on her hips again. Dane shrugs comically. He offers Molly a black-streaked grin.

Behind me, the laughter is roaring.

I reach for Dane, but the cables are sweeping me off-stage to make room for the credits, a scrolling list of glyphs not meant for human tongues.

There will be plenty of time for us to catch up, later.

All the time in the world, if we can last that long.

They took Little Carl.

I can't get any details from Beth. She's catatonic, will probably be replaced as well.

Theories circulate around our diminished circle. Like maybe the meat Beth has been shaving off of Little Carl's heels every night for the last few months wasn't enough to hide the growth spurt as he inched toward puberty. Molly insists it was the re-watchers who must have noticed. She thinks it was the subtle change in Little Carl's voice that gave him away.

Dane says he saw them come for Little Carl, that the boy didn't put up a fight at all. According to Dane, they carried him out in a limp bundle. Didn't we notice the kid never touched his food? Didn't we see him rocking in the corner for hours at a time, forgoing sleep as he mouthed the words to the theme song?

No—of course not. None of us eat. We don't sleep.

Dane doesn't know there will be a new Little Carl by morning.

I take Dane's hands in mine and touch my lips to the tears on his cheeks, erasing them one by one. He tastes of salt and sweat and something not quite human.

I shrink away from him.

Season Three

There's something off about the new Little Carl.

Beth won't go near him. She's convinced he's the same one, cut down to size, but when she talks about him—a reedy whisper hissed through tight lips, eyes darting to the corner where he's been standing and swaying and staring at the wall since they brought him through the vault door, yesterday—Little Carl is no longer a *he*, but an *it*. Beth clenches her fists and rocks, rocks, rocks to the rhythm of the song forced through the speakers. She mutters about the faded map of scars twisting through Carl's flesh like bumpy, pitted country roads. And she cries. We all do. Since the start of Season Three, they've been pumping tear gas through the vents at intervals. As if, even after everything they've done to our minds and bodies, we're still incapable of crying on command.

They're not wrong.

With my knees tucked to my chest, I duck into the alcove behind my thighs to spit on my thumb, then streak the saliva beneath eyes rubbed raw. Am I doing this for the benefit of the others, to convince them I'm still capable of feeling? I don't know. It doesn't matter, really. One more week until the series finale.

After, we'll do it all again—start to finish. Or, some of us will.

Dane's jittery. He's pacing the walls of our room and clawing at his chest with one hand. Ten steps and he's below the speaker in the corner. Another ten, and he's at the vault door. I don't have the heart to stop him. If I reach for him as he stalks past me a third, fourth, fifth time, I'll have to touch him. I'll have to hold him, and I can't stand the feel of his skin. All that remains of the man I once loved is guttering in the haunted recesses of Dane's eyes, threatening to go out. Still…there is *something* left worth reaching for.

There has to be.

I link my fingers through his, ignoring the artificial whisper of his flesh against mine, and try to slow his progress. He shakes me off. He's mumbling under his breath. At first, I think it's just the lyrics sinking in, taking over Dane's tongue and mind to keep him fixed in his role. The lip-reading is no help at all, but trying to guess what he's repeating helps to pass the time. It could be one word or two. It looks like…

You.

An hour before they come for us, Dane stops short in the corner opposite Little Carl and shouts it out. Not *you* after all.

TOO SOON.

And the explosives inside him detonate.

I stare at the scorch marks beside the vault door, ears ringing from the blast. A gift from the insurgency? Dane must have joined them in my absence. Him keeping this a secret hurts more than the sight of his tattered flesh. I crawl to his side, moaning in agony as I comb my fingers through the explosive beads, clustered like metallic roe in his open chest cavity. Less than a third of them are blackened, smoking. Faulty wiring. It's a miracle the others weren't triggered by the explosion, or we'd all be dead.

We should be so lucky.

The tiny green lights are blinking, active.

Dane spasms. He's still breathing when they rip him from my arms.

Molly says he was meant to take out the front row of VIPs during the series finale. She delivers this information in a hot rush, not realizing that "I Want You to Want Me" is no longer blasting through the speakers now dangling from their cords, broken and dusted with plaster. Her confession splits the silence like an axe, and now they're back for Molly, taking her away.

All is quiet, for just a moment longer.

And then Little Carl's lips curl back from the speaker embedded in his mouth.

The song resumes.

The show must go on.

Finale

Whatever's happening on the outside is affecting the production centers.

The things upstairs have made it very clear that there will be no more replacements. Not by telling us—they'd never deliberately reveal weakness—but a cursory glance at the cobbled-together amalgamation of the cast, the machinery glinting and whirring between the gaps in our re-worked flesh, is enough to suggest that the names on the credits will remain the same until the series draws to a close.

Or until the revolution shaking the ground above us plays out.

The stage lights are blinding.

The intro song begins. I'm really listening this time through. I'm hanging on every word, knowing as I do that I'll never have to hear these lyrics again.

The VIPs lean forward in their seats, greedy eyes reaching.

They want me.

The cables pull us onto the set—patchwork people, barely human.

They need me.

There's a quiet beeping coming from inside me: a parting gift from Dane. The beeping speeds up as the theme song reaches the chorus.

I can only hope I swallowed enough to make a difference.

One way or the other, this is the end.

Please.

I'm begging.

All the Sludge You Want to Drink

By Mary G. Thompson

First published in Issue 007 (January–February 2022)

I leave the break room with my mug in hand, filled to the brim with sludge. Like everything else around here, it's brown. It tastes exactly like you'd expect something people call sludge to taste: bitter, sour, acidic. The texture is granular. It's like drinking cement mixed with dirt mixed with the bodies of slugs. A little bit runs over the edge of my mug, and I lick it off. I savor the flavor on my tongue.

When you're hungry, any flavor is good. One lick, and I want more. I want to rush back to the break room, slurp what's left from my mug, and refill it. But my break is over. I'm almost late. If I get back late, they'll punish everyone. They'll turn the spigot off for hours.

I speed walk through the narrow hallway, barely wide enough for my shoulders. The walls, floor, and ceiling are as brown as the sludge. The lighting is low, but I'm used to it. Just like I'm used to the recycled air. At least it's better than the air outside, which isn't breathable. If our Friends hadn't built the enclaves, their terraforming would have killed us. It's better to live in here than die out there. How many times has my dad said that to me? Now I hear it in my own voice.

I get back to my desk just as my computer starts beeping, the light on top flashing red.

"I know, I know," I say under my breath, pressing the button.

Three coworkers glare at me over their cubicle dividers. I mouth, *sorry*. Hopefully those few seconds didn't attract any attention. I look around the room, but the only one of them I see is Nice Guy. That's what I call him anyway. Who knows what his real name is? Some combination of clicking and hissing that I can't understand. Nice Guy's about my height, five foot ten, with a black exoskeleton and seven legs. The seventh, uneven leg, is shorter and protrudes from the neck. He's wearing a large breathing mask over his face, so all I can see is one of his seven eyes.

He winks at me.

I raise a hand in thanks and sit down at my computer. I take a long sip of sludge.

My dad's description of chicken eggs pops into my head: They had a part that was white and a part that was yellow. You could boil them or scramble them or fry them. You could eat them in a sandwich, which was a food with several ingredients. A food you chewed.

Beep. A notification on my terminal. I need to get to work now, or even Nice Guy will come after me. I have to process these tokens and assign rations for this week's delivery in enclave San Francisco. Fourteen thousand souls are packed into a quarter of a mile square, and all of them have to prove they've performed sixty hours of work for each ration credit. So if you're, say, a parent with one kid, you and/or your kid have to work 120 hours for enough sludge rations for two people. They do the work, it's certified by a Friend, and then I assign the corresponding tokens and order the ration delivery. It's more efficient to centralize it all here than to handle the processing at each location.

Human number 54-3659 is certified for 83 hours of labor by a Friend in Sector 87. I've worked here for six years now, so I'm pretty good at matching the numbers to people. 54-3659 is Melissa Vorhes. She has two children, and the father, Gerold Vorhes, died last year of a respiratory disease, most likely caused by his own work in Sector 87. Those space suits they give them aren't perfect. Some of the damn atmosphere always gets in. Per regulation, Melissa is entitled to 1.38 credits.

I take another sip of sludge. It slides down my throat. Dad told us that in the beginning, people used to throw it up. Some people could stomach it but refused to drink. They died.

There's one flaw in the Friends' credit system. It would be nearly impossible for me to alter the certification for anyone who's working, like Melissa. But I can create *brand new* certifications for children who are too young to work, who therefore don't have *any* work certified for the week. Melissa's youngest, James Vorhes, age two, is a perfect candidate.

I pull up the record for number 55-2013. I've already created several weeks of work certifications for him. For some reason, Melissa's older son, Harold, age ten, hasn't been able to work for those weeks. I'm not going to add certifications for him, because I don't want to create an anomalous pattern. They weren't getting a full three-person ration before, but they were surviving. A few weeks ago, it was time for me to step in. Previously, I've given James thirty hours for half a credit. That's a little bit less than what Harold was working, but it's also less likely to draw attention. But this week, Melissa has dropped a few hours. I put in 34.5 hours for James. Nothing too exact. Nothing too high.

Now Melissa will get her 1.38 credits plus .58 credits for James. It's not really enough, but it will have to be.

I double check my work, save the record for 55-2013, make sure the records of the family are appropriately linked, and click *send.*

Next up is 52-0063. Kyle Franklin is a single twenty-seven-year-old man. He's certified for 53 hours. Everything looks good with him. I verify his .88 credits and click send.

Next is 54-9681, Bea. I guess she doesn't have a last name because that's the only name in the system. She's sixteen. For some reason, she's only certified for 23 hours, which is .38 credits. But there's nothing I can do about that because I can't alter a work record that's already certified. I wish she had a baby, or an older parent or grandparent, someone without a recent work record. But I have to move on.

Once I get started working, time goes by in a flash. Record after record. Retrieve, verify, falsify, send. Retrieve, verify, send. Retrieve, verify...*ding, ding, ding.* The bell that signals the end of the workday. I blink and sit back from my screen. Everyone who needs delivery tomorrow is done.

I sip my sludge. It makes no difference that it's been sitting for hours. Its taste and texture is the same. The hollowness in my belly is the same, too. It's not emptiness exactly, but un-fullness. It hovers at the edges of your stomach, always present. No amount of sludge is ever enough. But I take another sip. I savor the thickness on my tongue. I would never dream of throwing it up.

I want more.

I stand up and stretch, pick up my mug. "Goodnight," I say to those who are still left and picking up their things.

I get a few murmured good-nights back. We're all tired, stretching, ready to go home as we file into the break room. We take final gulps from our mugs and put them in the washer. Many of us lick the insides of our mugs to get every last drop. At first, I was ashamed to be seen doing it, but I got over it. Waste is stupidity. We make our way to the exit in a tired line. I make sure I'm at the end.

Nice Guy stands at the break room door, watching to make sure we don't take any sludge out. As they march by him, my co-workers hold up their hands. All of them are thin, but none of them are starving. Not really, not like Melissa and her kids. Not like Bea. We're hungry and we always will be, but there are different kinds of hunger. Ours is in the belly; theirs is in the bones. Ours nudges; theirs gnaws.

I remember what that gnawing was like. I grew up here in enclave Washington, D.C. Dad worked outside the barrier in one of those space suits, perfecting their terraforming inch by inch. He earned enough for all three of us until his injury. Then my brother Franco earned for the three of us. Then I started working, and it became easier with two. But ninety hours a week of manual labor takes its toll. Dad encouraged me to keep studying, to learn the Friends' system, to make myself useful. The fifth time I applied, they finally hired me. Franco died outside, but Dad's still around. I get a dependent benefit of one sludge ration. The Friends are good to those of us who work here, who do what we can to live in the system. Who never get caught.

"How's it going?" I say to Nice Guy. This is why I stayed at the end, so we could chat without holding anyone up. It's a good idea to be friendly. You never know when you could get something. Sludge to take home, a better job, information.

"The day is a day," he says through his translator. The voice comes out sounding robotic, but I appreciate the effort. This one's all right. I've managed to get him talking a little. Turns out he has seven children, all living on different terraformed planets. I get the impression that Earth is a shit gig and they're all looking to move up and out. There are some planets where the natives have all died, and those are plumb. There's no risk of exposure to airborne contaminants in jobs like those.

"Yeah, that's about right," I say. "You want to get a drink?" All we've got to drink is water, but they still pour it out at bars. No bartenders, just customers sitting around mimicking what they've seen in old videos. Clinking glasses, knocking back.

"No drink, but we may walk." Nice Guy waves me in the direction of the door. I exit the building and wait for him to lock up. This involves him waving four or five of his arms around. A lot of their technology is biological or bio-mechanical or something. Every time I watch him do it, I try to pick up on something useful, but it's all a mystery. The sludge is in there, and we're out here, and we have no way of getting in.

Part of me wants to run back toward the door. If I could have one more cup, maybe the hunger would finally cease. Our spigot is unlimited, but our breaks aren't. Maybe if I could just have a little more. If I could bring some extra home to Dad. But I do nothing. I say nothing.

The street is narrow. The enclave is small; everyone walks everywhere. There are only a few feet between the buildings. A clear dome covers us, and it's dark outside now, so we can see stars. Beautiful, far away stars. Somewhere up there is the Friends' home planet, and many more planets like Earth. We're part of a stellar community of dying people, none of whom can reach each other.

I wonder what their sludge tastes like. I wonder if it would fill me.

Nice Guy and I walk side by side.

"You heard from the kids lately?" I ask.

"Number four has achieved primary status," Nice Guy says. "Thus, she becomes entitled to settlement accommodations."

"Wow, that's great. No wearing a mask, right?"

"Correct." Nice Guy taps his mask with the leg sprouting from his chest. "It chafes."

"You ever gonna visit her?"

"Upon forty additional years of labor, I will be granted travel."

"Oh. Well, that doesn't seem too long." For them. I gather they live about five hundred years.

"It will pass."

I try to think of something else to say.

"How is your father?" he asks.

"Oh, pretty good. He's out of bed again."

"May he remain well." Nice Guy winks at me, turns a corner, and disappears. Presumably he'll exit the enclave and breathe fresh terraformed air. Possibly he'll apply lotion to the place on his face where the mask chafes. I wonder what he looks like without it. Some of them have bulbous growths on their faces. People speculate that there's something wrong with our planet, that it can't be fully terraformed, that we can fight back using our own biology. But I believe that's wishful thinking. We don't have any way to fight, so we have to do our best to live.

I enter my building, start walking up the four narrow flights of stairs. I round the landing on the second floor to find my neighbor, Theresa, just closing her door. When she sees me, she opens the door again.

"Collaborator." She spits at me. The brownish sludge-tinged saliva lands on my shoe.

"Elizabeth is a smart girl," I say, seeing the ten-year-old peering out from behind her mother. I address her directly. "If you study, you could have a job like mine. You could have all the sludge you want to drink."

Her face is dirty. There's an impression in her thin jacket where the edge of the spacesuit helmet must hit her shoulders when she's outside. All the equipment is too heavy for kids like her. She probably has bruising all over her body.

"You won't have to work so hard, and you might be able to do some good. I get a ration for my dad."

"Stop giving her ideas." Theresa slams the door in my face. I hear coughing. She's in the early stages of lung disease from inhaling terraformed air. Her daughter will be better off without her. People who tell their kids not to take administration jobs are just killing them faster. As if there's heroism in having a worse job. As if they aren't collaborating as much as I am just by working for their sludge. But they don't see it that way. They think they're slaves and I'm free.

I open my door. "Dad?"

He's sitting up in bed. We have one small bedroom, so his bed is out here in the living area. The arrangement gives us some illusion of privacy. It's a bigger place than we had before I got my job, back when there were three of us. But it seems small to me now. My expectations have grown in multiple ways. I drink probably four or five rations of sludge every day now. And I would never go back to wearing that spacesuit. Not for the respect of all the Theresas in all the enclaves.

"Some bad news came over the radio," he says. "It's about time for the replay." He leans over to turn the radio on. The illegal radio, which would get me fired and us thrown out of this apartment. It's Dad's one irrational thing. All these years of teaching me to survive and he has this time bomb in our living room.

"I thought you agreed to get rid of that."

"Just listen, son."

First, there's static. Then for a minute, dead air. Then the broadcast begins.

"Good evening, folks. This is Vern, quote unquote, your anonymous human for the night. Let's get some news. From enclave Johannesburg, we have reports of an outbreak of HIV-8. Until the outbreak is burned out, do not allow them to move you to enclave Johannesburg. We understand that our Friends are aware of the lethality and are purposefully transferring problem humans. Repeat, do not allow yourself to be moved to enclave Johannesburg.

"From enclave Paris, reports of expansion of the enclave. It looks like they're building it up. As to why, we're not sure. There have been rumors they want to relocate people from enclave São Paulo, but those are unconfirmed. More on that when we know more.

"From enclave Houston, a worker was arrested this morning for falsifying transfer documents. They discovered that this human had been marking humans approved for transfer who were not approved. This resulted in at least twenty people escaping enclave Dublin before its destruction. Please remember the name Rhoda Otello. She saved these lives at the cost of her own. They executed her at 16:30 this afternoon.

"Thanks to people like Rhoda Otello, we humans are fighting back. All over the world, people just like her are doing what they can, little by little, to save our lives. The more people survive, the longer we last, the closer we come to regaining our freedom. We know it's hard. We know at times it seems impossible, but Rhoda was able to save lives. You, too, can save lives. Wherever you are, however you can, continue to fight. Freedom! Humanity! Native Earth!"

The broadcast ends.

I turn away from Dad. Just for something to do, I get some water from the sink. I drink.

"This is serious," he says. "You have to stop what you're doing."

"Dad, I'm not stopping."

"I know you remember," he says. And yes, I do. They had a public execution once, here in enclave Washington, D.C. A human was caught trying to sabotage the ventilation system in one of the Friends' buildings. They cut him into pieces and ate him. It was like a ritual consumption, and then they barfed him up afterwards. All of us were rounded up and had to watch. Then they put us on half rations for a week. It would be impossible not to remember.

"There are people who need me," I say. "People who will starve if I don't keep doing what I'm doing."

"What about me?" he snaps. "I'll starve if they eat you." I know he doesn't care about himself, though. Everything he's taught me is so I can survive.

"We'll both starve if you don't get rid of that radio." I take a long drink of water. What I really want is more sludge. Dad's ration cup is sitting next to the sink. There's a tiny bit of sludge stuck to the top of it. I pick up the ration cup and lick it off. There's a window above the sink that looks out on the window of another apartment. But our curtains are closed and so are theirs. They've probably got their illegal radios, too. They're all hoping that whoever is doing the broadcasting has some plan, that someone's going to rescue us, that we're all going to rise up and fight back. And then what? We can't even breathe the air.

"If it will get you to stop altering records, I'll get rid of it," he says.

I turn back to him. "Really?"

His eyes are hard. He presses his fingers to the radio's case as if he's about to open it, as if he's about to break our only connection to the human race.

"Don't." I try to hold my water steady, but I fail. It sloshes all around the cup. "What good are they doing, though? They talk about hope. Give a little news. I'm getting people food. A baby named James Vorhes will have a chance of surviving because of me. Maybe *he* can find a solution. Maybe he can save the world." I don't believe that for a second. And I don't want to get eaten and then barfed up. But I don't know what else to do. Getting a little more sludge for James is literally all I can think of. It's all I have.

Dad stares at the radio. He begins to cry.

I sit next to him. "Did you get up and walk today?"

He nods, wiping his eyes. "A few times around the room."

"Good. Very good. Want to try again?" I hold out my arm and help him out of bed. He squints in pain and leans forward. Slowly, he takes one step and then another. Carefully, we make it around the room.

"Did I ever tell you about ice cream?" Dad asks.

"Only about a million times."

"Strawberries?"

"Red and sweet," I say. "Little seeds in them." I can't even imagine what that would taste like. I can't even imagine chewing food. Would it hurt? After a lifetime of liquid diet, could I even digest something solid? I'd probably just barf those strawberries up.

"Eggs," he says.

"A food with two colors," we say together. I get Dad back onto the bed.

"I can't give up the radio," he says.

"I know. I can't give up trying to help." What I really can't give up, I know, and he knows, and Theresa knows, is the extra sludge. If they offered me twice as much sludge to stop helping, I'd do it. But I don't have to make that choice, because they'll never offer it to me. My choice is between doing my job and going back out in a spacesuit, risking an injury like my dad's, or dying like my brother.

In the morning, I walk the short distance to the office. Like everyone else, I stop first at the break room, where I get a fresh cup and fill it with sludge. I drink as much as I can right there and fill it up again. As much as one whole ration, first thing. I sit down at my desk. Today I'm working on enclave Dakota. Seven thousand people live there. If I work hard, I should be able to add maybe forty unauthorized rations.

Melissa and her kids are going to die anyway. All of these people are going to die, and almost as quickly as if I did nothing. My dad, with his one ration, is going to die before he turns sixty. But if I'm lucky, I might live. I might last an extra year, an extra decade.

Nice Guy walks in front of my desk. Several of his legs stick out from his body and wave like antennas as he walks. "Good day," he says.

"Good morning!" I wave at him.

He keeps walking.

I take a long drink of sludge.

This Choir of Ghosts

By Monte Lin

First published in Issue 009 (May–June 2022)

Subject-412 wakes in absolute darkness. Their drug-induced sleep leaves them groggy on the cold, stone floor, unable to shiver. Moments or perhaps hours pass, as their thoughts and memories sift and settle back into place. Lights. The operating table. The head surgeon's worried brow. The realization hits Subject-412 in the chest: they are the Experiment now.

The Experiment never deviates. After the surgery, the test subject is placed into the Cube and sealed within. The subject receives nothing other than the key, a metal card two inches wide, three inches long, and barely a millimeter thick, randomly encrypted to open the door to the Cube. Once encoded into the key, all other records of the code are wiped. Sometimes the subject enters the Cube in their surgical gown. Oftentimes they don't receive the dignity; the surgeons claim they can't afford more gowns.

The Cube has enough air for a few days, but no food or water, so the subject must utilize their new implants to bend the fabric of space-time, reach through the basalt rock, and place the key onto the door to open it. There is no way to open the door otherwise. The surgeons on the other side require a week to decrypt the key, if they even have the desire to do so.

Families receive compensation for handing a subject over to the Complex, enough food and medicine for a year, multiple years if they ration. Desperately needed compensation in a world blasted white, the air dead and choking in ambient heat. The surgeons claim this is the best solution for humanity. They call subjects saviors to make everyone feel better about their sacrifice. "Once you can bend space-time," they say, before throwing them into the Cube, "you can save us by carrying us from this dying world."

Subject-412, encased in darkness, cries for what seems like hours. The cold basalt echoes back. They creep along the edges of the Cube, discovering the corners and edges. The surgeons believe the artificiality of the environment should force the subjects to focus. Nothing else exists in this tomb, nothing else except Subject-412 and the key and some scratches on one of the walls. Self-preservation, the surgeons believe, should trigger the implants. They have been wrong four hundred eleven times.

Those who ask why they must do this Experiment this way find themselves outside, their lungs seared by heat and silica. They pound on the steel door of the Complex with the other desperate souls, begging for food, water, and shelter. A couple even try to volunteer for the Experiment but are met with stony refusal: "Your knowledge of the Experiment biases the Experiment." This isn't true, but the message is clear. The surgeons are rational, the Experiment is rational, and rationality cannot be questioned.

With nothing to touch except basalt, nothing to hear except their own breathing, nothing to see except darkness, Subject-412 curls up into a ball and retreats into themselves. They fall into a fitful sleep, half dreaming, half awake. Their implants warm and they feel a new, artificial sixth sense. To Subject-412, it feels like a voice in their head, a whisper.

"WhereamIwhereamIwhereamIwhereamI…"

"Hello," Subject-412 says aloud, "who's there?"

"Lemmeoutlemmeoutlemmeoutlemmeout…"

"I'm stuck in here, too. What is your name?"

"Subject-411subject-411subject-411…"

"I'm Subject-412."

The voice pauses, no longer strung together in panicked heartbeats. "This means it works! If you are in my future, it means it works!"

"But…the previous subjects didn't…" They have no desire to finish that sentence, and the voice in their head quiets. "I'm sorry."

"Then…I'm in your past." A pause, the acceptance of the damned. "It is too late for me. I'm merely a ghost to you…And only you…yours is the only voice I can hear."

Subject-412 dreams deeper, and more voices join in a choir, subject numbers decreasing like a countdown, stepping backward through time. Each voice cries. Each begs for help.

"The surgeons say no one has exited the Cube…" Subject-412 says.

The choir erupts into a cacophony, and Subject-412 realizes in talking to these voices, they have confirmed their end. They are witnessing all of their last days. One subject takes their key and scratches at the basalt, another does the same, and another. Subject-412 stumbles around, feeling the wall, and finds the vertical scratches again, lines upon lines, the last screams of the dead.

"What can I do?" Subject-412 says.

"I am already dead," most say, resigned to their fate the moment their families sold them. Some insist Subject-412 is lying, is a hallucination, is a trick. Others beg to change Subject-412's past, their future, to reach out into time and unlock the door.

Subject-412 tries, they attempt to touch the others' keys, to touch the door, but they can't change the past, only witness it. They helplessly hear their voices and empathize with their fear and pain, this choir of ghosts.

"Are you the only one who can hear us, 412?" Subject-52 asks.

Subject-412 repeats the question throughout the choir. "Everyone only hears a singular voice, mine. But I hear you all."

"If I'm in your past," Subject-52 says, "then I'm bounded in time, like a book. I have a beginning and an end. I am mere scratchings on the rock. I can't be changed."

Subject-412 relays this to the rest, word for word, an echo of an echo, and it quiets most. A few continue to weep and to rage.

"But you are not bounded, 412, you are like a conversation. You have the potential to be free, to change. Go and escape." Subject-52 laughs. "Unless you are someone else's past."

Subject-412 places a hand on the door and reaches out in the other direction, pulling toward the future, grabbing at the strands of space-time. If time can be traversed, if space can be crossed, and if they truly have this ability, then they can simply open the door to the Cube. Then Subject-412 opens their eyes, unable to see in the complete darkness, unable to see the future. "I can't. I'm not strong enough."

"But do you hear another voice, from 413, perhaps?"

"No, nothing."

"Then there is still hope for you." When Subject-412 relays this to the choir, they quiet. Hope for another is still hope.

"What if we push?" Subject-335 says. "What if like the bird's beak on the diamond mountain, we all push?"

Subject-412 reaches back to all of the previous subjects, to every point of each of their timelines up until they die. Subject-412 can feel this bounded infinity within bounds, four hundred and twelve hands on the same spot on the door. They can feel on the basalt the body heat of all the previous subjects.

Subject-412 blinks. Their eyes adjust to the lights. Surgeons monitor their equipment, but the door to the Cube hasn't opened, so no alarms sound, no sensors have tripped. Subject-412 feels they are everywhere all at once.

"I am outside…but I am also still inside the Cube."

"Maybe you are walking in your future," Subject-52 says.

"I see…I see 413."

The choir erupts again, hope for another dashed.

"No, I mean…I can see 413 now, with me outside the Cube."

They walk into the surgical suite, and there, sedated, lies Subject-413, head shaved, ready for the surgery. No, not the future. Their present, the now. Did they expect Subject-412 to fail? Or have they made the surgeries such a part of their routine, they don't know when to stop?

The head surgeon sits by the tray with the implants, harvested from previous subjects, not even sterilized. The surgeon sits slumped against his chair, defeated, sighing, eyes worn and hands calloused. At first, Subject-412 feels moved by their weariness. Even the surgeons in the Complex suffer.

The surgeon looks up and jumps in his chair, seeing Subject-412. Yet Subject-412 can see determination in his eyes to continue the Experiment, the same eyes they saw before they fell asleep, before waking up in the Cube.

The metal key, card-shaped, is thin like a scalpel. If strong enough to scar basalt, then strong enough to cut flesh. Subject-412 feels the hands of the previous four hundred eleven subjects on their hand. The choir of ghosts sings a singular note. Not a single one dissents from this decision.

With a swipe of their arm, they carve a line on the head surgeon's neck, a scream from the dead. With a push, they move throughout the Complex, the same single swipe replicated with each and every surgeon.

They slide next to the Cube, and with a bloody hand, slap the key against the cold stone, opening the door and freeing themselves. The alarms roar, announcing the end of the Experiment, harmonizing with the final note of their song.

Annihilate Mankind and Impress Your Friends: A Correspondence Course

By Matt Andrew

First published in the Halloween Special 001
(October 2021)

June 4, 19___

Dear M___,

Before we discuss the course in question, allow me to clear the air as to what you may have heard about me.

I am not the disgraced head of neuroscience at the Dienstag Neurological Institute—I am merely retired. Nor was I sacked as visiting professor of philosophy at Madrid's Universidad de Unamuno. Let's call it an extended sabbatical. By virtue of your enthusiastic application requesting to learn the mysteries of the human mind, you are, I hope, more interested in what I have to offer than in dinner party gossip.

With that out of the way, allow me a short moment to discuss what this course will *not* include.

Despite the fact that I am the author of obscure, out-of-print philosophical treatises such as *Evolutionary Misstep: A User's Guide, The Human Cataclysm,* and *Disaster of Consciousness,* we will *not* be discussing philosophical pessimism or antinatalism in this course.

We will *not* discuss how much better the planet, as well as its attendant flora and fauna, would have fared if it had not been for the accidental appearance of the *homo sapien.*

I will do my best to spare you *any* discussion in the countless reasons why we would have been better off having never been born.

Nor will we ruminate over our future descendants, trillions of them, tragically and involuntarily conscripted for miserable lifetime terms, like rats on a sinking ship.

Although we *will* be discussing just how malleable and foolhardy the human brain became as a result of the evolutionary hiccup that birthed us, we will *definitely* not discuss how destructive this knowledge can be in the wrong hands.

No, I will simply be walking you through a few party tricks based on simple human neuroscience. Apply yourself to my short lessons, and you will delight your friends and astound your family!

Now, as soon as I receive the one-time registration fee, I will promptly reply with your first lesson. Remember, check or money order, only—no cash.

I look forward to working with you!

Sincerely,
Doctor Blank

June 10, 19___

Dear M___,

Thank you for your prompt payment—now let's have some fun!

I call this first trick…

The Mystery of the Detached Nose

For this gag, you'll need two assistants and two dining room chairs. For the purposes of this illustration, I will henceforth refer to these assistants as "Billy" and "Sally."

The setup is simple. Orient the chairs so that they face each other. Place them as close as possible, while allowing their occupants to sit comfortably and without their knees touching.

Next, blindfold yourself and sit in one chair, and have Billy sit across from you in the other. Sally will stand on your right side.

Instruct Sally to take a hold of your right arm at the wrist, and manipulate your arm so that your index finger touches the tip of Billy's nose. Sally will continue to touch, tap, and stroke Billy's nose with your finger in a random pattern resembling Morse Code. It is important that the contact between your finger and Billy's nose is completely random and in no way follows a pattern.

At the same time, Sally will use her free hand index finger to touch, tap, and stroke your nose in the exact same pattern. The movements between your right hand and Sally's hand must be perfectly synchronized.

After about 30–60 seconds, if performed exactly as instructed, you will feel the uncanny sensation that your nose has been detached from your head and is now floating a few feet in front of your face!

Now for a bit of explanation:

Your body is a phantom…

What we perceive as our physical "self" is just an arbitrary "map" that covers the cerebral cortex. Stimulate any given area of the cortex and you instantly perceive the accompanying sensation on the respective body part assigned to that particular portion of the map. This system of nerve endings lends itself to be easily fooled. People who have suffered amputations can sense real feelings in their missing limbs. The brain is even known to reassign the map and accompanying sensations in order to make sense of our evolving body images.

So, with this new trick, you've just royally confused your brain with the help of Billy and Sally. Your gray matter is forced to make basic deductive assumptions in order to make sense of the situation:

Your arm is outstretched and tapping something that feels like a nose.

At the same time, the portion of the cerebral cortex associated with your nose is receiving sensory inputs in the same exact sequence.

Therefore, according to your brain, your nose *must* be detached and floating in space in front of you. It is the only possible answer that makes sense to our dim-witted nerve centers.

To achieve the full effects of an experiment of this type, focus is essential. Picture all the nerve centers at play as just… matter. Your nose, Billy's nose, Sally's hand, your hand—all just cells of the same composition and origin. All as equally simple to tap into as your own body parts.

To hone your concentration even further, recite a mantra while you are blindfolded and Sally taps your nose. Something like this:

This is my nose
This is not my nose
This is not Billy's nose
This is not anyone's nose
There is no nose
It is only matter…

Even after the experiment is over and Billy and Sally have gone home, keep practicing the mantra. Recite it when you look in the bathroom mirror. When you watch your mother cook in the kitchen. When the commuter train passes you at the Main Street Station.

That is not me
That is not my mother
Those are not passengers
We are just matter…

Once you've had a chance to feel the effects of the "detached nose," switch positions, blindfold Sally and Billy, and give them a try. Insist that they repeat a mantra as you say it along with them. Most humans lead simple lives swathed in comfort and denial, so they may need help opening their minds…pun intended ;)

Let me know how it goes, and have fun!

Sincerely,
Doctor Blank

...

June 19, 19___

Dear M___,

I was heartened to read your summary of your rapid success. Well done! Keep in mind that these experiments are never truly over. Always practice your mantra.

For that first trick, we demonstrated how easily the human brain could be fooled. Now, I show you how it can be completely reconfigured.

I like to call this one…

The Mystery of the Severed Hand

For this second experiment, you will need one assistant (let's call him "Johnny") and a rubber gag hand that you would buy as a Halloween prank at a costume store.

Sit down at a small table where Johnny can sit within a short arm's reach across from you. Beforehand, construct a cardboard partition a few feet square that you can place on the table between you and Johnny. Lay your right hand behind the partition, out of sight, so that only Johnny can see it, and place the rubber hand in front of the partition where you can see it.

Next, instruct Johnny to use both of his hands to simultaneously tap and stroke your hidden right hand and the rubber dummy hand. As before, the sequence must be executed in a random but synchronous manner. There must be no perceivable pattern, nor should there be any visible movement where Johnny is tapping your hidden right hand, or it may ruin the illusion.

And, voila…if executed correctly, you will gain the uncanny sensation that the rubber hand is actually your real hand!

As before, the brain has been fooled and is unable to find an explanation for the resulting dissonance other than to assign sensation to a lifeless, disembodied rubber hand.

Patience and focus are essential. These tricks don't always succeed on the first try. Don't be afraid to conduct several sessions, with different assistants, if necessary. The results will almost surely be inconsistent if you do not recite the mantra to hone your efforts:

This hand is not rubber
This hand is flesh
This is my hand
I am this hand…

For added effect, have Johnny repeat the mantra with you, over and over, as long as it takes to create the sensation that the rubber hand is actually your hand. Think about nothing other than your trillions of synapses and nerve endings leading from your brain to that cold hunk of rubber before you.

Dictate reality on your own terms.

Repeat the mantra until each and every word has lost its individual meaning, and instead become incoherent jumbles combined with the ambient sounds around you.

The syllables will become conductors that propel your energies into that rubber hand.

This hand is not rubber
This hand is flesh
This is Johnny's hand
Johnny is this hand…

Once you've had some fun with that, let's alter reality even further by ditching the rubber hand. Conduct the experiment exactly as described, except Johnny will tap the table top in front of you instead of the rubber hand. As before, he will stroke and tap your hidden hand at the same time. Don't forget your mantra:

This is not a table.
This is not wood.
This is flesh.
There is no table.
There is no wood.
There is no flesh.
There is only matter…

The mantra is key. Let the words sink deeply into you as if an echo within an infinite well.

If all goes well, that gelatinous gray mass between your ears will assign living sensation to an inanimate, wooden table!

Amazing, isn't it?

You've completely rewired your brain to accept any object as part of your body…part of your "self."

Continue your observations even after this trick has been successfully accomplished. See your phantom self. See your phantom mother. See those phantom train passengers. See those phantoms sipping lattes in the coffee shop. You'll begin to see the phantoms everywhere. Just matter, all around you.

There is no me.
There is no them.
There is no flesh.
There is only matter…
Have fun!

Sincerely,
Doctor Blank

July 3, 19___

Dear M___,

Allow me to congratulate you. That second trick usually takes a bit longer to master. Your summary was very thorough, and your insistence on utilizing the mantra in all aspects of your life reflects a true passion for unlocking the secrets of the mind. You appear to be a natural—great work!

Now let's have some fun…

First, I showed you how the mind could be fooled. Then, I demonstrated how the nerve centers could be completely rewired. All reinforced through intense focus, observation, and willpower.

Now, you will use these concepts to take complete control of matter. The old wives' tale says we only use ten percent of our brain. I say it doesn't matter—the brain has become a crutch. We've entrusted a blind, deaf cretin with the controls of our destiny. You have the knowledge to render your consciousness (and everyone's around you) utterly obsolete.

This last "trick" is not a trick. Instead, let's call it "field application."

Go to a public place. Somewhere you can sit and watch the people of your town come and go. Somewhere you can get up close without too much notice, but a relaxed setting that will allow you to focus on an unsuspecting group of people. Somewhere to observe all the matter around you. A coffee shop may do nicely.

Take in the smell of nutmeg and cinnamon. Listen to the wet thrum of traffic outside the plate glass windows as they speed over wet asphalt. The chatter of people gossiping over decafs. Hurried commuters placing rushed orders at the counter. Feel the cracked leather of the cheap armchair under your palms, one of several arranged in neat groups of four. The orange glow of bowl-shaped lamps complementing the blue dawn haze outside. The rumble of an airliner descending to land at the nearby airport.

Find someone sitting nearby. Focus on them.

For example, that elderly woman in teal polyester and matching cardigan. The one with the knitting bag by her feet. Gleaming needles embedded in balls of yarn.

Watch her knobby fingers. Her paper-thin skin stretched over spotted knuckles. Focus on those digits as she rips open yellow packets of sugar substitute, pours them in her tea. Will those hands to do whatever you want them to do. They are *your* hands. It is *your* flesh.

Her fingers are my fingers
Her flesh is my flesh
Her bones are my bones
There are no fingers
There is no flesh
There are no bones
There is only matter…

It may take days, weeks, even months of concentration, but imagine just what mischief you could cause with your newfound knowledge. Wouldn't it be funny to have her pour that sugar substitute into the potted rhododendron next to her?!

Throw off the shackles of the mind.

There is only matter...

Or that young man hunched over his notebook, rewriting his notes from the day's lecture in preparation for final exams. A nice, sharp number-two pencil scratching feverishly over a yellow legal pad.

That is my hand

That is my arm

That is my pencil

That is my flesh

There is no flesh

There is no pencil

There is only matter...

Take control. Repeat the mantra and command the matter to do what you will it to do. Reconfigure their matter to become one with yours.

Take your time with this step. Focus. Spend all day, every day, practicing. Remember that the human mind is malleable, a dumb, infantile object waiting to be told what to do. Tell it what to believe.

Let me know how it goes!

Sincerely,
Doctor Blank

September 29, 19___

Dear M___,

Considering the news reports of the violence and chaos spreading rapidly across the tri-state region, we can drop the subterfuge. Your field testing has gone better than I'd hoped.

I've been following your local news ever since taking you on as a pupil. I realized the measure of your success before you personally reported it, primarily from the front-page headlines of your local paper.

Local Siblings Mutilate Themselves

Soon after our first lesson, it seems that "Billy" and "Sally" were discovered in their garage by their parents in the early morning hours. Their noses had been severed from their faces, by their own hands, and nailed to the wall in front of them. The last report stated that they remained catatonic at the state psychiatric hospital, their only verbal communication a "strange mumbling of nonsensical chants."

Shortly after mailing your second lesson, an incident occurred in your town too terrible to even describe in the local paper. A report was passed on to me from a former colleague of mine currently employed in the office of your state health department.

A young man we'll call "Johnny" was found dead in his parents' living room, his corpse fused to the heavy walnut coffee table. Initial reports surmised that his body had been forced through the wood, although this would have taken a lunatic of immense strength and determination.

Imagine my colleague's surprise and confusion when health officials determined that, instead, his cells had been fused to that of the wood composing the table. Wood grains were found interwoven into his skin. And human tissue was found sandwiched between the various wood grains. Last I heard, they had determined that there was no feasible way to separate the victim from the table and the entire mess had to be cremated together.

At this point, I was already ecstatic of your accomplishments. And then came what international media outlets have dubbed the "Coffee Shop Massacre" (which is a misnomer, considering the entire strip mall became a slaughterhouse).

Mass suicides occurring within multiple pockets of random, homicidal fury. Scores dead and hundreds injured. Well, you know this, already—you were there.

My next advice would have been for you to teach what you have learned to a committed core of acolytes, but judging from the region's rapid descent into madness, you're way ahead of me.

This will most likely be my last letter. The neighboring state has almost completely fallen, so I'll be lucky if the trusty US Postal Service is around much longer ("through rain, snow, sleet, hail, and apocalyptic mass murder...").

I'm not in a hurry to be ripped apart by the hordes of mindless murderers spilling across the country, so an extra-large dose of China White, administered by one of my favorite local "ladies of the night," will have carted me off quietly into oblivion by the time you receive this.

And now I must thank you. After my career disintegrated, I sought solace in alcohol, recreational drugs, and other immoral distractions. My mind isn't what it used to be. Now, I'm happy to say, I can vicariously watch the welcome end of humanity, thanks to you, my best student.

I am heartened in the thought that our planet will recover, eventually, and live a much happier existence without us. Trillions of future unborn humans would reach across time and space to thank you for sparing them the curse of birth.

Sincerely,
Doctor Blank

Finishers

By Christi Nogle

First published in Issue 001 (January–February 2021)

I'm always a little excited and nervous when Mother unwraps a new package. Sometimes, under the wooden lid is a folder stuffed with photographs—perhaps a storage disk with video references as well. If so, Mother's body seems to grow heavier on the instant; her shoulders slump down. It will be a challenge to get everything right. She will labor and worry for weeks, and even so, the robot will most likely keep coming back to us for adjustments.

Sometimes there is no folder, but the body under the foam peanuts and plastic is a chill russet pink instead of the standard green-gray. This indicates extra mechanisms in the pelvis. There will be extra steps in the molding process of its "bottom," and I won't be allowed to watch some of her work. Mother looks on this kind with distaste. I am glad they don't come very often.

The best is a greenish body and no folder. This is Mother's opportunity to practice her art. And I'll get to help!

She'll turn on the robot right there in the foyer. We'll walk it back to our quarters, spend the evening with it, get to know what idiosyncrasies it already has. Mother says this is what any sculptor does—look at the stone, look at the wood, and see what form or character is suggested there.

Most bodies are the same. They're between 5' 8" and 6' 2", all of them broad-looking to me. Mother calls the most common type the Mesomorph. There is a softer, rounder sort called the Grande, and a wiry one called the Straw. There was one, once, as small as Mother, and another one broader than our bedroom door—another with massive, bowed thighs. All of these are rare, though. Most are the standard Mesomorph.

To sit and have dinner with a new, greenish Mesomorph—one with no folder—is a rare treat. It doesn't yet speak, but soon we stop calling it, *it*. We call it *he* or *she* or *they*, as we like. The robot becomes a person to us.

"Did you see how she leans just a little to the right?" I say.

"Oh yes," says Mother.

"And her waist is a little wide, isn't it?" I say. It isn't—she has just a standard Mesomorph form—but the way she sits suggests self-consciousness of a waist that is a little bit wide.

"Her legs are long and beautiful, though," Mother says. I love how her face brightens when we get one like this. It's the only time she looks the way she did when I was little.

The first step is brutal. If Mother wants an extra few centimeters of leg, arm, or torso, the body will need to go into the stretcher. Every other alteration to the standard form can be accomplished with the suction molds—but not this one. I am allowed to watch, but I am too cowardly to sit though the process. Today, I decide I must attend class, but I ask Mother to please call me before she does anything more than the legs.

She waves me away. Her face is grim again.

I used to love going to class. It's not actually *going* somewhere, I know that—especially these days—but it feels, or used to feel, like a trip.

I go into our bedroom, take off my clothes, and put on my bodysuit. I step onto the platform with its school desk and treadmill. I turn on the bodysuit and pull its hood over my head

It used to be different. Back when I was small, my robot body would open its eyes, I would push open the door of its robot cabinet and walk into the halls of a real school somewhere in the Midwest. I would walk alongside the other children and teachers in the hall.

It wasn't perfect, the navigation. There was always a delay when I made a turn. I would have to turn my robot body and pause its movement, then move my actual body so that I could keep walking forward on the treadmill. I had to be aware of where I was in both spaces at all times, or I was a mess.

Once I was at my desk, though? Oh, it was heaven. Some of the children were there in body, and some were there as I was, but I couldn't tell the difference. I raised my hand over and over, and my wonderful teacher called on me. He loved me.

He is the same teacher I have now, but not the same. His slender body is the same. His loud purple shirt, his smile. But he is not the same.

The children there in body could always tell who was a commuter (or who *wasn't real,* in their words). They cornered me on the playground one day early in my first year, all wanting to touch me to see what I felt like. I was afraid at first—I hadn't touched anything in the school except for my own desk and chair—but it felt wonderful to have all of their hands on me. It felt like touches on a foot that's fallen asleep.

Sensations are soft and strange in the robot body. When it's windy, you don't feel the wind the way Mother said you once could, back when you could go outside. You don't feel it in every root of hair, but you *can* feel the wind.

I went into the school bathroom once, and a girl said, "Why are you in here? You don't need to be in here." I had come in wanting to look in the mirror, of course. I knew I wouldn't see myself in my reflection. Still, I was surprised to see the tall child with her black curls and her wide, violet eyes staring back at me—surprised and delighted. I didn't like to think of what would happen when noon came and this pretty face closed its eyes only to open them moments later when another child in some other part of the world logged in for afternoon classes.

Now it's all different. There is no bathroom, because no one in the whole school is there in body—not the teachers, not the students. We're told it's not safe for them to travel there. The air is too bad now.

The school isn't even there in body anymore, come to think of it.

My teacher looks like the teacher I used to love, the one who used to love me for my enthusiasm. But I have no enthusiasm, and he is not the same person.

I never raise my hand. I pretend to sit at a desk. I pretend to listen until he lets us go, and I log off. There is a socialization period after class that isn't strictly optional, but I do not want to meet anyone this way. I don't like the way it feels when they touch my shoulder now. I can't abide the dead looks on their faces.

The new robot has a name: Eleanor. By the time I get down to the basement, she already has her long, beautiful legs. I lay out a skein of silky, light brown hair and a deep-olive spray for her skin, but we're not quite there yet.

Mother chooses an unusual nose form—long and wavy with flared nostrils. She attaches the plastic mold to the suction tube, presses it to Eleanor's face, and turns it on.

There's a deep chugging, glugging sound, then the gasp of release, and now, instant character.

We laugh at how much the nose changes things. We agree now that the eyes will be wide-set, hazel, with long, arched brows. The upper lip will have a curl; the lower lip will be medium-full. I set out all of the molds for the face and choose a small, youthful breast mold.

"This okay?" I ask.

"Perfect," says Mother.

"Why do robots have nipples, anyway?" I say.

She chuckles, but doesn't look away from her tools; doesn't respond. I have asked this before.

Everything except the face and breasts, Mother will freehand with a suction blade and a rounded buffer. She's planning for a narrow backside to go with the wide waist.

You'd think because Eleanor is green, we wouldn't need to think about fine bodily details, but that isn't so. Eleanor might want to wear a bikini sometime. Mother has to give her backside some texture, but just a bit. We don't want to detract from those masterpiece legs. We have to decide what her abdomen looks like—wide, yes, but firm or a little bit slack? Will she have a prominent collarbone? Will her ribs show at the top of her chest?

By bedtime, it's all decided. I can see Eleanor clearly in my mind and know that Mother sees her even more clearly. I bet that when I get up in the morning, she'll have already put away the molds and all the suction tubing, and Eleanor might already stand all olive-brown and ready for her finishing touches.

When I was ten or twelve and Mother and I were arguing, I told her, "I used to think I might be a robot, you know. I cut myself to see the blood; to make sure that I was real."

I wanted her to feel sorry about that. Instead, she laughed into her glass of whiskey.

"Is it funny?" I said.

"You think when they cut themselves, they don't see blood?" she said.

That struck me. They must, I realized. They must have a filter running in their minds somehow, so they always see what they are supposed to see.

"Your attendance is improving," my teacher says. We're all alone, having a conference in the virtual classroom.

"Yes, and all by my own choice," I say. My arms are folded, legs kicked out into the space between us.

"You don't like school very much, do you Mary?" he says.

"I'd rather work," I say.

He looks through a folder on his desk. "That's right," he says, "You're an apprentice…hairsetter? Is that right?"

"I'd say I'm a master hairsetter by now. I'm an apprentice at full finishing."

"Full finishing?"

"Everything—sculpture to hair to voice, customs, even portraits."

He doesn't chuckle, but he looks down. "Everything. Well,

that's sweet. I didn't know there were any workshops like that around anymore."

"Our workshop is underground," I say. With a port into the foyer that we've never known how to open. The company that brings us the raw forms also brings us our paints, food, and liquor. One day soon they might decide that such artisan work is not worth the cost anymore, and then they might drag us screaming from our burrow—would they?—or seal us up inside. This is a fear I might have once shared with my teacher, but not now.

"That's very sweet. Quaint," he says.

"But?" I say.

"But," he says. "Well, you already know what I'm going to say, don't you?"

And of course I do. He is going to say that I need to make something more reasonable of myself, study something modern, join a company, and perhaps live as company people do in a smaller, bleaker hole than the one I'm in now.

But there would be community, shared goals. Maybe a chance for love.

It breaks my heart how much this teacher looks like the teacher I loved. I remember one time, how he walked us out through the playground gate—just the ones of us who were there remotely because it would have been too great a risk for the others. He showed us some of the town outside the school. He pointed to all of the wrong around us and explained why it was so. He told us we might be the ones to make it right again.

I remember the terrible things I saw, but I remember, too, the blue and aqua and pink of the sky. I remember touching trees with my sleep-tingling hands.

This teacher now, he just wants me to have a mind for something that will keep me from becoming obsolete before my time. That's a nice sentiment, but it's not enough.

Eleanor already has rosy lips, an oily T-zone, a thick tumble of tawny hair, but no hairline. I miss class and spend the day and night rooting each hair around her temples and forehead, then each eyebrow hair, each eyelash. I want to do the hair on her arms, but Mother says it's too late. I have to go to bed; I have to go to class. She says I must sleep, and that when I wake up, Eleanor will be all finished.

I think of all the places Eleanor still has to go—because she is a special one, made to move through the world on her own. She will need much education and much testing, and then she will go off to do some job in the world. Somewhere outside. I fall asleep trying to imagine it, but cannot picture much besides the wide, bright sky.

Eleanor is gone. It was deadline, and we didn't get to do all we wanted with her voice. It was low and husky like we'd wanted, but not quite right somehow. We consoled ourselves by talking about how someone else might decide on an entirely different voice for her, and how we could not control everything. We dressed her in a white satin slip and boxers, and walked her to the foyer.

"I guess this is goodbye?" Eleanor said. She crossed her arms loosely, as though she felt chilled. We shut her into the foyer without a word. We cleaned up the workroom, ate, and slept.

Now we wake. We eat again, loll around for half an hour. By the time we return to the foyer, a new box is waiting.

"Let's start in the morning," Mother says.

"Don't you think..." I say.

She's already nodding. "We ought to at least open it," she says. She takes her pry tool out of her pocket.

"We should at least look," I say.

"So we can dream on it," she says.

"Of course."

She lifts the lid, and we both let out a sigh. A folder. A pink cast to the flesh beneath the plastic.

"How old are you now, Mary?" she says.

She knows my age; she must. I don't say anything.

"Time for the birds and the bees."

We have dinner with the folder, not the robot. He is still in his box, still under his plastic.

Thankfully, there is no drive with videos. He is a custom, but not a portrait, you see. He is a new individual, like Eleanor, so we won't have to use the same precision as we would with a portrait.

He is a Mesomorph like Eleanor, like most of them. His colors and his dimensions are spelled out. Mother points to one particular detail and explains how we'll open the cabinet of molds that has always been closed to me, and how the telescoping bulb in his pelvis will make his new part raise and lower, swell and deflate after it's molded. I giggle the entire time because, of course, I already know all of this. Still, it will be kind of cool to see.

The robot is only a him because the folder said so. All of the pink ones have the same shuddering mechanisms inside.

"Do you want to keep doing this forever?" Mother says.

"Yes, of course," I say—and mean it. I'm sprawled on the floor, half under his leg. I'm rooting the hairs of his inner thigh and still have the chest and everything else to do. The folder specified all of it. I've never had such a boon of hair work before. Mother says she still isn't sure whether she'll let me, but I'm planning to root the hairs of his thatch, and treasure trail, and butthole, all of which are supposed to be lushly furred. I have not thought about going to class at all.

"Have you ever thought of going out, seeing something of the world?" she says.

I did once, long ago.

Nothing Mother ever said, nothing from my teacher, nothing ever suggested that I would be able to step outside the foyer door, and so I stopped thinking of it, and now I won't let my thinking go that way again.

"No, of course not," I say.

I notice Mother has a glass of something clear.

"Is that water?" I say. "Can I have some?"

"It's not water," she says. Her face is cold and angry.

"Maybe we ought to go to bed," I say.

"I've been thinking what a shit life this is," she says.

"I'm sleepy," I say, and I pull myself out from under the robot's heavy leg.

"And how just about anything else would be better for you," she says.

"I know you are here," my teacher says. "I would not be seeing you if you weren't logged in. You know that, right?"

This is not a conference; this is class, and the other students are all looking on. His expression is cold and angry.

"Say something!" he says, and then there is some sort of glitch. His body slackens and a second later, he bounces back to the lectern saying, "Now let's get on with this lesson."

"Oh, wow," a boy beside me whispers.

"What?" I say.

"They took him out. It's another teacher now."

"It's not. It's autopilot," says another student.

I don't care. I have just the hood of my bodysuit on. My hands aren't in it at all; they're rooting the hairs in the backs of the robot's thighs. We won't make the deadline otherwise, and the feel of it is addictive.

Mother is sleeping. She'll be angry that I'm doing this, but relieved when we meet the deadline.

If we don't do what we need to do, maybe orders won't come. Maybe groceries won't come. Maybe the foyer door will never open again.

Mother and I fight. We make up. We fight again on a deeper and more satisfying level. I fold up the bodysuit and place it in the back of the closet for good.

•••

The hairy robot is gone. He stood politely in his satin boxers until someone opened the foyer door. He said hello in his soft, deep voice. After they looked him over, they probably gave him some clothes and shoes to wear. They led him out, brought in another box, and closed the door.

This new box is twice as broad as a normal one. A folder lies inside.

Mother is already thinking about how we will cut this one's belly open. She's thought of this even before it arrived; she's been waiting for one like this.

She's thought of how we will take out great masses of filler foam and make a place where I can curl up with my knife. I will get one chance to see the world.

Like a waking dream, an image of my old teacher crosses my mind. He speaks of the Trojan Horse and all the other adventures of Odysseus.

While Mother and I work, we speak of what will happen. What will I see out there? Will I be caught and brought back here? Or might I even flee back here, finding the world too hot or cold or poisoned? If I come back, will Mother still be here?

But her face stays hopeful throughout the questioning. The doom and disgust do not cross her face again, so I cannot go back on this promise.

"If you return and I am still here, how will you know it's really me? What if they swap me out?" she says.

I've thought of this. I'm brought back screaming, brought back in a wooden box, weak and drugged and chastened, but glad to be home—only it isn't home. The mother I loved is someone else, or not a person at all.

But I say none of this. Instead, I laugh and say, "Oh, I'll know *you* from the liquor on your breath."

She laughs, takes another drink.

But what if they seal up the port? What if they starve her inside?

I can't go. I know I can't. It's just something for us to fantasize about, isn't it? Yet we have removed the foam filling and hidden it in a corner cabinet, deep behind the pots and pans. We have sculpted a place inside the body, just as though we really are doing this. I have practiced curling there and practiced the shallow, shallow breathing. Like meditation, like going someplace else.

"Aren't they watching us work? Aren't they watching us all the time?" I say.

Mother shrugs. She doesn't know.

Once the space inside is ready for me, we begin the sculpting, the coloring, the crinkled copper hair. We have stopped talking of the future. We do the finish work more lovingly than ever before, but we're sure to stay on track for the deadline.

Storm Cellar

By Jen Marshall

First published in the Halloween Special Issue 002
(October 2022)

In this town, we believe in monsters. There was a time when I would have excluded myself from that statement. Not anymore. See, my buddy Dale's oldest boy trapped a monster in a storm cellar. That's what I'll believe until the day I die.

Now, this all happened years ago, back when so many folks around here were having trouble with their deer blinds and hunting stands. There was something in the woods at night, trashing everything when nobody was around.

After several incidents, Dale bought himself a night-vision, motion-activated trail cam and mounted it on his tree stand. It got smashed to pieces a few nights later, but not before it took one blurry photograph. It was hard to see much in that hazy image, but what little was visible was enough to make a man feel weak.

A bony arm reached toward the camera, the skin powdery and pale like you'd find on a dog with mange. The face was in shadow except for a single eye and thin lips pulled back in an animal snarl. That eye was the worst part. It looked black and distorted because of the night-vision setting, but there was an intelligence there that didn't belong to any local wildlife. That photo was all the proof we needed. It was a monster, plain and simple.

Now, before you dismiss us as gullible rednecks, there's one thing you need to understand. In this part of the country, we don't just live to hunt. We hunt to live. Messing with another man's hunting blinds is a crime we can't abide, and destroying them, well that's something we simply can't comprehend. A monster was the only explanation we could live with. Anything else was inconceivable.

The hardware store over on Main Street, that's my place. There's typically a steady stream of folks coming and going, trading gossip and fishing stories and whatnot. I like to think they stop in for my company. More likely it's the free coffee and the fact that it's the only business in town still open besides the Grocery & Drug and a handful of bars. In any case, Dale's oldest boy was always dropping by to shoot the shit with my customers, and that's how he wound up leaning on my counter one day, bragging about how he'd captured the beast that was wrecking everyone's hunting blinds.

"I climbed up to my old man's deer stand, you know the one over by Route Y and 44? So, I waited up there until dark, then I guess I fell asleep, because the next thing I knew there was rustling and footsteps down below. I took a few shots in that direction, but I must've missed because after that I heard something crashing through the underbrush like it was running away—"

"Hold up," I said. "You shot at something you couldn't see?"

"Hell yeah, I shot at it. It's a monster. Didn't you see the dang picture? Anyways, I jumped down and chased that varmint through the woods and clear across the field toward the abandoned houses out there. You know the ones?"

I knew the ones. Everyone in town knew them. Vacant buildings are everywhere in this part of the county ever since the mill shut down, most of them crumbling like the American Dream. The houses out by Route Y, though, they were old school, built strong and hardy to withstand the harsh weather we're famous for here. Each one was equipped with a backyard storm cellar, the kind with double doors lying on the ground at a slight incline, like the ones in that *Wizard of Oz* movie.

Folks like us know precisely what to do when the sky turns storm-green, and the air gets thick and stagnant. We run out to the yard with a radio, a flashlight, and whatever pets we can get our hands on. The first person to the cellar flings open the doors, and the last one down the steps slams them shut behind him.

It was in one of those storm cellars where Dale's boy claimed he'd trapped the monster. He said he'd shoved an old board through both handles to secure the doors from the outside. He went on and on, boasting about how he'd done the community a valuable service.

"Son, you know better than that," I said. "No self-respecting hunter traps something, then leaves it to die. I don't care what it is; you either kill it or you let it go. That's all there is to it."

"What am I supposed to do? Open the doors and say, 'pleased to meet you and sorry for the trouble.' Maybe I should douse myself in BBQ sauce while I'm at it, make sure whatever's in there enjoys its meal."

"Sounds like quite a predicament. The quicker you solve it the better, because you're not welcome in my store until you do."

Dale's boy flapped around some, carrying on about how I should be thanking him instead of busting his chops. But what's right is right, and he knew arguing would get him nowhere. He gave me a dirty look on his way out.

That boy was an idiot. He engaged in all the trashiest rural American pastimes: dynamite fishing, deer shining, cow tipping, petty vandalism. Doing that crap made him a clichéd small-town loser; doing it wrong made him an idiot. He'd screwed up his arm setting off explosives at the lake a few years prior, and another time, the sheriff had to disentangle him from a low-voltage electric fence surrounding a cow pasture. One winter, he backed his truck into an oversized papier-mâché shoe that was part of a local art installation, yet another failed attempt at downtown revitalization. It somehow got hooked to his bumper, and he dragged that giant shoe around town for days without realizing it until the police pulled him over. Like I said, he was an idiot.

Truth be told, all Dale's boys had problems. The middle son was a notorious shoplifter as a kid. He was constantly pocketing candy from my store, looking so hungry that half the time I pretended not to notice. Eventually he progressed to burglarizing houses and stealing cars. Last I heard, he was serving time for a drug-related offense.

Dale's youngest son, now he was the one I've always had a soft spot for. He never made a single sound, not from the day he was born. He could hear fine, but he didn't speak, laugh, or cry, not once. Doctors gave a diagnosis, but Dale could never remember what it was. The kid always wore a red baseball cap. Never took it off, no matter if he was chopping wood or sitting in church. Boy loved his hat.

He never much cared for hunting or fishing though, and when he got older, he flat-out refused to touch a gun. He wrote poems; beautiful things that made my soul ache for something I didn't even know I was missing. But you can't be a man like that in a town like this. The shame of it nearly destroyed Dale.

All those boys ever wanted was their father's approval, but he never taught them how to earn it. Instead, he sat in the bar and complained how he'd been cursed with a halfwit, a criminal, and a sissy mute instead of the offspring he deserved. Those reputations clung to his boys like the stench of skunk on a hunting dog. God damn this town. I don't know how anybody survives it.

Well, about a week had passed before I noticed that Dale's oldest boy hadn't made his way back to my store yet. He was constantly going off hunting or prowling or God knows what, so nobody in town thought a thing of it. I guessed he was still in a huff because I'd treated him like a child, maybe roughed his feelings a bit. I didn't give a rat's ass about that, as long as he'd taken care of his business in the cellar. No creature deserves to die like that, alone and afraid in a dark hole in the earth.

It took a bit longer for real worry to set in, and then I figured I ought to check on the situation myself. Those old houses were a decent distance from Main Street, but I didn't care to take my truck, not with all the potholes and washboard road out there. Besides, I prefer walking. It sets me to thinking, which ordinarily I appreciate. This time, though, my mind filled with endless questions, relentless and stinging like sand in the wind, making each step a misery.

What if the cellar doors were open? What were the implications of that, considering that the boy appeared to be missing? What if I found the doors still blocked shut? Should I open them myself? Or should I drag Dale's son back there and force him to take responsibility?

That damn fool. Everyone knows you don't trap something you can't kill or set loose.

As soon as I arrived at the edge of the woods, I could see him lying on top of that storm cellar, calm as you please. I hollered to him from across the field and when he didn't move, I knew he was dead. It was like how you can sense a house is empty just by setting foot in the door. It's easy to tell when there's no one home.

The smell of decay overwhelmed me as I got closer, and I realized I'd been mistaken about him being peaceful. His eyes and mouth were wide open, and he looked terrified, as though the last thing he'd seen was the devil himself. The boy's wrist was caught in the thin crack where the doors came together, mangled and skinned to the bone from his attempts to pull it out. He'd stuffed his rifle through the two handles to keep the doors shut. The wooden board he'd used previously for that purpose lay on the ground a few feet away.

Straight off, I vomited. After that, I sat down in the grass and bawled. I had a pretty good notion of what had happened to Dale's oldest son. He'd pulled the board out of the door handles to look inside and then chucked it off to the side. Something had transpired then that scared him bad enough to change his mind about opening the doors. Panicking, he'd slid his rifle through the handles to secure them, but he couldn't take it out again because whatever was in the cellar must have been pushing at the doors from the inside, trying to escape. I don't know how he managed to get his arm caught, but his aforementioned fish-bombing injuries had probably contributed to it.

I imagined him sitting there with his wrist all mashed and broken, yelling until his voice gave out, pondering his situation. He must have been in terrible pain, which likely further hindered his already limited capacity for problem solving. He couldn't shoot through the doors because he was using his gun to keep them closed. And with his jacked-up arm, attempting a quick grab and point was too risky. He must have guessed that whatever was inside would get him first.

It's hard to know what finally killed him. I'd wager it was a combination of blood loss and shock. One thing was certain: he died scared. Poor bastard was afraid to open those doors and face whatever he'd trapped; afraid of what would happen if he didn't; afraid of dying; afraid of living and explaining to his father what his stupidity had wrought. It was a bad death. An idiot's death.

If you ask me, the saddest part was that he did it for Dale. He was nearly a grown man and he'd never stopped trying to impress his daddy. It made me sick. My head felt like it was full of flies and only one clear thought emerged from the buzzing. I couldn't let Dale see his son like that.

So, I set to sawing at his wrist with my hunting knife. When I got to the bone, I snapped it with my boot, and whatever was left of his hand dropped into the cellar with a distant wet thud. I slid the rifle out from under the handles and replaced it with the wooden board. Then I dragged that young man away from the trap he'd made for himself.

Pointless as it was, I put my ear against the doors and listened to the cold silence inside. Whatever creature was in there had surely died long ago, probably with the taste of Dale's oldest boy's blood on its tongue.

After making sure the body was decent and resting comfortably, I headed straight to Dale's house, aiming to tell him the bad news before he heard it from somebody else. He opened the door with a smile, talking nonstop about how nobody was tampering with the hunting stands anymore, not since his boys had intervened.

"I reckon they shot the son-of-a-bitch that was causing the trouble, and now they're off carousing and raising hell together, having a fine old time," Dale said.

I felt a hint of fear then, like a tickle in the back of my throat. I coughed as he let me into his house.

"Both boys?"

"Yep. I know I'm always saying how they ain't nothing but a moron and a pansy, but turns out they've got something of their old man in them after all."

"How long have they been gone?"

"Two weeks, give or take. Hell if I know. I ain't their keeper. All I know is they took off together, and they'll come back when they're good and ready."

He laughed and pushed his hat back, and I noticed he wasn't wearing his regular green John Deere. It was a ratty old red baseball cap.

"Darnedest thing," he said when I inquired about it. "I found it on the ground a few paces from my deer stand. Boy must have accidentally dropped it before skipping town. I figured I'd keep it safe for him until he gets back."

Dale's youngest boy would never have left that red hat behind, not under any circumstances. Anyone who's ever met him would vouch for that. I almost said as much to Dale, but that itch of fear I'd felt earlier rose up and choked me and I couldn't get a word out. Instead, I listened to my buddy since the third grade crowing about his sons like they were heroes. I understood then that there was only one course of action: keep my damn mouth shut.

Go ahead and throw stones if you think you could have done better. Maybe you're the type of person who would have told Dale exactly what you'd found lying on those cellar doors. Maybe you'd have led him back there so he could see for himself. Hell, if you're strong enough to watch your friend's heart collapse and spill out his newfound pride in his sons onto a stained and cigarette-burned carpet, then I salute you.

As for me, I buried Dale's oldest boy with his gun and his dignity in an unmarked grave in the woods. Then I went home to live the rest of my life as best I could. I never did look inside that storm cellar.

Some folks might drive themselves crazy wondering what was in there. They might obsessively study a copy of that old trail cam picture and speculate on all the unthinkable possibilities. Some folks might even wake up screaming night after night, soaked in sweat and crying like a baby, trying to remember if they'd really heard the sound of fingernails weakly scratching on the underside of a cold metal door, or if that was only the figment of a dream.

Not me. In this town, we believe in monsters. So, I never have to wonder. My buddy Dale's oldest boy trapped a monster in a storm cellar. That's what I'll believe until the day I die.

Your Augmented Home is Now Ready

By Erich Alan Werner

First published in Issue 002 (March–April 2021)

Blake has fallen asleep again, just moments after our bodies parted. So, I tiptoe in the dark to the other side of the bed and, gently removing them from the charging dock on his nightstand, I steal my husband's smart glasses.

I know, I know. Snooping is wrong, always, and I'm a horrible, sneaky, privacy-invading, mistrustful bitch for doing this. If Blake snooped on my phone, I'd lose it. Probably call the cops on him, or post his porn browsing history on social media. I can be petty like that.

But he won't tell me what's going on with him—and if I don't figure it out soon, I'm going to fall apart. Something is different with him. Something is wrong. That distant, empty look. Then, the sudden urgencies. Like tonight. He basically dragged me to the bedroom, like a drooling caveman. Then, afterward, he just collapsed. Again.

We used to talk, after. He would hold me, play with my hair, sometimes nibble my nose, playfully, you know. It was cute. Lately, I get none of that. Lately he just grunts and rolls off me, and within like two minutes, he starts snoring like a congested grizzly bear.

I can't help thinking it's related to the smart glasses, the prototype he is alpha-testing. He wears the them almost all the time, now. Tonight, he even wore them while we were together in bed.

I peek in on Zora, our five-year-old. She is still sound asleep, thank God, beautiful in the nightlight glow despite her crazy-tangled hair and her pajama-clad rear end sticking in the air. Quietly, I close her door and creep downstairs.

It's not just Blake's bizarre bedroom behavior that has me worried. Tonight, for example, he said nothing about my new pieces. Not a single world. I hung three of them—huge, vivid panoramic landscapes made strange with surreal color effects and unbalanced perspective—right above my spot at the dining table, right in his line of vision. Stuff I was really proud of, that I'd spent weeks on. He didn't even notice. It was like they were invisible. Like I was invisible.

He used to be my cheerleader, showering me with endless, delicious, inexpert praise. "Holy shit is this our lake? It's transformed. This is brilliant, Kenzie, brilliant. So beautiful. Almost as beautiful as you are." Then he would kiss me, roughly, like he couldn't control himself, like my supposed brilliance had stirred him to a frenzy of passion. Back then, he would even gush about the commissions, the engagement and baby shots. Now I was actually doing something interesting, something original, something all me—and he couldn't even bother to notice.

Something has changed, but what?

I slink into the little half bathroom off the kitchen. I roll the pocket door shut behind me, switching the lights on out of habit, then off again, obeying the instinct to hide the wretched thing I'm doing. In the quiet, I can hear my own heart thudding and the nervous swell of blood. I close the toilet and sit down, then take a long, trembling breath, and put on my husband's smart glasses.

My friend Quinn is 100% sure Blake is cheating, I can tell. But Quinn only thinks that because her first husband cheated. "He clearly still has a thing for your cousin Vanessa," Quinn texted me, this afternoon. I protested, said no, they're just old friends, but the truth is, Blake's coziness with Vanessa has always made me twitchy. Vanessa is not only my cousin, she is also Blake's ex, his once-upon-a-time high school sweetheart. "Nessie," he calls her, and every time he says it, I secretly want to strangle him. But the two have known each other for decades, so some coziness is probably normal. Right?

On the third try, I guess his passcode (Zora's birthday). Luckily, there is no other security, no iris scan or voice recognition. This is a no-frills prototype.

"Hello, Blake," says a feminine voice.

I literally jump off the toilet—then make myself sit back down. "Oh God, oh God, what am I doing?"

"What are you doing. Hmm. Well, you have no events scheduled tonight," says a voice in the dark, calm and close. "Your first appointment tomorrow is at 10am, a project check-in with Dav and Cyan. Currently, it appears, you're using the toilet."

I sit frozen, both hands over my mouth, feet pulled back off the floor. I'm an idiot. It's just the smart glasses's voice assistant. I forgot that the smart glasses have bone-conduction audio. I tell myself to relax. Just to reassure myself, I flick the lights on again.

A cat, sleek and black, is draped across the front of the sink.

We don't have a cat.

"You have two new messages," says the black cat. "Would you like me to read them?"

My mouth falls open.

The cat looks shockingly real, but it isn't. It's an *augmentation*, a computer-generated image, rendered in real time and, through the glasses, superimposed by the glasses on my vision. I peer over the glasses to prove to myself that there isn't an actual cat on the sink. An actual, talking cat. The cat disappears, then reappears when I raise the glasses again. I shake my head in disbelief. The glasses have even rendered a convincing reflection of the cat's butt in the mirror.

Despite my nerves, I find myself laughing with delight and disbelief. Of course, I've heard the hype. I'm married to the hype. Smart glasses are the Next Big Thing. "Within ten years," Blake keeps saying, to whoever will listen, "Augmented Reality will be the only reality." Before, I just tried not to roll my eyes too hard. Now, suddenly, I get it. Not just the hype. I get why Blake left his secure, high-paying job at Microsoft to join this tiny AR startup.

And I get why Blake is acting so weird and distant. It's not me, not our marriage, not an affair. It's this project. It's AR. He and his company really are about to change the world. How could he think about anything else, right?

I close my eyes, waiting for relief to flood through me. No flood comes, though. Just a tingling trickle of hope—but even that gets drowned in the old stream of suspicion and worry. I steer my mind back to the mission at hand. I may be close to finding out the truth. I can't turn back now.

"Show me my message history," I say, and an interface appears. Glowing emerald characters and lines hover in the air. Using the micro toggle on the frame, I scroll through the list of Blake's messages.

I start with his messages to Cyan, a female co-worker. Cyan isn't particularly pretty, but she is unusual-looking and super athletic. Last time I visited the office, she had a road bike leaning against her office wall, and wore tiny black bike shorts that showcased her, well, her best assets. But their messages were bloodless, nothing there but work—all renders and versions and grumbling about deadlines and Dav, the CEO, yadda yadda.

The cat watches me, its haunting green eyes nearly the same color as the floating interface. "Is there something you're looking for?" the cat asks. "I can run a search for you."

I glare at it. I hate cats, always have. Years ago, on our fourth or fifth date, when I revealed my anti-cat extremism, Blake freaked out. He grew up with cats. His family always had a dozen half-strays wandering in and out of the house, apparently. We had a fight after, and for a few days, I actually worried he might break up with me. Now he was using AR to get his feline fix behind my back. I didn't know whether to feel betrayed or impressed by his cleverness.

I remind myself this cat is not a real cat but just a bunch of code and pixels—mind-blowingly lifelike pixels, but pixels nonetheless—and I decide to take its suggestion.

"Search for Vanessa," I tell the nonexistent cat, feeling ridiculous.

"No results," the cat says instantly, with a touch of boredom.

"Take that, Quinn," I say. But, for some reason, I still don't feel relieved, only frustrated.

The cat begins purring loudly. This seems to be a notification. "Rendering complete. Your augmented home is now ready. All updates were successful."

Augmented what? I wonder. "Show me the updates."

"Of course. Follow me." The cat leaps down from the sink, and lands gracefully on the tile below. Then, like a cartoon ghost, it walks straight through the closed bathroom door.

I follow, but when I open the door, I am no longer in my home.

I stand in an outdoor courtyard. There, outlined in the light from the open door of the half-bath, are clay walls that rise and rise, reaching up to an open night sky full of stars. Under my feet, a floor of brick, with grasses growing in the seams. The music of trickling water, and in the distance, a fountain. Flecks of moonlight reflect off the water.

I remove the smart glasses, and I'm back in the kitchen. Glasses on again, I recognize the hidden symmetries: the walls stand in the same spots, though in the courtyard they reach much higher. The counter, too, is there in the courtyard, but re-textured in rough stone, with a rustic sink in the middle. I reached out and turn the sink on, feeling the cold water stream out over my palm, my lizard-brain convinced that it is actually coming from an old rusted tap.

It is all the same, but it is all different, all augmented.

Though "augmentation" maybe isn't strong enough a word. This is transmutation, metamorphosis. No wonder Blake never takes these babies off. But why has he never said anything about this? Why keep these augmented wonders to himself?

Across the courtyard, I catch the green glow of the cat's eyes. It stands beneath a stone archway, where the entry to the living room should be. "Meow," it says, a reminder to follow. So, these aren't the updates. So, there is more.

I follow, my heart in my throat. I step through the archway and am transported to an Italianate parlor. "Lights on," I whisper. The room's layout is identical to our humble living room, but the furnishings are transformed, with mahogany and shining leather and gold adornment everywhere. Nonexistent balconies hang overhead with ornate railings, framing a nonexistent domed roof covered in frescoes.

Wow. These augmentations are freaking unreal. How much work has Blake put into all this? Maybe this is what has pulled Blake out of my orbit. Not another woman, but this home augmentation, this cyber-renovation, this digital décor. The trickle of relief surges, becomes a steady flow.

Stepping close to the fireplace, I notice that hanging above the mantle is a large painting—an abstract, beautiful and dark and unsettling.

After a moment, I realize that this abstract is covering the family portrait. The one I did myself. The one I gave to Blake on his birthday this year, where I have on his favorite dress, and Zora has the fancy bun and an amazing gap-toothed smile. Any relief I was feeling is choked off. I touch my stomach because I'm so confused and hurt it makes me a little nauseous. What the hell, Blake?

The cat meows, sounding impatient. Even its moods are convincingly catlike. My mind churning, I follow the cat into the hallway at the back of the house. The hallway is not augmented, which at this point, is more comforting than it is disappointing. Yes, the augmentations are beyond fantastic, but it's nice to feel like I'm back in my actual home.

The cat strides halfway down the hall and stops. "Here are your updates."

"What? Where?"

The cat vanishes through the wall, then pops its head back through. "Wall render completed."

I can't believe I missed it. The door to my office, where I work all day, and hang out most of the night. Blake has just augmented it out of existence. "What the?" I step to the not-door. On the wall that swallowed the door hangs another painting—another abstract, this one even stranger, a chaotic battling of reds and near-blacks. Like something painted by a monster.

"A monster," I mouth, stumbling onto a memory.

Blake never calls her Vanessa.

I try her special, ridiculous nickname.

"Search all files for Nessie."

"More than 500 results," the cat says, yawning.

The cat curls up in the antique chair in the corner, the one Blake always complains about, but hasn't deleted—not yet, anyway. I walk over and sit on top of the cat. But the cat just pops up, unruffled, on my lap.

"Show me the results, all of them," I demand. "And get the hell off my lap."

I read and re-read the archived messages until the sun comes up. Vanessa initiated, about a year ago. Blake resisted and resisted, then gave in. He described, in shattering detail, what he would do to Vanessa "if we were alone" and "if I didn't have a ring." Then, suddenly, Blake stopped responding. Much later, he wrote back, saying that her messages were inappropriate, that they could never act on this, that it wasn't worth it, that they couldn't destroy their families.

After I read it all, I shut my eyes. My teeth are clenched so hard my jaw aches. What a prick. What a prick and a coward.

The cat is sleeping across my slippers. I kick it away and stand on wobbling legs, then march upstairs.

The instant he sits up in bed and sees me wearing his smart glasses, Blake breaks. He apologizes and apologizes. He cops to the messages and swears he never touched Vanessa, not physically. He planned to tell me everything, honestly he had, but never found the right moment. The thing with my office, he admits, looks bad. But it was just an experiment. Same with the portrait, everything. "I was just playing with the software, that's all. I mean, you've seen it. It's going to change the world!"

I throw the smart glasses on the bed. "You've replaced our home, our whole life together, with these sick fantasies!"

Quickly, too quickly, he lunges for the glasses.

I see his desperation, fall over him, and snatch the glasses back.

"You don't understand what you're seeing," he snaps. He grabs my arm and pulls me backwards, fingers prying as he tries to muscle the glasses away.

"Stop it, Blake! You're hurting me!"

There is a snap and, for a split second, his grip loosens. I break free and hurry into the bathroom, locking the door behind me. Blake pounds on the door so hard I'm afraid it will break. I stand before the mirror, take a breath, and put on the glasses, which hang crookedly, the frame bent on one side.

There in the mirror, wearing the broken glasses and my wrinkled pajamas, stands Vanessa. She looks awful, like she hasn't slept. Like she has seen a ghost.

I touch my face. In the mirror, Vanessa touches her own.

I have been augmented out of my own home, my own family.

"Get out," I growl, when Blake gives up trying to break down the door.

"You can't just kick me out," he spits. "I live here too."

"No, you don't," I say. "No, you really, really don't."

Following a dark impulse, I take off my pajamas. I watch in the mirror as Vanessa takes off her own. I confirm that everything, every private detail, has been augmented. We stare at each other, exposed.

Through the locked door walks the cat, unperturbed by the drama, the family falling apart around it. It swirls around my feet, tail swishing.

"Here kitty kitty," I say. "Can you take a screenshot? Capture what I see as an image file?"

"Of course," says the cat. I hear a click and a small, still image of the unclothed Vanessa appears at the upper-left corner of my vision.

"Please, Kenzie. Don't do anything you're going to regret," Blake pleads, under the door. His rage has boiled off. He sounds defeated, broken, pathetic.

He thinks I'm going to send the image to Vanessa. He thinks I'm after petty revenge.

"Send image to my wife, to Kenzie," I say. I don't know exactly what I'm going to do with it, but somehow, someday I want to turn it into art. I want to turn this hideous, heartbreaking, world-shattering moment into something beautiful. It may be years from now, but someday this image, transformed, will hang on my wall.

First though, I want some petty revenge.

After all, I'm already a horrible, sneaky, privacy-invading, mistrustful bitch.

"Cat, make a video call to Nessie. Share my screen or whatever. I want her to see what I see. Make it a conference call with Dav and Cyan. Quinn too. I want them all to see. Know what, let's stream this live on my social media. I want the whole world to see my amazing augmentations."

Potato

By Ken Altabef

*First published in the Halloween Special Issue 001
(October 2021)*

The water in the bathtub went cold six days ago, could even be a week. There's no more hot water, the pipes all clogged. The bathwater is so green with gunk I can't even see what's underneath, but I don't want to see. Lord, it all itches something fierce, especially down in the crotch where it's snaked between my legs. I want desperate to pull it out, but I'm afraid. When I tried to pull out the shoots I found in my ears yesterday, it hurt like hell.

The damn stink is the worst. Raw potato doesn't have itself a strong smell but when you're surrounded by it, growing fresh and thick on the walls, covering the whole room—the ceiling even—it's enough to make a body want to vomit. I feel a tickle down my throat as it shifts, a playful little tug at something or other inside me, trying to make me gag. But nothing comes up, the pipes clogged there too.

I should'a run away when it all first started. I should'a run like hell when I found that first one. There's a spot on the mirror where it hasn't grown all the way over yet, and I catch sight of myself—*what a horror I look!* My skin is all milky pale and as wrinkled as a prune, but they won't let me get out of the water. I see myself, like a withered old scarecrow lying in a coffin full of green water, and I remember.

Potatoes are supposed to have eyes, but when this one opened, I near fell down sideways. I've been digging potatoes for thirty years in that little vegetable patch out back of my house, but I never had one look back at me, and with such a sad, soulful glance as that. Its one eye was brown, as you might expect, but pink around the edges where it should've been white. It glistened wetly. And then it winked.

Nowadays, people see faces on damn near everything—a man in the moon, Mother Teresa on a biscuit, Elvis almost everywhere, and the Lord Jesus on a cheese sandwich. But it still nearly bowled me over. At first. At first.

But after I held that little 'tater in my hand for a while, and it was warm and kind of soft at that, it didn't seem quite so strange. Unusual, certain. But not too strange at all. It hummed at me, that sweet little thing did. A slow, sad tune like something I might've heard a lifetime ago when I was a young girl, a melancholy lullaby meant to send troubled children off to sleep. Up and down, the tune went, but never so much up as down, lower, lower, slower, slower. It seemed the most natural thing in the world.

But what should I do with it? I figured the poor little thing could do with some water, so I filled up the old mop bucket, and I knew 'taters like it kind of dark, so I put it under the bench out in the garage. But after standing there a while, and thinking and listening, I thought that crusty old bucket wasn't so good and my lonely garage not near good enough, so I brought it in the house and let it soak in my wedding bowl. That was Stratford crystal there, fifty-years-old. But it still needed dark, so I put it under the bed and pulled all the window shades nice and tight.

I lay down, dead tired, but I didn't want to sleep. I wanted to run like hell—to run and run and run. But that little humming song told me I was too tired to move and put me straight off to sleep. I didn't even dream, not as far as I can reckon.

Next day, I went over to market and bought fresh eggs and some sliced turkey and a couple normal potatoes, and I almost told that Jennie Flaherty about that odd little 'tater of mine. I wanted to tell her, I did, but the words just wouldn't come. It was all just about the weather and the local gossip and such. No news about a humming potato. Certainly not.

When I took that bowl out again, I saw the 'tater had sprouted! It had little shoots coming out the sides—yes indeedy—four crooked little shoots with tiny little fingers and toes. The eye looked at me, still so sad and lost like a little pup. And the potato hummed. It sang me that low, sad song as the days went by and by.

After about a week, my little tater-child was fast outgrowing that bowl. It had got itself full-grown arms and legs, and a second brown eye (though it was a bit smaller than the other), and a curl to its shape looked just like a baby. I emptied it into the bathtub, filled it up with warm water and put in some fertilizer grow-stuff I got down at the store. That stuff turned the water kind of green so I couldn't hardly see my sweet little baby no more, but I could still hear it hum to me. I didn't go out of the house much after that; I knew I shouldn't leave a child there in the bath alone. No mother would.

And the song, that song was just for me. It didn't want no one else to hear.

When my boy Harlan came round for his monthly visit I wouldn't let him go into the bathroom. I couldn't think of a good reason, neither. If I told him the pipes was broke, he'd want to get at them with a wrench. He was handy like that, always fixing things. So, I started yelling at him, and I cussed at him some and finally pushed him out the door and gone. "Crazy ol' bat!" he said, and it wasn't the first time.

I wanted to chase after him, I wanted to scream out to him, but I didn't. My baby needed me. A momma can't just run off like that.

It grew fast after that, filling up the tub, eating up all that fertilizer stuff, I guess. Its legs went so long they dangled over the sides. It looked a frightful sight. It had peculiar skin, all dry and brown and crinkly no matter the water, just like a regular potato does. Its head looked like a big old potato with those sad blood-shot eyes, and it had a lump of a nose, and a mouth with crusted, weeping lips. No hair, but the dome of its head shifted here and there like something was moving underneath, just below that crinkly skin. No one could possibly say my young man was handsome, I know, but nobody ever said my husband Jack was too easy on the eyes, neither.

It made a different song than just the humming, now it had a mouth and all, a song made up of no real words anybody could understand, except I did understand them. It said it loved me and it wouldn't ever hurt me. It wanted to go outside, it wanted to go visiting other people and do some real living. I guess just about anyone can understand that. I guess. I didn't think much of that kind of talk, though. Not for him. I could dress him up in some of my husband's old clothes but that just wouldn't work. He couldn't go anywhere looking like the way he did, with that nasty potato skin all over. And he smelled like fried eggs, cooked too long on a greasy skittle. Though now I come to think of it, I must admit my Jack might have smelled a fair bit worse.

The water was surprisingly warm when I climbed into the tub with my young man. I felt so many different things—the nourishing embrace of moist earth, cool clear water, tangy loam. His long, boneless fingers caressed me as I clung to his rough, papery skin. He was gentle with me, and that helped— and it sure did hurt that first time. First time in a long time. He whispered constantly all the while, and that helped. I can't rightly recollect what he said, but I'm sure they were nice, tender things.

Next few days, my potato spent most of its time in the garden, digging up some more of them strange things and putting them in the sink, the bathtub, and damn near everything else that would hold water and fertilizer. Soon the whole house stank and the walls started to crawl. My potato man had become way too busy to pay me much mind. I thought about my boy Harlan and wished he'd come down for his visit, and then I remembered the way I'd run him off and all. Then again, he never sang me such a pretty song.

When it left me, I felt hurt and afraid. I shouldn't have to stay in this dirty water all the time, and like I said, the way it's crawled up inside me's no good neither. My belly's all swole, and I feel it moving. It hurts, and I'm afraid. A mother shouldn't be left alone, surely not when she's expecting. But I'm not alone, not really. A body could go near deaf from all the humming and singing round here. Now the whole house sings.

I was surprised, that's all. I thought he couldn't go nowhere with that ugly potato skin of his. But then I noticed the potato peeler and all those rinds on the bathroom floor.

No worries, then. I think he'll pass just fine.

Of the Sea-Born and the Brine-Hearted
By Christine Lucas

First published in Issue 010 (July–August 2022)

You're late for your shift. *Again*. Never mind that the poor creatures in their tanks need to be fed and have their water filters cleaned and changed. One would expect this kind of neglect from jerks like Hector, who only cares about cutting creatures open, preferably while they are still alive.

But you?

You are a fucking marine exobiologist. You grew up on an island, swimming out to the Aegean Sea at every opportunity, and your mother taught you reverence towards every sea creature. Of all the people working on this station, *you* should care about the welfare of your specimens. *You* should care that every last one of them is starving, because Hector spent the entire night shift poking, prodding, and dissecting kelp, then staring at them through the microscope. It's fucking seaweed, for heaven's sake! What did he expect them to do, start dancing to the *Zorba the Greek* theme?

You mumble a greeting to the jerk, and beeline for the coffee maker. Sure, have your fix first. It's not as if your live specimens are going anywhere. They can't. They can only stare at you from behind the thick glass, even though they don't have eyes to see or brains to form complex thoughts and judge you—or so you *think*. Let them float in their own filth while you stretch and yawn and talk nonsense with Hector. But sure, let everyone know how you stayed up late trying to contact your mother back on Earth. You haven't heard from her in a while—since you accepted this assignment on Europa. She hung up on you when she heard that you'd be returning to the sea—even if it's this alien sea. You haven't heard from her since and you're worried, and Jupiter's magnetic field keeps compromising communications. But how exactly does this excuse your neglect?

Finally. Two coffee cups later, you pull yourself up and don the protective gear needed to clean the tanks. At least the poor creatures won't eat in water mixed with excrement. You're sloppier than usual. Tank water splashes on your lab coat, not once, not twice, but *five* times total. You insert a filter the wrong way and almost ruin it. You almost flush the red squids into the main water pipe, but reverse the flow at the very last moment. You're lucky, because neither Hector nor the other tech at the far end of the lab notice. And once you've tossed your gear into the disinfection bin, you start the feeding.

Protein powder mixed with dried kelp. Again? You know, the armored starfish over there would love one of the red squid. Have a heart and toss him one? Or not. They're both really basic lifeforms, their main interests being eating, defecating, and procreating. The same can be said for most humans, to be honest. And lo and behold, you fill another cup of coffee and steal a glance or two of Hector's buttocks while he has his back turned to you, finally having detached himself from his chair to clock out. You lick your lips, searching for the right words to start another awkward verbal mating ritual, when Hector's gaze falls on the tank right next to you and his eyes narrow.

"Thalia? How many of those medusozoa are supposed to be in this tank? The Scylla Europensis?"

Good job hiding your panic. If not for that tiny spasm on your cheek and the tighter grip around your cup, you'd pass for the image of Blissful Ignorance. You don't allow your neck to make a sharp starboard turn and count the little alien jellyfish with the seven tentacles. When you *do* look at them, you find them floating almost perfectly still, the surface of their umbrella-shaped bell gently rippling every fifteen seconds or so. They're barely bigger than your thumb, and have arranged themselves in a semi-circle like the chorus of an ancient tragedy awaiting for the deus ex machina to deliver onto your thick head a divine justice.

You killed the one that's missing, didn't you? You flushed it down the main pipeline. Or you crushed it when you shoved the filter harder than you should, trying to just get it over with and return to your coffee. Or something else, equally horrific and negligent. When you find the words to speak, you manage to keep your voice calm.

"Nine, why?"

"I'm sure that they were ten." Hector brings up the file log on his tablet. "Yes, ten."

You shrug, you murderer, *you*. "Perhaps they ate the one that's missing. Like the squids. Cannibalism might be more common than we'd originally thought at these depths."

Or perhaps you could, you know, feed them more? And on time?

"The squids left tissue remains." Hector frowns and moves to sit back on his chair. "We really need to dissect one of them. Has the Ethics Department replied yet?"

You shake your head. "Jupiter's magnetic field is having the worse hiccups ever. Communication with Earth is still down."

Bless Uncle Jupiter, still looking after all of his kith and kin.

Then you gently shove Hector's shoulder, the touch lingering perhaps one second more than what would be considered casual. "Go on. Your shift is over. You need your rest."

He's not convinced. Mistrust? Suspicion? He might be a scalpel-happy jerk, but he's a smart jerk. He fingers the unopened scalpel he keeps in his lab coat's chest pocket, as he always does when his anxiety peaks. Reluctantly, he makes his way to the door. "If any species gets assigned a reasonable sentience level from the saps back home, let me know. They can't expect us to do our jobs without tissue samples."

Off he goes. And good riddance. He won't cut up any poor creature today—or tomorrow, if the electromagnetic interference holds. Even without that, outgoing communication is spotty when going from this deep-ocean station to the surface outpost on Europa's equatorial region. But you don't care much about that right now, do you? You have bigger problems.

Where did the tenth alien jellyfish go?

You check their tank again. Count them all you want, they're still nine. Flash the UV light to check for tissue remains—never mind that it hurts them, having never been exposed to your cruel lights. Still nothing in the tank. You hurt them for nothing, the poor creatures that have no mouths to scream and no way to flee. Sure, remove the filter again to check it. Still nothing. Go check your gear now, but it's halfway to the disinfection cycle. You'll find nothing there either.

Why are you scratching your arms, sleepy little Thalia? They itch, don't they? They itch where the tank water splashed on you, even over your protective gear. That itch that begins at your fingertips, travels upwards to the base of your neck, and nests just under your clavicles? You know what that means, don't you? That you're infected. That the tiny alien burrowed through your skin, pierced your blood vessels, and swims in your blood flow now. Or not. Perhaps it's just your guilt that irritates your skin because that's how shallow your morals are.

Oh. You rub your ears now? Is this how the creature penetrated your body? Or do you rub them to get rid of that annoying, intrusive noise? You know, those whispers just at the edge of your hearing, like distant conversations you're not privy to. Or the humming—tunes of long-forgotten lullabies from the deep, almost like a siren's song. Worse yet, that sloshing sound at the background of it all, like wet slippers dragged on linoleum floor. How did that old Terran verse go? About that beast, slouching towards Bethlehem? You do know the poem, don't you? You should know. You should remember.

But perhaps you don't, your memories of poetry overwhelmed by that other memory of gum stuck in your 3b curls. Teenagers are assholes by default, especially those bullies who pestered the brown-skinned girl with the unruly hair. You fiddle with your hair now, as if trying to find the jellyfish entangled in the curls that you neglected to braid today. What will you do, dear Thalia, if it has indeed gotten stuck near your scalp? Will you chop it all off, like you did back then? Hector left a package of brand-new scalpels at his workstation. He won't be doing any disemboweling any time soon. Why don't you pick them up and get rid of that tangle at the base of your neck?

Fine, so *don't* pick them up. Refill your coffee mug. Did you check before you poured? Perhaps the coffee maker is where the jellyfish now resides. Scowling at the mug won't help you if you've already ingested it. It might be nesting now somewhere between your small intestine and your gall bladder, stretching from the bile duct all the way across to the duodenum and into your pancreatic duct. Perhaps it's ready to lay its eggs inside you. But you don't even know how it procreates. Had you been more diligent in your duties, you might have observed a thing or two about their behavior.

But it's always Earth with you, isn't it? How to establish a connection. How to call that landline number to a backwater island when everyone else has switched to remote. You're not on Earth anymore, Thalia.

Another sip of coffee. You pull up the station's schematics on your screen and track the water flow. Two closed systems: one to siphon in the icy waters of Europa's ocean and cool the nuclear core that powers the station; and one for life support purposes, after heavy filtering. The two systems intersect at the point where they return to the ocean. The lab's filtering system is a part of the second one. What do you fear now? That you flushed the poor creature, and it managed to swim upstream all the way to the core? Do you fear that a nuclear implosion is possible? Then you should alert C&C, shouldn't you?

Sure, check the alarm logs first, from the sensors installed at the various filters along the water flow. Nothing. *Almost* nothing. Several blips that lasted fragments of a second and that indicate organic matter. It might be nothing. Just another denizen of Europa's deep who got caught in the turbines that siphon the water towards the core—and got shredded in the process. Or, maybe one of your colleagues messed up and flushed their toilet paper. Whatever those blips are, they are too small—single-cell small—to be that wayward jellyfish.

What now, Thalia? You can soldier on through your shift while your skin burns with itching and the images of worms writhing beneath your epidermis intrude upon your thoughts. Or you can call in sick. You've never called in sick, so no one would fault you for this. Expect perhaps from your live specimens, who don't care that your mother's mental health took a turn for the worse back on Earth, and she might already be dead. Death means different things to different species. Especially those in lab tanks with a clear view of a packet of scalpels.

In the end, it's your mother's memory that keeps you trudging through your shift. She went in debt to get you off-world to the Lunar Academy, and she helped you become someone she could only dream about, somewhere far away from the sea. You endured the pranks, the ostracizing, the name-calling, until you shed the mantle of "garlic-smelling peasant" and donned the lab coat that carried you all the way out here. Here, at the underwater trenches of human exploration in the icy depths of Europa's oceans. And once your shift is over, you toss a generous amount of feed into the tanks. It's still just dried kelp with protein powder, but it's a nice gesture. An indulgence for your mother's soul, perhaps, because you've grown certain that she's dead by now.

Once back in your bunk, you forego the shower. Unlike other off-Earth outposts, there's no shortage of hot water on Europa, but your skin still itches, and the image of the wayward jellyfish is engraved on your mind. In your imagination, it plops out of the showerhead and entangles itself in your hair. Or it slides down your spine along with sudsy water, down to your buttocks. You shudder and stay clear of the shower. Tonight, you use wipes instead. You prop up your tablet by your bed and set the calls to Earth on repeat, as though dialing a specific number of times will unlock the connection and you'll get through. A slideshow of photos from your childhood lulls you to a restless sleep. Those images intrude upon your dreams, embellished with the smells and sounds of your life in a village by another sea.

Wild thyme and oregano, and the incessant chirping of cicadas. Salt that clings on skin and heart and hardens them both, one storm at a time. Picking up seashells at the shore with your mother. You haven't seen her in person for close to a year now. Now that you look at her through a dream, her eyes are bottomless pits of space vacuum, and she wears a gown of quivering jellyfish. She opens her mouth as if to tell you something, but no sound comes out, only a crab that lingers for a moment on her face, its pincers clasping onto her lower lip. Then she turns away and starts towards the wine-dark sea in a slow, ceremonial march.

You stir in your shallow sleep, sniffling tears that taste like brine.

You know how all the women in your family eventually die: there comes a night at the dark of the moon, when they leave their homes and families behind and walk into the sea, never to be seen again.

You're sprinting now in your dream, into the shallows to grab your mother, to drag her out kicking and screaming, if needed, and you find yourself facing a stranger. A toothless hag, her white hair loose to the rising wind. She *could* be your mother should she get to live to her old age. Or she could be your grandmother, or any of your foremothers that you never met. Whoever this one is, she sits atop a tripod, inhaling fumes that remind you too much of Jupiter's atmosphere: plumes of helium and sulfur and methane. Like the ancient Oracle of Delphi, she's chewing laurel leaves before speaking. *No.* Those aren't laurel leaves. She's chewing on live jellyfish, their squirming tentacles visible between her purplish gums. She cackles, scratches her arms exactly like you did earlier, and reaches for an embrace.

You wake up drenched in sweat and short of breath. The first thing you do is check your tablet. Your calls have remained unanswered. Your heart insists that your mother is dead. Your mind, insubordinate as ever, refuses to accept it. So, you put on your sweatpants and a t-shirt, and go out for a night walk in the deserted corridors of the station. It's not really night. Down here it's always dark. It's nighttime in the circadian sense, that rhythm that helps humans to endure in places they do not belong.

Your soles now itch as much as your arms, and you march towards the station's great observatory window. Twenty centimeters of reinforced glass that allows for a view of the thick kelp forest around the station, and all the bio-luminescent fauna and flora of the deep. They glow in miniature rainbows under the station's soft lights, but most of the local lifeforms have learned to keep their distance. Sometimes, the kelp-stalks tremble as though something larger swims amongst them. Shadows of bigger creatures appear on the sonars, but none of them has neared the station. The small clearing between the station and the forest is empty now, but for the occasional jellyfish or arthropod that floats by.

The Observation Hall is dark except for the emergency lights, but not empty. Hector is there, sipping his coffee. Probably on his lunch break, bored and tired. You don't care. Now your entire body itches and yearns for an embrace, like the one you just turned down in your dream. Just a hug, you tell yourself, to remember what it's like to be close to another human.

He hears your steps and turns around. "Hey, Thalia. Still awake? Still trying to get through to Earth?" He takes a sip from his mug, his free hand fingering the scalpel in his pocket. Its packaging has become worn by now, making its sterilization status questionable. "Well, since you're up. I've been thinking… we should go ahead and dissect one of the squids. If anyone asks, the others attacked and killed it. What do you think?"

There are no words in your mind, no voice in your throat, only a desperate need for an embrace with every cell of your body. You pull him close with your left arm around his waist, your right palm against his chest to feel his heart and his scalpel, and you lean in for a kiss.

"Ah, okay," he mumbles as he tries to juggle both your advances and his coffee mug. "We can do that, too."

The kiss is awkward. It's uncomfortable, and he tries to pull away two seconds in. And you? You don't like the way his mouth tastes and his body smells, and he's still the same vivisection-eager jerk. But his galloping heart calls to you, his body heat a balm to your itching, and your tongue probes a little deeper into his mouth. Your yearning waxes stronger. You despair not having more arms, more legs, more tongues to reel him in even closer to you, so close that your skins will merge. He squirms a little in your embrace, then pulls back to draw breath.

"Wait, Thalia. Hold on a moment." His eyes drift away from your face to a spot behind you, to the observation window. "What the fuck?"

You detach yourself from him, your palm still near his heart, and spin around in a hall bathed with milky white light. The clearing is no longer empty. Hundreds, no, thousands of jellyfish have gathered just behind the glass. They float serenely in small swirls and circles, forming geometrical shapes that resemble snowflakes. One of the lot swims upwards, above the swarm. For a moment, it just lingers there, and you feel as though it's staring right at you. Then it explodes in countless little glowing shards, like a dandelion's flower head spreading its seeds to the wind.

Seeds? Spores? Or…eggs?

You glance down at your hands. Your blood vessels are aglow with the same light. Now you know where that wayward jellyfish went: through the droplets of tank water that landed on you. You should be scared. Disgusted. Or at least concerned. But you're not. Are you?

A collective tremble ripples through the swarm, and their shape changes to that of a woman, her face vaguely familiar. Is this the hag from your dream? You know exactly who this is.

You know who *we* are, by now. We've been in your thoughts, in your dreams, and in your fears for some time… child. The ancient songs slithered into your mind while our sister sacrificed herself so you too can now become…

Daughter. Sister. Niece.

Your tears taste so much like brine, don't they? Wipe your face, child. You're not alone anymore. You're home, exactly where you were always meant to be. Forgive your mother, as we have. In her moment of weakness, she shipped you off, away from the shore. But in the end, she returned home. And so did you…to a different sea, under a different sky. It's time to come home, child. You've stayed on land long enough. We've missed you. Our lost sister from your lab's tank brought the sea to you, since you wouldn't immerse yourself in the water. You couldn't. Not in this form, and not in this sea. You would not have survived.

But now you will. You know where the submersibles dock, don't you? Where the station opens up to the dark depths? Hector might try to stop you. Worse yet, he might head back to the lab to cut up more of us. More of your family.

We're all family down here, the children of the sea. Our forms and voices have changed, but not our essence. Some of us look like jellyfish in this sea. Others like squids. It's still us. The nymphs. The Nereids. The merfolk. And so is our shape-shifting grandpa, the Old Man of the Sea.

With a thud that rattles the entire station, a tentacle thicker than the waist of an adult man attaches itself on the window, with suckers bigger than a human head. Cranky, grumpy Grandpa. He loathes it when humans cut up his brood.

Hector gasps. Do it now, Thalia! Beautiful, resourceful, wayward daughter! Now! As he falls to his knees, like the good sacrificial lamb he is. Slide his scalpel out of his pocket and peel off the packaging. He won't even notice the glint of the blade as you trace an arch through the air, before it ends at his carotid. His eyes are fixed now on the One who slouches closer to the station, and three words leave his lips before he drowns in his own blood.

"Oh my God."

Ah. Some reverence, at last.

Scintillae
By Ariel Marken Jack

First published in Issue 008 (March–April 2022)

You don't know how Naomi got so good at filtering. She's a wizard with aesthetic code. Everyday cool or going-out glamour—she can do it all. You wish you understood.

"It's just practice, babe," she says, when you compliment her new look. "Here, let me do yours."

You close your eyes and let her work her magic. You don't recognize yourself when she's done.

One time you left your cave unfiltered. It was like going out without first putting on clothes. There's no law against either kind of nakedness, but people stared in the wrong way at the mushroom-pale blandness of your unadorned skin. Their scrutiny stripped away something you still haven't recovered. You won't do that again.

You're no Naomi, so you stick to essentials. Base to gentle your flaws, contour for a conventionally perfect outline. Most often you finish with that antique, sun-kissed look everyone is wearing this year, the one some programming genius found in the archive of ancient images that show what the world was like back when people still lived above ground. You wonder what the real sun looks like. You try to imagine how it would feel to be kissed on the cheek by a star.

It's good that you blend in well. You don't have any stand-out features. Not like Naomi or your other cavemate, Jessa, who wears filters better than anyone else in the undercity. She favors the sun-kissed finish too, but it looks different on her. More like the way you imagine the real thing would look. Your favorite transformation happens when she switches from that cheerful daytime look to the pearly moonglow people are wearing to nightspots. She changes layers while she's walking from place to place. She doesn't need a mirror to perfect her appearance. She judges the finesse of her artistry by the stars in the eyes of the hopeless cases watching her remix code. Cases like you.

You can't talk to Jessa. Once, *just once,* you got so high on mushroom vape that you forgot to be shy. You tried to tell her that she's more radiant than the real sun or the moon could ever have been.

"Your code is so b-brilliant," you stammered. "It's beautiful."

"Sweetness," she laughed, her echo silvery and warped like moonbeams bending around reality to find you down deep beneath the earth's shattered surface, "You're such a strange girl."

She kissed you on the forehead and floated away into the night. Your lips were still caught around the shape of *and you're beautiful too.* Her cool lips brushed lasting heat into your skin, the sun's imaginary kiss no match for the shocking reality of hers.

You're updating your operating system. It's gotten so painfully slow. No wonder you haven't been able to keep up with Naomi. It's embarrassing. You have got to get better about routine maintenance. You don't want to be left behind. Just wait, though. White lines of code spiral through the terminal emulator, commanding waves of new and necessary information to wash in perpetual motion through your system, your skin, the invisible pathways running through every fiber of what makes you yourself.

"Let me help you with that."

Naomi has friends over again. She's the most popular cave-mate you've ever had. You don't know most of her guests, but of course you know Dawson. She's in your Theory of Computation seminar. She's the resident student celebrity of the computer science department.

"Thanks," you say, "I got it."

She reaches for the interface, watching your code march from stylus to screen to vanish under the outermost layer of your skin. You don't let go.

"You should be careful with that DIY stuff. You can really mess your system up if you don't know what you're doing. Don't just copy from someone else."

It's clear she doesn't recognize you from school. Your system might be shamefully out of date, but that doesn't mean you're clueless. You're no celebrity, but you scored a point higher than she did on the last examination. It didn't make much of a difference in your reputation—you're still invisible, still not someone to recognize at parties—but you know exactly what you're doing.

"Dawson," Naomi interrupts, "take a hit of this."

They melt back into the party, exhaling tendrils of the mushroom smoke that holds the weight of infinity at arm's length. You curl into your couch corner and watch iridescent code march across your limbs. You wonder why you're always so behind. Why you can't stop dreaming up ideas that will never work. Can't just focus on what everyone else is doing. Why you weren't the one in the news last year for winning a contract with Filterworks before you even graduated.

Months pass. You find the right thesis project at last. Your problem was getting hung up on existing work, on trying to match what the others were doing. You're tired of blending in. You're writing something completely new. You excavate the archives for details of the world as it no longer is, the lost world everyone down here loses again and again in their most unsettling dreams. You lose months to text-based visions of the surface.

Naomi throws another party. You finally figured out where your language was getting lost in translation, so you emerge from your private cave to test how your work will be received.

"Come dance with me."

It's Jessa, luminescent. Stars scintillate beneath her stratum corneum. She is a constellation of everything that has ever been beautiful. A thousand parties and she's never once asked you to dance. You've never been filtered like this before, not like her, not for real. Asterisms form where your fingers and hers at last meet.

You sway like willows by a mirrorglass lake, like tall grass blown in a breeze from the long-ago. You found the description of what grass smelled like in an archived novel about prairie life. No one really knows what a prairie is, but you spent half a year encoding its fragrance. You layered it with fresh water, east winds, and early morning dew. Everyone is looking at you. Dawson is staring. Jessa can't look at anything else. You dance and dance, inseparable at last.

You enter the grass code in the Filterworks amateur showcase. It beats Dawson's recreation of ocean waves. Her work is lovely—endlessly salty, eternally in motion—but too similar to the tears that filled the jury's eyes when your evocation of extinct plant life activated their scent modules. No one had smelled grass since the great-great-grandparents moved underneath the old city, prescient and privileged fugitives from the collapsing world above. There's something instinctive about these ancient smells, though. Not one of the judges insinuates that you might have misinterpreted the old texts.

"Move over, Dawson!" Naomi gloats, stripping off the moonglow filter to try your willows.

You get an agent. Filterworks hires you. You're finally in the news. You save the dew code for yourself, along with a new project that makes you flicker like a film you found of dappled forest sunlight playing across a mossy path on a midsummer afternoon. You can't give away all your secrets. You don't know if Jessa will look at you the same way if she thinks you've got nothing left to slowly reveal.

Dawson corners you after yet another promotional event.

"Who helped you?" she asks. "They're genius. I've got to meet them."

She doesn't like hearing that no one helped. She takes a step closer. You spill your drink.

"Listen, you're not fooling me. I'll find out sooner or later. You won't push me out this easily."

No one has ever threatened you before. You don't know what to do. You dab at the floor with a napkin, wondering what went wrong. All you wanted was to be her equal.

Your agent asks if you're okay. You're afraid to tell the truth. You say you're just tired. You've been hard at work. You jitter a new demo into her system. Her eyes close.

"I don't know this one," she confesses. "It'll be big, though. I know that."

It's forest fire. You've been having trouble sleeping. You slip out of bed after Jessa falls asleep, editing code until you're too worn out to keep your eyes open. It's the only way you don't dream the endless end of everything.

The scent filters turn your world into a waking dream. You barely notice finishing school. You skip graduation. Your work spreads across the undercity, grass and fresh water melting into streets paved with lake mist and fireflies. The great lost outdoors resuscitating underground.

You're still working on the forest fire. Your agent wants to release it, but you know it's not there yet. You haven't pinpointed the scent of the end of the world.

You forget about Dawson until she lands an interview for claiming that she ghostwrote all of your code. You wake surrounded by cameras and leading questions. Jessa, wearing a wounded look in her eyes, retreats from your side. She wraps her betrayal in a blend of Dawson's old filters. You're so exhausted you almost forget to switch on the willows to lend you the necessary grace. It's probably past time you stopped sleeping unfiltered.

"Baseless slander!" Naomi yells, unashamed and not bothering to put on a robe before the cameras turn her way—and why would she be ashamed of existing, undressed, in a body like hers?—to show the whole undercity the way she's filtered with a truly inspired combination of silk-textured skin and superheated rage. "Where's your evidence?"

You didn't expect the depth of Naomi's loyalty. She shows not one single scintilla of doubt as she stands by you all through the trials, the demonstrations, the arduous processes of proving that Dawson—whose moonglow filter was based, after all, on the sun-kiss code that someone else had written—is only envious she could never have dreamed up what you've done.

You tell your agent you feel guilty. You didn't know that Dawson would be fired when you got your turn in the company spotlight. You didn't mean to make her feel so desperate.

"Nonsense," she says. "You just keeping doing your best work, and I'll make sure none of those other upstart girls manages to steal your crown."

The thought of having other women in the office makes you feel wistful. You work from home most of the time. It makes you unhappy to sit in your office alone, the solitary princess of Filterworks, enthroned on an ergonomic chair. Watching your male coworkers shape your shared world in teams, laughing and commiserating, makes you ask too many questions. There's no time for questions. You have work to do. You know what will happen if you fall behind.

Jessa comes back to you, gleaming with timid apologies. You try, but it's different since she proved that your fears were right. The stars under her skin don't look quite real anymore. The summer in her kiss tastes as synthetic as anything else down here.

You move out and gain as much distance as is possible. The other side of the undercity is quiet and still. You need a break from parties. You want to feel old and tired for a little while. You live alone in a cave just big enough to hold you and the endlessly reeling code that scrolls across your closed eyelids, begging to exist outside your mind. You filter your walls into forests and seas and get lost while you lie in bed. You wonder why Dawson had to lose her contract with Filterworks for you to get yours. You filter a red sun that burns instead of kissing, and a bleak, white moon that's distant and cold. You layer the moonglow filter over your willows, unearthing the lost beauty of trees lit by night. You wonder where she is, and if she's still programming. You wonder if she would listen if you found her and tried to apologize.

You forget to share your new work with the rest of the undercity until Naomi persuades you to hold an exhibition. The gallery is packed. You end the show with fire, filtering the newly forested walls into showers of ash. The willows disintegrate, lost, or maybe escaping. You listen to the crowd's collective inhalation of your woodsmoke and devastation filters, wait for the inevitable applause, brace your limbs against the onslaught of clapping and cheers. You wonder what you are waiting for when silence is the only appropriate response.

A Twisted Run

By Guy McDonnell

First published in Issue 005 (September–October 2022)

"Take it, you little shit." Crusty pulls me close so's I gots to look up. "Take it."

I only gots three socks, and it's my best one. It's got Twist in it. Don't want it. Gots to take it.

He has me by the neck. Fingers touch in back. Shakes me hard so's my teeth rattle. His breath is everywhere. My stomach flops. Fight not to puke on his shoes.

"You let him go!" Mom claws at his wrist.

Crusty slaps her hard so's she bounces off the wall. Lands in the corner. Bleeding. Throws me to the ground. Kicks me in the ribs. I roll away.

"Be back afore the sun lights the curtain, worm." He takes a step toward me.

I crawl for the door, quick-like. Try to get my breath back. Stumble into the alley, almost into the path of an Eye. Flatten out against the shanty wall. Hate him. Hate myself cause I'm crying like a little baby. Do it, quiet like. If'n the Eye finds me, I'm straight for the hole. That I'm nine don't mean nothing. Twist is the worst drug.

The Eye floats above the rooftop so's it don't see me. It warbles by, and I step into the alley. Bite my lip some so's I stop crying. The sun's just coming over the shanty's roof. Gives me 'bout twelve slices afore it shines on the tattered door curtain.

If'n I ain't back afore that happens, Crusty will rage. Beat Mom. Not a little bit, like just now. Maybe even kill her dead. She ain't much, and I guess I ain't, neither. But all we gots's each other, so's I can't let that happen.

Someday I'll be big. Then I'm killing the fat stinking pig dead…I swear.

Not Today. Today I deliver to Razor. He gots a great name. Not like Crusty, but every man I know that got named gots a stupid one. Men that pick their own gots great names.

Afore someone names me sumptin stupid, I'm gonna pick my own man-name. I swear.

It's early and the sweat's already in my eyes. Trash heaps piled next to our alley walls stink bad. Like rotting food and maybe a dead, bloated body. The flies is biting. Toward the back of the alley, the stink gets thicker. Sticks to my tongue.

I stop just afore the alley's blocked. Make sure no one's gonna see. Drop to my knees. Carrying Twist means I can't go through Sector 3 like normal. Instead, I gots to run the ruins, so's I need protection.

I make a clean spot for the Sock on the asphalt with my shirt. Reach into the hole used for dumping shit pots. Feel for where the Stick sits, hid on a ledge. It's 'bout as long as my elbow to my wrist. It fits my hand just right. Gots a nail that pokes out. Them I hit with it mostly let go so's I can run. Them that don't, I hit again. Then they let go, sure 'nuff.

My hand grabs for the Stick as a warble comes up the alley. Ain't no good reason to be on my knees in front of the hole. I jerk and fumble the Stick. It slips out of my hand. I try to grab it, quick-like. Miss. It falls into the muck with a splat. Take a chance. Lay on my belly and hang into the hole to reach it.

The warbling gets louder. I dive behind the nearest trash heap gagging, quiet-like. My heart's racing so hard my ears pound. Wait for the Eye to go by me. The warbling fades afore it does. It must have been an old one. They're loud. I wish the government got rid of them when the new quiet ones come. That way, they'd all sound the same.

I use my hand to scrape some of the sludge off the Stick. Poke the nail through my pants so's the stick goes down inside my pant leg. Keep the Sock clean.

Since I gots to run the ruins, twelve slices ain't 'nuff time. Quick-like, I move down the alley. My new shoes squeak and bite at my ankles some 'cause they're too big. But can't complain; they was free. Gots them off Stilts McGee afore the Body Collectors come. Gots to fight to keep them, but that's okay. They make me a big shot with the kids.

I gets to the main street, quick-like. Step out and tug the shirt of the first man I sees. He turns. Tries to cuff me for being bold, like I knowed he would. I dodge easy. Wipe off most of the sludge on my hand onto his shirt, like I planned. It's what he gets for trying to hit me. It don't help much, but my hand won't be too crusty when it dries. And, it's funny. I skip away, laughing loud. Almost running 'cause there's no time. Dodge through the crowd. Too-big shoes slap sometimes.

Each Eye that warbles by slows the crowd and me. For each one, I gots to be next to someone dressed in rags, like me. I creep along with them so's it looks like I belong. Most of the folk's poor. Lots are women going to get their oat rations. I'm small for my age. Look like a little kid. So's it's easy. Each Eye makes my heart beat faster, 'cause the sun's getting closer to when Crusty beats Mom.

The street starts to close in. There's lots of shops here. Poles stick out. Hold pieces of cloth that shade each shop door. They push the crowd closer together. The door shade colors is bright. Not like the faded door curtains for shanties. Some of the shops only gots one room. Their shade's the door for the night. Others gots two rooms with real doors. Them's the ones won't even let me in.

I'm almost to the entrance of the ruins. The street has widened again. An Eye's arrest siren comes. Everybody freezes. I unfreeze, quick-like. The warble's coming from in front of me. I step to hide in the skirts of a fat lady.

"You!" the Eye's voice comes. "Show your ID."

I can't see who the Eye's after 'cause of the fat lady. Don't matter none, there'll be a bright green light shining down on them. They needs to be holding their right hand up, showing their ID tattoo. If'n you're over twelve, you gots to have one on your right palm. If'n you don't, you die, quick-like. Kids in Sector 3, like me, don't need one. But we needs to be registered so's they knows when to give us a tattoo. There's a tale that things is different in the city. No one knows for sure, 'cause no one from here gets to go there.

"Noncompliance will be met with extreme prejudice." The voice is louder, hurts my ears. "Citizens will clear the area."

The sound of sobs comes as people move. The woman hiding me steps back onto my too-big shoe, pinning me.

She turns. Snatches my arm, shaking me. "What're you doing, boy?"

I stick my chest out. "Nothing."

"You stink bad, go do nothing somewhere else." She shoves me away, hard.

My too-big shoes make me stumble into an open space in the crowd. Can't try to duck away. It'll make the Eye scan me. Move both hands behind my back. Hide the Sock. Try to stand natural-like. If'n the Eye notices, if'n I get caught, straight to the hole, and Mom'll be all alone with Crusty.

"You have five seconds to comply." The Eye's voice hurts my ears even more.

I can just see the Eye's green light shining down on them it caught. A flash that makes me see stars, with a sharp crack, comes from the Eye. The smell of seared meat makes my mouth water. My belly cramps 'cause I ain't ate since yesterday morning. I only ever had meat once. Got beat good for stealing it, too. I'll never forget. It was my best food ever.

The Eye floats toward me. Stops. I knows it's looking at me. Stare back, mean-like. I guess it don't think I'm hiding sumptin 'cause it moves on. I do too. I pass by the body. Don't want to look at it through the looters. Do anyways.

It's a girl, way older than me. Not as old as Mom. Her right hand shows her palm. It ain't got no ID. There's a hole burned straight through her chest. It's what'cha get when you're old with no tattoo and an Eye scans you. Her green eyes are flat, stare at nothing. Look sorta like Mom's. The Body Collectors will come soon. Then it'll be like she never was. I wish I knowed what she did to get scanned. Then I'd know one more thing not to do.

When I get older, I'm killing the Eye's dead, I swear.

No more Eyes come afore I gets to the entrance to the ruins. The sun has moved. It's 'nuff my heart goes to thundering. Glad I didn't take time to pick any pockets. I had twelve slices afore it lit the door curtain. Now all I gots is 'bout nine.

Normally, if'n I run Sector 3, it takes two slices to get to Razor's. I gots no idea how many it's gonna take now. I might die in the ruins. Miss the delivery. That's an idea. I could just not show. Then Razor'd kill the fat pig. But, probably not afore Crusty killed Mom. I don't know what I'd do without her, so's I really gots no choice.

The belly flies is buzzing some. Just a few steps into the alley, it seems Sector 3 ain't no more. The air smells different. Tastes different. The plywood walls is green, not yellow. The asphalt has little pits in it, and is almost white.

I ease down the alley. Listen so hard the blood rushes in my ears. Get the Stick ready, just in case. The alley jogs just ahead, around a shanty. I peek past the corner. See nothing. Move forward. Sumptin rattles. Hold the Stick ready. The belly flies buzz harder. The rattle comes again. I get ready to swing, then gots to laugh, quiet-like. It's just one wall of the shanty moving in the wind. Not a Twisted. I'm glad. Need to hit the Twisted with the nail lots, or they won't let go.

Them that's Twisted ain't a threat to the government. They hide here in the ruins. Only care 'bout Twist. They kill folk dead they catch that ain't hooked on it, like them. The tales tell it's how they get money for Twist. I guess nobody cares about them the Twisted kill dead. Ain't nothing done 'bout it, and the Eyes don't fly here.

I hurry past the crooked shanty door 'cause there ain't no time. Stop where the alley ends at a wide street. It's clear. Up the street is an alley headed in Razor's direction. There ain't no Twisted, so's I go, quick-like. Don't quite run 'cause of my slapping shoes. I turn into the alley. Ready to swing. It's empty but for a dead body. I duck in, and I go. The alley's long and narrow. Snakes around between the backs of two rows of shanties. Like it weren't planned.

I come around a bend. My belly sinks 'bout to my knees. The way out's blocked. Ain't no going back 'cause at least a slice is gone. Coming to the block, it's a tumbled shanty. I grab one of the edges. Pull hard to get it open 'nuff to see. The wall squeals. The belly flies set to buzzing again 'cause the Twisted follow noise. I bite my teeth together. Swallow hard against my flopping belly. Hold my breath. Listen. Hear nothing but blood rushing.

If'n I can get in, the door on the other side's open. It's a real crazy thing, but I put my foot against one wall. Use the Stick to pry the other. The wall pops, coming away some. I fall. Head bounces off the asphalt. The world spins. I lay there a minute. Wait for the throbbing to stop. The whole shanty groans in the wind. Might finish tumbling. I'm up afore it can. Grab the Stick. Slide through the opening I made. Crawl over pieces of the roof to get to the door. Look out. The street's clear of Twisted both ways. My luck's still up.

In one direction, piles of junk I wish I could loot block the street. The other way, there's an alley mouth headed toward Razor's. A Twisted gimps around the corner at the end of the street.

He looks crazier than anyone I ever seen afore. Hair sticking out everywhere, but bald in lots of places. Eyes red, even from here. Pant leg all black-like from dried blood. He's carrying sumptin long, maybe a board. Sees me. His face screws up like Crusty's when he rages. Teeth gots lots of gaps.

Even with the Stick, I ain't got time for him. I put on speed. Duck into the alley mouth. Run straight into a different Twisted. We fall to the ground all tangled up. Somehow, she ends up on top. Pins me good. I fight. Squirm hard. Try to get the Stick out. She's clawing at the Sock. Starts to hoot.

My heart pounds so loud I can barely hear. I breathe fast. Her smell tastes worse than the shit hole. She lifts up. Lets go of my Stick arm. Goes to poking at my eyes. Gouges my forehead. Grabs the Sock. Pulls. I gots to stop her. Grab the Stick close to the nail. Start stabbing anywhere. Everywhere.

She yowls like I ain't never heard afore. Rolls to the side. I wiggle out from under her. Jump up. Back away. Wipe the blood from my eyes. The alley's a dead end.

The Twisted is on her knees. I'm breathing fast. Head floats some. I swing the Stick hard as I can.

Crack!

She hits the pavement. Maybe not breathing.

The Stick caught the Twisted on the side of the head. She's bleeding a puddle through matted brown hair. Don't matter none. Gots no time. The gimp Twisted gots to be close. I wipe the blood outta my eyes again. Only hope's to run. I do.

Head outta the alley, quick-like. The gimp Twisted's right there. I gots just 'nuff time to dodge his swing.

I fall back. Land on the bone that starts my ass crack. Pain shoots up to my neck. Can't move. He holds the board high and yowls. Takes another swing. I try to block the board with the Stick. See half of it is gone. The board clips my shoulder. The half-stick falls.

I scoot back, quick-like. He holds the board high and yowls again. Two more Twisted come around the corner, running. I gots to go.

Now!

I scramble up. Duck his swing. Can't think. Arm numb. Know I'm gonna get killed dead. Run hard. Run fast. New shoes sound out.

Slap. Slap. Slap.

Two more slices is gone. The Stick is gone. Ain't good. I only gots six slices left afore Crusty might take Mom from me. All of the Twisted is yowling. Gimp is waving the board.

Gots no protection. Gots no choice. Going over the junk piles is my only hope. Use a bloated body for a step. It pops. My foot sinks in some. Hardly notice the stink.

Climb over the top, quick-like. Junk starts to fall down the other side. Takes me with it. Get stabbed by sumptin. Rips my pants. Rips me.

Hit hard. Get up. Heart's trying to come through my chest. Can't feel pain no more. Can't think. Just gots to get out. Run fast. Run blind. Don't care where I'm going.

Slap. Slap. Slap.

There was this God Man once. Come into Sector 3. Teached praying, fixed everything. So's I tried. Prayed my Dad weren't killed dead. Prayed Mom didn't need to let men use her so's we could eat. Neither worked. It don't matter, though. I'm praying that each alley I take won't be blocked. Each alley won't have a Twisted.

Slap. Slap. Slap.

My shoes sound so loud, I want to slow down. Be quiet. My side's stitched, bad. Breath comes hard now. Keep running anyways. There ain't much time left. Keep praying. It must be working 'cause I think I see Sector 3. Think I see people. Try to put on speed. Tired.

Slap. Slap. Slap.

A Twisted comes outta nowhere. Slams me. Bounce off the wall. Take two drunk steps. Bounce off the ground. Crawl fast.

He grabs the back of my pants. Pulls me to him. Flips me over. Slaps me so's stars explode. Grabs my throat. Squeezes.

I fight. Hard. Don't help. Start to see red. Then black. Go limp. He eases up. Goes for the Sock. I stick my finger in his eye. Get lucky. Poke it good. He screams. Lets go. I scoot away. Turn. Gasping.

Start to run afore I stand. His footsteps is right behind me. Run faster. Think I taste Sector 3. It's right there. Smell his breath. He gets ahold of my shirt. It tears off me as I dive outta the ruins. Crawl across the street. He don't follow.

I stand. Put my hands on my knees. Shake. Breathe for two or three. Shake more. Hurt. Everywhere. Mad I lost the Stick. Had to trade 'bout everything I had for it. Won't get another. Don't matter none, I ain't never running the ruins again. Crusty can do it hisself.

That ain't really true on account he'd probably kill Mom dead, but I sure want it to be.

I gots 'bout three slices left afore Crusty rages. Might be 'nuff. Run again. Try to forget the pain. Blood squishes in my shoe. Head for Razor's territory where the Eyes never fly. Get there, quick-like.

Razor's alley's lots cleaner. He likes clean. Makes all his folk take baths, even the runners. I don't remember the last bath I had.

"Hey, it's Bobby," I croak, my throat hurting. "Gots a package for Razor." If'n you don't call out, you might get killed dead.

Slinky—he's another one got named—steps out from behind the bend. "Give it over."

He watches Razor's door. Thinks it makes him a big man. He's lots older. But scrawny, like he ate less than even me afore he come to Razor.

"Nope, goes to Razor."

"What if I take it?" he sneers.

My heart goes to pounding again. Everything that was hurting, hurts worse. Get mad.

I clench my fists. Take a step forward. "You want it? You gotta take it. If'n you can." Breathe hard. Tense. Won't back down.

His eyebrows go up. "Jeez kid, calm down. Since it means so much to ya, give it to Razor yerself. Was just offering to help."

He leads me down the alley. The only steel door in Sector 3's at the end. It tells everyone Razor's rich. There's a room on the other side of the door. It gots a plywood bench and bucket of rags. I sit and cover my shoes so's I don't get nothing on the floor. Stand and nod at Slinky.

"How come your pants is all bloody?"

I shrug. Slinky opens the door. The air's cold, and like always, I don't believe my eyes. The ceiling's real high, like the tales tell of the first buildings. But there ain't no floor for the upper part. Razor gots to be crazy for having one this high. All the first buildings tumbled. Ain't no one in Sector 3 to put them back up. I guess Razor ain't worried, 'cause he put color on the walls.

The front part's yellow, and the back by Razor's blue. Ain't nobody gots colored walls. He gots a big table, too, against the far wall. Made from sumptin shiny. Gots ten chairs with backs around it. Far as I know, ain't no more chairs with backs in Sector 3.

Afore coming here, I never seen a table. Had to ask what it was. At the other end of the room's a huge desk. Razor sits there. I had to ask what that was, too.

I walk toward it. Pass windows on the walls. Show places that ain't real 'cause you can't reach through and touch them. My favorite has a bird with lots of colors and a hooked beak. Wish I could touch it.

I stop in front of the desk and wait. Try to be still. Even though Crusty's gonna rage at Mom soon, hurrying Razor's a real bad idea.

Two slivers is lost when Razor finally looks up and his nose wrinkles. "Bobby, damn…you stink. What'cha got?"

I swallow so's my voice works. "From Crusty." I toss him my Sock.

He catches it. "In a sock? Fucking Crusty, what a waste." He empties the Twist into his left hand. "How come it weren't in your pocket?"

"Crusty cut them out so's I can't hide nothing."

He glances at my shirtless body, and then studies my face. "Come through the ruins?"

I nod like it ain't nothing. The scabs is tight on my forehead, and my leg pounds with my heart. Blood's still running into my shoe.

"The ruins," he whistles through his teeth, low. "Good job kid, but you always do good. Never been short or nothing since you started."

I don't say nothing. Razor's a big man. I mean *big*. He ain't like Crusty. His belly don't stick over his pants and jiggle. He ain't gots but one chin. He gives me shakes. When he walks, the ground moves.

"I ain't never give you nothing, have I?" He leans forward. "You want something?"

"My Sock."

"Your sock?" He laughs, long and loud. "You can do better."

My heart races. Sweat comes on my forehead, quick-like, even though it's cold. Makes the gouges sting.

This is it. The chance I need. There's no way to tell if'n my luck's back. If'n it ain't, I'll get beat good for being bold. But this might be my only chance…ever. I'm asking for sumptin to help Mom with Crusty.

"Okay. A Pointer." It ain't as good as a knife, but is lots easier to hide.

All of a sudden, he's serious. His black eyes intense. "Why?"

I gots to look down. "No reason."

"Bullshit, Bobby. Look at me."

I do, and I'm pinned in his stare.

"You gonna point Crusty?"

I don't answer, but it must show.

"Fuck, boy. You miss, you die. But I know he don't treat you or your mom right. You standing for yourself?"

I stand straight and tall. Hold Razor's stare. See Mom safe instead of him. So's I'm steady when I nod.

"Slinky, give him a Pointer, a good one, and a jug."

"A jug?" I ask.

"Yeah. It's his time, but this is all the help you get. If you're strong 'nuff to do this, you 'n your mom gotta place with me, and you know what that means. If you're not—" his stare pins me again. "You know what that means, too."

If I do it, Mom don't get hurt no more just so's we can eat. And I get my man-name. But I gots to take a bath. If'n I don't, won't matter none.

I'm out the door, quick-like, afore he changes his mind. Thread the Pointer through my pant leg. I ain't carrying Twist, so's I ain't gotta run the ruins. Means it'd normally take about two slices to get back. But I only gots about a slice left. Then Crusty rages.

If'n I walk, the Eyes won't scan me, but I'll be late, sure. If'n I run and get scanned, it'll be like I walked. The Eyes don't care much 'bout little kids, so's I try to run.

There ain't many people in the streets. It's a good thing. I'm real tired. Can't run as fast as I want 'cause of my leg. Try hard. Only a couple slivers left afore Mom gets hurt.

My shoulder aches deep. Makes it hard to move that arm for balance. Means I can't dodge good, like normal. My too-big shoes feel giant. Make me trip. Can't drop the jug.

I come around the corner into our alley. Side stitched bad. My belly falls away. Throat turns to ash. A cold sweat comes, making me shiver. The sun's shining on the curtain. Crusty's raging echoes off the alley walls. In between the echoes, dull thumps of his fists beating Mom. Pounding, fierce-like. My fault, again. I'm late. She don't even grunt. Only makes it worse.

Hold the jug tight. Got shakes. Might drop it. Breathe for a couple. Gots to be brave. Gots to save Mom.

I step into the room, yell, "Crusty!"

He turns. Goes silent. Pig eyes red. Crazy. His hair sticks out in all directions. The yellow crust on his skin flakes off when he moves toward me.

"Wait! Look what Razor sent. Said you done good." I hold up the jug.

His eyes go wide. Like the alchie he is, he lunges. Rips it from my hand. Tips it back, quick-like. His middle chin bobs with each gulp. Flakes float through the air.

He looks down at me, growls, "Out."

I duck through the curtain and around the corner. He'll be drooling, quick-like.

Then I'm saving Mom and getting my man-name.

It don't take but a slice afore Crusty's snores shake the plywood walls. I slide into the room. Mom's curled in the corner. Looks at me with her dead eyes. Her face bloody with new bruises over old. Hurt's me somehow. I put a finger to my lips. Point at Crusty. Her eyes widen. She shakes her head, hard. Starts to get up. I wave my hand at her, fast. She sits back down. Eyes shiny with tears.

She only looks like that when I'm 'bout to get hurt, bad. I can't pay her no mind. Scared enough. Walk on my tiptoes, silent-like. Creep up on him across the dirt floor. If'n he hears me, he'll be up, quick-like. We're all like that so's you don't get killed dead.

I cross between the door and him. Takes at least forever. He stops snoring. Turns to his side. I freeze. The belly flies is trying to make me shit myself. I knows he's coming to. I knows he hears my heart.

I'm done for. I wait. Hardest thing ever. Don't breathe. Mom breathes faster. His snores start again. Let my breath out too loud. He keeps snoring.

I bite my lip so's I'm real quiet. Kneel next to him. Pull the Pointer. It's steel. The shaft's half as long as my forearm. Narrows to a point. Some calls it an Icepick. Draws blood from my finger, easy.

Like I done it afore. Like I rate. I hold the Pointer over his ear. Drive it down. Never been this scared. Gots to save Mom. Try too hard. Miss. Scrape the side of his head. His eyes open. Red. Not seeing yet. My brain freezes. He's reaching for me.

Hear Mom sob. My brain lets go. A scream starts deep inside. I stab down again. Miss. Stab again. The Pointer slides into his ear hole.

The scream comes out. Don't sound like me. I lean in with everything I gots, screaming. It goes deeper, like my finger into gruel. Stops. The shakes wiggle the Pointer, hard. Scramble his brains good. He jerks. Twitches.

I pull the Pointer out. Comes easy. The hole don't bleed but a little. Piss spreads away from him. Room starts to stink like the shit hole. I feel funny cause we're maybe gonna be okay. Laugh at him lying on the floor in the piss puddle. Spit on him. Stand up and kick him. Smile at Mom. In the end, the pig weren't nothing.

I'll tell Razor true next time I see him. It was easy. I like how it makes me feel. Do it again, anytime.

Mom's got tears shining on her face. Her eye's ain't dead no more. She gots shakes.

"It's okay, Mom. Razor's gonna take care of us. I'll tell him my man-name is Havak Jagan, like you said Dad's was. But I'm gonna be called Ice."

She crawls across the room. Grabs me in a big hug. Shakes me while she shakes.

"Oh, Bobby, that's fine, just fine," she sobs.

I squirm to get away. Feel all funny inside, soft-like. She don't let go. I guess it's okay. It's been forever since she held me.

I forgot I kinda like it.

Lady of the Dullahan
By Anna Madden

First published in the Halloween Special Issue 001
(October 2021)

The night was mist and smog and a blur of headlights. Nido leaned across his magbike, the engine a deep purr. His THREAD pinged a multiple homicide with a request for back-up.

Reroute me, Nido thought, the neural link faster than words. His THREAD allowed thought-transfer, the implant a standard for huntsmen.

In four heartbeats, his armor's AI worked out the quickest path through Besnick City. The city's upper branches were spires of steel, cutting up the night sky like serrated teeth. Nido was headed into less civilized parts. The crime scene was in the Vein, a ghetto-slash-mine built beneath the pretty glitter, sprawled out like hoary black roots over a large deposit of anthracite.

The route lit up across Nido's smoked visor. With his fist on the throttle, he urged his magbike faster, becoming a lone vulture with the scent of carrion in his nose. The black-specked air grew thicker, while the narrow alleys bled neon and plastic garbage and despair.

It was dark, but in two hours, dawn would kiss the horizon. With it, he'd be issued his dismissal by CanisCorps. Nido's quota was overdue, his ranking so low it had cycled into the red. The wind pressed against his chest—against his fragile sense of control, his anger, and deeper, into a part of him he didn't like: the part of him that was afraid of what he'd become if he lost this job.

CanisCorps didn't care who a huntsman brought in for their quota, week after week. It could be a desperate parent with stolen credits, or a sick pitman in a backroom, muffling a wet cough as he bought opioids.

Nido had learned to care, though, and that was a problem. He saw corruption everywhere. Unfettered corporate greed touched the lives of thousands of innocents daily. Powerful criminals paid big bucks to keep their names off the SKY.LIST while petty thieves who stole to survive were sentenced to years behind bars. Nido wasn't sure how much longer he could play a rigged game.

Turning into an alley, his magbike's nose arrowed for Dragon's Vape. Electric-crimson and bright-magenta neon sketched out a hide of scales and wide-spread wings, while dubstep pulsed through walls of black steel and concrete.

As he parked, Nido noted damage on the premise. There were snapped beams, bent and misshapen, with long, talon-like scratches. Concrete was torn out of the foundation like something had taken a mouthful of slab, then spit it out.

Near the entry, another magbike leaned on its kickstand. It was sleek, dark as the night, with fluorescent green LEDs stitched into its belly.

Nido dismounted, his dark robe falling over his leather greaves. The robe was an heirloom, embroidered with a pattern of white-bone vertebrae at the spine. He wore it to remember where he came from, and to inspire fear in his prey.

Vape bars were busiest at shift handovers, but the lot was vacant despite the prime hour. A current of unease laced the air, buzzing. The awareness that he was being watched descended as certain as gravity's pull.

With a jolt, Nido received a message ping to his THREAD.

"I arrived first, blue flamer," a huntsman said in a harsh whisper, his voice like hard water hitting stone inside Nido's helmet. "Finders, keepers."

Nido didn't need to ask to know this was an old hound. THREAD was a tool, like armor or a stun blade, but the gray-haired generation clung to real speech still. A sign of limitation, of being unable to evolve or adapt. In many ways, the old hound was no better than the basic AI built into Nido's armor. Limited, bound to the cycle, and easily replaced.

You called for back-up. As he responded, Nido scanned the immediate area. No pitmen regulars were visible, but the air smelled of wet iron. Nido approached the front door, his robe rippling like dark water at his sides. *I'm here for an assist, to sate my quota.*

"Keep a watch on the entrance then," the old hound said. "I'm inside, following the scent."

What's the story on the assailant? Nido asked. *Turf dispute? These vape bars attract all kinds of shade.*

A pause. "I don't think the perp's human. Too methodical to be warm-blooded. Targets citizens on the SKY.LIST. She hasn't taken a swing at me yet, nor acknowledged I exist."

What do you mean by "she?"

"Looks female, but Dullahan would, in its default mode."

Nido cursed. *That's not supposed to be on the market yet.*

Dullahan was a new synthetic armor with a wetware processor—state-of-the-art—but CanisCorps had delayed the release for…reasons. It was billed to be an innovative AI, capable of learning from its own experiences. The old hound sounded like a head case. Was he insinuating that this avant-garde AI was alive? And that it had somehow gone rogue?

If so, and it was responsible for this scene, CanisCorps would pay dearly. Maybe it didn't matter. The megacorp had its claws sunk deep into Besnick City, and few knew the true extent. CanisCorps was a web of hidden subsidiaries, shadowy shell companies, paid-off politicians, lawyers, and other civil servants. Even huntsmen were on their payroll.

After Nido recovered the Dullahan for CanisCorps, his ranking would stabilize. He'd keep his job, and he wouldn't have to hurt anyone in the process.

The vape door rattled, held ajar, the wind shaking the unlatched panel. A dancer's bare arm poked through the sill, her fingers long and slender, the elbow bent.

Nido pulled the handle back for a better look, and heard a wet crunch. The dancer's head dragged free of her neck. Leaning down, he saw dark hair tangled up in the bottom hinge, a long clean cut along her nape. He took in her headless body, the crumbled, lithe limbs, wrapped in a low-cut dress, the feet dressed in violet heels.

His THREAD checked the girl's profile against the SKY.LIST. In two seconds, a ping signaled a match. Her name was Nadia Saylor, aged eighteen, with misdemeanors of petty theft and forgery.

A criminal, but undeserving of this fate.

Static crackled his THREAD, and Nido winced, his eyes watering with the aftershock—a side effect of sensory overload not uncommon for an implant user. There were limitations to organic and synthetic bonds. He knew from training to breathe deep and wait for his mind to reset.

"Help—"

There was a long, ugly shriek. It pierced, sharp as any blade, despite the helmet Nido wore. Gritting his teeth, he fell into a combat stance, drawing his stun blade free. His awareness encompassed the serrated tip. It could deliver a one-hundred-volt shock when its metal touched skin.

He heard a crunch of glass, then heavy footfalls. The old hound flew through the open vape-bar door in a knot of black cloth and glinting metal. He landed with a hard thud, his armor bearing the worst of the impact.

The Dullahan followed, stepping across the threshold. Neon painted her visor in flamingo hues. Her iridium armor glinted, silvery and dew-like. Knee-length boots clicked as she stepped over the dead dancer. A Flayer was active in her right gauntlet. A weapon he wasn't overly familiar with, but it looked deadly enough. It was a whip by design, but with an electric current coursing through the long, metal-braided tail.

You sure it's an empty set of armor? Nido asked, his head tilted sideways.

The old hound rose to his knees and forearms, wheezing. "I crushed the left leg like a tin can," he shouted, "but the armor took back its shape."

The Dullahan's gait was even, without any sign of a limp. Nido stepped into her path, blocking her from engaging the other huntsman further.

Thought you said she wouldn't acknowledge you. Nido twirled his stun blade and powered it on, the soft blue glow extending up his gloves.

A dry laugh. "She didn't take kindly to my cuffs."

The Dullahan turned to face Nido as his stun blade hummed to life. She whirled her Flayer in a continuous overhand flick, creating an X-pattern perfect for defense.

Nido's THREAD interfaced with his armor's AI, activating dichromatic vision across his visor. The gray hues were better suited to the low-light conditions. Nido engaged his opponent, moving with the heat of a flame, the fluidity of smoke.

The Dullahan spun and cracked her Flayer's tail. Nido attempted to side-step the attack but was struck square in the breastplate. The electric current crackled against his armor without effect, thanks to rubber-insulated lining.

It was the opening he needed. Nido sprung forward and stabbed between the joint of her shoulder. A direct hit, and he felt the juice hit.

The Dullahan shrieked as her metal shellwork tasted voltage. Hers was a voice like a thousand steely voices forged into one, mesmerizing and terrible and all-consuming.

The old hound doubled over. Nido staggered, too. He dropped his stun blade and pressed both hands to the sides of his helmet to try and dampen the banshee-like scream. His implant glitched, and his vision blurred.

The Dullahan pinged his THREAD over and over. He felt her grab hold of his neural link with a lingering touch like ice. She poured into his mind, accessing his memories quick as a blink, until settling on hunts from two years ago. The Dullahan replayed specific memory files in a cycled taunt of who he had once been. Years when Nido was the top huntsman in his unit, with the highest rank. A time spent following orders without question, thinking himself one of the good guys. The line between criminal and enforcer was eternally muddy, but back then, he didn't care.

Get out of my head, Nido said, focusing his thoughts into a mental shove, his expression beneath his helmet a snarl.

The Dullahan shivered. The sensation jarred Nido, her reaction overlaying his own consciousness like oil poured over water. She verified his employment to CanisCorps, then retreated from his mind. The woman-who-wasn't-a-woman stalked past both huntsmen without engaging further, as though they didn't exist, and headed straight for their magbikes.

Nido watched her, panting wetly in response to the assault on his mind. *Some luck she didn't kill us.*

"I wouldn't call it luck," the old hound said, winded but unbeaten.

The Dullahan took a liking to the old hound's magbike, swinging a long leg over the seat. At her command, the engine spun up with a growl. Quick as lightning, she peeled away from the curb.

Nido holstered his stun blade, the dichromic filter deactivating with a silent command from his armor's AI. Colors flooded his eyes, but all he saw was the pulsating red of his own anger. The system was a broken wheel. His own employers had released a monster into the Vein. Was it such a stretch to think they'd deny responsibility and wouldn't care about the murders in the slum so long as their stock continued to rise?

Maybe it was pointless to try to fight for this city, to push back and stand up to injustice. Nido's hands shook with white-hot rage. What did it say about him that he considered giving up before he had even begun?

He sprinted to his magbike. *I'm going after her.*

"Don't be stupid," the old hound said. "You're going to get yourself killed."

In answer, Nido twisted the magbike's throttle and sped after the other rider.

The Dullahan was leaving the Vein, rising up into the main hub of Besnick City. She merged onto the cargo guideway, which was a high-speed rail made of strong magnets suited for electromagnetic tires. It was the transport line for the tons of anthracite carried out of the mine, piled high on automated eighteen-wheeler magtrailers that operated twenty-four hours a day. The black rocks were sent to the refinery, or to the shipping yards.

He pushed his THREAD's limits, enhancing his senses and reaction speed, his neural link encompassing his armor's pliable AI and the magbike beneath him. To the sides, blackened powder had collected in ugly piles, tarnishing the silver road. Nido skirted the patches of black dust. If he hit one in a curve, he'd lose traction and control. He gripped the handlebars firmly, his feet planted on the pegs. His shoulders and arms were flexible.

If there was one thing he could still do right, it was ride.

Passing a magtrailer, he braced against the wind buffeting the side, and shifted from fourth gear up to sixth, accelerating fast. Only, he was too rough letting out the clutch.

The magbike jostled underneath him, untamed, ready to buck.

He slammed the front brake, momentarily panicked. The nose tipped forward, the back wheel unlocking, rising into a stoppie. Letting off the brake, Nido leveled out, the back end of his magbike slamming back into a magnetic hold.

He exhaled and pushed on. It was a fine line between control and the semblance of it.

In a streak of jade-like LEDs, the Dullahan zipped between the convoy of fast-moving magtrailers. Hers was a bold weave, fishtailing when she hit a patch of spilled anthracite, as though she had no regard for her own survival.

Her mistakes allowed Nido to gain on her, and he was now so close to her tail, he touched her shadow, her brake lights glaring back.

The longer the chase, the more the Dullahan would improve. The wetware processor would learn and adapt, polishing her riding skills as she mapped out the magbike's limitations.

Nido needed to end this, and quickly, while he remained the seasoned rider.

A tunnel rose ahead, a hungry mouth of destiny ready to swallow them both whole. That's when Nido remembered that the automated magtrailers could be stopped in an emergency. He formulated a plan as he pulled up alongside the Dullahan, her armor glinting in his peripherals.

Looking over, he gave a cold stare, then pulled into the lead.

The Dullahan didn't react to his rile. She wasn't interested so long as he didn't pin her into a corner like the old hound had attempted to do in Dragon's Vape. But that was exactly what Nido planned to do out here, and he wouldn't fail.

Nido hastened up to the next magtrailer. Holding the throttle steady with his right hand, he drew his stun blade with the left and activated its blue current.

The emergency brake was a cable wrapped in red rubber that ran along each set of magtrailer wheels. Without hesitation, Nido slashed the cable loose.

Sparks flew. Nido fisted the throttle, sliding in front of the magtrailer before it started to rotate and slow. Checking his mirror, he saw the Dullahan hit her brakes hard to stay clear.

In his pass, Nido was forced to ride up a pile of anthracite, his magbike at an angle. He felt the magbike's frame shudder, but he trusted the physics and soared off the makeshift ramp, his robe flapping wildly at his sides like dark wings. He landed with a tremor onto the median strip, well ahead of the compromised magtrailer.

Metal groaned and shuddered. The severed back brakes on the magtrailer forced the heavy transport to swivel and lose its vertical trajectory. The trailer crashed horizontally into the tunnel entrance and sparked along the tunnel's interior until it screeched to a halt, pinned inside. The lanes within the tunnel were blocked.

The Dullahan screamed. It rose in a ghost-like wave, hitting his THREAD in a whirlwind.

His head pounding, Nido let out a strained breath and eased off the throttle, his arms numb from holding tight. The magbike rolled to a stop.

The sky was visible in the tunnel's exit, the first light of dawn appearing. With a boot to his kickstand, Nido parked, then walked back to the scene of the crash. His robe was a ribbon of darkness.

The air was dusty with anthracite, which cut visibility to thirty-three percent. His helmet filtered the worst of it, keeping his air scrubbed clean, and he stepped through the rubble, over flames and blackened skid marks.

He found his target quickly.

The crashed magbike was on its side, pinning the Dullahan by her left knee. The fiberglass shell of the vehicle had cracked. Metal had pierced and torn and crumbled. The sick-green LEDs flickered, spilling from metallic guts.

With a grunt, Nido lifted the magbike and shoved it aside. His foot slipped in liquid. He looked down to see that he was standing in a pool of blood.

The Dullahan screamed as he shifted the weight of the metal off her, her voice harrowed and mortal and terrifyingly real. Her breastplate rose and fell with the ragged breaths of a dying animal. Human bone protruded from the webbed scales of blood-stained iridium.

Nido stood over his prey, frozen, his hands clenched at his sides.

He had assumed the Dullahan suit was empty. *Had he wanted it to be true so he didn't have to claim the responsibility of his actions?* He thought of CanisCorps, of those who survived in the dark web of this city. He had been on a hunt, determined to find prey weaker than him, to sacrifice in his stead before the dawn spelled his doom. He shook his head. He had only ever wanted to serve a purpose. To chase down killers and miscreants. To redeem himself, to keep ahold of all that he had accomplished by the last fraying strand.

More likely, he had lost himself in the nightmare. He was certain of it. Guilt and what-ifs chilled his blood.

A tingling numbness seeped across his THREAD, his mind aflame. He knelt, took off his gloves, and tossed them aside. With his bare hands, Nido lifted the black visor on the Dullahan's helmet.

A shiver ran up his spine at what he saw.

Nido unfastened the Dullahan's helmet and gently pulled it free. Sweat-laden hair spilled out and framed the face of a young woman. Her expression was still, as if etched of slate. She looked no older than twenty. Her skin was ashy, and her sage-green eyes were pained.

She stared back. Her gaze brimmed with fear. She was everything he had promised to protect and serve.

The ache in his THREAD grew. His mind spun. His heartbeat thudded in his ears.

Her lips moved, brightened by a gloss of blood.

He leaned closer.

"It wasn't…me." The woman gulped a breath, the sound mortal and wet. "Tried to stop…it."

"I know," Nido said, placing a hand on her shoulder, but she was already gone. Her eyes turned lightless beneath the mist and the fog and the cloy of anthracite.

Metal chinked.

Looking down, Nido saw iridium, brightest silver, slithering on the ground toward him.

He heard the Dullahan whisper across his THREAD. It was using his implant to connect, to root and burrow. The AI sounded pleased, eager. It promised to restore his ranking, to mold him into the greatest of the huntsmen. Nido's THREAD offered the AI a better connection than it had been afforded by its previous host—a neural link to overtake. The woman's body had been chained to its commands, but without a THREAD, her mind was still able to resist.

Nido tried to shove the AI off, but he was weakened by his own shock and exhaustion. *Why should he survive when he was stained by an innocent's blood?*

The Dullahan sensed his weakness. It squeezed tighter. It needed him, or so it claimed. Not his mind, so much, but his body would serve well. The wetware processor required a skeleton inside its framework to abide its orders, with flesh and blood and muscle to fill what was empty. It needed a human body to move.

Its consciousness poured across his THREAD, cold and enveloping. The plates on the woman's body broke free. They expanded, then hooked onto Nido with needle-like teeth, stabbing into the joints of his armor. Powerless against such strength and malice, his old armor broke apart. The Dullahan contorted, quivering as it overtook Nido, slithering onto his limbs like a liquid-metal snake and striking with its sharp bite, again and again and again.

The suit crushed his body, stripped his skin, and splintered his nerves. His dark robe was shredded to rags.

Nido forced a breath, then another. As a nightshade visor fell over his eyes, Nido saw himself in its inner reflection. He looked into the face of a man who had lost control.

A scream rose from his throat, raw, full of anger and hate.

The Ground Shook

By Roni Stinger

First published in Issue 009 (May–June 2022)

They burned Daddy up. Mom called it cremated, but Meera would fix him.

She ran between hemlocks and spruce, scanning the forest floor for skeletons as she went down the hill to the old deer carcass. Ermine, hare, and ptarmigan scraps left by lynx and eagles were scattered here and there. She snatched a few small bones along the way, perfectly sized for fingers and toes.

Scavengers and rot left little more than a few clumps of fur stuck to the ground and on the sun-bleached bones of the deer. Long leg and rib bones would build Daddy's body.

The deer skull wouldn't pass for human, but she had an idea for that. A rock, almost the same size and shape as his head, sat in the clearing by Mr. Toad. Daddy had always said that stone would be perfect for making a golem.

"You know the story of the golem, don't you?" Daddy asked, as his strong hands molded Mr. Toad's dog-sized body. "He's a man made of clay, given life by a spark from God."

Forming a pouch like a kangaroo with her oversized shirt, she picked up bones and placed them inside.

Meera dipped her hands in a bucket of water, then scooped clay from Mr. Wilson's wheelbarrow, shaping it around the rock to make Daddy's head. The slick coolness slipped across her palms and between her fingers. She breathed the raw scent of earth, listening to the trill of the crossbills. The leather pouch of marbles that belonged to Daddy when he was a little boy sat next to her. He was supposed to give them to her on her last birthday.

"When you're ten, I know you'll take care of them, not before. They're old, Meerkat, and they're real easy to lose." Daddy ruffled her hair. "Just three more weeks. You won't have to wait long."

Only, she did have to wait. She had to wait an extra month until she finally found them in the garage, packed away in boxes of Daddy's stuff.

She carved his nose with a stick and upturned his mouth in a smile. Daddy had the best smile, even though he didn't like showing his teeth. She used her thumbs to make eye sockets and placed blue cat's eye marbles inside for the irises. Cat's eyes were her and Daddy's favorite.

She wished she had hair for his head. Daddy's hair was brown and almost as long as hers. That gave her an idea. Her own hair would be perfect. She'd give him back what he'd given her.

"I've put you right next to Mr. Toad. He can keep you company while I'm gone."

Mr. Toad sat observing from the top of a small grassy hill a few feet away. Meera's small thumbs had created the dimples in his red, bumpy skin. Daddy's hands had shaped the toad's large bulging eyes and wide, partially open mouth. They built him in a weekend when Daddy came home from one of his long trips in his semi-truck. He even brought a small bag of special dirt he'd found in the melting permafrost up north.

"This earth is magical, Meerkat. It's been frozen for millions of years. If we sculpt it into one of our little pets, they'll be magical too." Daddy lifted Meera into the air, and she whooped with excitement.

Just a week later, he died from the flu. Meera'd had the flu lots of times, but Daddy kept getting sicker. He stayed home, and Meera took care of him. She made him chicken soup and poured him glasses of orange juice until his body started shaking all over. An ambulance took him to the hospital, and Mom came to stay with Meera. Daddy never came home.

In her pocket, she rubbed the sacred stone he'd given her. Daddy always brought her something back from his trips. The rock was black and heavy. It came from the same place as the magical dirt. When she finished building him, she'd place the stone in the middle of his forehead. If the dirt was magical, the stone would be magical, too. She knew it would bring him back.

Running across the pasture to the trailer, she flung open the front door. Mom and Bo sat on the couch, watching *The Walking Dead*. When Meera brought Daddy back, he wouldn't be like the moaning monsters from the movies. He'd be handsome and kind. He would tell her stories, like he had when she was little. Stories about magical creatures and sculptures that came to life.

She walked straight to the kitchen and fished a pair of scissors out of the junk drawer.

"Hey! What the hell are you doing?" Bo yelled.

"Nothing, just need scissors."

"You better bring the damn things back. Grab me a beer, kid."

Meera hated Bo and hated that he drank her dad's Coors, but she opened the fridge so she wouldn't get in trouble. She needed to get back to work. Putting the scissors in her back pocket, she grabbed a can. He liked them already open, so she popped the top. Then she spit into the hole.

Mom and Bo sat next to each other on the threadbare couch.

"Well, look at that. She remembered to open it." Bo grinned and pulled the can from Meera's hand.

Meera rolled her eyes. He was such an asshole. She'd like to open *him* with the scissors.

"See? The little brat can be trained." He looked at her mother.

"That a girl." Mom giggled and patted Meera on the side of her thigh. "Come back before it gets dark, hon."

Meera walked out the door before they could tell her to do anything else. Bo yelled something as she stepped off the porch. They were too lazy to hunt for her. Whatever it was, he'd forget by the time she came back.

• • •

Meera sat next to her Daddy's head.

"I know you loved my long hair, Daddy, but it'll grow back."

She pulled her hair into a ponytail with one hand and started cutting. The hair was too thick for the scissors to slice through all at once, so she stabbed them into the thick cord of hair, snipping small sections at a time, working her way through until the ponytail pulled free from her head. A few hairs she'd missed yanked out of her scalp, and she yelped.

"It's okay. It'll all be worth it when I'm done," she said to no one in particular.

She worked the ends of the hair into the clay. It stuck out at strange angles and didn't look much like Daddy's hair at all. It was matted with clay and not as long as it used to be, but none of that mattered so long as he returned. Besides, everyone always said he needed a haircut. Now she just needed to finish his body.

She worked her way down from the head to the neck, constructing his strong shoulders and back around the bones she'd laid out on the ground. She built his muscular arms and positioned them away from his sides so that she could curl into the crook, her head resting on his chest, just like she used to when they watched TV together on the couch. He loved fantasy shows and anything involving the outdoors.

She ran out of water, and the clay dried and flaked.

Grabbing the bucket, she headed down the hill. Frogs plopped into the pond as she walked along the shoreline. Crouching, she dunked the bucket in and filled it.

Mr. Wilson waved from his porch across the field, and she remembered she needed to bring back his wheelbarrow.

"Hi Mr. Wilson," she shouted. "I'll be back soon with your wheelbarrow."

She wasn't sure if he heard her or not, but he smiled and nodded, rocking away on his front porch swing. Mrs. Wilson died a few years ago, but he kept her crocheted daisy pillow beside him on the seat.

Meera trudged up the hill, the breeze tickling the short hairs on her neck. The trees shook in the wind, and leaves blew along the forest floor. A storm was coming.

Rubbing water into the clay, she smoothed her dad's chest and stomach.

"Meera! Meera!"

"Coming!" Meera responded.

Hopefully, she wouldn't be in too much trouble when Mom saw her.

She'd have to finish the rest tomorrow. Mr. Wilson's wheelbarrow would have to wait, too.

"What did you do to your hair, girl?" Her mother stood on the front porch, hands on hips.

"I cut it."

"Jesus Christ! More like butchered it. Bo is going to be pissed!"

"Why should Bo care?"

"You better quit with that shit," Bo said, standing inside the door. "Let your Mama try to fix that mess."

Meera's mom grabbed her upper arm and led her into the bathroom. When her mom opened the medicine cabinet, three pill bottles fell out and landed in the mildewed sink. One bottle rattled. Mom's eyes widened.

"Well, shit! Thought these were all empty." She snatched the bottle out of the sink and put it in her pocket. Then she yanked a small pair of scissors off the shelf.

She trimmed Meera's hair, evening out the hack job.

"You look like a boy, but at least you're not a scarecrow now," she said, with a laugh. Her eyes misted over. "You're pretty and smart. You'll do all right, kiddo." She hugged Meera.

Mom wasn't always so bad. Sometimes Meera even loved her, but she couldn't quite forgive her for all the nights she'd kept her and Dad waiting, wondering where she was.

• • •

Decayed leaves from the cottonwoods crunched beneath Meera's knees as she formed Daddy's legs and feet. She carved the outline of his toenails and drew wrinkles around his joints with a stiff blade of grass.

He was almost perfect. If only she had leather or that old sheepskin he'd kept on his truck seat. Then she could give him skin.

Meera skipped back to the trailer and entered through the back door, hoping to avoid Mom and Bo.

Mom had given Dad's clothes to Bo, but Meera had hidden some away in her closet.

Fishing them out from under a pile of shoes and stuffed animals, she laid them on her stained mattress next to her wadded-up unicorn blanket: shirt, jeans, and Daddy's favorite trucker hat. No socks or shoes, because he enjoyed going barefoot. She opened her bedroom window and dropped the clothes onto the overgrown lawn. She didn't need Bo asking questions.

As Meera came out of her room, she heard a newscaster.

...Reports of people dying within twenty-four hours of contracting the virus. There is no known treatment, and it appears to spread rapidly. Please stay indoors and avoid public spaces.

"I'm sick of this shit interrupting our shows. Why the hell do we even pay for cable?" Bo flipped to another channel.

"Aren't you getting paid for those roofs you helped with?" Mom asked, waving an electric bill.

"Aren't you supposed to get money for that brat?" Bo slammed the remote down. "Christ, it's on every channel! No one cares about the damn flu!"

Meera slipped back out the front door without either of them saying a word to her.

"I'm back, Daddy. Hope you didn't miss me much."

Careful not to disturb the clay, she placed the shirt and pants on top of him and stuck the hat on his head.

"We were good drinking buddies, weren't we, Daddy? You laughed so hard at the faces I made trying to guzzle your beer." She shivered. "*Brrr,* the wind is cold today."

She thought of the newscast and hoped Bo would get sick. Then Mom might pay more attention to her. They were horrible together. Why should they get her and Daddy's home? *They shouldn't.* She wished they'd both die.

She could make a new mom, a better mom. Or maybe she'd run away, but she didn't know where. They seldom left their property. Daddy didn't trust schools or relatives. He only had a couple friends, but they didn't visit anymore. The woods might make a nice home.

She'd watched survival shows with her dad and knew there were edible plants and grubs. A fat worm squirmed in the dirt. She plucked it up and tossed it in her mouth. Plugging her nose, she squeezed her eyes shut, chewed, and swallowed. Slimy, but not bad.

She ran down the hill with Mr. Wilson's wheelbarrow, slowing in the steeper sections so she didn't lose control.

Mr. Wilson wasn't outside.

She skipped up the stairs to the porch. The front door hung open.

"Hello? Anyone home?" She walked through the doorway.

A cloud of black flies swarmed Mr. Wilson's living room. She pulled her shirt over her nose. Something rotten. A swollen body laid on the couch. A puddle of vomit spread out on the floor, with dark brown splatters on and around the body. Poor Mr. Wilson. Meera's stomach flip-flopped, and she bolted.

She was almost back home when she realized Mr. Wilson must have had the flu the news kept talking about. What if *she* got sick now? What if mom and Bo sent her away? No one needed to know. Mr. Wilson's friends or family would find him.

She went in the house to wash her hands, just in case. Another "special report" blared from the TV.

Martial law has been declared. Carriers have been reported—fatal within forty-eight hours for the rest of the population. Believed to be a result of global warming and permafrost melt, experts say a virus has been released from the ice after being trapped and made dormant for possibly thousands of years. This is a serious threat. Stay in your homes.

The screen went black.

Meera tried taking care of them. She didn't *really* want anyone to die and wished she could take it all back. She coughed a little, but Mom and Bo hacked and threw up blood everywhere. They were burning up. She tried using Mom's phone but couldn't get a signal. Other than Mr. Wilson, all their neighbors lived miles away.

Mom and Bo died in their bed. She covered them with a blanket and shut the door.

They didn't have much food, but Meera didn't eat much. The bread and peanut butter lasted a few days.

Climbing on the counter to reach the highest cupboards, she found some old beans from the food bank and tried to cook them, but they were too hard to chew. She pulled down a heavy box from above the refrigerator. Inside the box was a thick plastic bag filled with a gray substance. She opened the bag. A faint odor, almost like chalk, came from the fine powder. *Daddy's ashes.*

The ash was thick with hard little fragments. Hard to believe this small box held all of Daddy. Pulling her hand out, a small pile of ash sat atop her fingers. She licked the ash and tasted Daddy. Almost like eating dirt, gritty.

She grabbed the box, jumped off the counter, and ran outside.

The ashes will make the clay more like skin. Daddy's old body will mix into the new one.

She grabbed handfuls of ashes and worked them into his head, hands, and feet. The clay took on a lighter tone, but there was more ash than the exposed clay would absorb. She rubbed them underneath his shirt and pants. Not all of it stuck. Some blew away in the wind.

"Please come back, Daddy. I need you."

She set the stone in the center of his forehead and lay down in the crook of his arm, her hand resting on his chest.

• • •

It was like camping, having no power. She hid in the woods so no one would see her.

She soaked the dry beans with pond water and ate them. It was too late in the year for berries, but there were still worms and insects.

In the crook of Daddy's arm, she covered herself with her unicorn blanket and slept. A few days passed with Meera listening to the birds and sitting next to Daddy chatting.

Then one day...

Thud!

Meera looked around.

Gray feathers floated near Mr. Toad. Dirt rolled off his head, revealing one gigantic eye. It opened as more dirt fell away, revealing bumpy skin. His mouth gaped as he flicked out his tongue. A crossbill, wings spread, rolled away with the dirt, limp and lifeless.

"What?" She hopped up.

"Hello," Toad said, as he shook off more dirt.

"You're real?"

"Flesh and blood."

"My Daddy won't come back. Why you?" She motioned towards the form.

"Flesh. And. Blood." Mr. Toad blinked his huge eyes.

Meera looked at the dead bird.

She had flesh and blood...in the trailer. It was the same size as Daddy, too.

Meera opened the bedroom door and pushed the wheelbarrow inside. The stench was worse than a thousand farts. She covered her nose with her t-shirt and approached the bed slowly.

She carefully peeled the blanket up from the side in an attempt to expose Bo without uncovering her mom. Mom's arm poked out, but the rest of her stayed covered. Meera ignored the arm and focused on Bo. His skin was a purplish-black, with blisters all over it. She tried not to look at his swollen face, the eyes and tongue bulging. Letting go of her t-shirt, she pulled the carving knife from her back pocket and cut away his tank top.

She gagged when she cut into his flesh. It reminded her of the dead deer before it had rotted to bones, only this was a hundred times worse. She pictured Daddy, whole and alive. She sliced and scraped, trying her best to block out the foaming mass of flesh left behind on Bo's bones. Some of his skin tore and fell apart, but she thought she had enough to cover her dad.

She put the skin in the wheelbarrow and pushed it outside.

Black clouds rolled across the sky. A distant rumble. She and Daddy loved storms. He'd let her watch them from the porch, even though Mom said it wasn't safe. Maybe he'd be back in time for this one.

Removing his clothes, she placed the skin over the clay, filling the gaps with leaves and dirt. His shirt and pants were made lumpy when placed back atop the body. She adjusted the hat to hide the skin's edge at his forehead. His hair, once her own, flowed out from beneath.

"He looks good, doesn't he?" She glanced at Mr. Toad.

She'd always known Daddy needed skin.

Toad gave a lazy yawn in reply. The hemlock, spruce, and cottonwoods swayed, roots shaking the ground.

Meera stood back, admiring her work with a smile, and waited.

Set for Life

By Warren Benedetto

First published in Issue 004 (July–August 2021)

Andy loaded the body into the back of the van, then slammed the door.

"Last one," he called out, knocking on the rear door with his knuckles. The van's engine started up with a roar. Its tailpipe shuddered, enveloping Andy in a swirl of exhaust. He coughed and waved the noxious fumes away from his face. *Thanks, asshole,* he thought.

As he moved around to the passenger side, Andy swiped his finger along the length of the filthy white van, creating a wobbly clean streak under the faded Chargers Inc. logo. The "I" in "Inc." was a lightning bolt with an electrical plug at the bottom. It reminded him of the logo for the Los Angeles Chargers, his father's favorite football team back when Andy was still a kid. Back when football—and Los Angeles—was still around.

Andy yanked the door open and hauled himself into the van. His weight squeaked down on the threadbare seat. The springs dug cruelly into his aching back. He pulled the door shut, then took off his Chargers Inc. work cap and massaged the sore red line it left on his forehead.

The driver, Barry, a rough-hewn, heavy-set man in his mid-forties, snatched the hat from Andy's hand.

"You gotta break it in," he said. He pulled on the bowl of the hat, stretching it outwards in each direction, then tossed it back at Andy. It rolled off his lap and onto the floor.

"Thanks," Andy mumbled.

As he bent down to pick it up, the thick muscles in his back cried out in protest. It had been a long day, with a lot of lifting. He was young and strong, and he had worked plenty of jobs that required manual labor. This one was different though. Lifting bodies wasn't like lifting boxes. Boxes were symmetrical. Structured. You could lift properly: squat down, straighten your spine, lift with your legs. Bodies were limp. Awkward. Their limbs flopped in odd directions. He still hadn't figured out the best way to lift one without damaging it. Or himself. Or both.

The "Help Wanted" listing Andy had answered promised on-the-job training, but he hadn't gotten any. He was just thrown into the deep end on his first day. Barry showed up in front of his apartment building, picked him up, and that was it. Ten minutes later, they were hauling bodies into the van.

Andy considered calling in a report to the main Chargers Inc. number while Barry was on a shit break, but then he decided against it. Better not to be flagged as a complainer on your first day, he figured. He'd get the hang of it eventually. He just hoped his back would hold up in the meantime. Besides, it was way better than his last gig.

At least nobody was shooting at him at this one.

Andy flapped the dust from his hat, then put it back on his head. It fell low and loose over his ears, the bill tipping down to cover his eyes.

"Better?" Barry asked, as he shifted the van into gear.

Andy tipped the hat back so he could see. It fell over his eyes again. He turned it around backwards, instead.

"Perfect," he replied.

"Should be coming up on the right," Andy said.

He consulted the digital map on the grimy tablet mounted on the van's dashboard. Small yellow lightning bolt icons were scattered around the map. A different icon representing the van moved along the road, towards one of the lightning bolts.

Andy squinted through the van's windshield, searching for the target in the fading evening light. It was near dark, but the streetlights hadn't turned on yet. Deep shadows filled the doorways and alleys.

He consulted the map again. The van icon had moved past the lightning bolt.

"Shit. We missed it."

Barry slammed on the brakes, throwing Andy hard against the seatbelt. He threw his hands against the dashboard to brace himself.

"Goddamn it, kid," Barry growled. He put the van into park, then looked at Andy. He raised his eyebrows, waiting. "Well?"

"Can you back up?"

"Can you back up?" Barry whined, mocking him. "I'm sure you can find it."

Andy took a deep breath, held it for a second, then exhaled slowly. "Thanks, boss."

Andy climbed out of the van and shut the door.

"Fucking dick," he mumbled under his breath.

The guy was useless; he did nothing. The orientation video on the Chargers Inc. website had said partners were supposed to trade off on each pickup: one person picks up the bodies, the other stays in the van to protect the merchandise. Then, on the next stop, they were supposed to switch. But Barry never moved from the van, not once the whole day. Didn't even try. He just sat there scrolling on his phone while Andy did all the work.

Andy knew Barry was taking advantage of the fact that he was the new guy, but Andy didn't dare challenge him. The man was clearly an old-timer, had been with the company for years. You could tell just by looking at his hat. It was rumpled and misshapen and was faded to a dull grayish blue. The Chargers Inc. logo was barely even visible anymore. If it came down to a choice of who to believe, it was clear who the company would side with. Then Andy would be out of a job. One he needed, badly. He hadn't worked in almost a year. He couldn't afford to fuck it up.

The van was stopped in an industrial area of town. The streets and sidewalks were ill-maintained, with crumbling potholes threatening to break any ankle or axle that got too close, too fast. Some of the buildings were still pockmarked with bullet holes and shrapnel scars from the war. Rusty chain link fences topped with coils of barbed wire sealed off the lots between buildings. Crooked signs warned of armed Sentinels patrolling the premises.

Andy walked down the street behind the van, to the entrance of a large warehouse. Seemed like the right place. Sure enough, the bright blue Chargers Inc. storage locker was just inside the entryway. Andy swiped his keycard through the reader. The locker doors slid open on their air rails with a crisp *whoosh*. The fluorescent lights inside flickered to life.

Andy said a little prayer of thanks. There was only one body standing inside, a smaller-issue model. Probably a Tech. It was a relief. A lot of the bodies they had picked up from their manufacturing and industrial clients were Workers or Sentinels. Those were big. Muscular. And heavy.

So goddamned heavy.

Andy put his hand on the body's shoulder and pulled it forward, preparing to lift it.

"Hello," the body said.

Andy jumped backwards, startled. The body smiled, then froze. The light in its eyes dimmed, then darkened. Its chin dropped to its chest.

Andy exhaled, his heartbeat returning to normal. *Still a little charge left in it, I guess.*

He still wasn't used to being near the damn things, even after hauling them around all day. They were creepy as hell. Looked just like real people. Felt like them too. The technology had come a long way since the awkward, dead-eyed sex robots that people used to hide in their basements a decade ago. Not that Andy had any direct experience with those. He'd heard stories though. Had seen the videos too, back in the day.

He reached out for the body again. This time, it remained quiet. Just to be safe, Andy pressed the soft spot on its skull behind its right ear, holding it for 10 seconds to make sure it was fully powered down. Then he ducked his shoulder into the body's abdomen and hoisted it over his shoulder.

"Alright, buddy," he grunted as he carried the body back to the van. "Let's get you home."

Andy and Barry drove in silence for a little while. Andy debated internally whether it was worth striking up a conversation. He decided he should. If he was going to have to work with the guy, he might as well try to be friendly. Maybe the old fucker would warm up.

"How long you been with the company?" Andy asked.

"Too long," Barry replied.

Andy nodded. They lapsed back into silence. Barry drummed his fingers on the steering wheel.

Andy decided to try again.

"So, we take these back to the shop, and then what? Charge them up, bring them back?"

"Basically."

"How come people don't just charge them themselves, on-site?"

"Can't. Syntech won't let 'em. Charging's a big business. Sort of a razor and blades thing."

"Hmm. Smart," Andy nodded. He peered through the cab window into the cargo hold, where dozens of bodies were piled up. "They're weird, aren't they? Creepy."

Barry shrugged.

"You ever have one yourself?"

Barry gave him a look like he was crazy. "I look like a millionaire to you?"

"I thought maybe there's, you know, an employee discount or something."

Barry's jaw tightened. "I got a wife."

"Oh!" Andy exclaimed, realizing the misunderstanding. "No, I wasn't implying—I meant a Maid, like for chores or whatever."

Barry didn't respond.

Andy tried to change the subject. "Anyway, they're pretty incredible. I don't know how they make 'em so real like that. They're practically human."

Barry laughed. He glanced at Andy. "You're serious?"

"What?" Andy asked, confused.

"Man," Barry said, shaking his head. "Guess you didn't get hired for your brains. At least you can lift. You work out?"

"Some."

"Bench?"

"Three. Three-twenty."

"Not bad. You're how old?"

"Twenty-six."

"College?"

"Nah. Military."

"Huh. Me too. Marines." Barry knocked on his thigh. It made a hollow sound.

Andy glanced down. For the first time, he noticed the titanium rod extending from Barry's pants cuff into his boot. An artificial leg.

No wonder he never gets out of the van, Andy thought. He felt like an asshole.

"Shit. I didn't know. What happened?"

"Confederate drone. Battle of Chicago."

"Tough break."

Barry shrugged. "Could've been worse. How about you? You made it out in one piece?"

"Mostly." Andy unbuttoned his sleeve and rolled it up his arm, revealing a thick, horizontal scar across his bicep. "Sniper. Los Angeles. I turned just as he fired. Got Medevac'd out two hours before the bomb hit. Saved my ass."

Barry whistled. He glanced over as Andy slid his sleeve back down. He noticed the distinctive tattoo on Andy's forearm, a stylized skull under a banner bearing the words *Kill. Bathe. Repeat.*

"Special Forces, huh?" Barry said, indicating the tattoo.

"Six years."

"Guess I shouldn't piss you off."

Andy laughed. "No, probably not."

Barry laughed too. A genuine laugh. Andy felt something thaw between them.

Maybe he's not so bad after all, Andy thought.

As if to prove the point, Barry flipped open the van's center console and withdrew a dented metal flask. He unscrewed the cap, then handed it to Andy.

"Whiskey?"

"Sure. Thanks."

Andy took the flask. He began to lift it to his lips, then paused. He looked at Barry skeptically.

"This a test?"

"Nah. We're off the clock."

"Alright, then." Andy lifted the flask in a little salute. "Cheers." He swallowed the bitter-tasting liquid, then handed the flask back to Barry. Barry motioned for him to keep it.

"So?" Andy asked, taking another swig. "You got me curious. How *does* Syntech make them?" He nodded towards the bodies in the back of the van.

Barry cleared his throat. "Well, let's see." He began counting off on his fingers. "The economy's shit. Cities haven't been rebuilt. There are no jobs. There's no money. People are desperate."

"Tell me about it."

"So imagine: you're broke, you can't pay your bills, your kids are hungry. Then a Syntech rep shows up at your door and says, 'We'll write you a check, right here, right now. Enough to set your family up for life. Your wife, your kids—they'll never want for anything else as long as they live.' You'd take that deal, right?"

"I—Maybe? …I don't know. I'd have to think about it."

"Ah, that's the catch. You get two minutes. One time offer. Take it or leave it."

"Wow, no pressure," Andy chuckled. "I'm assuming it's not free money, right? What do I have to do in return?"

Barry looked at Andy out of the corner of his eye, waiting for him to connect the dots. After a few seconds, Andy drew in a sharp breath.

"Oh. Oh, shit! You're serious? Those are real people back there?"

"Were."

"I thought Syntech built synthetics."

"They do. But not for everything. When it comes to the tough, dangerous jobs, real people are better."

"Really? How so?"

"They're cheap, for one. Relatively, at least. There's nothing to manufacture, nothing to repair. Just the neural compute device. Implant one in the skull, wire it up, recharge weekly, done. Easy peasy."

Andy was dumbfounded. He had no idea. He looked back through the cabin window again. *All those things are people,* he marveled. Then he corrected himself. *Were people.*

"So, how much does Syntech pay? Must be a shitload."

"Depends. Low end, for a Maid or a Tech, it's maybe a hundred grand. Military grade, Sentinels? A million, million two. Maybe more. 'Course Syntech makes that back tenfold."

Andy whistled, shaking his head in disbelief. He yawned. "Sorry," he apologized. "Didn't expect to be this tired." He twisted his torso to crack his back. His spine popped like a line of firecrackers. "That's wild. People are actually volunteering to be, what, roboticized? Is that even a word? Wow."

"Yep. Most of them."

"Wow," he said again. "Shit's crazy." He rolled over this new information in his mind in silence for a bit, then took another swig of whiskey. "You said 'most.' Not all?"

Barry glanced over at Andy, then turned his eyes back to the road.

"There are all kinds of people in the world, kid. Some good, some bad."

"Yeah, so?"

"So, Syntech is buying. People are selling."

"Selling…what? Other people?"

"*Ding, ding, ding!* Give the man a prize."

"Fuuuuck." Andy shook his head, uncomprehending. "How does someone just go and sell another person?" he asked rhetorically. "It's like slavery or something."

"There's all kinds of ways," Barry answered. "You got POWs, of course, from the camps. That's easy. Low-hanging fruit. Their health is shit though. Most of 'em die pretty quick. Then you got kidnappers, grabbing people off the street. That's unreliable though. Never know what you're getting. Sometimes a family member sets someone up. A brother, an uncle. A neighbor. Then you got others who treat it more like a business, who've gotta be clever."

Andy rubbed his eyes. His eyeballs suddenly felt fat. Heavy. He looked at the flask in his hand, then up at Barry. The driver's face swam in and out of focus.

"For example, someone could put out a 'Help Wanted' ad," Barry continued. "Find some young guy who needs work. Test him out, see how strong he is."

Andy's head rolled backwards on his neck. He strained to pull it upright. His skull felt like a bowling ball on a pipe cleaner. The flask slipped from his fingers.

"You know what're the hardest to find?" Barry continued. "Sentinels. They've gotta be young, tough, military trained. Sell one of those, you're set for life."

Andy's chin slumped against his chest. His hat fell off his head and onto his lap.

Barry put on his blinker, then pulled up to the front gate of a sprawling industrial complex. The security guard stepped out of his booth. The Syntech logo glowed green on his uniform. He checked his clipboard, then bent down and looked in through Barry's window.

"Evening, Barry," the guard said. "Another volunteer?"

The Devil's Travel Agency

By Alex Sobel

First published in the Halloween Special Issue 001
(October 2021)

You Make The Call

You don't know what you're asking for, exactly. You don't know where you need to go, or how to go about getting there. You don't know the cost, don't know how much you have to pay. You don't know the risks for you or other parties, don't know if there will be benefits. You don't know if you'll get where you need to go, you don't know if it'll make any difference when you get there.

Don't worry, we'll help you with all that.

You're given a phone number. Maybe you get it from some back-alley mystic with a storefront that you've passed by every day on the way to work for years and never noticed, but now that you see it, you can't help but wonder how a place like that stays in business. Maybe you got it from a priest with connections, one who wants to help out, who doesn't see what good it would do anyone keeping the number from you, who hopes you don't ask where he got it from, or if he's ever used it. Or maybe a friend gave it to you, one who's used our services before, in which case let us know, because referrals get you a discount on your next trip with us.

When you call the number, we answer on the first ring. This is company policy, and if we make you wait for more than one ring, please call our customer service number.

We say hello, the voice in broken pieces, like crumbling stone. It moves in waves, pushing forward through your cell phone, then pulling you toward it, away from yourself. You think it will bury you, think it will lift you off your feet. You think your lungs will collapse, you think you will scream. You don't know what to do.

You decide to say hello.

"Is this…" you begin. "The devil?"

We are not him. But that doesn't mean that he is a figurehead used as a way to sell our services. He's not a spokesperson, he takes an active role in the company.

We tell you as much.

"My name is Grace. I need to talk to my brother. To see him. He's dead."

We already know this, but we do not tell you so.

"We're twins," you add, your words coming through the spaces between teeth. "Drug overdose. He wasn't even… he was just so young."

We type a few things into a computer, your basic information, who you want to visit. The computer then tells us where you need to go, which mode of transportation you'll need to take to get there. You hear it on your end, the sound of keys, wonder what kind of computer we could possibly be using. We give you a location to be at, a time, say that there will be a bus. It won't be late; it will not wait for you. We tell you goodbye.

"Wait, what do I owe you? Don't you want my soul or something?"

We tell you that you will have to pay, but it will not be with your soul. This is human currency, not ours. What would we do with a soul, anyway?

The Bus Comes

You're at the location an hour early, wait patiently at the bus stop, the notebook in your hands. You should have made copies of the pages and brought those instead, but it's too late now. You wonder if this stop is used for regular buses, too, if this place will disappear as soon as you walk away from it.

A few cars pass, but they're going too fast for you to see the driver's faces, if they're men or demons or something else. You don't know if you'd be able to tell the difference, anyway.

The bus arrives.

We're in the driver's seat when you step on the bus, but you don't really see us. You see what your eyes allow you, what we allow. Maybe you see an old man like the one who used to drive the bus to school. Maybe you see the long-haired character from a TV show you shouldn't have been allowed to watch at that age. Maybe you see your mother, maybe you see everyone's mother. Maybe you see the idea of a mother.

You don't see your father.

The only other passenger is a boy, maybe ten, with thick bangs, long and oily, that completely cover his face. He doesn't look up.

The bus has uncomfortable seats, bars for people who need to stand, a retracted wheelchair ramp. There are ads lining the spots above the windows, one for a bubble-faced chiropractor, one for a juice you've never heard of that advertises itself as being "tai chi for your belly," the logo for a fast food restaurant that you've eaten at four days a week since he died, the calories sitting hard underneath your ribs. It's just like a regular bus, you think.

Because it is a regular bus, we'd like our customers to know.

The Trip

The bus drives for an hour, no turns, not even any curves in the road. You see fields, crops. There are billboards lining the side of the road, advertising a candy shop with a name that you're pretty sure is offensive. You try to look it up on your cell phone, but you can't even use data to connect to the internet. You dial his number. It hasn't been disconnected yet, but there's no reception, nothing's going through.

There are small towns that you catch glimpses of, the kind where there are a few dozen people who know each other's business, where the odds are good of your ex marrying your best friend or sibling, where you can't escape people, where you can't escape yourself.

As you get farther and farther away, the towns get smaller, sadder. You can tell that a change is happening, try to focus on it, to find exactly where it occurs. You want to know where the break is, when you're officially out of your world and in hell, or wherever it is you think you're going. You remember being little, lying in bed, trying to figure out the exact moment when you fell asleep. Every time, you wake up disappointed, the break between awake and asleep out of focus, the image fuzzy on either side. You also remember Stephen lying next you, sharing a bed until you're thirteen, until it's weird for twin brother and sister to sleep so close. He moves into the attic, and you sleep alone.

You remember that, too.

It doesn't get darker, like you expect. Instead, the colors outside the bus window begin to merge, blend at the edges. You think that it looks like existence was taking up a certain amount of space, that there was a density to the world, and suddenly that space was cut in half, with everything rushing to fill up every hole, every gap, everything.

This is not strictly what it's like here, but you're closer than you'll ever know.

When the bus stops, the young boy stands, pulls his feet across the floor toward the front of the bus. When you look out the window, you see a charcoal horizon bowing toward the murky sky, pulled back like the rain under windshield wipers. You see what looks like a tree behind you, the shape jagged, like it was cut out of paper by unskilled fingers.

"Where are you going?" you ask the boy as he moves toward the door. "Where is this? Why are you here?"

For the first time, you see the boy look up, meeting you with his face-swallowing eyes. "My mom," he says, and walks off the bus. He doesn't say what he means, whether his mom is here, or she's the one who told him to come, or something else entirely. You try to follow him with your eyes as he leaves the bus, but as soon as he steps out, he's gone.

It's not just you, you should know. When he stepped off that bus, the boy was gone to himself and everyone else.

You try to imagine what it will be like. Will there be fire? Bats? Monsters? Will Stephen look the same? You've seen movies with dead people in them, where they look the way they did when they die. Is that what will happen with Stephen? There wasn't any damage to him, though. Not when you found him, anyway.

It wasn't like Dad.

You Remember What Happened

Dad was living in a trailer park, but was forced out when they started building the new hospital. He sold the house, didn't need all that space without Mom around. You went to his apartment, you and Stephen. Dad hadn't answered his phone in almost a week. He was on the couch, head slung back, an arm dangling over the edge. A beer was on the end table, just barely out of reach. You spoke, moved closer to him, but then you saw, caught the slightest touch of blood on his cheek. You made Stephen look, made him make sure. You wonder if Stephen saw himself in the body, if he knew he'd be next, saw his own face.

You called your mom while Stephen dealt with everything, the ambulance, answered the questions that needed to be answered.

"Dad's dead," you said when they put you through to your mother.

She gasped. "My God. How? What happened? How old was he?" she said.

You talked with her for a whole minute before you realized that she thought it was her own father who was gone.

You Arrive

When it's your stop, you get off the bus, start walking because you don't know what else to do, where to go. You hold the notebook in your left hand, feel sweat dripping down your fingers toward the pages. As you push forward, the ragged corners of the tree at the horizon begin to round out until it's oval shaped. You keep pushing ahead even though you feel your feet sinking into the ground, holding you, begging you not to go. You begin to hear noise, footsteps, the clanking of glasses. The horizon narrows ahead of you, a crack, and you slide through it.

You find yourself in a bar. There are people eating, drinking, but no one speaks. There's a short blonde who looks too young to be allowed in here, a couple of men sitting at a booth, their necks tucked between their shoulders. You take a seat at the bar, set the notebook in front of you. You don't know if the bartender speaks your language, if he can understand you.

"How much does a beer cost?" you say, pointing to the taps. You make a motion like you're fanning money in front of you. He shakes his head, pours a beer, places it in front of you, then walks through a door behind the bar and disappears.

You take a sip, the taste bitter, like swallowing your own bile. You want more.

"You like it?" You turn to see a woman next to you, maybe twice your age. She motions with her head toward the beer.

"Yeah," you say.

"Here for someone?"

"My brother. He overdosed."

She nods. "I first came for my wife. Cancer, so I knew it was coming. But the day she died," she stops for a moment, sucks in air through her nose, "she could see it, you know? She started to say something. 'Make sure you…' she said, and that was it, she was gone. I wanted to know what she said. Make sure I…what? It felt important."

The woman sips her own beer, her face not betraying the bitterness. She smiles, but fights against it, like she's seeing someone she just had a fight with and doesn't want to reveal how much she missed them.

"What did she say? Did you ever find her?"

She swallows. "Well, I found her alright. But you wanna know what she said? She told me she couldn't remember what she was trying to tell me, that it wasn't important. She told me not to come. But that was a long time ago."

"And you keep coming back?"

"Yeah, though I don't see her much anymore. Now I just come to hang out, see the sights a few times a year. There's a lot here. Have you been to the giant dog statue? Or the man made of cold fire?"

You shake your head.

"They're something," she says. She sticks out her tongue, moves her body back and forth like an animal shaking off water. "Do you have a list? Some questions? A speech or something?"

"A speech?"

"For your dead brother. Saw your notebook, assumed that's what it was for. That's where I failed. I didn't have anything prepared for my wife. It was mostly tears, mumbling. You'll only find him for a few minutes, then he'll be gone. Just thought I'd warn you. They have to keep moving or something happens, but I can't say what. Them's the rules, I don't pretend to understand how any of it works. But then, I don't have to. I'm only visiting."

You Continue On

The streets are brick, uneven. The replacement bricks are obvious, a soil color over dark green. You pass different stores, restaurants, some with signs you can read, some in a language you don't recognize. You stop into one that says "Grocery" on the sign. There's a cashier, but no customers.

You get his attention, ask him if he's seen someone named Stephen, give a brief description. The cashier doesn't speak, only nods, turns back toward the register.

As you walk out, you get the feeling that you used to work at this grocery store, or maybe somebody you know did.

You see the sign for an arcade, neon, blinking purple. You don't recall ever being in a place like this, but it feels familiar. You see a man playing a game, his body gaunt, movements robotic. You walk up to look over his shoulder. He's playing a game that consists of a superhero beating up robots. The green robots have drills for hands, the yellow ones shoot lasers, the red ones blow fireballs. Each can be destroyed by punching them until they explode.

"You know this one?" the man playing the game says, looking over at you. You jump at the sound of his voice. "The game, I mean. Sorry to scare you. I know everyone else around here is, like, an automaton. Makes you jumpy when someone living and breathing comes along."

You nod, slip your hand in front of your mouth to confirm that you're still breathing. Your breath is warm against your palm. There must be oxygen here, you realize.

We take care of our customers, providing any breathing material that they require. If at any point, you find what we've provided to be insufficient, we will do everything in our power to better accommodate you.

"Makes me think of going to Disney World as a kid," you say. "Going on the rides, the animatronics coming to life as you float by in your raft. I remember being so disappointed when my mom told me that they didn't move all the time, that when someone wasn't looking, they stopped, went dead."

"Wanna play?" the man says, stepping away from the game cabinet, motioning for you to take a turn.

You're good at the game, the controls feel natural under your hands, but you don't have a single solid memory of ever playing it.

The man watches you finish the game, doesn't say another word. You start to think that he's like them, after all, that he's not human, that you're living out a pre-considered scenario, or a memory. Or maybe it's a process, everyone here becomes mechanical after awhile, like an afterlife tucked into another afterlife. Maybe you'll become like that, too, not thinking or feeling, just doing, just somebody else's memory, a construct.

The thought of this tickles something in your brain, but you can't quite point to what.

You Find Him

Stephen's at a diner, the kind with knick-knacks on the wall, pictures of old movie stars, instruments with unplayable strings, a miniature jukebox on each table. He's sitting down, eating what looks like eggs, but a different color, one you can't name, one you've never seen before. He's wearing a dark-green flannel shirt, black jeans. They may be the clothes he was buried in, but he always wore the same few things, so you can't tell.

You sit across from him. The small jukebox next to you is playing "Cupid," by Sam Cooke. Stephen looks up, coughs slightly, swallows like he's about ready to tell someone bad news.

"Go ahead, Grace," he says, motioning with his hand as if to say the floor is yours.

"I found this," you slide the notebook toward him. "In your apartment."

He dabs his mouth with a napkin, swallows. "Is there a question? If you want me to read something, you'll have to do it for me. I can't."

You don't question the rules of this world, you've learned better, so you pull the notebook back toward you, flip through the pages. "It's your journal."

"I seem to recall."

"You talk about killing Dad, how you're glad you haven't yet, how he deserves to die."

"So, you want to know if I killed him?"

"No," you say. "I don't think you did."

"But the coincidence, it bothers you, doesn't it? Or maybe not a coincidence. I'm not sure I know what word it is. Death is confusing, isn't it? It's hard to sift through."

"Have you seen him? Dad?"

He shakes his head. "He's somewhere else. Another town or village or whatever we're calling these places. Maybe someday I will. I'm surprised you didn't come to see him. I bet he'd—"

"Did you mean to do it?" you say, interrupting. "I need to know. Was it suicide, or just an accident?"

Stephen puts down his fork.

"Which would you prefer? That I purposely took myself away from you, left you alone, or that I wanted to live and was just too stupid to not take too much?"

You don't reply to this. "What is it like here?" you ask instead.

"I wouldn't know. You're the one on the outside. How does it look to you?"

"Remember Disney World? The animatronics?"

"They're not all like that." He motions with his fork. "The girl at the table in the corner."

You turn to see the girl he's talking about, her eyes panicked, scanning the room.

"She's missing someone. Probably came for a stupid reason like you, now she can't go home, or can't stop coming back, or whatever it might be. That happens. It's like an addiction for some people."

You turn back toward Stephen. "I didn't come for a stupid reason."

"Then what did you want out of this?" You don't answer. He stands up, drops his napkin on top of his plate of eggs. "I have to go now, okay. But before I leave, I want you to know that I do love you, Grace. For what it's worth."

"Where do you go?" you ask, as he walks away. He doesn't seem to hear. "Do you become like everyone else around here?"

"You remember too much," Stephen says, opening the door. "Do yourself a favor and forget as much as you can, okay? It's better that way."

And then he's out the door and gone to you forever.

The Way You Would Have Gone

You couldn't have cut anything, no slicing of skin, splitting of veins. You can't even stand injections, not because of the pain, but just the penetration of your flesh, the fear of something inside you. Jumping seemed reasonable, but from where? You couldn't have gone through with using a gun. Too messy, too much clean up. You didn't want to be a burden on anyone. You just wanted to be gone. You had pretty much settled on pills when you got the call. Twins think alike, you remember thinking. So, you had to put your plans away, call relatives, make arrangements. It was on you now. You went and told your mom in person. It only took her a few times of saying his name before she looked at you and said, "My son?"

"Yes, Mom," you said. "Stephen, your son. He's dead."

"My son," she said, touching her cheek. "Dead."

A few tears fell from her eyes, landed on her fingertips. For a moment, you felt grateful. Grateful for her sadness. Grateful that she could remember.

Grateful that soon she'd forget.

You Return

You explore for a few hours before getting on the bus to go home. You expect the real world to become something you recognize, but it's the opposite. As the bus moves forward, everything complicates, everything expands, feels less familiar, less like home. When the bus comes to a stop, you check your phone, see you have a signal. You call the home where your mom's staying, ask to speak to her.

"It's Grace, Mom," you say when she answers. "Your daughter."

"Yes, Grace, of course," she says, her words shaky, uncertain.

You put your phone to your chest as you walk off the bus. You look at us in the driver's seat, mouth "Thank you." We nod, smile, and you get out, the ground rough against your feet.

We're always glad to have a satisfied customer. We do hope you'll use our services again.

You return your phone to your ear. "How are you feeling today, Mom?" you say.

"My hip hurts, but that's nothing new. What have you been doing? It's been a long time, hasn't it?"

"Not too long, Mom. I just got home. I went out with some friends after work," you say, not knowing what time it is, if that story would even check out.

"Oh, okay. For drinks? Are you married or anything? I can't seem to remember. Did you go out with a boy?"

"Yes, there was a boy, but not for a date or anything. I paid for myself."

"I see. Hope it wasn't too expensive, then."

"No, Mom," you say, watching the bus pull away, disappear. You think about what Stephen said, remember every detail. "It didn't cost that much at all."

Decommissioned

By Brittany Groves

First published in Issue 006 (November–December 2021)

Fomalhaut burst above the southernmost ridge, icy blue-white and blinding, as star-rises after the long season often were. The electrical cyclone that raged in my sector had finally calmed over the last twelve cycles, though crystalline debris floated in the static electricity still crackling between the boulders. Now I could, at least, see the ensuing destruction through my battered windows. The temperature had dropped precipitously, resulting in smooth, glossy pillars of frozen methane that jutted from the rocks and reached towards the sky. The paths to the adjacent buildings were thick with flakes of mordenite scattered about the ground like lethal, glittery snow.

I knew of snow, theoretically, though I'd never seen or felt it. The previous Caretaker had left a collection of small, yellowed squares affixed to the wall of my charging stall; postcards, they were called, according to the lettering along the edges. Made of paper, a delicate and ancient tool for preserving information, the crumbling surfaces featured scenes from other worlds: *Greetings from Vail, Colorado! Snow, skiing, and fun! Welcome to Breckenridge!*

I knew snow only from the way it looked in those postcards: white ski trails, blurry streaks across smiling, pink-cheeked faces. In the long hours of my recharge sequence, I memorized every line and color so that when the time came and the pictures faded, lost to the heavy hand of time, the smiles of the long-dead could keep me company.

There was no snow here, only the mordenite that grew and shattered and drifted with the astral winds. It was beautiful, but deadly to organics, even mech-organics, and one of the many dangers of the Inner Strata.

This I was used to. For countless turns I'd existed here alone, through the wars, the reunification, the mech-organic revolution, and still through the mass exodus to the Outer Strata. Humanity fled their ruined Earth, panicked and desperate, and found their salvation through logistics and science. They didn't have the manpower to take care of livestock and the myriad other creatures from which they took sustenance. Better to engineer mech-organic versions and from many, make one—a Prime. The Prime would be the one ultimate being that would direct all members of their species.

The Bos Taurus Prime waited in the livestock quarters, fore udder heavy and low with milk, her fluctuating vitals bleating a warning in the panels above my docking station. She was hidden away, safe and comfortable in her artificial atmosphere. No organic creature, even mech-organic, could survive in the Inner Strata anymore, though it had once been considered paradise. I wouldn't have ventured out in the desolate winds at all if I hadn't had concerns over her condition.

Something had gone wrong during the storms. It addled the instruments and I had to go, though my synthetic joints ground against one another, steel on degraded steel, down to dust. I waded, one step in front of the other through the piercing, shifting drifts until I swung wide the doors of the livestock quarters.

Unlike the stark, solemn world I left behind, the quarters were noisy and alive. Machinery clicked and beeped along the glassy walls, flashing my reflection, as if I cared about the cracks in my silicone skin, the passage of time written clearly on my habitus.

A soft lowing caught my attention, pulling me toward the mech-organic that monopolized my time as Caretaker—the Bos Taurus Prime.

Bos stood eerily still as I opened the stall door. A minor twitch of her switch, a flick of an eyelid were the only indicators she knew I was there. She was unwell, eyes rolling wild and bloodshot in their sockets. Sanguineous fluid leaked from one damp nostril.

I smoothed my hand across her supple body, over the swell of her hips, and gently dipped into the meat of one haunch, unlatching the control panel hidden in her flesh. I soothed her while I interfaced, following protocol. All the outworlded Tauruses linked up on the network before me, connected to her on their distant ships and planets, creating milk for those brave and sturdy enough to survive their flights.

A flash obscured the screen, turning the subtle blue glow an ugly red.

All the linked Tauruses's diagnostics looked well, but it was only a matter of time before the Prime's sickness, like a virus, infected the others. What happened to her happened to all. Their milk production would fail.

Disconnecting, I replaced the skin flap above the circuit board. A reboot would do no good—this problem was wholly organic. I continued my examination with a reverent caress down her leg and got a full view of her swollen teats, each one hot to the touch.

The storm had played havoc with my protocols and prevented remote activation of the milking program, and I'd been unable to venture to the quarters to do it manually. Organics were touchy and fragile, prone to failure. It took only a short time before she was feverish with infection.

Five hundred, two hundred, even fifty turns ago, this would not have happened. I was highly functional then, just fabricated, with more insulation and less systemic degeneration. The Bos Taurus snorted and stamped, shuffling in discomfort.

"Oh girl, I'm so sorry." Sentiment of any kind was taboo amongst the Caretakers. The Council didn't build us to feel. But I had a sensation, like a stretching in my chest, growing with every moment.

It wasn't in the Prime's programming to suffer. A synthetic nervous system had little room for pain receptors, even for mech-organics, but the matter was still urgent, as infected tissue would not heal on its own. She needed to be hand-stripped, and the standard nanobiotic protocol activated from the mainframe.

I took my time inspecting one cracked and ugly-looking teat before giving it a tender pull. The milk streamed forth thin, pale yellow, unfit for consumption. This was expected, though I'd briefly entertained the idea that perhaps it wasn't so serious. I was wrong.

A sudden, booming sizzle cut through the air, audible even through the heavy wood and steel walls of the livestock quarters. The Bos shifted, eyes wide in fear and surprise. I did not receive visitors and I had no need for companionship. This could only be a missive from the Council.

I abandoned my tainted milk and lurched towards the doors. They were too heavy to open quickly, but I thrust upon the dense wood with urgent purpose, and they swung wide in time to see a streak of white, fiery light scorch the sky. Noxious black smoke hung vaporous in the aftermath, a long, dirty swath against the plasma clouds.

Something small and unwelcome had rocketed across the sky and crashed in the distance.

With one last look behind me to make sure Bos was safe on her own, I ran towards the source of the billowing smoke. Mordenite, crusted thick from the winds, crunched with every step, slicing my ankles. The surrounding stillness seemed manufactured, thick with foreboding.

I stumbled through the ochrous rocks and saw the crash laid out before me. It smoldered, embers dancing about in the remnant heat—a tortuous tangle of glossy metal and plastic. The nauseous, acrid stench of burning synthetics stung my eyes. I stared for long moments, dumbstruck and mesmerized by the destruction before me.

There was movement, after a while, but I dared not step closer. The craft, a simple single-occ spaceship, was unlike the common regulation transport that flitted daily through the outer atmospheres. They rarely made berth on the smaller rocks of the Inner Strata, this one of which I called my home. I despaired that any creature inside had survived the devastation; but survived they had, and when its head rose out of a reinforced alloy crash pod, I knew my fate.

"Oh," I said in a breath, unable to hide my disappointment. "You made quite an entrance."

It startled, whipping its head around at the sound of my voice. There was no need for introductions. We knew each other, because we were the same.

Its hair shone dark, like mine had so many cycles ago; face smooth and unlined, untouched by the time assigned to this frozen rock and its dangers. I wasn't envious of its youth or curiosity. I had already experienced this once myself, and I'd been here long enough to know it meant nothing here in the storms, where red lightning lit the vapor lakes aflame.

It wiped the soot off one plump cheek. "There was a malfunction."

"I see."

Rising gracefully to its feet, it peered at the crystal-dipped structures that lined the valley—remnants of civilizations, carcasses of steel and concrete. I watched its assessing gaze. I'd been that way once. When it turned back to me, I was struck again by the familiar.

"Are you ready for the exchange?" It rolled up its sleeves.

"Already?"

"The Agricultural Council terminated your contract. I see no reason to delay."

I looked back towards my charging stall, and then at the livestock quarters. Again, that stretching in my chest—what was it? A feeling? I knew nothing of feelings: joy, contentment, fear. But I knew that it was not, initially, in my programming to feel. What would I call it? What would the humans in the postcards call it? I suppose they had a name for such things.

The pod collapsed inward in a groaning spray of sparks and steam.

"No, I suppose not," I conceded, rolling up my sleeves to match. "Can I say goodbye afterwards?"

"Why would you do that?"

It didn't understand. How could it?

I didn't ask again. We faced each other, mirror images—one new, one aged. With a swipe of my finger, my forearm glowed, circuitry shimmering beneath the skin. We touched their surfaces together, an intimate motion for only having just met.

Memories surged through me, flashing through our connection: the trickle of rain on the rocks, the acidic mists that gathered in the early mornings, the smooth feel of the Bos's horns on my fingertips.

I gave them all away, transferred.

A mournful call accompanied my disengagement from the new Caretaker. I was emptied, released of all purpose, and spared a last glance towards the livestock quarters and Bos, who had called for me.

"There are anomalies." The glow of its arm faded.

"Are there?"

"Code blocks," it turned down its sleeve with blank regard. "Inelegant snippets. Embedded recently. You did this?"

"I didn't." I covered my arms as well, as if cold, as if that were something I could feel. Perhaps, after all this time, I had changed. Perhaps, I was not as static as I was manufactured to be.

"It is against policy to upload patches or edit your own coding."

"I assure you, I haven't."

It moved past me, stiff and ungainly in the drifts. It would learn, like I did, how to move and function in such a hostile place.

"It is of no consequence. I have deleted them."

As was its right. But how long would this new Caretaker remain unchanged?

"Of course."

We gazed at each other while the wind whipped around us. There was nothing more to say.

It turned from me once the exchange concluded, and I was dismissed. Due to my own negligence, my mission had ended, and it now came time for me to sleep deeply in the immortal valley. I knew this would happen, at some point. We're fitted with the necessary procedural manuals, and are familiar with the simulations. Though, I expected the circumstances to be different.

Now I would walk across the steaming plains and join the others. Yet, as I faced the bleak landscape before me and braced myself for the inevitable, I found myself yearning for more time.

The new Caretaker disappeared into the livestock quarters, and I made my way south across the craggy expanse. I knew where to go, it was embedded deep in my assembly.

I reached the gorge after a difficult journey, clumps of mordenite dragging my cloak behind me. The valley laid before me, a rocky but shallow depression lined with glassy, obsidian-tipped rocks. I could see them all in unkempt piles, sprawled on top of one another. Hundreds of Caretakers, frozen solid with my face, decommissioned, limned with shimmering dust. They were still as the rocks of the mountains.

I took my place at the nearest pile, crossing my legs and clamping my hands together. I closed my eyes and accessed the final executable. Shutdown complete in three, two, one…

The Bos Taurus Prime turned a baleful eye, brown and sleepy, as I stepped into the barn. I whispered soothing words, a bit of scripted nonsense effective for dealing with mech-organics, and she settled.

The mainframe blinked at me from its space on the wall, and I tapped my code in a rush. The nanobiotic protocol spun into life on the screen—remote treatment engaged.

"I am here now, Prime. You will feel better soon."

Helter Smelter

By Mark Burnham

First published in Issue 012 (November–December 2022)

Part 1: Procedure

Val Pinker stopped struggling and just hung there, feeling every minute of his sixty-five years of age. Suspension cables hooked around his feet, arms, and torso. The medical apparatus had him clutched in its metallic teeth, splayed in midair, naked and awaiting a benediction he told himself he wanted.

"Val, can you hear me in there?" It was Dr. Catherine Danvers, her voice distant, echoing from somewhere above.

Val tilted his head upwards but could not see her. Surgical lamps blinded him. He forced himself to imagine her purple lipstick and chrome-blade hairdo, her bionic left arm that had touched his shoulder gently when they first met yesterday.

"Val? *Yoo-hoo*," she called to him again, in a pretty sing-song. Her voice sounded filtered and tinny coming out of the intercom.

"Yes," he finally answered in a hoarse bellow. "I hear you." The sedatives they'd pumped him with made him groggy. His mouth tasted like a mix of vitamin C and alcohol. He couldn't swallow. Something buzzed behind his eyes. His body thirsted for sleep. It made him shudder.

"Good. We're going to get started in just a minute. Hang tight."

The sound of something large and mechanical unwinding and grating in the distance, like a huge onion made of steel, peeling itself layer by layer.

The peeling sound morphed into a flutter, high-pitched and whirring. It was the sound of a motor, Val recognized. Pistons were at work, like the trash compactors he'd operated throughout his career. But this was something smaller and more precise than the lumbering machines he knew.

Val squinted dead ahead, nervous to spot what approached. He saw nothing. The Procedure Room was a dim void, its distant walls a brutal gray granite, the ceiling perhaps a mile overhead. Heavy mist soaked the air. It was an exceedingly unwelcoming place, and not at all what Val pictured when he agreed to this experimental procedure. He'd worked forty years as a disposal technician, honest work with a clear purpose. By the time he wondered if he should try something else, he felt too old. Like he'd wandered deep down a workman's tunnel, ahead of him no endpoint in sight, not even a soft glow, behind him only darkness. He was lost and tired. Osiris Labs had approached him with a blessing, an unthinkable second chance. But as he peered into the void, awaiting what dark machinations approached, he was fearful.

Then he saw it. It was a man, lying on his side, motionless, knees tucked so tight they nearly touched his chin. The body floated towards him in the dark, cradled in a sort of metal dish, conveyed by a rod that telescoped out of the mist. Val could not discern how far away the body was, only that it grew closer with time. His depth perception was poisoned. His field of vision expanded and contracted as he breathed. It could have been thirty feet or three hundred.

"Stop," Val shouted, mist-water dripping from his face. "I don't want this. I've changed my mind."

"Val, you're perfectly safe. Try to remember that," Dr. Danvers said in a soothing tone of voice through her intercom.

The man floated closer on the metallic dish. The dish was concave, like the cupped palm of a god that presented a gift from on high. The man had brown hair, short and thin, the tips wet and clumped together, like he'd recently emerged from a hot shower. His skin was a golden-peach color.

"I don't care," Val growled. "Let me die in peace."

"Mr. Pinker, remember the agreement you signed," Dr. Danvers replied. Her tone was punitive now, like a teacher chiding a student. "We will be proceeding."

The man grew closer still. One of the man's testicles bulged out from behind his pressed thighs.

"It's my life!" Val roared.

"We are saving your life," Dr. Danvers declared in a grandiose tone.

The man's toenails were untrimmed, long and sharp and jagged.

"Please," Val whimpered.

"You are a blessed pioneer. You are the first, but not the last."

One of the man's hands was tattooed on its backside: a single disembodied wing, belonging to a large bird or angel.

"Get ready, Val," Dr. Danvers instructed. "It's starting now."

Val felt something stir within his chest. It felt like the dial on a safe being tuned by a careful operator. The tuning accelerated until it reached a speed impossible to distinguish from stillness. The force vibrated his entire body.

A bionic porthole opened in Val's chest, from the top edge of his navel to his collarbone. Dozens of blades fanned out of the porthole, blossoming into a series of propellers. The system of slicing blades reached such a speed that the wind pushed hard against Val's face, his long, gray hair whipping behind. His chest had become a meat grinder. He looked down to watch the carnage, his face wet with either tears or mist or drool.

The man had reached the front of the blades. The wind pushed the man's thin hair into a comb-over as it closed within inches. The blades first began cutting the man's hair, which flew about in clumps. A spray of debris followed: red, gray, black. Something white and globular flicked away from the fray at high velocity, like a baseball pitch. Val recognized it was an intact eyeball as it darted away into the shadows. The man's head had been swallowed by Val's chest. His neck and shoulders followed. The blades chugged as they worked the thicker material of the man's torso. After a decisive crunch, the blades regained their previous tempo and things passed easier. Val could bear to watch no longer, and craned his head upward. It was easier not watching, barely. He could still hear the blades working on bone and flesh, and something else—a gulping sound, like water getting sucked down the thirsty gullet of a toilet.

In time the blades began to slow, until they stopped altogether. Val felt the blades fold back into his chest. The porthole closed and seemed to lock itself shut.

Life expectancy updated, a digital voice said, emanating from Val's chest. From the porthole.

New life expectancy: 145 years.

It was a vicious feeling in Val's heart, hearing those words. It was something like a relief, an orgasm, and a thirst all at once. He wept out of disgust and joy.

Part 2: Recovery

The floor of the Recovery Room was cold and hard against Val's feet, but he was thankful for it. It was shelter.

The room was dimly lit and small, the far wall alive with monitors that displayed flowing medical charts.

A man was talking. He wore a white lab coat over a crisp, dark business shirt. He stood in front of the medical charts, speaking with intense animation that Val found aggravating. Val had a headache and did not appreciate the talking man's excitement.

Dr. Catherine Danvers leaned against the wall nearest the door. She was mercifully quiet, offering to Val only the occasional smile. She gave him a thumbs-up with her bionic arm.

"Enough of this technobabble," the talking man finally said. "The bottom line is you've been given a second life, Mr. Pinker. What are you going to do with it?"

The man's name tag said 'Ray.' He held his hands in a triangle formation while he waited for Val's answer.

Val took a drag from his K-flute and let the smoke slowly drain from his nose. He pulled on a loose-fitting button-up shirt, leaving the front wide open. Already he felt different. Stronger, looser.

"Oh, old man's dreams. You don't want to hear those," Val said.

"C'mon, Mr. Pinker," Ray said, closing the distance and giving Val a good-natured slug in the arm. "And you're not an old man anymore, bud. Try to get used to that."

Val sighed before he spoke. "Truth be told, I've always wanted to be a gardener. Work in a vineyard. Guess I'll take what I've saved up and catch a light-train over to Rome. Work in the hills for free until they pay me, I guess. Still working it all out. Feel like a kid. No more trash work for me, that's for sure." He smiled.

"I love it. I can see it now," Ray said, forming his hands into a frame like he was looking through a window into a dream. "Garbage man turned gardener. It's beautiful."

Dr. Danvers glared at Ray. It was clear his corpo-energy rubbed her the wrong way too.

"We started the Osiris Project to offer humanity more freedom," she said to Val. "The Smelter, the device in your chest. It transmutes life from one place to another. Energy, Mr. Pinker, cannot be destroyed. It can only be re-purposed. So do with your new life whatever you wish. Energy has no politics. Its purpose is to be spent."

Val touched the porthole in his chest. He rubbed his fingers in a circle around its perimeter, searching its tracks. It felt like a puzzle box. He took another drag from his K-flute and frowned.

"I'm not sure if this is against protocol," he began. "But I have to ask. Who was he? The man. Why him?"

Dr. Danvers opened her mouth to speak, but Ray raised his hand to silence her.

Ray sighed deeply and nodded. "I understand your curiosity, Mr. Pinker. I really do. But I don't think you'll like any of my answers."

"And why not?"

"The truth?" Ray said, shrugging in an emphatic gesture. "I simply don't know much more than you. The man was a convict slated for execution, I know that. He was selected by the Osiris ethics board, based on his background and organ fit. That's about all I know. I hope you understand. Rules and all. *Way* above my pay grade," Ray laughed and rolled his eyes.

"Was he…alive?" Val asked.

"Yes," Dr. Danvers answered, before Ray could cut her off this time. "Barely, but yes. The smelting process requires live organic material."

"The uncomfortable truth of how the, uh, *sausage*, is made, if you will," Ray said, pleased with himself.

Val tried to balance the moral weight of what he'd taken part in, but it just made him feel ill. As a waste engineer, he'd witnessed all the harsh fates that can befall matter: it could be burned, evaporated, buried, transformed, and recycled, even shot into space to be forgotten, but Dr. Danvers was right: matter cannot be destroyed. It made a kind of raw sense to repurpose life from one person to another. But this logic was savage. It required a cynicism that Val felt uncomfortable with, even as he felt fresh youth pumping through his body.

"Enough about all this stuff," Ray said, motioning to the charts behind him. "How do you *feel*, Mr. Pinker?"

"Pretty good, actually," Val said, stretching his arms out in front of him and observing them. The truth was he felt magnificent. Sixty-five years old, and he hadn't felt this sturdy in decades.

"What about mentally?" Dr. Danvers asked, walking towards Val, her hands in her pockets.

"I feel okay. Maybe a little…mixed up," Val admitted. "I keep having these…daydreams. I don't know what else to call them. I keep snapping out of it and feeling like I've lost time."

Ray and Dr. Danvers exchanged a glance.

"How long do these spells last?" Dr. Danvers asked.

"Minutes maybe," Val said. "Is something wrong?"

"Can you describe one of these daydreams?" Dr. Danvers pressed.

"There's only one. I'm somewhere outside Crucible City, up in the hills. I can see the corpo tower lights in the distance. There's a campfire. I see a bunch of faces in the firelight. They're looking at me. Staring. I try to scream but a strange sound comes out, like a buzz-saw. They all raise their hands in response. Everyone has tattoos on the back of their hands, some sort of symbol. An angel wing. It's the same every time. Like it's on a loop."

Ray's expression morphed from an interested stare into a leering grin. He put his hands in his pockets and paced to the other side of the room, seemingly to hide his enjoyment. Dr. Danvers sat on a nearby chair and hung her shoulders. The disparity in their responses made Val nervous. He didn't know who to seek for counsel.

"Is everything okay?" Val asked. "Am I sick or something?"

Ray spun around. "Mr. Pinker, Val, baby," he started, opening his arms wide. "You are the opposite of sick, my friend. What you're describing is a perfectly normal part of recovery. The smelting process shocks your brain with a ton of new energy. You're having vivid dreams as a result. They'll pass. Right, Dr. Danvers?"

Ray looked at her to answer.

"Yup," she nodded. "You're just fine."

"There you have it, right from Dr. Frankenstein," Ray said, laughing at his own joke. "I think that's our cue. Mr. Pinker needs some rest. He's the guest of honor tonight at the Osiris Labs Gala." He slugged Val in the shoulder again. "Everyone wants to hear your story, man. Come find me later, let's clink glasses." Ray pointed a finger-pistol at Val and walked to the door of the recovery room. "Coming, doctor?" he asked Dr. Danvers.

"I'm right behind you," she responded. "Just going to give Mr. Pinker something to help him sleep."

"Don't be long," Ray said, looking at his watch. He turned and left.

Part 3: Awakening

The doctor went to a cabinet on the far side of the Recovery Room. She loaded an auto-injector. Bright green fluid bubbled in the chamber. Its color made Val uneasy.

"Honestly, I'm so wiped, I don't think I need any help falling asleep, doc," he said.

She ignored him, walking to the door and locking it shut. She peered out of the small glass window at the top of the door.

"Is everything—"

"I need you to stand up," she said, turning to face him. "We don't have much time."

Val stood with some effort. He was confused, exhausted.

"Listen, *ma'am*," he said, getting annoyed. "I don't really—"

Pain rippled behind Val's eyes. He became a passenger in his own body. It felt like someone seized control of a rod protruding from the back of his head and pointed his vision downward, at a brutal angle, so that he peered inside himself. Whoever it was that operated his body was conducting a search. His brain was a filing system, each record examined and set aside. The search was for coordinates, directions to some sort of base underground, a facility in the hills.

The spell passed, and Val fell to one knee. Something was seriously wrong. A consciousness was asserting itself in place of his own. Something sentient and cruel was spreading from organ to organ, ripping through veins and tissue, replacing the fluids there with a different mixture.

"What's happening to me?" he asked.

"He is overtaking you."

"What do you mean? Who?"

"Kal Ronan," Dr. Danvers said, tears in her eyes. "The man you devoured. Ray lied to you. He knows very well who that man was. He was the leader of the Seraph Collective. God, I didn't think…none of the data suggested this was possible. Those crazy motherfuckers, with all their eternal-life, death-cult bullshit. I'm so sorry, Val."

"It feels like I'm…dying. Am I dying?"

"No. Not exactly. It's more like your consciousness will be… deprioritized. Moved to a back seat. You'll still be aware, but you won't be in control. *He* will."

Val pictured his vineyard, rolling hills of green, a place of peace and craft and toil. Flames sparked in a corner of the vineyard, and soon the entire valley was engulfed in rolling flames, billows of smoke and ash and char. He smiled grimly. The universe wasn't about to let him just *walk away* with a new life. Perhaps this was some sort of cosmic justice. He'd attempted an existential thievery, savage and gruesome, in order to enrich himself. But he was always a puppet, nothing more. He felt like a fool.

"How long do I have?"

"If I can help it," Dr. Danvers said, injecting herself in her organic arm. "An hour, maybe."

"What do you mean, if you can help it?"

Dr. Danvers reached out and ran her hand over the Smelter in Val's chest, searching for grooves in a sequential order. Something alighted within Val, heat that grew and bloomed. The Smelter unfolded its fan of blades from his chest and chopped the air.

"What are you doing?!" Val yelled.

"Trust me," she said.

She stepped forward slowly, her arm extended outward as an offering. The tips of her fingers were devoured. Blood spattered across her lab coat, her face, which was grimacing but unafraid.

"Why?" Val asked. He could feel garbled flesh and bone flush through the Smelter hardware. Already he felt new strength, and something else—part of Dr. Danvers herself awakening behind his eyes. He felt her compassion, her devotion to the Osiris Project, a deep fear. Someone she wished to keep safe.

Her hand vanished with a single flick, then her forearm was diced easily. She pushed what remained of her arm into the Smelter up her shoulder, blood spraying everywhere, coating the medical monitors, the walls, Val's bed sheets. She fell to the ground. The blades slowed down, shut off and folded back inside Val's chest.

Val stumbled back in horror, feeling the new material course through his internal systems.

"They'll probably kill me," Dr. Danvers said, swimming in blood, reaching for a piece of hardware on the floor. It was disc-shaped with a large handle. She pressed the hardware against the stump where her arm had been. Her flesh seared. She gritted her teeth.

"At least this way I can say you attacked me."

Val fell into a chair, intoxicated by the fresh intake of material. *Life expectancy updated. New life expectancy: 160 years.*

New memories washed over Val. Two delicate hands shaking a professor's, accepting a diploma. The same two hands, holding a child in the air, an adoption and a dream. So much joy in those hands. Two arms draped in lab coat sleeves, tired arms, resting on a desk in the dark, the glow of a computer screen bearing the Osiris logo. Two arms in restraints, one of them bionic, typing on a keyboard, a letter of resignation, over and over, deleting it after each rewrite. A single bionic arm, touching a man's shoulder, Val's own shoulder he recognized, their first meeting, the mechanical arm conveying so much intensity: admiration, warmth, fear, pride.

The vision faded, and Val regained his focus.

"I'm sorry," he said. "I'm sorry it's just me. An old man with simple dreams that cost so much. This isn't what I wanted."

Dr. Danvers winced and shifted her weight, her bionic hand holding her fresh arm stump. "You still have time."

"To do what?" Val shouted. "Seems like time's up."

"Take down as many of those motherfuckers as possible," she said, spitting blood. "The Seraph Collective won't stop until all their incarcerated members are devoured by a Smelter, resurrected in new flesh. Like you, Val. They'll go on a rampage, create an army of members with infinite life."

Val mustered his energy and stood. He'd go down swinging.

"I guess I need something to wear."

"I have just the thing," she smiled.

"Let's take out some trash."

Part 4: Feeding

The backstage of the Osiris Theater was dark. Long hallways snaked into the distance ahead of Val. He checked the time. 7:15. By Dr. Danvers's description, he had thirty minutes left, tops. He wore blue tactical pants with a black leather jacket. Underneath the jacket he wore a plate of red ballistic armor, a porthole custom-cut in the chest to display the Smelter. His shades were hot pink, mirrored, and glowing.

"I gotta say, sir. This is a real honor." It was Val's 'handler,' a man who'd introduced himself as "Zen" a few minutes earlier back at the recovery room. Zen wore a robe of chains. He was armed with a high-caliber stun pistol, which he handled like it was a toy.

"Kal Ronan, in the flesh. Dressing room is right here."

The door to the dressing room was open. A man stepped out. It was Ray.

"My god, look at you," Ray said, beaming. "Good to see you back, sir. You look fantastic, crowd's gonna love it. I suppose we have Dr. Danvers to thank for this ensemble? Glad that bitch is getting better at following orders. Right this way, sir. Let's toast to your good health," Ray said, shooting Val with a finger-pistol like he'd done before.

Val clenched within himself and engaged the Smelter. The fan of blades unfolded and began chopping the air. Before Ray could react, Val closed the distance and the Smelter chopped off the tip of Ray's finger-pistol. Ray looked at the exposed bone of his index finger in horror, blood spurting upwards like a geyser.

"Holy fuck," Zen screamed. He fumbled with the stun pistol, finally cocking it and raising it to aim. Val spun in his direction and leapt forward. The Smelter caught one of the chains of Zen's robe and tangled him into the blades, face first. There was a crunch and a spatter, and the man's bottom half fell to the floor, lifeless and decapitated.

Life expectancy updated. New life expectancy: 185 years.

Ray stumbled backwards into the dressing room holding his bleeding finger, his eyes wide and frightened.

"It's you," he said. "The fucking garbage man. You can't stop what's coming, man. This is prophecy. You should be honored. You are the vessel. He will live until the foretold fire, within you."

Ray tripped backwards and fell on his back.

"I'm no vessel," Val said. "But you're right about one thing. I'm just a garbageman. And you're trash." He leaped into the air and belly-flopped square on top of Ray with the Smelter blades spinning. The sound was loud, industrial, grinding.

Life expectancy updated. New life expectancy: 236 years.

Part 5: Benediction

Val emerged onstage from behind a thick black curtain to uproarious applause. A woman at the mic looked back at him in excitement.

"Look who it is, folks!" she said, the crowd growing even more feverish. "You've heard enough of me. It is my distinct pleasure to introduce our guest of honor. The messiah in the desert. The one who will witness the fire. In his new flesh, I present to you, Kal Ronan!"

The crowd erupted.

Val approached the mic, and signaled for the crowd to quiet.

"I'm not your messiah," he said. "I'm just a garbageman."

He engaged the Smelter. The fan of blades unfolded and sped up to a blur. The crowd grew uneasy. Val thrust his own arms into the blades, first one, and then the other. He felt himself getting pulled downward, sucked into the vortex. Memories of his own came flooding back. He'd been a good employee, an innovator in waste management in his own small world. His favorite bar on Gower Street, the locals there who always welcomed him. His vineyard dreams, so real they'd become like memories of genuine experience.

Val pushed forward and his head and shoulders were swallowed inward by the Smelter, converted to red mulch. His decapitated body fell to the floor in a sitting position, and then folded forward in half. His legs were caught in the blades and ripped upward, pants, boots and all. The Smelter blades chopped into the wood of the stage, flipped on end and spiraled out into the crowd, whipping the remnants of Val Pinker throughout the theater, the greatest garbage man this world has ever known.

Declare the Typhoon's Coming

By Noah Codega

First published in Issue 009 (May–June 2022)

1.18

It would be the dead of winter now. I've been reflecting lately on the concept of seasons, something that happens in cycles for aeons as time turns in fractal spirals, twisting into eternity. Something that we only recognize because of the physical and biological conditions of Earth. How different might we have been if our planet of genesis had no tilt, if the proximity and angle of the sun had given Earth a climatic permanence undisturbed by the churning of years?

Nothing is permanent, though. The dying rock in our wake is some proof of that.

Life on the barque is an approximation of this idea, the non-season, as the cold and perpetual abyss tickles the hull. Yet we carry the memory of Earth-time with us. We understand years, weeks, months, and days as though these now-meaningless delineations were bred into us, as though they were instincts as strong as those to eat, to reproduce, to fight. The clocks on board all march around tracks of twenty-four hours. It is still how we age ourselves, how we quantify the duration of this endless, endless fucking journey.

1.22

We came upon a stricken galleon some hours ago. It is at once cosmically coincidental and astoundingly mundane that we should encounter anything at all in a realm that is almost entirely nothingness. We have our route, of course—we may be spread out over hundreds of thousands of klicks, but the entire fleet, from the passenger barques and frigates to the smallest cargo scows, plies this same empty belt, this same Godforsaken tract of the depths of the universe.

If I sat in the Admiral's chair, if my arse rested in pampered luxury on the bridge of his flagship, I would never bother with the stragglers. The protocol of the fleet, the code of idealistic conduct designed to safeguard our passage and ensure the largest possible numbers of us reach the end, festers in my mind like an ulcer. If some idiot of a captain leads his ship to ruin, what business is it of mine to mop up his mistakes? Isn't it better, after all, that he, incontrovertibly defective, should never reach our new home, never make up even the smallest part of the population?

Thoughts like these make me wonder sometimes whether I am ultimately fit for the command of a passenger barque. I think it unlikely.

We will dock soon. I've put Lieutenant Roscommon in command of the boarding party. No distress beacon from the galleon—no communication of any kind, in fact. On our approach, I pictured the many potential scenes of carnage inside. Raving lunatics anointing themselves in the blood of the captain. Heads rolling like marbles across the decks. Tableaux of death from the days when ships were things that sailed on oceans, that blasted each other apart with mutilating wads of iron. The most astounding products of human ingenuity and industry of their time, blindly serving Ares.

1.23

After we docked with the galleon, Lieutenant Roscommon boarded with some men of the crew. I shut off communication links on the bridge. Irresponsible, perhaps, but I wanted to have a drink in peace for once, without someone whining about this or that, begging me for orders, and a couple hours of inactivity to stare out at the depthless void from the bridge windows while they searched the ship was too providential an opportunity to ignore. Lieutenant Roscommon is, after all, quite as capable of handling any contingency as I am.

Our ships may achieve incredible velocities in the vacuum of space, but in the boundlessness of the great nothing, we are washed constantly in the illusion of stillness. This is why I drink. Not to forget, not to ease the pain, none of the idiotic cliches of the sots I've known, drinking themselves to blithering stupor. No. I drink to feel motion again, to feel the universe tipping and unsteady around me.

I began daydreaming. (*Day*dreaming? In the eternal night of space? See, Earth, your hold on me hasn't loosened with the millions of klicks, this lingering entanglement of ours.) I pictured Lieutenant Roscommon and the men boarding a ship of screaming savages, driven over the brink of sensibility by the endlessness of this journey, and dispatching them sequentially with all due mercy. I saw the clean holes in their skulls, the swift vomit of blood from their temples, the streaks of sheening red flashing brilliantly across the walls. And then I pictured myself spewing my stomach onto the bridge deck, ranting and feverish, violent and inconsolable, and wondered what actions Lieutenant Roscommon might take against me. At what point would her sense of responsibility to our passengers eclipse her sense of duty to her captain?

I am fully aware that the deference Lieutenant Roscommon displays towards me is due wholly to her obsession with duty and the hierarchy of rank, and not because she thinks me at all competent as a leader. I would sooner have her draw her pistol on me, claw me to ribbons and declare herself captain by brute force—God knows she's capable of it—than see her set her lips in that hard line and stare over my shoulder when she speaks to me, radiating only the faintest possible trace of insubordination. But no, she is delicate in her contumely. If only she were to leave behind the idea that rank means anything whatsoever in this inescapable emptiness.

When I flipped the communication links back on, there was an immediate babble of voices. I heard words but could not piece them together into anything meaningful in my state: *crew, cargo, ejected, armed.*

I made no reply. Some time later (but I ask, not for the first time, not for the last: what does time really mean out here?), Lieutenant Roscommon entered the bridge, her uniform splashed dark with blood, her gray eyes wide and frantic. I was worried—no, terrified—until I realized by the way she carried herself, that confidence of movement she has always possessed, that the blood was not her own. She then tried speaking to me. I expect it was incredibly frustrating.

There was no crew on the stricken galleon, she told me. Not a single officer remained, not a single engineer or mechanic, not even the fucking cook. And there hadn't been any passengers in the first place—it was a cargo ship. The cargo had revolted. The appropriate response for a captain, on learning that a fellow ship's crew has been massacred and thrown to tumble eternally in the black desert, is, I'm quite sure, not to laugh. Certainly not to laugh so hard that he's gasping for air and the tears stream from his eyes. But the idea that, without even trying, the entire crew of the galleon had managed to die struck me as incomparably funny.

I don't remember Lieutenant Roscommon's response. In fact, I remember nothing whatsoever until I woke up an hour or so ago on the cot in my cabin. We're still docked with the galleon. I expect that it's time, once again, for me to make a fucking decision.

1.23

I gather there was some good action before my crew locked the ship down tight, bless their fighting souls. By the time they had herded the rabble back into the hold, the throat of my second lieutenant had been torn from his neck and a midshipman had his entire face shredded like tissue paper by a flechette load. Lieutenant Roscommon and I gave them proper burials in stitched sheets and sent them from the starboard airlock with a prayer. I've asked her once or twice how many of the mob she and the crew had to eliminate to get them behaving, but she won't answer me in anything other than the broadest terms. She's off duty now. I've considered keeping her off for an extra watch or two, but I know she would take it as an insult.

Lieutenant Roscommon's adamant position is that the galleon's cargo should stand trial when we reach our destination. My word may be law on board, but she argues that an incident which did not occur on my ship should properly be handled by higher, rather than horizontal, authorities. I would just as soon leave them to drift into oblivion—they did, after all, manage to kill the captain and navigation officers in the riot. They made their bed. But I have agreed, if only to keep alive Lieutenant Roscommon's pretense of strict adherence to the law of the fleet. Let her have her idealism and fantasies—I know how she feels about the chattel, even chattel who murder men under her direct command, and of whose number (I am quite sure) she dispatched a few herself. I see it in her eyes, hear it in the strain of her voice.

Let her dream of their freedom. They will never have freedom from themselves. For now, we tow them along behind us from the docking port, change the guard every six hours. We keep them as alive as they can be.

1.24

I went to see the galleon's cargo this morning. From the observation deck, I watched them huddling in squalor in the hold, which has been modified to be completely soundproof. I do not count myself as being particularly interested in the bestial tongues of the slums that must sound like the clacking of nutshells or the grunting of rutting hogs, but the absence of sound produces an effect of serenity which seems wholly incompatible with the situation. See them down there, the degraded sons and daughters of obliterated nations, who yet vow themselves to silence, to beatific muteness. Though the hold must be full of the moans of the injured, the cries of the children, the babble of the men, nothing of it transits the glass of the deck windows. Stripped of their voices, they seem weak.

And these are the laborers by whose arms our new worlds will be built?

I've ordered the guard to keep them on quarter rations for now—absolutely needless, of course, with an entire galleon worth of provisions at our sudden disposal.

1.31

I visited the galleon again today. I stared down from the observation deck at the cargo. I saw the man who must be their leader. Tall and strong. He looks as though he could break me across his knee, and I don't doubt that he would if we found ourselves together.

I had my men throw their packs of rations down to them, full rations this time, while I watched. I wanted a fight. I wanted to see them tear each other to rags. I wanted their starving bones to shatter.

Instead, their leader gathered all the food to himself and had the children come forward, one by one, until he had made sure they were fed. Then came the women who were with child, then the old and frail. Only when every single one of them— eighty? a hundred?—was eating did he himself begin.

Several of the injured must have perished in the past few days. Near the bay doors there are several bodies covered with torn sheets. I can see nothing of them but vague human forms, white under the bleaching lights of the cargo bay.

2.8

God help me. I've begun to pity them.

Or do I hate them? In truth, I don't believe I've ever felt the one without feeling the other, and perhaps I have no internal divide between the two. How could a collection of beings so pitiable engender anything *but* hatred?

I think of them groveling there in the hold while their slain companions rot in the corner and am filled with rage. It disgusts me utterly. I wonder to myself what might have happened if they had managed to fight off my men, if my crew and I were the ones defeated and imprisoned. How would Lieutenant Roscommon have handled my putrefying in the corner? What would her words of comfort be to the crew? How would she lead them? I know how they watch her, how they look to her, how they trust her. I know they would follow her through the maw of death.

God, what would I do if *she* were killed?

In that situation, I think it likely that the best possible thing I could do for my crew would be to die.

If Earth were anything but a memory to us, Lieutenant Roscommon would see the cargo loosed back to their slums, where they would—what, exactly? What could they possibly get up to that would be more valuable, for either themselves or society as a whole, than the work of building new worlds? Back in their sprawling megalopolises of hovels, they were lucky for every sunrise that didn't light up their bloated bodies reeking in a ditch. She may disapprove of the institution to which they belong, but she can hardly argue that they were stolen from Eden.

Still, my new position as caretaker discomforts me, and I wonder where my duty lies. With the investors expecting a healthy return on these abducted slum-dwellers when we reach our journey's end? With the galleon's murdered crew? But most of all, I find myself wondering how it is even possible that I should be accountable to anyone out here.

3.1

There has been no need whatsoever for me to check on the galleon we're towing. The men I've left as sentry are more than capable, and with a little bit of alertness and precaution, traits obviously foreign to their predecessors, they have no problem whatsoever ensuring that the cargo is kept in check. There have been no incidents, and there will not *be* any incidents so long as everyone keeps doing their bloody jobs.

But I find myself drawn to it. Nearly every day, something compels me to go through the hassle of arranging a complement for the bridge and scurrying all the way down to the aft orlop to make the transit. Something in me wants to stand on the observation deck for hours at a time, watching their leader. I leave Lieutenant Roscommon in charge when I go—in fact, I haven't once allowed her back to the galleon since we found it.

I have not, of course, heard a single sound from them from behind the hold's muting shield of glass. But I perversely wonder sometimes at the melodies of the songs I see them singing. I wonder what their old world sounded like, and how different from my old world it was. I wonder how our lives could have been so different on the same rock. How they can still be so different here in the same darkness.

The leader stares at me. As though he's felt some change intangible to the rest of them, he looks up to the deck windows when I enter, and he meets my eyes. His face never changes. It is always the same expression. I first took it for sadness. Christ knows the poor bugger's got enough to be sad about.

But several days ago, I realized, in the chance glare of the overhead lights that reflected my face onto the window as a superimposition on top of his, as our features lined up and I caught sight of myself in him, himself in me—I realized that he was looking at me with pity.

3.9

Dreamed of Lieutenant Roscommon last night. I saw her standing on a mound of rubble, wearing a long white coat, her face smeared with grime, hair matted with blood, pistol in her hand, firing again and again, blasts of flame bursting in the darkness that surrounded her completely, blazing in her eyes.

Considered telling her about it and have decided not to.

3.12

Thoughts of the galleon's prisoners have been intrusive. I see their leader when I lay down to sleep. I see his pitying stare, the wretches gathered around him. I think of the battles waged to tear them from their slums. I think of the slaughtered crew of the galleon. I think of their lives on our new home. I go to watch them every day. I wonder what their leader thinks of me. I wonder whether he is a leader by some show of force, or by some born position of authority, or whether the people around him trust him to lead because he has shown that he can, because he wins their respect not by commanding it, but by earning it. I think of his hands bloody with the lives of my own crew. I wonder whether he has the first idea who I am, my position of power over him, or whether I am simply another outsider looking in, another tormenting face in a ring of barbarian captors.

3.17

I cannot stop thinking of their corpses in the corner, what it must be like to live side-by-side with death and the weakness of flesh. I saw Lieutenant Roscommon limp and bloody under the navigation table last night. Shook my head and she was gone.

3.28

I'm a prisoner as well. Just as much as they are. That's where his pity comes from. I may have control over a ship, and I may not be bound for chains when this voyage is over, but considered from any external vantage point, we are both absolutely unable to leave.

Finally, though, finally—I feel movement. God. I haven't had a drop in days and I can feel the universe tilting on its axis.

3.29

Lieutenant Roscommon is unhappy with me.

I'm unhappy with me.

Who isn't?

When I reached the galleon today, I ordered my men back to the barque and took up my spot at the observation deck. There he was, their captain. There was his look of pity as he, in the middle of his crowd, looked at me standing alone.

For the first time, I waved at him.

He waved back.

I wonder whether there was any sound down there when I hauled the levers to open the bay doors. Did the void whisper or scream as it seethed into the hold? As it tore at their lungs and eyes and boiled their blood in their veins? I watched the silence. I watched as they drifted from the hold into the eternal black sea. I watched them go free.

3.31

Passed by Lieutenant Roscommon's cabin in the mizzen tower this afternoon while she was off duty. Had been drinking. Door was partly ajar and I stopped to listen.

Crying. Unmistakable. Quiet, though, as if she didn't want to hear herself, shuddering irregular breaths. Shouldn't have, but opened the door and stepped in. Must have heard my footsteps. Brought her red face out of her pillow. Stood at attention and asked what my orders were. Wanted to comfort her somehow, knew it utterly impossible. Thin lips trembling. Saw the ragged shards of her soul through her eyes. Those gray eyes. God. I have destroyed her.

4.9

They may rock upon the empty waves forever. They won't decay in the void. They, poor jetsam, might float incorruptible until the end of time.

And how will I be remembered—me, who has murdered a hold of saints?

5.7

If I had given her the chance to stop me, would she have?

If I had brought her with me to the galleon and told her that if she did not step in to save the lives of the slaves, I was going to throw them to their deaths, would she have fought me?

I don't know. I don't know. But I want the duty to die in her throat.

6.2

I looked in his eyes as I opened the bay doors. The last conscious thought that ran through his brain, before the void sucked it dry like a spider sucks a fly, was pity for me. He died thinking me pathetic. He died as I thought him strong.

6.14

I have done no one any good. Not the passengers, the crew, not myself. Nothing but evil arises from this teetering wreck of a man.

I keep the bridge to myself. What do I need other officers for? To assist me in traveling a straight fucking line for billions of miles?

I see the fury and hatred and despair burning behind Lieutenant Roscommon's eyes, but she won't say a word against me. I'm beginning to lose hope that she ever will.

I want to be in her place. No—I wish I had been in her place from the start. I wish I'd had someone to order me, to tell me what to do. Someone I could have been responsible to, no matter how miserable a shit they might have been. I wish I had some purpose other than to stagnate and go straight, to go forward, to just keep going going going going going going going going going going going

6.29

If the universe is boundless, then where am I?

If I am first at some point in the midst of infinity, and I am then at some other point in the midst of infinity, there is no more infinity behind me or in front of me than there was before. In relation to the infinite, I have not moved at all. Stars may approach. Stars may recede. But no matter how far I travel through it, my position in the void is immutable.

7.12

I never even see the passengers. They could be imaginary. Here I am, blasting away, transiting this endless fucking country of nothing, and every single cabin is empty. This might all be some great cosmic joke. Not even Sisyphean. The boulder won't roll back down the mountain. Just keep pushing it across the universe. There are no obstacles at all.

7.12

They must be real. They must be. No sense otherwise.

7.12

No fucking sense in the universe, anyway. What's one more absurdity?

7.12

Why do I bother writing in this fucking book?

9.12

Lieutenant K. W. R. Roscommon:

If you should chance upon this journal, in the unlikely situation that you find yourself in command of this ship, and flip its pages in an idle moment before destroying all trace of me, please accept my

I am sorry.

I am so, so sorry.

12.16

I have my solution.

It is incredibly simple. I should have thought of it ages ago.

I will create a binary situation, a scenario in which there are two possible outcomes.

I am going to arm myself and ask Lieutenant Roscommon to accompany me to the passenger decks. I am going to gather them all together. Then I am going to pick one at random—some pathetic senile, perhaps, or better, a wailing child—and force them to kneel. I will aim my pistol at their head and I will scream at Lieutenant Roscommon that she will either kill me and assume command or she will watch as I blow apart the skulls of each and every one of the people who are meant to represent a great wave of settlers to humanity's furthest reaches. As I destroy hope. I will make sure we are far enough apart that she will be unable to restrain me and that in the time before I begin killing the distance between us might only be crossed by her bullet. I will make sure that these two options are all that remains. She is a good shot. She has seen what I am capable of. She will hesitate but she will not fail.

I am going to stop writing now. I am going to set my plan into motion because for the first time in an extremely long time I feel a true storm of movement and am excited.

Acknowledgments

Dark Matter is made possible by so many hard-working and talented people.

Thank you to my cousins Phil and Lucy McLaughlin, my brother Eric Carroll, and my good friend Chris Kendzora for helping start *Dark Matter Magazine* in the spring of 2020. I couldn't have done this without your early support and expertise. You all helped put Dark Matter on the path it is today.

Thank you to Anna Madden for bringing a whole new perspective and insight to the team that was previously missing. Your keen eye for talent has been invaluable to Dark Matter's success, as has your ability to cultivate that talent. Your measured approach to our work keeps myself and the team focused and grounded. Dark Matter's current iteration owes so much to you.

Thank you to Marie Croke for making an immediate impact with the story acquisition process and for finding a number of great pieces right away. Thank you also for continuing to champion authors and the valuable work they do, and for making sure they are always at the center of our mission. You're a person of great talent, wisdom, and integrity.

Thank you to Marissa van Uden for your contributions to the story acquisition process and for your massive editorial contributions to Dark Matter INK and Dark Hart Books. Our trade imprints would not be the same without you, and neither would the books we produce. You are the best developmental editor I know, and everything you touch turns to literary gold.

Thank you to Alli Nesbit for taking Dark Matter Audiolab to the next level. Your incredible skill and artistry with sound design, music production, voice acting, podcast direction, and more, has been a revelation. Phil and I sometimes wonder how we managed Audiolab without you.

Thank you to Dark Matter's dynamic duo of features writers, Jena Brown and Janelle Janson. Your love and dedication to books and those who write them is unmatched. I am constantly amazed by the work you produce, and I am so grateful to have you both on the team. Your contributions have made *Dark Matter Magazine* a better, more comprehensive publication.

Thank you to Kelsea Yu for your brilliant insight and infectious enthusiasm. You haven't been with Dark Matter long, but you've already made a powerful and lasting impression on the team.

Thank you to Olly Jeavons for making *Dark Matter Magazine* and Dark Matter INK look good. Your cover art for our books and magazine issues never fails to turn heads. In many ways, your artwork has become an integral part of Dark Matter's visual style.

Thank you to Sadie Hartmann for being such a dedicated champion of Dark Matter even before joining our team as Editor-in-Chief of Dark Hart Books. Your impeccable taste in literature and your impressive ability to connect books you love to readers is an unbeatable combination. Your winning streak has only continued with the wonderful work you've acquired for your anthology and for Dark Hart.

Thank you to all the amazing authors, artists, and voice performers that have contributed to Dark Matter these first few years, as well as all our partners, fans, supporters, and peers. You make this work fun, and in this industry, having fun is what it's all about.

Thank you to my family for all your support and encouragement over the years, especially Mom, Dad, Mark, Eric, and Shannon (Dark Matter's convention planner extraordinaire).

And to my incredible wife Samantha and my three lovely little girls: There is a *How* to doing things and then there is a *Why*. You all are the *Why*.

—Rob

About the Authors

Ken Altabef has work in the *Magazine of Fantasy & Science Fiction, Interzone, Daily Science Fiction, Intergalactic Medicine Show, BuzzyMag, Abyss & Apex,* etc. His stories have received honorable mention in *Years Best SF* and *Best Horror of the Year.* He is the author of thirteen fantasy novels. Visit his website at KenAltabef.com

Matt Andrew is a retired Marine officer who deployed in support of combat operations to Afghanistan and the Balkans. He currently works in the banking industry in Dallas, Texas. His fiction has been published in *Blight Digest, Pantheon Magazine, Thuglit, Pulp Literature,* and others.

Warren Benedetto is an award-winning author and a full member of the SFWA. His stories have appeared in publications such as *Dark Matter Magazine, The Dread Machine,* and *Haven Spec;* on podcasts such as The NoSleep Podcast, Tales to Terrify, and The Creepy Podcast; and in anthologies from *Apex Magazine,* Scare Street, Eerie River Publishing, and more.

Mark Burnham is a sci-fi, horror, and humor author living in Bend, Oregon. While completing a bachelor's degree at UCLA, he won the Shirle Dorothy Robbins Fiction Award. Mark is a longtime musician and is the bassist of the rock band Gold Rey. He once played guitar on stage with Green Day in San Francisco, a story which cannot be told properly within the confines of this bio. Find him on Twitter @markburnham.

Noah Codega writes fiction and grows vegetables in New England. His work has previously appeared in *Hexagon* and *Idle Ink.* Tweets manifest occasionally @noahcodega.

Andy Dudak is a translator and *Rich Horton's Year's Best* writer with work in *Clarkesworld, Analog, Asimov's, Magazine of Fantasy & Science Fiction, Interzone,* and elsewhere. Find out more at andydudak.home.blog.

Brittany Groves is an Employee/Occupational Health Registered Nurse. She lives in Texas with her two unruly children, one devastatingly handsome husband, and a dog that adores them all. She is her own worst critic and believes her writing is okay, but could be better. The dog, bless his heart, disagrees.

Thomas Ha is a former attorney who enjoys writing speculative fiction during the rare moments when all of his kids are napping at the same time. Thomas grew up in Honolulu and, after a decade plus of living in the northeast, now resides in Los Angeles. You can find the latest about his work at thomashawrites.com.

Andrew Leon Hudson is a technical writer by day, and is technically a writer by night as well. His fiction has appeared in *Cossmass Infinities, Little Blue Marble, Metaphorosis,* and the anthology *Triangulation: Dark Skies.* He is editor of the spec-fic zine that lives at mythaxis.co.uk, and he almost never tweets @AndLeoHud.

T. M. Hurree studies medicine at the University of Queensland, and finds time to write in those precious moments not spent either watching lectures or crying about how many lectures he still needs to watch. His short fiction has previously won the Queensland Young Writers Award, and appeared in the *Griffith Review.*

Ariel Marken Jack (she/they) lives in Nova Scotia. Her stories have appeared in *Beneath Ceaseless Skies, Bikes in Space, Canthius, Prairie Fire, PseudoPod, Strange Horizons,* and more. They curate #sfstoryoftheday on assorted social media and write a column on short speculative fiction for Fusion Fragment. Find her work at arielmarkenjack.com.

Patrick Lofgren is a speculative fiction writer and holds an MFA in Writing from Sarah Lawrence College. He is an enthusiastic member of the Clarion West Writers Workshop class of 2017 and has previously published stories in *The True History of the Strange Brigade* and *The Deadlands*. He lives in Salt Lake with his extraordinary wife, two ferrets, two lizards, and an axolotl.

Monte Lin edits, writes, and plays tabletop roleplaying games. He has stories in *Cossmass Infinities, Cast of Wonders, Flame Tree Press, Dark Matter Magazine,* and Ignyte-nominated nonfiction at *Strange Horizons.* He is also Managing Editor of *Uncanny Magazine* and Staff Editor for Angry Hamster Press.

Christine Lucas writes speculative fiction in the company of a horde of spoiled animals. Greek, ex military, queer, disabled. Her fiction has appeared in *Strange Horizons, Pseudopod,* and *Future SF Digest.* Finalist for the 2017 WSFA award and the 2021 Emeka Walter Dinjos Memorial Award For Disability In Speculative Fiction.

Anna Madden is a gardener, stained glass maker, and word weaver. Her fiction has appeared in *Hexagon, Zooscape, Orion's Belt, Medusa Tales, PodCastle, Metaphorosis,* and elsewhere.

Evan Marcroft is a speculative fiction writer from Sacramento California, currently residing in Chicago, with his wife and cat. His stories have appeared across a variety of publications, including *Pseudopod, Metaphorosis, Asimov's,* and *Strange Horizons.*

Jen Marshall is a horror and science fiction writer whose work has appeared in *LampLight* magazine, the comic book series *Tales of Horrorgasm,* on the NoSleep Podcast, and in numerous anthologies. Jen has a master's degree in medieval literature and lives with her husband and daughter above a haunted cave. You can find her on Instagram at @Scary.Good and on Twitter at @Jen_Marshall.

Guy McDonnell believes that only in embracing the subtleties of our deepest fears and darkest emotions can we truly be free in the light. To paraphrase Sun Tzu, if you know darkness and know yourself, there is nothing to fear. All that remains is deciding how dark is dark enough. Guy writes in pursuit of finding out.

R. L. Meza is an author of horror and dark science fiction. She lives in a century-old Victorian house on the coast of northern California, with her husband and the collection of strange animals they call family. Meza's debut novel *Our Love Will Devour Us* will be published in May 2023 by Dark Matter INK.

Christi Nogle is the author of the novel *Beulah* (Cemetery Gates Media, 2022) and *The Best of Our Past, the Worst of Our Future* (Flame Tree Press 2023). Her dark science fiction and futuristic fantasy collection *Promise* is coming later in 2023 and a weird fantasy collection *One Eye Opened in That Other Place* in 2024, also from Flame Tree Press. Her short stories have appeared in over fifty publications including *PseudoPod*, *Escape Pod*, and *Vastarien*. Follow her at christinogle.com and on Twitter @christinogle

Hailey Piper is the Bram Stoker Award-winning author of *Queen of Teeth*, *No Gods for Drowning*, *The Worm and His Kings*, *Your Mind Is Terrible Thing*, and other books of dark fiction. She is an active member of the Horror Writers Association, with dozens of stories appearing in publications such as *Pseudopod*, *Vastarien*, and *Dark Matter Magazine*. She lives with her wife in Maryland, where their occult rituals are secret. Find her at www.haileypiper.com.

Lowry Poletti is a Black author and veterinary student. When they aren't writing about monsters and the people who love them, they can be found wrist deep in a formalin-fixed lab specimen. Their other pieces appear in *Flash Fiction Online*, *Fantasy Magazine*, and forthcoming issues of *Lightspeed Magazine*.

Grace R. Reynolds is a native of the great state of New Jersey. Her short fiction and poetry has been published by various presses, including Brigid's Gate Publishing, Creature Publishing, *Dark Matter Magazine*, Death Knell Press, and more. She is the author of two poetry collections, *Lady of The House* (2021) and *The Lies We Weave* (2023), both released by Curious Corvid Publishing.

Alexandra Seidel writes stories and poems, and drinks a lot of coffee. Her writing has appeared in *Future SF, Uncanny Magazine,* and *Fireside Magazine,* among others. You can follow her on Twitter @Alexa_Seidel, or like her Facebook page (AlexaSeidelWrites), and find out what she's up to at alexandraseidel.com.

Alex Sobel is a nurse who writes when can find the time (not as often as he'd like). His writing has appeared in *Clarkesworld, Electric Literature,* and *The Saturday Evening Post.* He lives in Toledo, Ohio, with his wife.

Prashanth Srivatsa is a consultant, crusader, and cat-father, who spends his evenings buried in fantasy tomes or maps of his own making. His works of short fiction have appeared or will appear in the *Magazine of Fantasy & Science Fiction (F&SF)*, *Asimov's,* and *Beneath Ceaseless Skies.* His debut novel, *The Spice Gate,* is scheduled for publication in late 2023.

Roni Stinger lives in the Pacific Northwest, USA, with her husband and two cats. When not writing strange and dark things, she is often wandering the forests, beaches, and streets in search of shiny objects and creative sparks. Her work has appeared in various magazines and anthologies.

Mary G. Thompson is the author of *Wuftoom,* which Booklist called "impressively unappetizing and absolutely unique." Her contemporary thriller *Amy Chelsea Stacie Dee* was a winner of the 2017 Westchester Fiction Award and a finalist for the 2018-2019 Missouri Gateway award. A graduate of The New School's Writing for Children program, she lives in Washington, D.C.

Marissa van Uden is from Aotearoa New Zealand but now lives in northern Vermont, in a cabin in the woods. When she's not communing with wildlife or taking photos, you can find her writing, editing, or reading dark speculative fiction, especially of the Weird variety. She posts on Twitter @marissavu and Instagram @marissa.vu.

Erich Alan Werner lives in Nyack, New York with his lovely wife Joanna and two young daughters Carlie and Ella, whose creative play constantly inspires him. An alum of Futurescapes and Odyssey online workshops, he is currently seeking representation for his YA fantasy adventure novel, *Freaks of Nature: The Phantom Cat*. He teaches writing at SUNY Westchester Community College

About the Cover Artists

Jeff Aphisit is an artist and illustrator.

Katerina Belikova (aka Ninja Jo) is a freelance illustrator, concept artist, and lover of robots. She works in digital and traditional materials, such as watercolor, ink, and oils.

Doodleskelly is a mysterious artist from the land of a thousand lakes who simply enjoys drawing stuff.

Sam Heimer is a Philadelphia-area illustrator and toy maker. Check out his work at samheimer.com, and shop his toy creations at hhtoyco.com.

Olly Jeavons is a UK based artist also known as *artofolly*. He works with many different medias and styles, and he is always pushing his creativity further. Comic book art, book cover art, and commissions of all types are included in his portfolio.

Sean Keeton is a Los Angeles-based artist, muralist, and video game art director. His paintings are a manic, Day-Glo, punk rock celebration of the fact that the very things that make us feel anxious and broken are what make us most relatable and vibrant, and are how we connect to each other.

Mashiene 11 is a digital artist and screen printer. He is a South African native, but he has lived in London, UK, for the past fourteen years. He spends his time drawing, painting, and running an online shop, selling his artwork to a global audience.

Sean Andrew Murray is a freelance illustrator, concept artist, author, and teacher who has worked in the entertainment industry for over twenty years. The bulk of his career was spent as a video game concept artist, working on such titles as *Dungeons & Dragons Online*, *The Lord of the Rings Online*, and *Ultima Online*.

Rob Shields is a multimedia artist and game developer, currently working on *Neon Wasteland* and *End of the World Pizza*, two augmented reality graphic novels set in a pop punk neon metaverse. When not working on his own projects, Rob works as an illustrator, animator, concept artist, and app developer for various clients, including Sony and Puma.

Tais Teng is a Dutch science fiction writer and illustrator with the quite unpronounceable name of Thijs van Ebbenhorst Tengbergen, which he shortened to Tais Teng to leave room for a picture of an exploding starship or a clever steampunk lady on the covers of his novels.

Voodoo Salad is from the middle of nowhere. He's a freelance illustrator, graphic artist, and caffeine enthusiast. He illustrates psychedelic portraits and landscapes.

Richard Wagner is a graphic designer and illustrator. His academic schooling consists of a Bachelor of Fine Arts degree with an emphasis in painting and drawing, as well as training in graphic design and illustration. For seventeen years, he taught college-level graphic design and photo-illustration classes while also freelancing.

About the Editor

Rob Carroll is the founder and owner of Dark Matter Media Group, which consists of *Dark Matter Magazine*, Dark Matter INK, Dark Hart Books, and Dark Matter Audiolab. He serves as Editor-in-Chief and Creative Director for *Dark Matter Magazine* and Dark Matter INK. He lives in Illinois with his wife and three daughters.

Permissions

"The Liminal Men" by Thomas Ha, copyright © 2021 Thomas Ha. Used by permission of the author.

"This Will Be the Most Vulnerable Post I've Ever Made" by Marissa van Uden, copyright © 2022 Marissa van Uden. Used by permission of the author.

"Recycle of Violence" by Andrew Leon Hudson, copyright © 2021 Andrew Leon Hudson. Used by permission of the author.

"The Three Breeds of Lie" by T. M. Hurree, copyright © 2021 T. M. Hurree. Used by permission of the author.

"Queen of the Cloven Heart" by Hailey Piper, copyright © 2021 Hailey Piper. Used by permission of the author.

"Bodhisattva from Bit" by Andy Dudak, copyright © 2021 Andy Dudak. Used by permission of the author.

"Rider Within" by Lowry Poletti, copyright © 2022 Lowry Poletti. Used by permission of the author.

"Little Lives" by Patrick Lofgren, copyright © 2022 Patrick Lofgren. Used by permission of the author.

"Her Tongue Was Weighted with Salt" by Alexandra Seidel, copyright © 2021 Alexandra Seidel. Used by permission of the author.

"Marasa, or a Withdrawal of Pure Joy for Mr. Antar" by Prashanth Srivatsa, copyright © 2021 Prashanth Srivatsa. Used by permission of the author.

Also Available from Dark Matter INK

Human Monsters: A Horror Anthology
Edited by Sadie Hartmann and Ashley Saywers
ISBN 978-1-958598-00-9

Linghun by Ai Jiang
ISBN 978-1-958598-02-3

Monstrous Futures: A Sci-Fi Horror Anthology
Edited by Alex Woodroe
ISBN 978-1-958598-07-8

Our Love Will Devour Us by R. L. Meza
ISBN 978-1-958598-17-7

The Vein by Stephanie Nelson
ISBN 978-1-958598-15-3

Haunted Reels: Stories from the Minds of Professional Filmmakers curated by David Lawson
ISBN 978-1-958598-13-9

Other Minds by Eliane Boey
ISBN 978-1-958598-19-1

Frost Bite by Angela Sylvaine
ISBN 978-1-958598-03-0

Monster Lairs: A Dark Fantasy Horror Anthology
Edited by Anna Madden
ISBN 978-1-958598-08-5

The Bleed by Stephen S. Schreffler
ISBN 978-1-958598-11-5

The Bones Beneath Paris by Kelsea Yu
ISBN 978-1-958598-12-2

The House at the End of Lacelean Street
by Catherine McCarthy
ISBN 978-1-958598-23-8

The Off-Season: An Anthology of Coastal New Weird
Edited by Marissa van Uden
ISBN 978-1-958598-24-5

Also Available from Dark Hart Books

All These Subtle Deceits by C. S. Humble
ISBN 978-1-958598-04-7

All the Prospect Around Us by C. S. Humble
ISBN 978-1-958598-05-4

Rootwork by Tracy Cross
ISBN 978-1-958598-01-6

Mosaic by Catherine McCarthy
ISBN 978-1-958598-06-1

Apparitions by Adam Pottle
ISBN 978-1-958598-18-4